BETRAYAL
ᴵᴺ PARIS

Doris Elaine
Fell

ABOUT THE AUTHOR

DORIS ELAINE FELL holds a B.A. in education, a B.S. in nursing, has pursued graduate studies in education, and has studied Bible and Journalism at Multnomah Bible College. Christy Award finalist and 2003 SPU Medallion Award winner, she is the author of sixteen novels, two nonfiction books, and articles in secular and inspirational publications. Her multifaceted career has taken her all over the world and has inspired a six-book Seasons of Intrigue series, as well as *Long-Awaited Wedding* and *The Wedding Jewel*. She presently lives in Huntington Beach, California.

Our purpose at Howard Publishing is to:
- *Increase faith* in the hearts of growing Christians
- *Inspire holiness* in the lives of believers
- *Instill hope* in the hearts of struggling people everywhere

Because He's coming again!

Betrayal in Paris © 2003 by Doris Elaine Fell
All rights reserved. Printed in the United States of America

Published by Howard Publishing Co., Inc.
3117 North 7th Street, West Monroe, Louisiana 71291-2227
In association with the literary agency of Alive Communications, Inc.
7680 Goddard Street, Suite 200, Colorado Springs, CO 80920

03 04 05 06 07 08 09 10 11 12   10 9 8 7 6 5 4 3 2 1

Edited by Karen Ball
Interior design by John Luke
Cover design by Kirk DouPonce, UDG|DesignWorks

ISBN: 1-58229-314-7

OH, WHAT A TANGLED WEB WE WEAVE
WHEN FIRST WE PRACTICE TO DECEIVE!
—Sir Walter Scott

PROLOGUE

Nightmare!

Month after month, the same nightmare jerking him from a troubled sleep. Blinding flashbacks. In his dream he is running. Plumes of choking dust and smoke fill his nostrils. The earth is coated with ash. The stench of death closes in on him. He stumbles through the debris, shrieking her name.

"Kristina! Kristina, where are you?"

He wakes, sweating. Sits bolt upright on the edge of his bed in a dark room. The moist spring air wafts through the open window. Sheer curtains sway, ghostlike. He reaches instinctively for the other side of the bed. It is empty. The pillow fluffed, untouched. His wife no longer there. Gone forever.

His personal loss spun in garish Technicolor in his mind—an intrusive reflection, as though it were happening now. The present moment crumbled to dust like the E-Ring of the Pentagon on that September morning.

On that black Tuesday he rose from his desk at the Pentagon at exactly 8:20. He straightened his uniform jacket, checked his watch. The watch, a gift from his wife, was as familiar to him as the Washington skyline across the Potomac. He ran his thumb over the flat sapphire crystal and took note again of the four time zones

1

displayed there. His life was regimented, on schedule. No matter where he traveled, he always knew the hour back home. She had told him that timing was everything to him, that it defined him.

But time with his wife was on hold.

His secretary frowned as he shoved several classified documents into his briefcase. "Colonel, you're not forgetting your meeting with Mr. Rumsfeld at ten?"

"I won't be long."

With rapid strides, he made his way down the long polished corridors to his wife's office on the E-Ring. He hesitated in the door, the lump in his throat doubling as he gazed at her. She was as beautiful as ever, with her flawless complexion and classic features. Shiny hair cascaded around her face; her mauve lips were full, desirable.

In his mind, the Tuesday morning reel moved forward. As his shadow fell across Kristina's desk, she glanced up, her cornflower blue eyes wide, startled. "Oh, it's you."

"Yes, me." He leaned forward, his palms flat on her desktop, his voice competing with the overhead TV monitor airing the morning news. It could have been a mindless cartoon for all the attention it was getting from the civilian employees in the room. "I called your hotel last night. They said you had checked out."

"We moved home with Mother." Her announcement had a final ring to it. "Mother likes having her only grandchild with her."

"Kristina, you're my wife. I want you back home where you belong. Six weeks is long enough to be apart."

Her mouth tightened, but the tremor of her lip gave her away. Tears balanced on her dark lashes. "Don't you understand? It's over."

"You can't take my son and just run out on me. I love you. I love you both."

"It's over," she repeated. "You're just not the same man I married."

"Then who am I?"

"I wish I knew."

"Kris, that's crazy. We've been married ten years."

Fiery flames burned in her eyes as she glared at him. "And you keep shutting me out. You're so secretive these days. Withdrawn. You're up pacing half the night."

"It's my job. Extended hours. The unending demands. Military briefings, classified documents—strategy planning. It never ends."

"Stop it. It's always the same excuses. It's *you*. Not your job. Not your duty. You've changed."

Before he could defend himself, the familiar face of a newscaster filled the television screen. "We interrupt this broadcast with late-breaking news: At 8:46 this morning a hijacked American jetliner crashed into the North Tower of the World Trade Center in New York City."

Kristina gasped. "Oh no! No."

He darted around the desk, his arm circling her shoulders. He rocked her with a gentle touch. Her gaze remained riveted on the screen where billows of smoke rose from the North Tower. The injured fled through the front entry. Bleeding. Terrified. Colliding. Their clothes covered with ash and blood. Their eyes blinded with soot.

His arm tightened around his wife. Their own private war seemed small indeed.

"It can't be! I have friends working there."

So did he. Friends in an investment firm and Secret Service agents he'd known in the past. His cell phone rang. His secretary's efficient voice came through a pitch above normal. "Have you heard, Colonel?"

"We're watching it right now."

"They've upped your conference to three minutes ago."

"I'm on my way." His chest tensed as he watched a second jet rip through the South Tower, tearing through it as though it were papier-mâché. Another fireball erupted.

"Terrorists. It has to be terrorists, Kris."

Her face went chalky. "Then it can happen here. I have to go home to my son and mother—"

"No. Duty demands that you stay at your post." He squeezed her shoulder. "You're safe here. Trust me. What's happening is happening in New York. So hold tight, sweetheart. The Pentagon was built to withstand anything. This whole area has just been renovated with blast-resistant windows. Nothing will happen to you."

The images on the television shouted otherwise. The towers on fire. Steel melting. Invincible structures imploding, crumbling.

He kissed her on the cheek. She didn't resist. "I have to go, Kris. I'll call your mother and tell her you're all right."

"Wait... There's something I haven't told you."

"There's no time now. Tonight—"

"I know you'll be displeased."

He barely recognized the frightened face looking up at him. "What are you talking about?"

"We're going to have another baby."

A baby? He towered above her, making her appear even more vulnerable. For a split second he stood with his back rigid, holding his shock in check. He was good at that. "I love you. I'll call you this evening. We'll have dinner together. We'll talk about the baby—about us."

Without a backward glance, he strolled out of her office and broke into a run down the long corridor, bumping shoulders with admirals and generals and civilian employees. The world was in crisis, but so was he. Wasn't one child enough? A second child would disrupt his life.

His cell phone rang again. His commanding officer bellowed, "Where the blazes are you, Colonel? Terrorists have attacked New York City. We're on full alert. The secretary of defense has called an emergency briefing in the Command Center. Get here on the double."

"Yes sir. Tell Rumsfeld I'm on my way."

Televisions blared live coverage updates as he ran past the open doors and headed for the stairs. Peter Jennings and John Miller sat side by side—their somber words relating rumors of a third hijacked airliner heading toward Washington.

He knuckled the handle of his briefcase, his palm clammy as he tried to process the news. His training kicked in. A hijacked airliner could be heading toward the White House or the Capitol. He glanced at a wall clock: 9:37. He knew the routine. The Pentagon's emergency evacuation drills would already be in effect. Disaster procedures followed with precision. The crisis action teams alerted. Military forces standing by. F-16s in the air. The Aerospace Defense Command combing the skies for the American passenger jet. And the president—God help him—forced to make a split second decision to blow an "enemy" aircraft out of the sky.

Another check of the time—the minutes were ticking away: 9:38. 9:39. 9:40. As he sprinted up the steps, a thunderous explosion rocked the west side of the building. A whooshing roar echoed through the halls. The building shook, the violent tremors buckling the walls behind him. The jolt tossed him into the air. He landed on his back at the foot of the steps, the jarring excruciating. In the choking dust he crawled on hands and knees, groping for his briefcase. It took him seconds before he pushed himself to his feet and raced back toward the flame-scorched corridor of the E-Ring. Into the rubble and debris, with its smell of acrid smoke and jet fuel.

Back to his wife and unborn child.

An admiral restrained him, and he fought to break free. "It's no use, Colonel. A skyjacked airliner hit us full power. No one could possibly make it through that."

"My wife—"

The restraint tightened. Wailing sirens pierced his ears. The admiral shouted above them, "It's nothing but a black, gaping hole back there. A combat zone."

"My wife—"

"No one had a chance. We have to evacuate, Colonel. That's an order."

Even in his darkened bedroom, the images of that day were painfully vivid. His rage at the admiral's command was as deep now as it had been seven months ago. Rage at his loss. Rage at the attack.

Rage that a dust-covered stranger had forced him to run out on his wife as he had run out on his friend a dozen years ago.

He buried his face in his hands but could not block out the picture of the marine helicopter carrying his dead wife to Dover Air Force Base for identification. His wife and his unborn child in a body bag. Bound together in death.

The vision of the chopper's rotating blades burned in his mind, whirling him back to the Iraqi helicopters zooming in low over Kuwait City at the start of the Gulf War. Back to that moment he could never forget...the moment he had betrayed a friend in the Kuwaiti invasion.

On orders from the top, he had reduced his friend's life to a star on the Memorial Wall, a name in the Book of Honor.

Now, as he sat alone in his bedroom, his temples throbbed, the wracking pain blinding him. His wife's smiling photograph at his bedside did not erase the memory of her burned face, her singed golden hair, her lifeless blue eyes. His numbing grief came in fresh waves, the cavernous crack in his heart tormenting him.

Kris had wanted to go home to their son. She'd died in that smoldering wreckage because *he* had demanded she remain at her post. *Duty. Honor. Country.* His facade. His pretense. His cloak of darkness.

The emptiness overwhelmed him, but he found some comfort in the fact that his beloved wife would never know about his past. She would never know that he was a traitor to his country. An impostor. Worse than a terrorist.

Worse than an infidel.

CHAPTER 1

AUGUST 2, 1990
KUWAIT

In the light of the lemon-slice moon, a rawboned, shadowy figure crept across the desert sand, his bruised and blistered feet scraped raw by his sandals. As he took refuge among the towering palm trees that edged the superhighway, his cotton robe flapped at his ankles. Under the robe, his camera and infrared binoculars jabbed his ribs.

Jon Winters had grown gaunt and skeletal from dysentery. His angular body felt wasted, his face pinched. Dawn would bring its searing temperatures and the intense humidity of another August morning. Even now beneath the Kuwaiti headdress, sweat dotted his feverish brow. For weeks he'd hidden from the scorching sun, sleeping through the daylight hours. Night after night he'd stolen from Hamad's house and crawled through the darkness, a deep-cover operative noting the Iraqi buildup around the Rumailan oil fields. Tonight he noted the increasing number of tanks and troops fanning out along the border. An attack was imminent.

Jon leaned against the tree, willing the strength to come back into his body. He had entered a country braced for an Iraqi invasion. Security was tight, foreigners unwelcome, a non-Arab viewed with suspicion. His passport bore another man's identification and nationality—and his own blurred photo.

How many more nights could he avoid capture? Or fight off the chill of the desert nights as he crawled across the dunes, risking encounters with scorpions and sand beetles and desert snakes? Without weapon or survival equipment, he had only his wits and ingenuity to fight the elements. And if he was discovered with his infrared binoculars and camera and the coded messages in his pocket, he would surely be killed.

Hawks swooped low in the clear desert air. He called back to them in Arabic, his words harsh, angry; it was as though they knew he had entered their country under false pretenses. Between their cries, he heard the faint click of his miniaturized transmitter, his watch—a trick of the trade. He dropped to the ground and flattened himself on his belly.

As he pressed the wristwatch to his ear, Hamad's tension crackled over the high-frequency transmitter. "My friend, the Iraqis have crossed our border."

"You're certain?"

"I do not lie, my friend. My father says you must leave at once. You must try to reach Saudi Arabia."

Jon's stomach muscles tightened. "They won't let me in without proper identification. Tell him I have done nothing wrong."

"My father says you overstayed your visitor's pass. His debt for our friendship is paid. I begged him. It is no use. My father has known you too long to think that you are just a visitor in our country." Remorse filled his voice. "He found the ground transmitter in your room."

"Tell him it's a shortwave radio for rock music."

He sensed Hamad smiling. "Do you think you have sheltered with us these three months and not aroused my father's curiosity? My father is a wise old man. He saw you slipping out of the house night after night."

"He must know I'm a restless sleeper."

"My friend, he has guessed that you are an intelligence agent, part of America's increased surveillance against the Iraqis. He loathes the danger that puts us in."

He loathed himself. His adrenaline kicked in with a futile attempt to defend himself. "But your father never questioned me."

"Because I begged him to help you. But now he calls you a deceiver—an infidel playing the part of an Arab."

"I have never lied to him."

"Nor have you told him the truth."

Hamad was right. For weeks Jon had carried his covert assignment in his memory, his fear of discovery stuck like a burr in the back of his mind. He did a rapid mental replay. He was to do intelligence reconnaissance: monitor the threat of war and report back, ferret out Iraqi agents, recruit and run sources within the country, form a Kuwaiti resistance group, and send back operational status reports through the American embassy.

How much had Hamad's father suspected?

"Tell your father I'm sorry."

"Your apology comes too late."

Had he wasted his efforts? Trained the wrong man? "Has Mahmoud guessed that I recruited you for the resistance movement?"

Melancholy crept into Hamad's voice along with the static. With Hamad, loyalty died at a snail's pace. "I would shame him if he knew. He would disown me. You must understand. As part of the ruling family, my commitment is to them. The resistance belongs to those without royal ties."

"You can't back down now, Hamad. The resistance needs you. Have you told your father that a terrorist cell has a stronghold in Kuwait City?"

Anger burned in Hamad's answer. "Many of those men have sworn allegiance to the resistance movement."

"And you believe them?"

"They are my Arab brothers."

"Let me talk to your father. He treats me as a son."

"No, my friend, you can no longer pass as one of us."

The grit of the desert sand stung Jon's eyes. "Is this over that heated discussion I had with him at mealtime?"

"You were wrong to tell him there would be a war."

"As if he didn't know." Jon switched the transmitter to his other ear. "I just wanted to convince Mahmoud of the imminent danger."

Hamad fought back with disdain. "He was right. You have such limited knowledge of the Middle East. You and your book learning. What do you know of us as a people?"

Earlier in the evening Jon had sat cross-legged on Mahmoud's carpet, dining on Mahmoud's mutton boiled with onion and garlic and sampling the spiced seafood. As they sipped biting black coffee, Jon had argued about the possibility of an Iraqi attack on Saudi Arabia and the certainty of one on Kuwait.

Without warning, Mahmoud's words had grown impetuous, vehement, his usual pleasantries abandoned. "Iraq will not attack us. You do not understand my people. Arab brother will never go against Arab brother."

But Arab brother had done the unthinkable.

Now Hamad's voice broke through the static again. "It will not go well with us that we have harbored you, not with my father serving as a cabinet minister."

Jon had depended on Mahmoud's position, depended even more on the fact that Mahmoud was a distant relative of the ruling family. Mahmoud's home was the perfect place to hide, to headquarter. "Hamad, please destroy the equipment in my room."

His throaty whisper crackled over the line. "I cannot. My father has already threatened to use it against you if we have to. Remember, Jon, my father says you are no longer welcome. You must leave. You speak our language well, but it will not take the Iraqis long to know who you are—*what* you are."

And what will happen to you, Hamad, when your father or the Iraqis find you are working with the resistance? Every muscle in Jon's body ached. Without the tree bracing him, he would topple to the ground. He had entered Kuwait with no escape route marked out for him. If caught, there would be no official inquiry about his safety. But he had to get word to Langley about the increased buildup along the oil fields and his concern about terrorists infiltrating the resistance. Whatever happened to him, he must get one final report through to the American embassy, and from there to Langley.

"Hamad, I need the ground transmitter."

"If you come back, my father will treat you as the enemy. Be careful, my friend—and may Allah go with you."

The transmitter went dead. His skin prickled. The silence was deafening, the seconds endless before sheer bulldog courage set in. He waved his knuckled fist into the desert darkness. "My survival is not dependent on you, Hamad. But your survival *is* dependent on me."

Jon's one hope lay in slipping through the enemy lines and reaching the embassy in case its communication lines were still open—in case one more diplomatic pouch could make it out.

He struck out, darting through the night on silent sandals. As he neared the city, the pain in his feet hindered his progress. Iraqi helicopters swooped down like birds of prey through the darkness, bringing in their loads of Special Forces. He heard the distant explosions. The rumble of tanks. The sound of vehicles approaching. A row of cars came into view, fleeing from the city with their headlights off.

Suddenly the nerves at the back of his neck tingled. He was not alone. A short distance away, someone shared the shadows with him. He fumbled for his binoculars, cursing the darkness and his fears. Sudden streaks of light illuminated the sky around him as a lone chopper skimmed the treetops. An Iraqi soldier fired from the chopper. Death rained down on the long row of cars. A vehicle careened off the highway, its gas tank erupting in flames.

In the blaze that followed, Jon saw the man who shared the darkness with him signaling the pilot. An Iraqi perhaps. An enemy, but a man like himself—a foreign agent on Kuwaiti soil. The blades whirred as the chopper lowered. If the Iraqis took Jon hostage, Islamic law would label him an infidel in Arab dress. He'd be tortured. Executed.

Jon ran, stumbling in his sandals. As he fled, he loosened the wide band from his watch and lifted the tiny transmitter to his mouth. "Hamad. Hama—"

The strafing exploded around him. Searing pain tore through his leg then through his shoulder. He pitched forward; his wristwatch slipped from his fingers into the sand.

Moments later he came out of his stupor as rough hands tossed him on his back. His wounded leg twisted beneath him. Jon screamed as the bone snapped, tearing through the skin. Blood spurted.

An angry face loomed above him. Confused, Jon choked out the words. *"You! Not you. I thought—"*

"Yes, me." The hands probed, searched. "Where is it, Jon?"

"I thought you were an Iraqi."

His bloody shoulder throbbed. He'd never known such pain, such fear. He had no strength to fight back. Last week's bout of dysentery had weakened him. His intestines rumbled and cramped. He knew he would spew his guts, or his bowels would explode. Retching, fighting off the unbearable pain, he stared up into the face of the man hovering over him. "What are you doing?"

Deft fingers snatched the papers and camera from beneath Jon's robe. "You won't need these any longer."

"I've got to get that report through to Langley."

"You're a fool, Jon. You should have left Kuwait while you had the chance. You were told to leave before your cover was blown." His words were as scorching as the pain. "You gave your location away using that transmitter."

Hamad, don't call back. Don't signal back.

"Come on. I need the whole report. Don't waste time. Don't make things worse."

Jon remembered the third man on their team. "Rick—where's Rick?"

"He left. But you had to stay and play the hero."

Jon retched again. The sand in his mouth was wet with the acrid taste of blood, the bile of his innards spilling out. He heard the click of the transmitter, muffled by the sand. *Stop transmitting, Hamad. Stop trying to reach me.*

He screamed as he stirred the sand with his good foot. Burying the transmitter was one safety measure he could offer Hamad and his family. That, and dying as an unknown Arab.

He looked at his betrayer. "Please. Please help me."

"You have come to begging, my friend. You, the boy who had everything. My orders are to leave you behind, Jon."

"Your orders? *Whose* orders? I don't understand—we came in together. We—"

"You volunteered for this mission."

"All three of us did—"

The man kicked Jon's leg, sending excruciating jolts through his body. "Did you think I could let your reports go through? You wanted to convince Washington that a terrorist cell has infiltrated the resistance movement. You *fool*. Couldn't you let well enough alone?"

He roughly toed Jon's leg again. "You don't get it, do you? You were never intended to leave Kuwait. You wouldn't have gotten far anyway. You're bleeding. Your leg is shattered—I can see that even in the darkness."

Fighting against the blinding agony, Jon slid his hand down his thigh and felt the jagged fragments of bone. He felt his friend's betrayal even more. "You sold out—"

"I didn't plan it this way, Jon. But I have my orders. There's only transportation out of here for one of us. The crown prince and his father are already en route to Saudi Arabia. They will be safe. That should please you." He stood and gave a mocking farewell salute. "For three months you hid and lived like a Kuwaiti. Now die like one of them."

Jon took inventory as he grew faint: Mouth dry. Throat tight. Thirst unquenchable. Breathing difficult. Pulse irregular.

He feared dying. Dreaded the eternity of the damned. He forced his eyes open. Sucked in another breath. His body was clammy with sweat and blood. What if blackness and emptiness lay ahead? What if his father's God *did* exist?

He had thrust faith aside in his anger at God—umbrage at the God who had allowed his father's humiliating downfall. But hadn't Dad called his dismissal from Paris *Father-filtered?*

Now Jon had stared into the face of his own betrayer—and realized it was the face of his father's betrayer as well. The truth fanned out from Paris, circled the globe, and ended at Winterfest Estates.

Minutes passed with the drone of more planes overhead. Jon

dragged himself in an agonizing crawl to the next tree, his breathing compromised. He had no strength left to push himself to a sitting position. With every move, his leg bled more. He rested. Drifted. Fought his way back to write his fiancée's name in the sand with his finger—that pretty girl with the faint splash of freckles across her cheeks. He would never caress her again. Never make her completely his own. He had called her from Paris three months ago to propose. No kiss to seal the commitment. No ring to sparkle on her finger. He had asked her to tell his folks…to tell them…

What was it he had wanted her to tell them? Jon blinked against the encroaching blackness, but it did no good. The blackness won.

When he came to, his homesickness was as overpowering as his nausea. The grinding roar of the helicopter was gone. His betrayer had left him as he would an Arab, dying in the desert sands. As Jon lay sprawled in a shallow depression, time lost all meaning. Through the predawn clouds, the moon had spread a gossamer whiteness over the desert sand. Now the chill of the night was giving way to the first rays of daybreak. He tried to focus his eyes and saw a gushing pool of water cascading over the sand dunes. The mirage bubbled. Sparkled. He stretched his hands toward it—and the pool evaporated.

In his confusion, the illusion turned the hills into snow-covered slopes—the beloved Colorado mountains where he sometimes skied in the winter, where he hiked in the spring. He sensed the old exhilaration of standing at the mountaintop, felt the utter freedom of taking the slope on skis. He reached again, his fingers weightless.

But his mountain disappeared. Gone. Like his strength.

Something wet and sticky trickled from his mouth and over his bristled chin. He tasted it. Blood. It took a long time to die. Agonizing minutes. The sands of Kuwait were splattered with his blood. He hadn't known how dark his blood could make the sand. A muddy brown, like the ocean waves washing a sandy beach, pooling into a child's bucket. His bucket.

No. Adrienne's.

The beautiful, bratty kid sister with her light, skipping steps on the stairs at Winterfest. He wanted to tell her the land would be all hers now, but the dusty lump in his throat choked him. He should have warned her about Paris—should have taken her into his confidence about their father's betrayer.

He tried to move, but the stabbing pain in his leg drove him to the edge of madness. He would never ski again. *Could I have imagined the betrayer as I imagined the mountain?*

He forced his eyes open and watched the desert sands turn into the blazing shades of autumn. He was climbing. Climbing higher. He struggled to turn over, to lift his head, the effort monumental. In the distance, his beloved mountain turned to reality—a skyline of mosques and domes and minarets, an ultramodern city where the new and the old existed side by side.

Kuwait—a place without alpine trails or snow-covered mountains. A city—a country—under siege. He imagined the familiar wailing that called the faithful, oil-rich Kuwaitis to prayer.

His thoughts drifted. His leg no longer throbbed. He felt nothing.

He awakened sometime later and knew that within hours he would die with the sweltering Arabian sun beating down on him. Again blurred images of his family and the pretty face of the woman he planned to marry gripped him.

Behind him he heard muffled steps on the sand. A stray camel? A goat? An Iraqi soldier creeping up on him?

Please, God. Not my betrayer.

In his uncertainty, he called out for help. Cried for his sister, his girl, his mom. "Adrienne...Kristy...Mom..." His speech slurred. "Hamad?—*Allah!*"

No, not Allah.

A prayer formed on his lips to the God of his boyhood. He fought to stay alert, but the pictures of those he loved—and those he feared—faded into nothingness as a canopy of darkness closed over him.

CHAPTER 2

AUGUST 2, 1990
LANGLEY, VIRGINIA

The news reports pouring into Central Intelligence Headquarters changed with the hour: Iraqi troops and tanks swept across the Kuwaiti border at 2 A.M. local time. General Schwarzkopf's security assistance team trapped in Kuwait. Two hundred Kuwaitis believed dead. All contact with the American embassy lost. Communication with the CIA station chief cut off. Two of a special CIA team made it to safety. The third man left behind. Presumed dead.

As far as Sheridan Macaroy was concerned, the young operative left behind in Kuwait became a security risk the moment the Iraqis launched their attack. All ties with Agent Jon Winters were severed. A-436, code name the Fourth Season, had become expendable.

Macaroy stepped from the elevator on the seventh floor at the Langley headquarters and was admitted at once into the deputy director's office. A sleepless night showed on the chief's square face, the lines around his eyes taut. He pointed to the intelligence reports stacked on his desk. "Mac, I have a briefing with the president in an hour, but sit down. What do you have for me?"

Macaroy eased into a chair and balanced his briefcase on his lap; inside lay the latest report on Jon Aaron Winters. Ignoring their own involvement, he said, "Nothing that you don't already know, sir. The Iraqis made the thirty-seven miles to the capital in just four hours—"

With a brisk wave of his hand, Webster silenced him. "I know.

16

The Kuwaitis woke to a two-hour artillery barrage—tanks racing down the highway, helicopters dropping in Special Forces. And no organized resistance."

"Chief, there wasn't time."

"Time, Mac? We've studied intelligence reports. We knew about the Iraqi buildup for months." He finger-brushed his dark hair. "Diplomacy doesn't work with madmen like Saddam Hussein. He launches a massive attack while we busy ourselves table talking over aerial photographs. When will Congress wake up? The Arab world is important to us."

"At least the oil fields should be."

Webster adjusted his cuff link and splayed his fingers. "We knew war was imminent. What I need is some good news."

"The emir and the crown prince are safe in Saudi Arabia. So far, that's the only good news."

"But American citizens were left behind."

"The embassy is less than a mile from the palace."

"What about the reconnaissance team you sent in?"

"Two of them reached Saudi before the border closed. The third man didn't make it out." Grinding his back molars, Macaroy unlatched his briefcase and handed the intelligence report across the desk. "This is just in."

Webster's glance sharpened. "Jon Winters? Harry Winters's son injured—dead? Mac, you were to advise our people to leave Kuwait days ago."

"We're not certain Winters got our message…should I notify his family?"

"Let's wait. We should be getting more reports."

"How? The Iraqis seized all communications. Winters knew the risks. He knew if the mission failed, we could not acknowledge his whereabouts or attempt any rescue."

"And who gave that order?"

Mac clamped his back molars again, sending a fierce pain along his jaw. "You know the policy, sir, about this Gulf thing. All intelligence was supposed to go through U.S. Central Command straight to Stormin' Norman."

"To General Schwarzkopf, you mean."

"That put the military in control. I thought you were in agreement." He met Webster's glare. "We needed a covert operation to gather our own intelligence and establish a resistance force. Winters was single. No immediate attachments. As it turns out, it was best that way."

"Mac, you're wrong. His parents and a younger sister make their home here in Virginia. His father told me his son was engaged the last time we spoke."

"That's unofficial. There's no public engagement."

Webster's gaze remained fixed on the wall beyond Macaroy. "I knew his father. State Department. A good man. But there was some scandal—"

"A scandal that won't die."

"People won't let it die. Nothing was ever proved. Poor man. He left Paris in disgrace some years back. Perhaps that's what drove the son—a desire to redeem his father's name. And now this." He thumped the report. "He was definitely his mother's favored child. That family has had its tragedies. Another son was stillborn when they were stationed in the Middle East."

"But they still have a daughter left?"

"Adrienne would be fifteen or sixteen now. Good-looking like her mother. Speaks French like a native."

"Let's not recruit her."

Frown lines ridged Webster's brow. "If she's anything like her parents, she'll make up her own mind."

"What about Winters? Should we leave notification of next of kin to the State Department?"

"My goodness, Mac, the invasion isn't twenty hours old and you want to write him off?"

Mac worked his jaw. "You set the policy. If a covert operation is blown, it had better make sense to the American people. We weren't supposed to be there, sir."

The director heaved a sigh. "And this one won't have the right answers for the watchdog committees in Congress."

"Not if they discover that Winters linked up with a high-profile Kuwaiti family—a distant relative of the ruling sheik. Congress would blow on that one—it threatens the relationship between our countries."

Mac hoped his message got through in time: Terminate Winters. *His cover's blown. If the Iraqis take him hostage—and they will if he survives his injury—it would mean trouble for everyone involved. It would be much safer to wipe Winters from the slate. Better for national security. Better for me.* "What about his family, sir?"

"Let's make certain Winters isn't coming back before we tell them. It will be tough enough to tell the president today. You know how he feels about casualties in any government posting."

Mac nodded. *But I already know for certain Winters isn't coming back. I have my sources, but I won't risk bringing questions down on my own head.* He stood and placed Winters's file in his briefcase. "Sir, I'll have this sealed and assigned to the vault."

Macaroy's stomach jerked as the elevator descended. He had chosen his Kuwaiti team with care. Winters was the kind of man the Company took pride in recruiting. Capable. Intelligent. Gifted with languages. A solitary man committed to the job. In spite of his artistic temperament, he lived on the edge. Thrived on undercover work. Too bad he was sometimes driven by his own agenda.

Winters despised bureaucracy and political wrangling. He scoffed at electronic intercepts and technology as the weapons of choice in the fight against terrorism. Now, Jon Winters would be nothing but a code name and a number. Another statistic. Another brilliant career ended.

He might be a favored child in the Winters's household, but at Langley he would be remembered only by his code name: the Fourth Season. In a matter of weeks, Langley would see to it that they placed a star on the Memorial Wall and a space in the Book of Honor for Jon Winters—with or without his name disclosed. That was the least they could do.

War is hellish—his hands fisted as he stepped from the elevator—*But it would be the same fiery furnace for me if they learn my mistakes in sending the Fourth Season into the desert.*

If the truth were uncovered, Macaroy's career would be over. He couldn't live long enough to make it into any Book of Honor.

AUGUST 23, 1990
WINTERFEST ESTATES, VIRGINIA

Fifteen-year-old Adrienne Winters tugged at the reins, bringing the thoroughbred to a breathless standstill on the crest of the hill. Her horse was her constant companion in the isolated world at Winterfest. She leaned forward to rub the sweaty neck. "Good boy, Rocket."

She gazed out over the land, so close to the city of Washington, yet so private, so far from the capital and its teeming crowds. The land came from her father's side—sprawling acres that had belonged to her grandfather Harrison. It was the same spectacular setting where her father had run as a child. Well-trimmed lawns sloped down to the river's edge. Behind her lay the wooded hills with the private riding trails, and down the hill stood the white stucco mansion. One day it would be hers. Hers and Jon's. She wanted the riding trails and stables. But what would Jon lay claim to? He spent little time at Winterfest.

She shifted on her worn saddle as summer clouds glissaded through the ocean of space. Clouds tagged clouds, skimming through the patches of blue. Her father saw the muted vastness as God's canopy; her mother always countered with a weather forecast, predicting a sweltering heat wave or a storm that would ruin her golf game or send the guests at her outdoor tea party running for shelter.

Adrienne remained curious about the heavens and what lay veiled behind the billowy clouds. She was in agreement with her father about the God he worshiped, yet feared that God's agenda did not mesh with her own. "There's plenty of time," she confided in Rocket, "for religious pondering. Right now I'm too young." Studying the drifting clouds again, she voted in her mother's favor. Given another two hours, it would be a blistering hot day, an East Coast heat wave.

A flash of sun reflecting against a moving vehicle caught her eye. She frowned as a government limousine pulled through the front gate. It crept like a funeral dirge up the winding driveway—coming much like the coroner's silver hearse that had come to take her grandfather Harrison away six months ago.

Three men stepped from the limousine. The stocky man was a stranger. But when she recognized Bedford Taylor and his son, she froze. Bedford was her father's colleague from the State Department, but he was no longer welcome at Winterfest. Rocket tugged at his reins, snorting. His prancing matched her hammering heartbeat.

She nudged Rocket and galloped down to the house. She slid from the saddle and left the horse grazing.

As she ran up the steps, Rolf swung the double doors open. He'd been with the family for years, more her father's confidant than butler. He gave Adrienne a slight bow as she gripped his arm. "What's going on, Rolf?"

He hunched his shoulders. "With your father home early and Mr. Taylor here, it must mean trouble. I've notified your mother that she is expected in the sitting room."

"Is Dad all right?"

"A bit gray around his mouth. Nothing more."

"He's not having chest pain again?"

"I encouraged him to take his nitroglycerin, but you best ask your mother." He nodded toward the stairs.

Her mother swept down the carved staircase in a flowing blue gown as though it were the most natural thing of all to welcome company at ten in the morning.

"Oh, Rolf, please hold all calls—and do something with Adrienne. I don't think her father wants her in on this meeting. He sounded quite upset on the phone—"

"That was an hour ago, madame. Mr. Winters told me he wants the whole family present."

Her jaw jutted forward. "Well, that excludes you, Rolf. And Adrienne? She can do as she pleases—isn't that the way she does everything?"

He winked at Adrienne. "I believe it is, madame."

"Someday Harry will wake up and stop spoiling her."

"And maybe stop pampering you," he mumbled.

Her mother gave him a withering glance and sashayed across the hall, a striking figure as she entered the sitting room. For a moment, Adrienne lingered beside Rolf. He was tall and spare, strong of spirit, ageless in a way. He had taught Adrienne much of what she knew about nature and horses. He scowled after her mother's retreating form, a flicker in his honest hazel eyes—not of anger, but of determination to win her mother's favor.

Don't bother being kind to her, Rolf. She will always treat you like a third-class citizen.

From the sudden silence in the living room, she was certain that everyone had risen to greet her mother. "Harry dear, what brings you home at this hour? And, Bedford"—Adrienne grimaced at her mother's gushing—"what a pleasant surprise."

"Mara, I asked Harry to meet us here at Winterfest."

Rolf patted Adrienne's shoulder. "Would you care to go riding, Miss Adrienne?"

"No...I'm staying."

"Then I'll take Rocket back to the stables for you."

She hugged him as he closed the massive front doors, then followed her mother, hesitating in the archway as her mother turned to Bedford's son. "Colin, I thought you were still in Paris."

Adrienne glared across the room where Bedford's son stood by the windows. He was tall like his father, their faces chiseled from the same Spanish mold. Colin was near her brother's age, but he had his father's arrogance.

"Colin...I was talking to you." Clearly she was displeased that

Adrienne had distracted him. "You were in Paris with my son, weren't you?"

"I came home to reenlist."

Her mother touched the tips of her fingers. "I hope Jon Aaron doesn't have that same crazy idea. I know General Schwarzkopf advocates a swift buildup of troops, but I don't think the sand dunes of Kuwait are a viable place for young men. Let the Arabs keep their oil wells."

She dismissed Colin's reenlistment with a flick of her hand and turned to the stranger standing by the fireplace. He was a solidly built man with a leather attaché case in his hand. His mouth was tight, his gaze cold as he looked at her. Adrienne's dislike of him was immediate. Most men drew to her mother like a magnet, but this stranger seemed unaware of her mother's charm. "I'm Sheridan Macaroy, Mrs. Winters. I'm afraid we have bad news for you."

Her mother's smile withered. "It's Jon, isn't it?"

Macaroy whipped an official envelope from his briefcase and unfolded it. "The State Department regrets to inform you that your son, Jon Aaron Winters, was killed in Kuwait—"

Adrienne's throat constricted. She couldn't make a sound, and yet a piercing scream echoed through the room. She'd never heard her mother scream before. She'd seen her angry, defiant, arguing with her father. But her mother never lost control as she was doing now.

Adrienne's father rushed to his wife's side and eased her into the nearest chair.

Her mother's scream softened to a whimper. "No, Mr. Macaroy. That's impossible! My son is in Paris. Tell him, Harry"—her fingers gripped his shirt front—"Bedford, you tell him. Our sons have been in Paris. They always do things together."

"I'm sorry, Mara. Jon Aaron is dead."

The trembling in Adrienne's legs wouldn't go away. Her brother dead? Her hero. Her best friend. Her worst enemy.

Her father's face twisted. "No, Mara dear, he was in Saudi

Arabia when we last heard from him."

"Your son was visiting a friend in Kuwait City, I believe." Bedford again, his smooth tone placating.

"You believe nothing of the sort, Bedford!" Her mother's anger snapped through her tears. "Otherwise you wouldn't be here. And Harry wouldn't be home from the State Department."

"You must believe me, Mara. Jon was killed when the Iraqis invaded Kuwait."

Her father said what Adrienne would have said herself if only she could find her voice: "Three weeks ago! And you are just now notifying us?"

"We had to be certain, Harry."

"No," he shot back. "It's not done that way anymore. Identification is immediate. Next of kin notified at once."

"We waited to confirm the report, Harry. There was an explosion... with the situation in Kuwait City, communications are difficult. We were lucky—"

"*Lucky?*" Her mother's strangled laugh echoed in the room. "Lucky to get word that my son is dead."

"Mara, we believe he was there on special assignment."

"With the State Department? A moment ago you said he was visiting a friend." Mara glanced up at her husband. "So you had your way, Harry. He followed in your footsteps. I *never* wanted him to do that."

His eyes misted. "Mara, you know his ties were with Langley."

"He wanted to be an *artist*. Should have been one."

"Your dream for him, dear."

"No, Jon's dream. He was off on the other side of the world for *you*, Harry. Trying to clear your name."

In the background, Macaroy's voice droned on. "We're here on behalf of the president—to express the gratitude of a grateful nation for your son's sacrifice."

"I want to see my son."

For a moment no one answered, then Bedford cleared his throat. "Mara, there was an explosion. There is no body. And even if there was, the Iraqis wouldn't release him—"

"Get out." The ice in her mother's tone startled Adrienne. "Get out of my house with your lies. I lost my first child. Don't tell me my other son is dead."

I'm still here, Mama. Look at me. I'm still here.

Her mother turned to Bedford's son again. "Tell them, Colin. Jon was in Paris with you. His last postcard to me was mailed from there. He said the two of you—"

Colin jammed his hands in his pockets. "Mrs. Winters, he left Paris several weeks ago. He didn't explain…"

"Get out. Get out, all of you."

Adrienne stepped back as the stranger rushed past her. When Colin reached her, his tangy cologne reminded her of Jon. "Adrienne, may I call you this evening?"

My brother is dead and you want to call. "No, don't."

Bedford refused to budge. He leaned down and kissed Adrienne's mother on the cheek. "Mara, if you and Harry need me, call. Even if it's the wee hours… As we learn more—if we learn more—Macaroy or I will get back to you."

A̶n hour later Adrienne found her father in the garden with Robbie Gilbert. Her father had always been a tower of strength, tall, broad-shouldered, a dignified man committed to government service. But he always made time for her. Yet in just an hour of grief he looked old.

"What are you doing here, Robbie? Can't you see my dad wants to be alone?"

Robbie met her sullen gaze across the flower bed, his brilliant blue eyes sympathetic. He was a lanky sixteen-year-old, his dark red hair as disheveled as it had been on the day they met at the American Academy in Paris. "I came in my father's car the minute I heard about Jon."

"You don't even have your driver's license."

"But I had to see you. I had to tell you I was sorry."

"Robbie, go away. Go away forever."

She turned her back on him and took her father's arm. As they wandered over the sprawling grounds toward the trails, her father scolded, "That was unkind. Robbie is your friend."

"He's like a bad penny, always coming back. I wish he would grow up and tuck his shirt in and comb his hair."

"Your friends like his wavy hair and casual ways. He's a good lad. More grown-up than you know. He's loyal. Ambitious. He'll make a fine journalist, like his father."

Adrienne let that one ride. She had her own priorities, and they didn't include Robbie. She didn't even take time to write about him in her journal anymore. Actually, she didn't keep a journal now that she was older—she kept a datebook. In it she recorded things like her recent holiday abroad before returning to the private girls' school in the fall, today's tennis lesson, the Washington Ball next week, the movie with her latest heartthrob.

No, she didn't want to talk about Robbie. She wanted to talk about Jon, but his name lodged in her throat. Her father's breath shortened as they climbed the hill. "Dad, I don't want to believe Jon is dead. I never told him I loved him."

"He knew."

"But we always argued. You said so yourself."

He nodded. "Brothers and sisters do that. They call it sibling rivalry. I was an only child"—he smiled—"I never had the pleasure of a brother."

"The last time I saw Jon I told him to go away and never come back." Like she had just told Robbie.

"You didn't know it would be the last time."

"I don't want him to be dead. I don't even know what being dead means. I just know I'm going to miss him."

Tears moistened his thoughtful gray eyes. "I already do, Adrienne. I'll miss our fishing trips. And spending our evenings playing a game of chess… I'll just miss talking to Jon. He had a brilliant mind, a world vision."

"I won't have anyone to argue with. Or a handsome brother to show off to my friends." She was crying now and uncertain what to do with her tears. She had envied Jon's closeness with their parents and felt left out of their political ramblings. But what she wouldn't give now to have him here, debating the world's woes with their parents. "Mother will miss everything about him. She's always boasting about Jon. About him skiing down the mountain slope. About mountain hiking with him."

About his muscular good looks. His charm.

"He was special to her. They are so much alike. Cut from the same fabric."

Sometimes Adrienne thought of her brother as her mother's son, as though they were strangers, not siblings. Jon was dark and handsome, and—thanks to their mother's Spanish ancestry—dashing. She was fair, like the Winters's side of the family. She didn't enjoy skiing and mountain climbing as much as Jon did. She was more into fashion magazines and horseback riding and tennis.

Her father's voice cracked. "Most of all, I think Mother will remember Jon's strong hands molding a piece of clay. She wanted him to be an artist—and now we'll never know whether he was another Michelangelo or not."

"He was the favorite with both of you."

He stopped and stared down at her. "Adrienne, both of you are special to your mother and me—each in your own unique ways."

"I should have died. Then it wouldn't hurt so much."

He patted her cheek. "Don't say that, sweetheart. We love you."

"Not the way you loved Jon."

Again tears moistened his eyes. "I'm so sorry if we've made you feel that way."

She clenched her fist. "Mom does all the time. Daddy, did you ever regret marrying Mother?"

A trace of a smile touched his face. "Regret marrying your mother? I love her, Adrienne."

"But you're so different. It's more than her spending her childhood in Spain. She surrounds herself with friends and partying and leaves you to spend your evenings alone."

"We understand each other. Your mother will need the safety of Winterfest even more with Jon gone."

She loves the land more than you. "What about you, Daddy? What about the times you've needed her since Paris?"

"She lost a lot when we left Paris."

"So did you." His reputation. His position with the State Department. The respect of old friends. Oh, the top dogs at the State Department had recanted on their accusations, but there had never been a public apology. No reinstatement to his old position. None of the previous top-security clearance permitted.

And so the scandal lingered. The rejection from his colleagues never quite went away. And the old friendship with Bedford Taylor remained tainted. Scarred...

And now Jon. Adrienne feared her dad would crumble at the loss of his son.

She stumbled forward over the rocky ground, blinded by tears. Her father's chest was heaving when he caught up with her. "For Jon's sake forgive your mother, Adrienne. She wanted what was best for all of us."

"She's the reason we came home in disgrace."

"The blame is all mine. Even Jon's death is my fault. He gave up art to go into government service in an effort to salvage the family name."

"What happened was *not* your fault, Dad. Jon said you were too honorable a man to ever betray your country."

"*Our* country, Adrienne. Always remember that."

She brushed at the tears streaking down her cheeks. "Daddy, someday I'm going back to Paris and find out what happened. I'll finish the job Jon started."

Her father pointed across the river to the city he loved. "The truth is there. Buried in classified documents."

"You don't believe they told us the truth about Jon either, do you?"

"Half-truths, perhaps." He stopped again and cupped her

cheeks, his hands rough against her soft skin. "That was disloyal of me, but we're all in shock, sweetheart. Losing Jon is unbearable. In time the pain will ease, but it will never quite go away. He will always be part of us."

His attempted smile failed. "With Jon…with Jon gone, you will inherit the land, Adrienne. That was your grandfather's wish, but promise me that there will always be a place for your mother here at Winterfest."

"I promise, but I'll never understand why Grandpa didn't want to leave the land to Mother. Didn't he trust her?"

Her father winced. "He was afraid that Bedford Taylor would move in and take over. Perhaps even sell it at a loss."

Since Paris, her father had treated Bedford Taylor with a tolerant politeness for his wife's sake. "Sweetheart, you know Mother and Bedford spent several years of their childhood in a small farming village near Madrid."

She squiggled her nose. "Childhood friends?"

"More than that—distant cousins of some sort."

"Does that mean I'm supposed to treat him like King Tut? Robbie and I grew up in Paris, but I don't kowtow to him."

"You should be much kinder to him than you are…Robbie would not mistreat the land."

She leaned against her father. "I was seven when I first saw Winterfest Estates."

"Eight years ago—before our move to Paris."

She smiled at the memory. "I was so enchanted with all the nooks and crannies where I could hide and the private gardens where I could wander unafraid."

They'd been home for holiday between her father's overseas assignments. She had tumbled over the grass, picked flowers without her grandfather scolding her, chased butterflies around the flower beds, and learned to ride the pony along the trails with her father or Rolf beside her.

"My father adored you, Adrienne."

"I know. I loved him back a thousand times."

All that holiday, she played hide-and-seek with her grandfather, hiding behind the Doric columns on the porch and screaming with laughter when he found her. For three magnificent weeks, she ran through the corridors of the big house, from room to room, as though the whole historic place had been nothing more than a playroom.

"Mother kept telling me to stop making so much noise. She was so afraid I would break something."

"And what did my father say?"

"Grandpa Harrison told her to let me be a child because childhood was gone so soon."

It was gone by the time Adrienne was little more than thirteen, when her father was recalled from Paris. After that their lives were shattered, but nothing could take this land from her father. It was his refuge, his inheritance—an inheritance he promised to pass on to his children.

As they continued their climb at a slackened pace, her father's pallor frightened her. "Dad, let's stop and rest. Rolf put some benches along the trails. There's one quite close. We could rest there."

"I'd like that. I forgot to bring my nitroglycerin."

"Oh, Daddy, I'll run back and get it." She eased him onto a rustic bench. "Will you be all right? Are you having pain?"

"No, stay with me. The woods are comforting. I'll just rest a bit. When we get back to the house I must notify Kris—Kris—"

"Kris Keller? But, Daddy, she's not family."

"She would have been had Jon—" His voice failed.

"Did Jon like her that much?"

"Freckles and all." His shoulders convulsed as he covered his face with his hands. "She called us several weeks ago and told us they were engaged. Not an official engagement. Your mother insisted on that. Mother wanted to throw a proper engagement party when Jon got home."

"Oh, Daddy." She gripped his trembling hand. "I'm so sorry. Mother won't have to throw a party now—"

Though it was a hot summer day, Adrienne shivered as though a winter's wind had swept across the Potomac and engulfed them.

Her father leaned down and kissed her on the forehead. "Adrienne, someday you will be even more beautiful than your mother. Jon predicted it. You'll be beautiful—inside and out. Your mother will have her hand in the one, but God will make you beautiful inside. I pray toward that end. But whatever you do or become, make Jon proud of you. Make all of us proud of you."

"I wanted Jon to be here for my sixteenth birthday."

"I know. We all did. But he left his present—just in case he didn't get back in time."

"He did? What is it?"

"If I told you, it wouldn't be a surprise."

"Is it big or little?"

"It will be big enough."

"A new saddle!" She sobered and teared up again. "I saw it in the stables, but I won't feel much like celebrating."

"When the time comes, you will. We'll do something special. We're not going to stop celebrating you, Adrienne. You're all we have left."

In the months that followed Jon's death, Adrienne's mother refused to attend the Washington socials. She said she couldn't stand how everybody pitied her because of Jon. Her father went deeper into himself, spending hours alone in the library reading his Bible and books on history and politics. As her sixteenth birthday grew closer, Adrienne longed for them to take notice of her.

One day as she sat in the library with her father, Rolf stomped into the room and slapped blueprints on her father's desk. He pointed through the French windows down toward the river. "Harry Thaddeus Winters, it is time to stop mourning. Time to turn your ashes into beauty. That area down there used to be filled with guests and music."

"Mara knows she can still have her garden parties."

"Look at the lawn, sir. Brown patches everywhere."

"We have automatic sprinklers."

"And no gardeners to tend them. Your wife fired every one of them."

Adrienne shrank back as Rolf pointed his finger at her. "You can't expect Adrienne to take over. She's still a child, Harry. She's hurting, too, you know. If I weren't suffering an arthritic back, I'd do the gardening myself."

"You have enough to do, taking care of my family."

"Harry, it's time for you to assume responsibility again. Winterfest is turning into briars and brambles and thorns while you grieve for your son. Jon would hate that. I know I do. I ache for what is happening to you, Harry."

Adrienne hugged her knees as her father's face turned ashen. "Have I neglected the land so, Rolf?"

"Yes. And you have shut everyone out, including your daughter."

Her father stared at her, all of the old tenderness crossing the room to engulf her. "Oh, sweetheart, I'm so sorry. I thought everything was all right with you. You've kept busy. You seemed happy."

"What else did you expect from her, Harry? But her friends seldom come around anymore. It's too sad here."

"Bedford Taylor always slips through to see my wife."

Rolf's tone hardened. "Not my doing, sir. Cousin or no cousin, I'd never let that man in if I had my way." Rolf pointed through the windows again. "Look out there, Harry. Down toward the river. There's a vast section there, sir, where I want to develop a memorial garden in your son's memory. Once it's developed"—he hesitated, his cheeks flushing—"once it starts blooming with life again and seasonal flowers—Mrs. Winters will like it."

"I'd forgotten her pleasure, Rolf. You never do."

Adrienne closed her eyes against the anger brewing within her. *Because Mother shuts you out. But what about you, Daddy? Will the garden take away your sadness?*

In that first spring following Jon's death, when the land was restored again and the Washington cherry blossoms were in full bloom, the Winters were invited to a private ceremony at Langley to receive Jon's posthumous Intelligence Star.

Adrienne's mother entered the Old Headquarters Building on the arms of Bedford Taylor and Sheridan Macaroy. Adrienne fell in step behind them, her hand in her father's; Jon's girl, Kris Keller, walked beside them.

The spacious lobby seemed to swallow them up. In front of them, the Agency's seal filled the floor space. Her mother's heels clicked across it; her father stepped around it, as though it was sacred. Though her father was only in his fifties, he had grown old since Jon's death. But this morning he wore a new suit for the occasion and a bright red tie Jon had given him one year for Father's Day.

Her father's smile steadied Adrienne as they faced the north wall. The Memorial occupied a large space with the American flag to the left, the Agency's flag to the right. She wanted to run when she saw the rows of stark, black stars. Her mother touched Jon's star with her gloved hand, her emotions raw, exposed. Adrienne felt her own tears welling.

Her father leaned down to her. "No tears. We're doing this for Jon, honey."

That meant with pride. With military reserve. Without display of emotions. Adrienne stared down at the Book of Honor lying open inside its locked display case. "Dad, Jon's name isn't in the book."

Macaroy spoke up. "Covert names are not revealed. National security. It could endanger the men Jon worked with... The year of his death is there. That's all."

She flicked a lock of hair from her cheek and met Macaroy's cold stare. "He was born with a name, Mr. Macaroy."

"But his mission was sensitive, Miss Winters."

If he expected her to accept that, he was very much mistaken. She recoiled inside. Mr. Macaroy seemed to see her brother as little more than a name or a number. But her brother had dreams. A girl he wanted to marry. Mountains he wanted to climb. Did they chisel a star in marble and expect the families to forget? The dead to cease to exist? The fiancée to go on her way rejoicing?

Macaroy hustled the family together. "We must hurry. The director is waiting for us in his office."

They rode the elevator to the seventh floor in silence. As they entered his office, the director rose to meet them. Adrienne busied herself studying the spacious room with its paneled walls and the large painting that reminded her of a John Constable. She dropped into one of the chairs at the conference table and spun around until she caught her father's warning scowl.

The director took the open box from his desk. Her father clasped the man's hand, but the director pulled free. They were old acquaintances; it was an awkward moment. The director looked beyond her father, clearly unwilling to meet his eyes. Her father stood taller, his eyes on the medal. Adrienne wanted to scream. As if a medal could substitute for his son! She found herself resenting the political correctness of her father's stance. And she pitied the pale, freckled face of Kristy Keller, who stood motionless, her misty eyes her only sign of life.

The director didn't look at his notes to recall Jon's name, but he should have. His voice was solemn. "This is the much coveted Intelligence Star given for a voluntary act of courage. With it, our country honors your son. For Jonathan Aaron Winters—"

Adrienne blurted out, "His name wasn't *Jonathan*. It was Jon. Jon Aaron. Jon Aaron Winters."

He caught Adrienne's eye as his neck turned scarlet. "For *Jon* Aaron Winters's courage and sacrifice under hazardous conditions...given for valor...under grave risk...with courage he put himself in harm's way on a mission fraught with personal danger..."

Her focus wandered. Several electrical cords snaked up from the floor to computers and phone consoles. She had an urge to go to the bathroom and wondered whether the one door led to the director's private facility.

With an apologetic glance at Kris Keller, the director picked up the Intelligence Star and passed it from his hand to Adrienne's father. Dinner in the director's private dining room was offered and refused. It was over within minutes, and they rode the elevator back down to the lobby.

Adrienne glanced toward the Memorial Wall as they left and felt nothing but confusion. A chiseled black star on the wall. A nameless number in a book. Not one word was said about the place where Jon died. About his mission. It was all nebulous. Vague. An obscure, hateful cloud hanging over them.

A nameless person had died in a nameless place for a nameless cause.

One day she would retrace Jon's steps from Paris to Kuwait. She would find out what made Jon put duty above all else. There was more to it than a handshake. More than a few noncommittal words of condolence.

Now, though, she smiled for her father's sake. The medal had somehow comforted him. She took his arm as they left the building. "That was nice, wasn't it?"

"Jon would have liked it."

The woman who escorted them to the door gave Kris a reassuring hug, then turned and shook Adrienne's hand. "I lost a brother, my dear. I do understand. You can't absorb everything in just one visit. If you and Miss Keller want to come back, call me. I'll arrange for another visitor's pass."

Adrienne flinched. *Come back here? Never. Never.*

CHAPTER 3

SPRING, 2002
ARLINGTON, VIRGINIA

At twenty-seven, Adrienne Winters knew all too well she turned heads when she swept into a room bringing Southern elegance and the delicate fragrance of Shalimar with her. She spun magic with her presence, prompting whispers of approval and envy, stirring soft whistles from men. Friends told her she seemed to feather-glide when she walked, like someone spreading her wings and never touching the fashion runway. Women adored her gentle Southern manner and admired her silky complexion—fair as a delicate rose, soft as a velvety petal. Men were enamored of her large mahogany eyes and full glossy mauve lips. They found her charming and sophisticated, but she kept them at a distance.

For Adrienne knew the truth about herself. Inside, she was fragile as crystal. She would not give her heart away and risk losing someone she loved again. Too often, memories of a childhood rivalry against a brother already dead tormented her.

Even in death, the favored brother was still favored.

Jon Aaron's death in the Kuwaiti invasion had curtailed some of her career goals and limited her overseas opportunities as a fashion buyer. But she was breaking free at last. Another business trip to Paris lay at her fingertips. And she was packing.

Today at noon, she was leaving.

Adrienne gazed out her bedroom window at the splendor of spring—a row of cherry blossoms in full bloom and a magnificent array of tulips carpeted the north lawn of the Winters estate. The white stucco mansion sat on a sprawling hillside just outside of Arlington, its lofty Doric pillars framing the wide front porch. She gazed the length of the property down to the gentle winding river, then turned her attention back to the open suitcases lying on her canopy bed. But what to do with the unpacked outfits—the periwinkle suit, the cable sweater and jasmine skirt for the cool nights, and her favorite evening dresses?

"I'd take all four gowns."

Adrienne turned to find her mother rolling her wheelchair into the room and straight to the bedside.

Adrienne smiled down at the upturned, oval face. Her mother's lips were a delicate rose, her brows plucked. But at sixty-two her body was already wasting away. Adrienne winced at the tremor in her mother's hand as she ran her fingers over the beaded silk Georgette with its plunging V neck. "This is my favorite, Adrienne."

"You insisted I buy it."

"Did I? I'd forgotten." For a moment the memory lapse seemed to dismay her, but she was quick to recover. "You have a degree in fashion design, my pet, but I still know style. Don't worry, you look good no matter what you wear."

"If I run out of clothes, I'll go shopping in Paris."

Wistful charcoal eyes stared back at her. "Weren't those shopping sprees just marvelous?"

Adrienne sought escape by staring out the window. The shopping? The social whirl? Was that all her mother remembered of Paris? But why not? Her mother cared about her looks. Her closet was jammed with exquisite designer dresses for the Washington parties she would never again attend.

"Darling, I hate to see you go so far away, traveling all alone. I'll worry the whole time."

"Security at the airports has never been so good."

"Something could go wrong. Engine failure. Or worse."

"Nothing is going to happen to the plane or me."

"I pray they will have a sky marshal on board. And whatever you do, Adrienne, don't sit beside him."

"It could be a she. And she'd no doubt fly economy. I'll be in first class."

"Small comfort. Colin should be traveling with you. Maybe he could arrange for fighter jets to accompany you."

Adrienne smothered a chuckle. "Fighter pilots have more important things to do. They're flying hundreds of sorties a month to protect our country from another terrorist attack. I'll be just fine. I'll call the minute I land at de Gaulle. I'll call every night if you want me to."

"No, don't fuss over me like that. Besides, dear, you know that Rolf will never desert me."

Rolf—the bone of contention between mother and daughter. As sole owner of Winterfest, Adrienne had persuaded Rolf to stay on to oversee the care of the property and her mother. Her mother still called him the butler, but he was far more than that. He was, as Adrienne reflected on it, one of her best friends. He was an endearing man, more endearing for his ability to overlook her mother's snobbery. "I'm glad Rolf is here."

"Of course, you are. *You're* the one who kept him on after your daddy died. You just had to keep up the Winters's tradition—Rolf overseeing everything. As though we couldn't think for ourselves." She clapped her hands. "So with our regular staff and the nurses— and hiring them was *ridiculous*—I can survive for three weeks. As long as Rolf doesn't hover over me and you don't stay away forever, I'll be fine."

No time like the present. Adrienne dropped her bombshell. "I might stay ten more days."

A faint whine crept in. "Whatever for?"

"For a holiday."

"From me?"

Yes, from you. From the past. From the sting of rejection from Father's friends in Paris—friends who had to know what happened all those years ago. Jon searched for answers; now it's up to me to unravel the truth.

Mara placed her hand on Adrienne's wrist. "We do need a break from each other, don't we? I'll be all right."

"So will I. I spent the best part of my childhood in Paris. I just want to look up familiar places."

"Promise me you won't go to the American embassy. You know Americans are still targets."

"Not even to look up Daddy's old friends? Don't worry. Once the fashion show is over, I want to visit some of the gardens and museums that Jon loved. The Louvre, for one. And the Tuileries Gardens. And especially the Rodin Museum."

"So you remembered?" She smiled. "Jon loved going to the Rodin Museum, didn't he?"

Adrienne nodded. "So did Daddy."

"Will you go to Notre Dame and St. Etienne du Mont? Your father found such solace in those old sanctuaries."

Adrienne's throat caught at the mention of the two cathedrals her father loved most. Majestic Notre Dame was the only place her father ever seemed small to her, his height dwarfed by the immensity of the building. "I'll see how my time goes."

Even as she spoke, her thoughts fled back to that last time at Notre Dame, days before they left Paris. She had sat stone still beside her father as ribbons of light poured through the Rose Window and painted rainbows of color on his face. He sat, head bowed. At last he reached out and squeezed her hand. When they stood, he seemed distant, but at peace with himself and his God.

"We'd best hurry home. Mother will be waiting for us."

But no one was at home waiting for them. Jon was out with his friends, and her mother had scribbled a note that she was off attending a charitable event in Paris... Adrienne sighed. Perhaps she would go back to Notre Dame and let those ribbons of light pour through her own heart and soul. Perhaps she'd find the inner peace that eluded her now. She met her mother's questioning gaze. How long had she been silent? She dared not admit she planned to go to the American embassy and to the old neighborhood, digging for truth. "I'll rent a car and drive out into the countryside where Jon and I played as children."

Her mother stiffened. "That won't bring Jon back."

"But it will make the memories sweeter."

The grip on her wrist tightened. "Darling, I wish you were more like your brother. He and I could talk about everything without him fussing at me. He made me feel so special."

"You are special." Pricks of jealousy jabbed at her. Jon Aaron, the brilliant, charming brother she had adored. The brother who teased her. Taunted her. Watched over her. The dead brother.

The brother she could never quite live up to.

Yes, Mother, Jon understood your need to be noticed, to be the center of attention. And why not? You're a beautiful woman. Illness hasn't robbed you of your flawless features.

Her mother's lip formed a perfect pout. "You're angry at me, Adrienne. Why must we be at odds when we talk about Jon?"

"I don't like living in Jon's shadow. He's dead, Mother. He's been dead for twelve years."

"And who knows that better than I? Jon stood up to your father to defend me, to take my part from the day we were sent home from Paris. And your loyalties, Adrienne—even then—were always with your daddy."

"And that still bothers you?"

"What bothers me is that you blame me for your father's dismissal in Paris. Me—your mother. What did I know about politics or the State Department? How did I know he would be demoted and sent home in disgrace over some trivial..."

Over some trivial matter? No, more like a bitter betrayal. "Let's not argue, Mother. I was only thirteen then. I was leaving my friends, leaving everything that was familiar to me. But not Jon... He stayed on when the rest of us came home."

At this fresh anger at her brother, Adrienne made a concentrated effort to smooth the wrinkles from her vicuna suit before packing it in her case.

"Darling, they do have irons in Europe."

"Do they? I think our maid took care of the laundry."

"What a spoiled young woman you are."

Adrienne brushed away the tear sliding down her cheek. "Jon always called me a hotheaded, nonconformist. Strange, but I think I'm going to feel closer to him in Paris."

"Look at me, Adrienne... It's all right. Jon and your father loved Paris. We all did. If going back makes them seem closer, then I'd like to go back someday myself."

"Get better and I'll take you."

Her mother tilted her head back, a touch of the old vibrancy showing. "I warn you, I'll dance the night away. I was the belle of the embassy balls."

"Yes, Daddy was always so proud of you."

Yes, the belle of the ball. Her mother had been that. She'd had many suitors, her beauty unmatched among her circle of friends. So why had she chosen to marry Harry Winters? Adrienne had long wondered at that. Her parents were so different—her mother outgoing, vivacious; her father a shy man given to reading poetry, a man who expressed deep inner yearnings for God. A man who walked with God. Trusted Him.

During those secret moments when Adrienne tried to determine what made her mother tick, she decided that it was Winterfest that had drawn her to her father. Why else would she have married him? The land represented position and power, and making an impression was important to Mara Winters. Or was it the glamour of overseas postings in Paris and Rome?

With sudden compassion, Adrienne realized the emptiness her mother must feel without Harry Winters at her side. "You miss Daddy, too, don't you?"

"More than you will ever know, Adrienne. More than he would ever dream." Her body jerked. "I never knew how much he meant to me until I lost him. But in those last few years, your father was never quite sure of me."

"Don't say that. He adored you."

"But he changed after Jon died. It was never the same for Harry

41

after that. I wasn't much help to him. I know that now. Thank God he had Rolf to talk to and that Bible of his to sustain him. But I was angry—even angry at your father's God for taking my son away."

"Daddy understood. He loved you. Prayed for you."

"I know. And I never told Harry how much he mattered to me. After his stroke, I didn't know what to say to him. He was always the strong one—I hated seeing him in that wheelchair." She threw up her hands. "Now look at me. Confined to this miserable contraption myself. Poor Harry."

She avoided Adrienne's gaze, studying her hands as though she despised the tremor there. Another tremor shook her voice. "Your father was so handsome. That's the way I like to remember him. The striking diplomat with silver hair. Bless his heart, he stayed on the sidelines, befriending diplomats from other countries."

"That was his job." *And his mistake.*

Her mother's gaze drifted up to meet Adrienne's, the old sparkle back in those charcoal eyes. "You think I should have sat on the sidelines with him. Well, I didn't. I *liked* dancing. Did you know Colin Taylor's father was always a great dancer? Bedford was light on his feet. Full of rhythm—Oh, Adry, will you take me back to Paris?"

"Of course."

Her mother's voice faltered again. "But no one will recognize me. My hands tremble. My head shakes."

"It's the Parkinson's, Mother. But I promise. I'll take you back someday, if you really want to go."

Her mother fingered an unpacked silk blouse. "I'm such a burden to you."

She'd heard it a hundred times. The same whiny voice. The same pity party. But she patted her hand. "It's all right, Mother."

"Oh, Adrienne—I almost forgot! Colin called. He's leaving the Pentagon early to take you to the airport."

"But Robbie Gilbert is taking me."

"Then we're in for trouble. You know those two go head to head whenever they're in the same room. I'd think Robbie would be too busy on his Washington beat for a drive to the airport. If you would just marry one of them, I wouldn't get so many headaches. Darling, I assume you wouldn't consider marrying Bedford Taylor's son?"

Adrienne didn't reply, and her mother tossed a sigh at her. "Don't use that silent treatment on me, young lady. I'm your mother... I know, I know. You're distant cousins. Two or three times removed. But surely Colin would have been your father's choice. He is mine, what with his position and power. He'd take such good care of you."

"If Colin's wife didn't want him, I don't either. Colin and his son don't fit into my plans anytime soon."

"Poor Gavin. A six-year-old needs a mother."

"He had one."

Adrienne had known Colin forever. Their fathers' postings in the diplomatic service had taken them to Kuwait, Rome, and Paris together. But their fathers were dead now. Her father gone five years. Bedford's sudden death came six months ago, a month after 9/11. They were buried in different cemeteries—Bedford with military honors, her father in a grave on a Winterfest hillside, a long way from Arlington National, where he had wanted to lie.

"Why do you always turn your suitors away? You're twenty-seven, Adrienne. Elegant. Fashionable. I was married at twenty."

"Colin is too old for me."

"Nine years older."

"Nine going on twenty-nine years older."

They heard the front door open and close. Colin's deep voice echoed down the hall, "Anyone home?"

"In here, Colin."

Her mother released the brake on her wheelchair. "You could do worse than a man like Colin. An investigative journalist like Robbie simply would not be my choice."

"Mom, when the time comes. I'll make the choice. But my friends say Robbie is the catch of the day."

"They would. You young people think alike. But I do admit,

Robbie's like a rock. As solid as the foundation beneath our family mansion. And don't think I haven't noticed what a handsome man he's become."

"We're just good friends. Stop trying to marry me off."

"I want someone to take care of you when I'm gone."

"I have my career."

"A career can kiss you good-bye, but it will never kiss you good night."

As Colin entered the room, he bent down and gave Adrienne's mother a quick hug, then turned to Adrienne. "About ready?"

She crossed her arms. "Colin, Robbie is taking me to the airport."

"What?"

She met his frosty gaze across the open suitcases.

"I left work just to—"

"I didn't ask you to."

His features darkened. "So Robbie wins again?"

"Colin, it wasn't a contest. He offered first."

Colin's eyes, his strongest feature, turned sharklike in his anger. His life was routine, regimented. He left town each morning with an attaché case in his hand and often returned by commuter train late in the day, his uniform looking as spotless and unruffled as when he left. He had admired Adrienne's dad, but his friendship with her brother had been edgy, and his dislike of Robbie never ending.

Colin touched her hand, stopping her from slipping another blouse into the suitcase. "Adrienne, if you want my opinion, you're foolish to go back to Paris."

"What happened to my dad happened a long time ago, Colin. I was happy there. Going back won't change that. This isn't my first trip back, you know."

His face clouded. "I hope it won't be your last."

"Is that a threat straight from the Pentagon? I get so tired of you pulling rank on me, Colin."

"Don't be ridiculous. But I think you're still trying to unravel your father's recall to Washington. Let it go."

"For crying out loud, Colin, that happened half a lifetime ago. What about my brother's death? That matters to me too."

His gaze sharpened. "Adrienne, you always told me Jon volunteered for that mission."

Score another point for Colin. He never stopped throwing the family demons across her path—tossing the old question marks about her brother's death and her father's humiliation into her face. Her innocent father—that godly man who never defended himself—who, shored up by prayer, took his shame and tried to live above it. Why wouldn't she want to clear his name? Wasn't that what drove Jon Aaron?

"I'm sorry, Adrienne. But what happened to your father in Paris, what happened to Jon in Kuwait, are both—"

"Ancient history?" She set her jaw. "Not to me, Colin."

As she pressed the last garment in place and closed the lid, Colin gave an impatient shrug. "Here, let me." Forcing the lid shut, he locked it. "You're certain you won't let me drive you to Dulles International?"

"I'm certain. It's best this way, Colin."

"Then I'll leave your luggage in the living room and get back to the office." At the door he turned back, scowling. "For my sake, just be careful in Paris. Decide on those ready-to-wear clothes and accessories and get home safely."

CHAPTER 4

Adrienne paced in front of the living room windows. Why did she allow Colin to upset her? She glanced at her mother dozing in the wheelchair. Streams of sunlight poured through the wide windows, making her mother's dark hair glisten, her creamy white skin glow.

Adrienne felt as vulnerable as her mother looked.

At the fireplace mantel, she picked up her favorite photograph of her parents and Jon. She had much of her mother's beauty and her brother's traveling bug. But it was her father's strength, his belief that God had not rejected him, that molded her. Her father's faith had been unshakable. At times her own faith was as rocky and undulating as the hills that sloped down toward the river. This was one of those times. She could not look at her father's picture without remembering his quiet endurance, his refusal to fight back. *But who were you protecting, Daddy?*

Adrienne blew the dust flecks from the picture frame and replaced it on the mantel. In spite of her love and loyalty, her father had died a broken man. But she could not look at his face or her brother's without missing them.

As the door chimes rang, her mother awakened with a start. "Answer it, Adrienne. It may be my son."

Adrienne's hand froze on the doorknob. "Mother, don't you remember? Jon Aaron is never coming home."

Her mother's wide eyes blinked. "Oh! I was dreaming about him—I do that so often."

The door chimes rang again. Adrienne swung the door open, and Robbie stood there, his auburn hair disheveled. Dear Robb! Unsophisticated, yet successful and well-respected by the older

46

journalists who trained him. He'd never be picture-postcard perfect, with his shirt sleeves rolled to the elbow, his striped tie loose, his classy jacket slung over his shoulder. His rugged good looks were his greatest calling card. He was the pillar in her life, the old standby that wouldn't go away—the man her friends would snatch from her if she'd let him go.

He smiled down at her with those smoky blue eyes. "Wow! I like that outfit. You'd make a great model on a fashion magazine."

He, on the other hand, would never make the front cover of GQ.

He glanced Mara's way. "Good morning, Mrs. Winters. Great day for your daughter's flight, right?"

"Go ahead, Adrienne. Tell him what I just did."

"When the bell rang, she thought you were Jon Aaron."

Kindness filled his features as he strode over to the wheelchair and put his hand over hers. "No, Mrs. Winters, it's me. Robbie Gilbert. I'm here to take your daughter for a ride."

"You two aren't running off to get married?"

"Don't I wish! But it's just a quick run to the airport."

Adrienne's mother bit her lip. "You take good care of her for me."

"I will." He turned back to Adrienne. "Ready?"

"Robbie, I want to say good-bye to Mother. Alone."

"Sure thing. I'll stow the luggage in my T-Bird."

Adrienne bent down to embrace her mother. "I'm leaving now, Mom."

"So you are going? Your brother would never run out on me when I needed him."

Adrienne bit off the words that would end in a bitter quarrel. Hurrying to the door, images of Jon ran like taunting couplets: Jon scooping her up in his muscular arms when she was small; Jon sending her away with careless indifference when she tagged after him and his friends. Jon explaining the Renaissance masterpieces with infinite patience or playfully boxing her ear when she couldn't solve a geometry problem. Jon giving her a hug against his sweaty hiking togs and then erupting when she dropped his sculpture of a mountain lion.

When Adrienne reached Robb's car, he held the door open. "Are you okay? Is your mom okay?"

"I'm just worried about Mother waking up like she does and expecting Jon Aaron to be there. It could be the Parkinson's. Or maybe she doesn't hurt as much when she slips into the past. Do you understand what I'm saying?"

"Of course I do. We all miss him."

"It's just a bad time for me to leave her."

"You know there will never be a good time. But don't worry. Rolf will watch over her. You have to get on with your own life." He slipped into the driver's seat. Turning the key, he took a final look at the house with its magnificent view and grinned. "Harrison Winters knew how to pick a winning location when he bought Winterfest."

"Yes, Grandfather wanted to be close to the politics he loved, but far enough away to maintain the lifestyle of a Southern gentleman. Dad was just like him. He never wanted to be far from Washington either."

Robbie shifted gears. "You're like both of them, Adrienne. You have that same fierce loyalty to the land."

"I know. My father made me promise that Mother would always be free to live at Winterfest. Now, with her so ill, I wouldn't think of moving her anywhere else."

But it wasn't until I moved back home after graduate school that I came to truly appreciate this old historic place, with its deeply coved ceilings, walls boasting priceless paintings, and Father's library with its magnificent Italian-carved mantelpiece.

"You should marry me," Robbie teased as they drove along. "Then you'd have a man in the house to help out."

"Oh, Robbie, don't you ever get tired of asking me?"

"No, but I wish you'd get tired of turning me down."

"I won't. It's important for me to keep the Winters name until I can bring honor back to it."

"*Gilbert* should be a name you could live with."

"Because it bears no scandals? No shame, like the Winters faced?"

"Nothing was ever proven, Adrienne. That's why they kept your father on at the State Department."

"They demoted him. Humiliated him. Friends turned against him. Don't you understand, Robb? My dad would never betray this country. Never steal secrets from it. But he went to his grave with that taint on his name."

He glanced her way, then back to the road as he merged with the traffic around them. "Someday I'll unravel the truth for you. Right now, I just wish I weren't so uneasy about you going to Paris alone."

"Please, don't start in on me about security."

"I didn't have security on my mind. You'll be gone three weeks. If my assignment to Europe had come through, I would be flying to Paris with you."

She laced her fingers. "No matter what I do, I can never live up to Jon. He ended up sacrificing everything."

"Adrienne, you gave up a lot too. You've missed some splendid career opportunities."

"That didn't exactly bother you, did it? It kept me here at home." She saw his frown and sighed. "I'm not very good company, am I?"

"You've had better days." He glanced at her as he found a parking space at the airport. "So what's troubling you?"

"The other day I mentioned the Gulf War to a fly-by-night at the office. He didn't know what I was talking about. I understand people not remembering my brother—but the Gulf War and the fighting in Bosnia? What happened, Robbie?"

"September 11, 2001 happened."

He got out of the car and came around to her side, then held out his hand and helped her from the yellow T-Bird. "Afghanistan and the war against terrorism happened." He squeezed her hand. "The invasion of Kuwait and Bosnia are relegated to past history."

"And my brother with it. It's not fair. What do these people want me to do? Forget Jon?"

"Never. He was part of your life. But he wouldn't want you to go on chasing ghosts."

"All these years with no body to bury. We just don't know what happened to him, and I never believed that story about an explosion. Neither did Dad. I think the government lied to us to protect someone. That's what I live with."

"I wouldn't let anyone in Washington hear you spouting that theory. Why they'd—"

"They'd what, Robbie? Audit my income tax? Dad said all the secrets are buried in Washington."

He found a luggage cart and loaded her suitcases onto it. "Then I'll be the gravedigger."

At the airport checkpoint, she gave him a gentle smile. "This is as far as you can go. I meant for this to be a happy time together, but I've spoiled all your fun."

He raked his hair into place. "I like to think I'm always there when you need me." As he leaned down to kiss her, another lock of his auburn hair brushed her cheek. "If you get in trouble, Adry, just call me. I'll catch the next plane."

"Oh, silly. I'll be just fine."

"If anything happens to you—I'll never forgive myself for letting you go."

She slapped her purse and briefcase on the conveyor belt. "Robbie, this trip to Paris was my idea. When will you and Colin realize I don't need your protection?"

Chapter 5

Early that morning in a high-rise complex overlooking the Potomac, the Impostor—for that is how he viewed himself—sank into the leather chair by the windows of his luxury apartment and stared across the river. Washington lay in a swirl of pale gray clouds. As night slipped away, dawn broke, painting the dome of the Capitol on Jenkins Hill with strokes of crimson and primrose.

His air conditioner hummed. A gilded ceiling fan whirled above him. Neither offered much relief from the muggy heat wave that had engulfed the East Coast. He had already showered, but the back of his smoking jacket was drenched with sweat. He massaged his eyes and went back to scanning the *Washington Post*. A retired air force captain had been charged as a spy after evading arrest for seven years. The Impostor imagined himself caught and charged with espionage, exposed as a *sleeper*—a double agent for a foreign government. He flipped the pages to the story of IRA terrorists arrested for training Colombian guerrillas in the use of plastic explosives and mortars.

Fools.

He applied the same term to those searching for a mole at the Pentagon. Another penetration of U.S. intelligence was suspected, the computer system considered pregnable. Since the attack on the Pentagon, eavesdropping and surveillance techniques in the war against terrorism had been compromised. Rumors died down when the E-Ring collapsed, but the rumors were back. Rumsfeld and Ashcroft wanted action.

With the blunders in the Bob Hanssen spy case still causing jitters, a new full-blown investigation was underway. Electronic surveillance had narrowed the field down to a short list of eight suspects. It was nothing but allegations, and so far his own name was not on the list. Thanks to his ingenuity during one of those closed sessions, two men had lost their security clearance. It kept the odds in his favor.

It helped that he had access at the highest level: secret, top secret, sensitive. He passed classified material on satellites and lesser known projects, making it appear there was more than one mole. The operational director insisted that the classified materials had ended up in the hands of China or Russia, but he was looking in the wrong direction. The Impostor's handlers were of the Arab persuasion—wealthy men from the Middle East.

So far—as far as he could determine—his living quarters hadn't been bugged.

He smiled. The fools are looking for me.

Once, pleasing his father and a hunger for wealth drove him. But money no longer controlled him. Nor did ideology. If anything held him captive, it was his fascination with his gun collection and an obsession to emulate Erwin Rommel, the Desert Fox. He had no convictions of one power being greater than another. Vengeance was his chief motive now. He loved this country—would choose to live nowhere else—but he wanted America to pay for the loss of his wife and child.

He stretched his lanky legs in front of him, his longing for his wife agonizing. And yet in the heat of an argument, she had called him double-minded. His facade was one of strength, but compromise had destroyed him early on. It still held him in its grip.

How long did one pay for wrong choices? How long could an impostor stay free? Five years? Ten? Twenty? Bob Hanssen gave it a long run, outwitting his FBI colleagues. Aldrich Ames risked high stakes as well. But he found these men contemptible, his mind separating himself from their treachery.

Still... How many more years before some slip-up made his life a headline? Hanssen and Ames traded freedom and the adrenaline rush of betrayal for life in a security cell in prison garb. The Impostor would not settle for such a fate.

If capture were ever imminent, he'd take matters into his own hands.

Midway between the national news and the sports section, his attention riveted on another headline: GULF WAR SECRETS DECLASSIFIED.

The newspaper slipped to the floor; the ceiling fan fluttered its pages. His Gulf code name lay hidden in those secret documents! How long would it take once that name was uncovered for the world to identify him?

He grabbed his phone to dial one of Langley's secure lines, but his friend would not be at his desk for another two hours. He slammed the receiver down, his numb fingers still ensnared in its cord.

Since his wife's death, his mind often played tricks on him, thrusting him back to that August morning when Kuwait captured the world's attention. Images of the Iraqi forces crossing its borders merged with images of the man he'd left in enemy territory—the ultimate betrayal. Presumed dead on a covert mission. A political deception. A cover-up. Sealed files buried in the vaults. *Sealed files declassified.* For what? An unnumbered bank account in Switzerland? Or to cover another bitter betrayal in Paris?

He gazed up at the blades of the whirring ceiling fan, but saw instead the blades of the helicopter as plane after plane screamed over Kuwait City during the invasion. The Impostor leaned forward, his face in his hands. The breeze from the fan buzzed his crew cut, but nothing could cool the searing images or blot out the memory of Jon Aaron Winters entering Kuwait—and dying there.

Hours later as Adrienne Winters's jet soared toward Paris, the Impostor stood by his window high in the Bradbury Towers and watched the city glowing in the evening dusk. His eyes burned with sleeplessness. The traffic on the streets below and the unrelenting pounding at his temples echoed like drumbeats.

He saw Jon's face reflected in the windowpane—as though the man stood beside him now. Winters's strong profile. His skin sunbronzed, like an Arab's, his hair jet-black. His thick mustache was much like a Kuwaiti's, but that easy smile was all American.

The Impostor's own legacy of deceit forced him to backtrack from Paris, where they'd met, to the suffocating memories of the desert sand dunes where he had betrayed him. Last night's phone call from his old friend at Langley told him what he already knew. Jon Winters's sister was flying to Paris. He had no occasion to stop her, but he would have her followed and pursued.

And, if she walked too close to the truth, terminated.

As Adrienne's plane rumbled over the Atlantic, day turned to darkness. Passengers around her dozed without comfort. Adrienne stayed awake, a crick in her neck and her feet cold from the draft on board. Her mind kept filtering the memories—chasing their ghosts. Images of Paris. Shadows from the past. The semblance of peace in the family home. Impressions of her father and Jon. Phantom tentacles of betrayal.

What had happened between her father and brother in those last visits together? Those two men who had once been so close, so much a caring father and son. Had those last debates in the library at Winterfest weighed heavily on her father after Jon's death?

Beating with the uneven rumblings in the belly of the plane came the echoes of joy and laughter in the family home in Paris. And after Paris—after her father's betrayal—the discordant tones. Jon on overload. Sometimes impatient. Often angry. Strident. Jarring. Savage. Her father lamenting the past. Grumbling about betrayal. Then refusing to defend himself.

During her father's and brother's last debate in the Winterfest library, they raked over the intelligentsia in Washington. Their words—no, *Jon's* words—mocking, clashing, grating as the two of them beat their heads against the proverbial brick wall. Her father licked his wounds in silence at first, then by quoting a verse or two to steady himself.

It was easy, in the dim cabin of the jet, for Adrienne to picture it all again. Jon had called men like Bedford Taylor nothing but think-tank intellectuals controlling the bureaucracy. Jon hammered on his old kickback: "Dad, look at the mess those enlightened bohemians are getting us into in the Gulf."

Her father sat in the leather chair behind his cherry wood desk, toying with a letter opener as he defended the guardians of war. "They're good men, son—the *top brass*, as you call them, were once my friends."

Jon's eyes blazed. "Who wants to die for oil wells just to back a friendship?"

"I made some good friends in Kuwait City when I was stationed there. Your brother was born and died there."

With an impatient sweep, Jon had whipped strands of jet-black hair from his forehead. "It doesn't mean we should get involved in *their* war. Why, they'll snatch Robbie up and make a soldier out of him. How would you like that, Adrienne? To have Robbie be a soldier boy like Colin?"

She met his glare without flinching. "If he were older, he'd go as a war correspondent. That's how his father got his foot in the publishing door."

While they argued about the upper crust of the military, Adrienne sat curled on the sofa, hugging her knees. "Instead of persecuting the top brass in Washington, you ought to think about how to prevent the war. I don't want any of you dying in a war zone."

Jon raised his right hand. "Little sis, I promise you, I'll come out unscathed."

"You can't make that guarantee."

He conceded, his eyes amused. "I don't plan to join the army. Does that put your mind to rest?"

"But you're going back to the Middle East, aren't you?"

"Yeah, maybe the second Tuesday of next month. Maybe sooner. What about Robbie, Adrienne? What's his take on those who walk the sacred halls at the CIA? Bohemians? Heroes?"

"He doesn't approve of their methods."

Jon laughed that deep amused chuckle of his. "Adry, what would you say if I told you that I'm one of them?"

"You can't be. Mother insists you're going to be another Michelangelo or Rodin."

"But I have other plans."

"Does Mother know?"

"She closes her ears whenever I try to tell her I'm with Central Intelligence." He glanced down at his hands, hands that had molded so much clay so beautifully. Then he met his father's gaze. "Washington will respect the name Winters again, Dad. Count on it!"

"Let it alone, Jon. Don't hurt those we love. I still have a desk job, Son. Let it go at that."

"But you're no longer privy to classified material."

"Does that shame you?"

Jon leaped to his feet. He ruffled Adrienne's hair. "A week from now I'll be back in Paris."

"With the military?"

"Little sis, you know I think uniforms are too restricting. But I can tell you that it's my job to defend this country—even if it means heading for the Arabian Peninsula. Does that help?"

"It scares me."

Jon turned to their father. "Does my working for the CIA scare you, Dad?"

Their father splayed his fingers on top of his well-read Bible. "This is where I will find my comfort, Jon."

Adrienne sighed as her memories faded. Outside the plane window it was still dark. Night had not yet turned to day. But wasn't it always the darkest just before the dawn? Why, then, did she feel apprehensive, so frightened of what lay ahead in the City of Light?

CHAPTER 6

On that first morning in Paris, Adrienne woke to a dismal gray dawn, with raindrops tapping on her hotel window and a gusty spring wind sweeping the rivulets of water across the windowpane. Her haunting dream and painful memories collided.

She tried to snatch back the fragments of the dream: Her brother trying to scale the iron girders of the Eiffel Tower, at risk of life and limb. Her father's somber face at the embassy ball. Her mother thrusting aside the wheelchair and dancing with someone else, with Bedford Taylor.

All snippets of truth. Remnants of the past. Shreds of yesterday. And all gone now, like the cobwebby storm clouds drifting away in darkness.

Her head pounded from the grogginess of jet lag and the whirring noises of the air conditioner. She eased her aching body to a sitting position, fluffed the thick pillows, and sank back against them. Finger whipping her tangled hair, she took a survey of the mess she'd made.

Her first-class hotel suite looked like a disaster zone—the way the house looked on that long-ago day when her father was recalled to Washington. Last night Adrienne hadn't even bothered to unpack everything. Her traveling shoes remained where she kicked them, and her luggage lay sprawled on the floor, like steppingstones to the bathroom, like bitter links with the past.

Her treasured size-six Doncaster suit and evening dresses in teal and plum hung haphazardly in the mirrored wardrobe where she had tossed them at the midnight hour.

The teal gown was Robbie's favorite. Adrienne's gaze rested on his snapshot, upright on the bedside table beside her. He insisted that she bring it. It was so like him—that uncontrollable curly hair looking as though he'd been caught in a wind tunnel. That familiar boyish smile that matched his carefree manner to perfection. His eyes twinkled as though he were right in the room smiling at her.

Robbie's roses and the lingering fragrance of the broken Shalimar bottle scented the air. *Let the maid clean up the spilled perfume, but what do I do with the cryptic man who sent the flowers?* Robb Gilbert was charming and clever, gifted and persistent. A rogue and a sweetheart all packaged in one. But all she could think about was the wistful smile on his face as she left him at the airport and his reluctance to let her go.

In his own way, with his e-mails and his bouquet of roses, he'd followed her all the way to Paris. He wanted to be here with her, but she was glad his assignment to Europe had not come through. She wanted the freedom of enjoying Paris alone. Tomorrow's maddening schedule would take her to the fashion houses as a buyer for ready-made fashions. She didn't want Robb tagging along.

Robbie, of course, would focus on Paris from a journalist's perspective, through those gentle, smoky blue eyes of his. She just couldn't respond to his ardor, his subtle advances, his hints of marriage. And she wasn't even sure why. She cared about him, so why did she draw back whenever he got too close? Why did she shut down? Close off her emotions. Push him away.

Adrienne rubbed a hand over her aching eyes. She knew why. She couldn't open her heart to another when pieces of her life were missing. Clearly, the melancholy she'd felt last night still held her. If only she knew why. With another brooding sweep of the room, she spotted the crumpled cable from Colin Taylor. Her hand fisted. Late last night, when she threw his cable across the room, she missed the wastebasket and toppled the perfume, spilling its contents on the glass-top table.

Score another one for Colin. His warning to be guarded on the streets of Paris piqued her irritation. If she didn't shake off his foreboding, she'd be looking over her shoulder for the next few weeks.

The cell phone by her pillow rang. She tugged her earring free and pressed the receiver to her ear. "Hello."

"Adry, it's Robbie."

"Robb—it's 2 A.M. there! Is everything all right?"

"Your mom's fine. It's just me. I miss you."

He waited, but she couldn't bring herself to repeat the words to him. "Robb, go back to bed. Get some sleep."

"Can't—I'm onto a news story."

She sucked in her breath. "Which senator this time?"

"Would it matter? You hate what I do."

She didn't hate what he did. She was proud of him. An investigative journalist, top quality, like his father. She admired his quest for truth. Robbie's beat covered the Pentagon and White House. On that terrible September morning, he'd been at the Pentagon within minutes of the jet careening into the E-Ring; in the aftermath he spent sleepless nights reliving the horror, the loss of friends. His coverage of that story had been filled with sensitivity, backed with prayer. Survivors thanked him for his kindness. But he wasn't always welcome on Capitol Hill or back at Langley.

"Someday you're going to end up on the losing end, Robb."

"I've been on the losing end for a long time." At his wry tone, she knew he was referring to her indecision in matters that related to him. "Adrienne, I spent the morning on Capitol Hill—and the afternoon at the National Archives."

Robb was dogged in his pursuit for truth. He seemed to take pleasure in toppling senators and diplomats. "The past doesn't matter any more, Robb."

"It does if it was a cover-up. I have great news. They opened more files on Paris and the Gulf War. Twenty years' backlog, free for the taking. Getting into those files may tell us what Jon was doing in Kuwait. But at the same time, opening those files focuses the public's attention on the past instead of the present Middle East conflict."

He was off on one of his pet pursuits. "Adry, we're spreading ourselves thin by sending Special Ops troops into the hotbeds of the world. Half the public hankers after more military action, not knowing the facts about the shaky politics in the Middle East. The other half—well, they have no opinion at all, if you can believe the polls."

"Robb—"

"So the government opens this Pandora's box to divert criticism. I'm telling you, today's headlines are important. Not just the fashion runways there in Paris."

"Important to you. You worry too much."

"About you? Always. But headlines are my business. I keep mulling them over in the back of my mind."

"And sometimes you don't even hear what I'm saying."

He laughed, a spontaneous chuckle that winged over the wires and warmed her. "That's what I say about you."

"I only do that when you talk about marriage. But go ahead. It's your phone card, not mine."

"Funny girl, don't forget Kuwait is a friendly, but when their emir suffered a brain hemorrhage, it threatened a change in their government, a threat to our own... Jon gave his life for that man and his country."

"We don't know that for certain."

"We know that the United Arab Emirates cut diplomatic ties with the Taliban. That was good. And we know that French intelligence exposed a planned attack on the American embassy there in Paris that saved lives."

"So I'm safe. Please, don't get so involved, Robb."

"I have to. I'm onto another story. I bag that one, and I can take you on a fancy honeymoon."

The man was incorrigible. "I'll pass on the honeymoon, but go ahead. You won't be satisfied until you tell me what you're up to."

"Rumors are buzzing about another mole in Washington. Maybe more than one. Nameless, so far. The way I figure it, they could have ties with terrorist organizations. We may have another Pentagon analyst channeling classified information to Cuba or who knows where."

"That analyst had a name, Robbie."

"Yes, and I can't even stomach saying it."

She switched the phone to her other hand. "I'm going to hang up."

"Don't. I wouldn't hang up on you if you were discussing your fashion shows."

"You wouldn't understand them either."

"I'd at least try."

"I am going to hang up. You make me nervous talking about moles in Washington."

"Don't hang up. Please. I have mercy for unredeemed men, but not for traitors. Not for terrorists. God has to mellow me on that one." He hesitated, and she was glad to hear his voice calmer when he continued. "Fourteen years ago, someone betrayed your father in Paris, Adrienne. That someone could still be at the top echelons of government. We don't know what happened. And like you said on the way to the airport, we've never known why Jon was left behind in Kuwait."

She felt that old ache in the pit of her stomach. "You know I think about those things all the time."

"What I'm doing, Adrienne, I'm doing for us. Declassified material on Paris and Kuwait are search engines to the past. Once the ghosts of your past are vanquished, I think you'll marry me."

"Don't count on it."

He rewarded her with his silence, and she regretted wounding him again. "You're certain that everything's all right at Winterfest?"

"Your mom's fine now that she isn't worrying about your plane crashing in the Atlantic. Nothing can go wrong at your home, not with Rolf managing Winterfest. Colin's the only problem. He's already stopped by to make certain things are going well."

"Did he have Gavin with him? A child in the house might upset Mother."

"You don't know your mother. She and Gavin are great buddies. But he's with his grandmother this week. Besides, Rolf knows how to handle kids, even if Colin doesn't."

She could hear the steady murmur of Robbie's voice over the wires, but her thoughts drifted. Would she never stop comparing Robbie and Colin? Colin, so professional, in his well-cut, tailored suits and uniform. Robbie with his rugged good looks, a "handsome hunk," as her friends said. And always proposing at the most unexpected moments.

"Adrienne. Adrienne, are you listening to me?"

She tried to squeeze her headache away. "I'm here."

"Colin got a jump on me. He's already knee-deep into those declassified reports from the Gulf War."

"Isn't that his job? He should know those frontward and backward. I don't want Mother to know about this."

"Colin already informed her."

She heard the rivalry in his voice. They were so predictable. Robbie was his own man, willing to stand against the odds for what he believed in. But Colin sidled up to those in authority at the Pentagon, using his brilliance and military expertise to the best advantage. But the thought of the two going head to head over this newly declassified material…it didn't bode well. "Robbie, don't get into it with Colin. Let the Gulf files alone. That was Colin's war, and he never questions the government's involvement."

"Well, Colin and I agree on one thing. He's trying to track down the mole at the Pentagon. But let's forget about him, or I'll end up at the drugstore buying digestive pills. Let's talk about us. What are you doing, Adry?"

She wiggled her toes and flipped the wrinkled sheet over them. "I'm thinking about driving out to the countryside and walking barefoot through a field of sunflowers."

"I'll go with you. I could be there in ten hours."

She glanced out the windows. "It's pouring buckets."

"It wouldn't matter. I'd like walking in the rain with you."

She heard the longing in his voice and was surprised when she was struck with a tingling of her own. "Robb, I'm going by the American Academy this morning, for old time's sake. That should please you."

His words came across lighthearted, but his voice tensed. "See if that rusty old bench is still there."

She laughed. "That's where you first proposed to me."

"Yeah! And you turned me down that time too."

"I was only thirteen."

"I know, but you were leaving Paris, and I just wanted you to know that you were my girl forever."

She sank deeper into the pillows. He was sprouting tall even then, the son of a journalist racing down the steps of the Academy with a rucksack on his back—and embarrassing her because he was toting a Bible along with his books. "Robb, are you sure everything's all right at Winterfest?"

"Positive. The mansion is still standing. The tulips are flourishing. And your mother is fussing up a storm at the nurses. Everything is normal—but like I keep telling you, God has everything covered. It's just... I don't like you being so far away."

"Nothing will happen to me. Now, I must run."

"Don't go chasing any ghosts from the past... I love you. I'm here for you."

She hesitated. "Give Mother my love."

"Am I to save any for myself?"

Before she could answer, he was gone. She pounded her bed-covers and resisted thoughts of the warmer, comfortable moments in Robbie's arms. She reached out and put his snapshot facedown. It didn't block out his smile or the sound of his laughter, but it made her feel better. Safer, less pressured.

Flinging back the sheet, she slipped out of bed, determined to forget the entanglements back home. But Paris was filled with memories of her brother. Jon Aaron's death had been without closure. A death without a body to bury.

No wonder the ache for him never quite went away.

As Adrienne dressed, she recalled her brother's last good-bye on that miserable morning when he came down the stairs at Winterfest, his suitcases packed. He dropped them by the door and turned to her. "Mom and Dad aren't coming down, Sis."

"Why?"

"Because I'm going away. I told you that last evening."

She pouted. "You just came home."

"You knew I wasn't staying."

"Will you be back for my birthday, Jon?"

He shook his head and tried to coax a smile from her. "I'm off to solve the problems of the world. It may take awhile."

She thumped his chest with a doubled fist. "Then go play your old war games and don't ever come back."

"You don't mean that, little sister."

Adrienne closed her eyes now, trying to remember how he looked that morning—but all she could see in her minds' eye was his injured expression. He was sporting a thick, dark mustache back then. She remembered realizing she'd hurt him, thinking she should apologize, but saying instead, "Jon Aaron, you look like an Arab sheik."

He gave her a caustic smile, the left side of his mouth twitching. "Then I will play my role well, little sister."

CHAPTER 7

SPRING 2002
RIGHT BANK, PARIS

Jacques d'Hiver stood at his window and watched the water surge over the quayside, stirring angry whirlpools into the River Seine. The downpour lashed against the window panes, fogging his view, obliterating the church spires in the distance.

The dampness caused the stump of his leg to swell, the nerve endings to throb. He turned and limped across the room to where four-year-old Claudio sat cross-legged on the hardwood floor. His son's nose was runny from a cold, his feet shoeless, his kneecaps bony.

Jacques ruffled his son's hair and glanced at the beautiful woman who shared his life. Brigette stood in the bedroom door, her robe tied in a knot around her narrow waist. Her eyes were full of caring. His, in return, must appear to her as empty. He thought, as he often did, *You could have so much more happiness if you had not met me.*

"Are you going away again, Jacques?"

"What makes you ask that, chère?"

"You've grown restless. You never came to bed last night. You stay away longer at the cafés each day."

"I like to stroll the streets of Paris in the springtime. But a man needs two good legs to walk and run."

"An artificial leg is nothing to be ashamed of."

The prosthesis was his constant reminder of all that he had sacrificed. And for what? Like the multifaceted city of Paris, Jacques was difficult to define, an enigma even to himself. But Brigette found strength, clutching their small white terrier to her breast.

"Jacques, I won't mention marriage again. I promise."

"Then you have not spoken to your priest this week?"

She shook her head, strands of her burgundy hair sweeping across one cheek. "I will not do that again."

He agonized for her shame. He wanted to go to her and embrace her, but that would be like promising to stay forever. In this last decade only Brigette had chipped away at his shell and found her way into his heart. He smiled because he loved her. "I wish I were free to marry you."

"Is there someone else?"

Jacques paused, remembering his first love. "No one."

In the beginning of their lives together, Brigette asked few questions for fear of losing him. Now her very existence depended upon the answers he could not give. In spite of him, she still believed in her God as he had done as a boy. But more and more, living outside of marriage tainted her soul, tormented her.

He knew from the workings of his own heart that he had crossed the line—had abandoned everything he once believed in—God, the sanctity of marriage, the integrity of life, loyalty to the Company.

He felt damned, a man in need of redemption.

Brigette shrugged, resigned as their daughter slipped past her and went to her father.

"Jacques, will you take Colette to school for me? I don't want Claudio out in this weather. Not with his cold."

"I'm expected at Angelo's studio this morning."

"You are always expected somewhere when I need you."

With a sideways glance at the Flemish tapestry hanging on the wall, he bit both his tongue and his thoughts. The tapestry did not blend with the otherwise practical furnishings. It hid the locked door from the children and demarcated another compartment of his life, off-limits even to Brigette. He spent sleepless midnight hours in that room, pouring over the Arabic intelligence reports, still translating them, interpreting them for the Company that despised him. And what of the other hours away from the condo that he could not explain? He forced himself to meet her gaze and saw the pain of betrayal in those woeful brown eyes. He steeled himself from crossing the room to her and mouthed the empty words, "I'm sorry."

"So you shut me out again, Jacques? Is that it? I am never to ask any questions. My only job is to mother our children and love you? Can you not do small favors for us?"

In spite of his resolve, his tone sharpened. "You know our agreement. Colette could go to the American Academy, but I must never be called upon to visit her there."

"You force her to make excuses to the other children."

Colette, at six, was a tiny replica of her mother. Wistful childish eyes sought his now. "My friends don't think I have a *père*."

He cupped Colette's chin. "Papa cannot go."

"They would not make fun of your leg."

He leaned down and kissed the top of her head. "No, you would not let them."

For a moment she let him hold her against him and then mumbled, "Mama says you will run away again, but Claudio and I like it here. Please don't make us move again, Papa."

They'd stayed here for more than a year now, longer than any place. Jacques looked around, savoring the contentment he had known here. The clouds darkened over the River Seine as the squall battered against the magnificent old building where ivy climbed up the pink walls and a flower box filled with drenched red geraniums hung from the wrought-iron balcony. He had chosen this complex on the Place du Pont Neuf with care. It was a small condo now, but it was still the home of his youth, that lifetime ago when the name on the mailbox had been different and the walls vibrated with laughter.

Claudio and Colette loved watching the barges on the river and sailing their toy boats on the lakes. No, he would not move them. Where else could they look out on the city he loved and on the river that lay in the shadow of their home? Where else could a man throw back the shutters on a clear day and peer out on the peaceful willows that overhung the quayside? Or look up at church spires that still stirred deep longing within him? He wanted his children to love Paris as he did.

He hugged his daughter and met Brigette's gaze. "I will never ask you to move away from here again."

For their safety *he* would go, but not his family.

Adrienne strolled along the streets of Paris, twirling her lavender umbrella above her. A sense of elation accompanied the tapping of her trim Italian boots on the wet pavement. She needed this break—this chance to delight in the scent of a rain-washed city.

The cleansing reached deep inside her, tugging at the old family demons. Still their steely tentacles left her with fragments of guilt for abandoning a sick mother back home. She pushed the unwelcome thought away and went to the Louvre for the sheer pleasure of wandering in its galleries and stepping back in history through the paintings and sculptures of great artists. Adrienne had come here often as a child—sometimes with Jon Aaron and Robbie—and always she came back here on her trips to Paris.

Here she could slip away into the world of art, caught up in the brush strokes of creative people who painted their dreams, their joys, their sorrows on canvas. By taking a blank canvas or shapeless piece of clay, they had walked from their own art studios and crossed the barriers of generations to touch hearts with their beauty. To touch her own. She tiptoed from artist to artist and three hours later left the da Vinci and Botticelli paintings refreshed, alive.

Across town, the Eiffel Tower rose high above the mansard roofs, piercing the rain clouds and the few patches of blue sky. Last night's fragmented dream came back—Jon trying to scale the iron girders of the tower, doing the impossible, the forbidden. Ignoring the stairs and the elevators, he risked everything, as adventuresome in her dream as he had been in life.

But he wanted more than anything to become a sculptor. To be another Auguste Rodin. No, better than Rodin. Remembering one of his favorite places, she crossed to the south side of the river, to a narrow, cobbled street shaded by chestnut trees, drawn with an irresistible urgency to the obscure gardens of the Rodin Museum.

For ten minutes the heavens darkened. Lightning flashed. Strangers in the street ran for cover. Another thunderous clap of thunder sent Claudio racing to his mother's outstretched arms. As the rains slowed to a steady downpour; a fragment of a rainbow arced across the sky.

Jacques could wait no longer. He slipped into his trench coat and took his weather hat from the hall closet. Brigette stood by the console, the white terrier still clutched in her arms, licking the palm of her hand.

"Do you remember the day I met you, Jacques?"

"How could I forget? I fell in love with you that day. You were holding a wounded white puppy that day too."

"Will you always remember?"

"Always."

He left the apartment, his promise to Brigette echoing in the silent room. She went with him in his thoughts, for the most pleasant part of his waking hours was thinking about her. Meeting her played always in his mind, in his heart. He had been walking through one of the terraced gardens on the Right Bank of Paris when he saw her, a petite beauty kneeling on the lawn, her hand extended to that wounded puppy. He had leaned on his cane, smitten by her gentle, upturned face.

"Bonjour, mademoiselle. Is the puppy yours?"

"He doesn't seem to belong to anyone."

Like me. "Then why don't *we* claim him?"

They sat on a nearby bench and talked until the afternoon chill set in. The puppy stayed nestled in her lap, smothering her hand with its kisses. She asked about Jacques's family. How long he'd been in Paris.

"I'm alone. I moved back here three weeks ago."

She blushed. "I'm glad. Will you stay?"

"Now that I have met you."

They met the next day and the day after that. And soon it was a permanent arrangement. She was his happiness. If he had to leave again, run, disappear, she of all people would always remember him.

Jacques crossed the bridge to the Left Bank, his mood as dark and ominous as the weather. A short subway ride later, he reached Angelo's Art Studio, where the students welcomed him. He was one of them. An artist. A man with a dream. His present molded to his future. His past, whatever it might be, did not trouble them.

The instructor, with his thick chest, wide-rimmed dark glasses, and a sagging triple chin, made an odd friend in this crowded city of strangers. Apart from art, Jacques and Angelo had little in common, yet he trusted Angelo as much as he trusted anyone. He needed Angelo's friendship and wise counsel. Jacques felt Angelo's eyes on him now as he passed the cluttered desk without dropping anything in the outbox for his handler.

No, Angelo my friend, I will not make you my messenger today. I will not risk your safety this time.

As he turned, he caught a flicker of relief in Angelo's expression. The instructor wore his familiar clay-smudged smock, his black beret pushed back on his balding head. His fingers were covered with clay as he moved from student to student. He gave a curt nod as Jacques put on his apron and took his place at the work-table.

Angelo was not given to overt praise, but warmth glowed in his eyes as he moved among his students. When he reached Jacques, he frowned down at the shapeless mound of clay. Massaging his jaw, he murmured, "Jacques, a man who keeps starting over never finishes."

"It just doesn't come together."

Bushy brows lifted above the glasses. "I am certain that Michelangelo felt that way too."

"And Rodin?"

"A troubled man, like you, my friend. But a great artist."

Jacques felt the corner of his mouth pulsate. Felt the pain of unfinished work. "Have you forgotten? Much of Rodin's work was never completed."

Angelo shrugged as though that was a small matter indeed. "Incomplete works, yes. But, ah, my friend, much more of Rodin's art lives on in bronze and marble around the world. Like you, Jacques, Rodin wanted to be remembered."

As Angelo ambled on to the next student, Jacques glared down at the clay-covered armature in front of him. He had intended a figure in motion, its arms outstretched as though in battle. No, that was yesterday's plan. What he wanted now was the reclining figure of a man wounded in battle, a man at peace in spite of war. As the idea crystallized in his mind, he pushed aside the abstract charcoal sketches and went to work; but the idea at his fingertips was hampered by blurred memories. The clay was drying too fast, maddening him. He moistened the figure again, ran his broad fingers over the irregular lines. He sensed Angelo eyeing him from across the worktable, scowling.

Jacques retreated within himself. His fingers ran down the rough textured clay, and without preamble he hated what he was doing. He could never create a work of beauty. He could never be another Rodin, but like that great Parisian artist, Jacques was more a native Parisian than many of those so born. Like Rodin, he failed to legitimize his own son. His own children.

Jacques studied his work again from all angles. His figure of clay looked static, misshapen. As though it was collapsing against its own weight. It did not please him. It lacked grace, reality, it was far from the figure he imagined. In a fit of despair he shoved it aside and covered the shapeless form with a wet cloth. But why preserve it? He stood, resenting his own awkwardness. Leaning against the worktable, he tore off his apron and flung it over a hook.

"I'm a failure." He scowled at Angelo as he reached the door, then extended his hands, bits of clay still caked under his fingernails. "Angelo, my hands won't cooperate."

His instructor tapped him on the chest. "*This* is where you are failing. You are trapped in there. You are a gifted man. I know it. I believe in you. God still believes in you. Let what's good come out, Jacques. Find what your heart wants to sculpt."

"I've tried."

He thumped Jacques's chest again. "You have tried out of your pain. Your dreams will crumble that way. Find out what's here, Jacques…"

"Stone."

"No, Jacques. Clay. And clay can be molded." He smiled, his piercing eyes narrowing behind the thick lenses. "Go back to Rodin's Gardens. Study his work. Learn from him. And come back tomorrow and try again."

Jacques entered the gardens of the Rodin Museum through the gate in a high stone wall. Just ahead of him lay the museum, an eighteenth-century mansion. He turned right off the main walkway, away from the reflecting pool and the floral gardens, where he often brooded over his failures. He limped past neatly trimmed hedges and roses still wet with the rain and followed an angled path toward the cone-shaped shrubs that surrounded *Le Penseur*. Rodin's bronze statue sat lifelike atop its marble pedestal, its immobile chin resting on one hand. As the image of *The Thinker* shimmered in a rain pool, Jacques considered it Rodin's masterpiece.

Jacques's leg throbbed with each wary step. As he reached the statue, he was aware of another visitor on the gravel path to his left. Her steps sounded vibrant, alive, a mockery to his own unsteady gait. As their paths converged, the woman's perfume permeated the air around them. He asked himself again why he must go through life without a leg, handicapped of spirit and mind. What did he have to offer Brigette? Nothing but secrets, a faceless past, and this blasted artificial limb.

His faith was dead. It died in the Middle East—died the day Kuwait was liberated and his repatriation denied. He had been shoved into oblivion, a man without a passport. Without identification. Without a country. Thrust aside for national security.

Jacques stood at the foot of the statue and thought about Auguste Rodin—a man rejected by the National Guard. An artist rejected by the established schools of his day. A man who spent decades plying his art and seeing himself as a failure, as one rejected by the social elite and yet known by them.

"Like you, Jacques, Rodin wanted only to be remembered." As Angelo's words came to him again, his stump throbbed. He fixed his angry gaze on the statue. *You know no pain like this. Your legs are strong and sinewy. Muscled and powerful. The way I was once. You have two feet. I have one. I'm only thirty-six, but I feel like an old man.*

Adrienne browsed in the museum for more than an hour, but when the rains stopped, she went back into the gardens. Cimmerian gray clouds scudded across the sky, swirling westward out of the city. As she closed the distance to the sculpture, she could almost see the molded muscles flex, could almost feel the artist's heartbeat.

Another visitor, a Frenchman with a cane, paused—as she had—to gaze up and admire the depth of detail in Rodin's work— the bulging veins, the gripping toes, the deep lines etched in the face.

The visitor stood with the crook of his cane over his arm. Adrienne sensed the disquieting strength of his presence. He was an imposing figure, a proud man, she decided. Tall and dark-haired, his trench coat still damp from the rain. Even from a sideways glance, she knew he was younger than she first suspected. Probably midthirties. Surely not forty. Standing immobile, he seemed a man as aloof and contemplative as *The Thinker*. But like the statue, the man commanded his space and brought his brooding into it.

Stepping back for an unobstructed view, she decided that Auguste Rodin might well have sculpted the tormented profiles of both the stranger and the statue. As she studied the man, he palmed his hand to his lips, a simple gesture that stirred a memory...

A cold chill swept over her. A ghost from her past had come back to fling itself at her.

The stranger turned. Their eyes locked.

For Adrienne, time stood still. She jammed her trembling hands into her Burberry. As the clammy chill settled around the nape of her neck, she tried to speak, but no words could escape her tight throat. Her brother had been killed, yet it seemed she was staring up into the face of her mother's son—a man who had been dead for more than a decade!

CHAPTER 8

J on?" The name slipped out, barely audible.

For seconds, his gaze held hers. Curious at first. Then annoyed. Defiant. His jaw was firm, stubborn like Jon Aaron's had been. But this man's eyes seemed aged, more deep-set than her brother's.

"Jon?" she whispered again.

He stared at her without recognition, a pensive scowl forming between his brows.

As he turned back to face the statue, Adrienne trembled on rubbery legs. *Oh, God, if it is Jon, he doesn't remember me. I've grown up. I'm not the teenager he knew. I am a stranger to him.*

His profile was like a bronze statue, his features cold like marble, his unsmiling face frozen in time as she was. It *had* to be Jon, but what had happened to his photographic memory? A head injury? Amnesia? Had he been injured in the Kuwaiti invasion? Whatever had happened, calling his name could not summon him back from the waters of oblivion.

The space between them felt like a granite wall. She took a step closer, second-guessing herself. Had she spoken to a total stranger? Was she caught up in one of those phantasmal games of the mind? A trick of her own imagination? An illusion brought on by jet lag? A will-o'-the wisp aberration, like her mother experienced so often nowadays? She opened her mouth but could no longer whisper his name. Her mind had deceived her. She was making an utter fool of herself. Wanting to see Jon alive had fired her imagination, twisted her thoughts.

With a terse nod, the man gripped his cane and left the gardens. At the exit, Adrienne saw him glance back, his frown puzzled. Her feet seemed set in marble like the statue. She glanced about and saw the gardener trimming the hedge. "That man—the one with the cane—who is he?"

The gardener with weathered skin went on trimming.

"Monsieur..." She repeated her question in French.

He eyed her, perplexed. "He comes here often."

"Do you know his name? Do you know where he lives?"

The gardener waved his clippers. "He lives in Paris. Where else? We never speak." Sizing her up, he broke off a dying rose and dropped it in the waste receptacle, then thumbed the edge of his clippers. "He seldom goes inside the chateaux—just stands here, leaning on his cane."

"Has he always been crippled?"

He gave the clippers another swipe. "Only the gods know who is born that way or comes that way by accident."

"I'm sorry for troubling you."

"We never talk, mademoiselle, but he finds solace walking in my gardens. If you have questions, ask him."

The gardener went back to clipping the hedge. Beyond the gate, the stranger had already turned on the Rue de Varenne, walking with a limping gait toward the Dome Church with its glittering golden roof. She could not live with herself unless she knew the truth, no matter how painful.

Adrienne rushed from the gardens, the rain puddles splashing her Italian boots. Shortening the distance between them, she stayed far enough behind so he wouldn't notice her. She matched her pace to his labored steps. Her pulse quickened. *Go back, Adrienne. You're a grown woman, and you are trailing this stranger like that pesky kid sister running after her brother. You're chasing a memory. The past. The dead.*

But she refused to slacken her pace. She needed answers for her mother, for herself. She followed the man through the ticket turnstile and into the Metro underground. Taking a seat two rows behind him, she kept her eyes fixed on the back of his well-shaped head. When he left the train, she followed. They came out again on top, at the Place de la Concorde, which led to the tree-lined Champs Élysées. Moments later, as she crossed the boulevard, Adrienne lost sight of him.

Frantic, she retraced her steps, peering into shops and bistros. She searched the faces of those in line at the cinema. Men stared back. Women turned away. Adrienne felt crazed, distracted. At last she spotted him, hesitating in front of an open-air café; the tassels on the red awning still dripped with raindrops. He ducked beneath them.

She ran to catch up with him and watched from the door as he wound through the narrow aisle to a back table. A waiter reached the spot first and wiped the glass-top table with his towel.

With a curt smile at the waiter, the stranger took possession as though the space had been reserved for him. Women, stunning in the latest fashions, and men in casual sweaters and black berets occupied every other table.

A waiter in an ebony waistcoat appeared at her side. He shrugged. "My apologies, mademoiselle. We are full."

She stole a glance at her quarry. The likeness was uncanny. Would he send her away as Jon had done so often when they were children? Would he point his finger and say, "Go away, Adrienne. Be a trouper. Get lost. Go play with your dolls." Or would he tease her? "Write one of your ridiculous poems for Robbie. That will keep you busy."

She cried when he went away the last time. She was crying now. She'd come too far to turn away.

"Mademoiselle, the tables are full—we have no room."

Undaunted, she pointed to the table where the stranger sat. "But, monsieur, there's an empty chair back there."

He reprimanded her with a scowl. "Not with Jacques d'Hiver. Monsieur d'Hiver always sits alone."

Jacques d'Hiver, she mused. *D'Hiver. Winter.* The name struck a familiar chord. *Winter, in either language.* "Perhaps this one time, he won't mind having company."

She brushed the waiter aside and negotiated her way around the tables to reach Jacques d'Hiver. She nodded at the empty chair. "Would you mine if I joined you? The other tables are occupied."

The waiter breathed down her neck. "Pardon, Monsieur d'Hiver! Mademoiselle insisted—"

The man at the table half rose, his dark eyes burning. "It's all right, Aleem."

With a smug smile at Aleem, she settled in the wicker chair. She could not take her eyes from the man across from her. He looked so remarkably like Jon. Would he recognize her now? Or had she changed that much? Jon would be thirty-six. This man was all of that, his thick black hair already streaked with silver, his complexion olive enough to have their mother's Spanish blood coursing beneath it.

Long ago Jon had gone away looking much like an Arab sheik. Now he looked like a Frenchman. Was he playing his role well, or had he by no fault of his own become somebody else? A man who did not know his way home because his memory was gone. Amnesia did strange things. As did twelve years.

Adrienne wiped crumbs from the edge of the table and then stared up at him again. Some clever plastic surgeon might have changed Jon's features; the once crooked nose that was broken when rock climbing was now Romanesque and striking. The skin stretched taut across the stranger's high cheekbones narrowed his face. Jon's old sparkle and daring were missing, but the surgeons couldn't change his eyes. Could they? For this man's eyes were a deep ebony darkness, a raw burnt umber, like their mother's. They seemed almost black now in their intensity. Beneath his unsmiling expression, she saw nothing but emptiness and lost years.

With a sweep of his hand, he pushed the basket of breads and jams aside, spilling his café au lait. "If you have finished studying me, perhaps you can tell me why you followed me here?"

Adrienne drew back. "You knew I was behind you?"

His brows arched the way Jon Aaron's did when he was curious or angry. "I knew. I do not know why."

"You look so much like someone I knew once."

"Someone who mattered to you?" His voice was deep, resonant. Almost gentle. "So you followed me here?"

"No—well, yes. Just from the Rodin Museum."

"Are you accustomed in your country to stalking people?"

She swallowed her embarrassment. "You're the first."

A solemn smile caught the corners of his mouth. "Then I should consider myself honored." His French was flawless.

He beckoned for the waiter to return. "Aleem, mademoiselle is ready to order—and you'd better bring me some red wine this time."

The waiter stood, pencil poised. She took note of him now. Tall. Striking. Jordanian perhaps. His lack of a smile could be his anger at her. Or perhaps he was always solemn, guarded. A white apron fit smoothly over his waist, but the flush at his neck above the bow tie warned her of his displeasure. "Please bring me a sweet roll and hot tea."

"She might like some brioches." Aside, Jacques said, "That's an airy muffin. Wash it down with your tea."

A *muffin?* Yes, she had eaten them as a child. Right now that was all her churning stomach could take.

The waiter returned, bearing a large silver tray. He held it against his waistcoat, where small pockets were filled with coins. He glanced over his shoulder, and she traced his gaze to the maître d' standing in the doorway, a heavyset man with a brush mustache.

Jacques drew her back. "What is wrong, mademoiselle?"

"The maître d' keeps watching us."

"Don't be concerned about Cavell. He wants his waiters to be quick with their service."

"But I think he's studying me, not Aleem."

The tautness of Jacques's mouth softened. "Monsieur Cavell always takes notice of a pretty woman."

As Aleem walked away, he said, "Now, tell me, are you touring Paris, mademoiselle?"

"I lived here for several years when I was a child."

"Your French is good."

"And yours perfect. I come back now and again on business trips, so knowing the language is helpful."

"Then you are one of those American businesswomen who lives alone and travels abroad. In pursuit of what? Fame? Fortune?" His lip curled. "Or perhaps a Frenchman?"

She stemmed her irritation. "None of the above. I'm a buyer for ready-to-wear fashions. But I'm here for the spring fashion show as well."

He gave her a fresh appraisal. "The haute couture on the Avenue Montaigne? Or do you go for Italian elegance?"

"On the Rue du Faubourg St.-Honore, this time."

"Models from around the world! I should attend."

"It's by invitation only."

"How unfortunate to keep all the beautiful women in Paris on one catwalk."

"Not all of them. Paris is a mosaic of beauty. The faces you pass. The city. The buildings. The ancient cathedrals. I love Paris. And what do you do, M. d'Hiver?"

"In a way, I'm retired. For health reasons." He patted his game leg. "But I study sculpture on the Left Bank. I often go by the museum after my art class. Rodin's is only a scant walk from Angelo's Studio." He kept his eye on the maître d' moving among the tables.

Adrienne's pulse jumped. "So you're an artist?"

"I admire the work of Michelangelo and Rodin."

Was he taunting her? Teasing her? She sipped her tea and studied him over the brim of her cup. The tremor in her voice gave her away. "My brother wanted to be an artist."

He managed a ghost of a smile. "I have the heart of an artist, but not the skill. Even if I did, it would do me no good to find another Sistine Chapel to paint." He braced his lame foot on the wrought-iron table leg. "My artificial leg would betray me."

Like you betrayed us by never coming home. Why? Or was it her own madness, jet lag twisting her thinking?

"At least in Paris I can admire Rodin's works."

"Then you're a bona fide sculptor, Monsieur d'Hiver?"

"I would like to be. My instructor, Angelo, keeps encouraging me." He held up his strong, supple hands and plucked some clay from his fingernails. Satisfied, he palmed the wide hands toward her, his tongue seemingly loosened by the red wine. "But these hands of mine, they don't obey my commands. I tell them to form a war memorial. I tell them to mold an immortal being..." For a moment his eyes brightened. "I tell them to shape a beautiful face. A face like yours—perhaps I could do a face like yours."

The momentary flicker of artistry shattered. He thrust back his chair and rose to his feet. "Good evening, mademoiselle."

"Please don't go. I—I need to talk to someone."

He glanced at his watch and eased back into the chair, the effort awkward. Their eyes met again over the wine carafe. He spoke first. "A few minutes longer perhaps. It would be rude of me to leave without knowing your name."

"Until now, you haven't asked. I'm Adrienne Winters."

He gripped the edge of the breadbasket, his eyes piercing. "Miss Winters, you've lived here in Paris, so you don't need directions to the Louvre or Eiffel Tower. You don't need my help. So why did you follow me here?"

Tears burned her eyes. She had been upset at Jon Aaron for so long—angry and unforgiving because he had gone away and never come back. Now she wanted to step back in time to make things right. But this man—this stranger—was he just Jon's look-alike? She wanted to shove the dishes to the floor and reach out and shake him. She wanted to say, "I'm Adrienne. I'm your sister!"

They sat in silence. She couldn't force him to remember, not if trauma had robbed him of his past. She couldn't resurrect the dead no matter how much she longed for Jon to be alive. D'Hiver's expression remained that of a stranger. She touched her brow, expecting to be burning with fever. Inside she felt the fool, a blinded idiot.

Jacques's eyes darkened as the waiter approached. He waved him away. Uncertain, Aleem lowered a silver tray with a white envelope on it. "But I have your—"

Jacques snapped, "Later, Aleem."

As the waiter retreated, Jacques glanced at Adrienne. "I want to know why you followed me here."

"Because I—I thought—oh, it doesn't matter. My mind is playing tricks on me."

"Go on. You owe me that courtesy."

"I thought I knew you." She felt tongue-tied. "I thought you were an American."

"No, I am a Frenchman. And like the waiter said, my name is Jacques d'Hiver."

He counted out the money for the bill and laid out each coin with a precise, deliberate motion—enough to cover her tea and muffin. Then, his eyes blazing, he said, "I really must go, mademoiselle."

"Will you come here again tomorrow? You said you like their bread and cheese."

"I seldom go to the same café two days in a row."

If she could see him again, perhaps he would remember. She looked around. "There's one across the street—the one with the blue awnings. I could meet you there."

He scowled at the maître d' hovering nearby. "Perhaps. Should I bring my children with me?"

"Children?"

"Yes, children. Does the thought surprise you?"

"Yes."

He was married. Anger boiled within her. This man who looked the spitting image of Jon was married! Not to the girl back home, but to some stranger here in Paris. There were children. More than one. The rafters at Winterfest should be exploding with the happy cries of children. She was an aunt. Numb at the thought, she was unable to ask, "Boys or girls?" Afraid to ask, for her emotions ran wild.

"I have shocked you? So do I bring my children or not?"

No, not the children. Not yet.

"Please, come alone. I must talk to you again. I'm only here for a couple of weeks… If I've offended you, I'm sorry."

"Offended me? You have helped me pass the hours. But you would be safer to never see me again."

"I'd risk everything just to talk to you."

"Why would you do that?"

"Because you're so much like my brother, Jon Aaron. When we were children, my brother was my hero."

Jacques d'Hiver pushed himself from the chair and steadied his balance with the cane. His eyes were distant, aloof, unapproachable. "Your hero, Mademoiselle Winters? Then let him go on being your hero." His voice dropped to a murmur. "And I will go on being a stranger."

CHAPTER 9

Outside the café, Jacques d'Hiver turned right on the wide, tree-lined boulevard, setting his course toward the twelve avenues that branched out from the Arc de Triomphe. The sun was setting behind the Arc, twilight forcing its way into the Parisian sky. He liked this time of night, when the street lamps and the warm radiance from shops and cafés illuminated the ancient city. He never tired of a brilliant sunset reflecting off the soaring towers of the cathedrals and turning the ornate fountains into rainbows of colors.

But tonight he sought the shadows. He kept close to the chestnut trees, his cane scratching the sidewalk flower beds. As he limped along the boulevard, he felt naked, exposed—as though those missiles of light had been turned on him. His security, his very existence here in the city of Paris, was threatened by this woman who could push him deeper into the shadows.

Once he believed a man could find peace and anonymity in Paris. That's why he had come back. In the pressing crowds of this sprawling metropolis, he sought to be a dark thread in a mosaic of strangers.

But now peace eluded him.

As he labored up the Champs Élysées, a street of victory parades and endless tourists, the traffic sped past him, racing toward the Arc, guiding him to nowhere. In his youth he believed in honor and valor. Youth? Was that so long ago? At thirty-six, he was ensnared in an escaped prisoner's freedom—an aimless wandering through the streets, existing without joy, living in fear of discovery.

And now it had come. She had discovered him.

Using the cane to propel him, he took long, deliberate strides to put distance between himself and the American woman. His steps came down harsh, strident against the pavement, every other step a heavy thump. His leg ached, his whole body protesting the pace. The smoldering tentacles of the past reached out for him, but he could no more go back than he could rid himself of the bitter memories that haunted him.

Adrienne Winters's presence here in Paris had awakened the sleeping giant inside him. She threatened his safety and her own. If it took another twelve years of silence on his part, waiting for Langley to unravel the truth, he would bide his time until he could clear the Winters's name. He owed that much to the memory of Jon Winters.

Another sleeping giant—that terrorist attack on America— had thrust the Persian Gulf and all of the Middle East back into the headlines. He wished himself back in the thick of battle, strong enough to serve his country as a covert operative in the Middle East. Whole enough to stand up on two legs and fight. On sleepless nights, he envisioned himself parachuting into enemy territory with a band of British Special Forces. Or crawling on his belly beside a French soldier from mountain cave to mountain cave, ferreting out the Taliban terrorists or participating in military maneuvers on the deserts of Kuwait.

Just beyond the international hamburger chain, he stumbled. Regaining his footing, he let the tourists and Parisians surge around him. Enemy agents had undermined the resistance movement in the Kuwaiti invasion—he was sure of it. Iraqis, Iranians, Libyans trained in terrorist camps. Men committed to the destruction of Kuwait. Some of these men could be hiding out in those caves, committed to a holy war. A war that Jacques would never understand.

And yet it was his war. His battle.

Why had she come back into his life? Didn't she understand? He had a job to do. Ahead of him the Arc glowed golden, a national symbol of other men's campaigns and military battles. The unknown soldier lay there, an eternal flame flickering by his burial site. The flames lapped at his own soul.

As he neared the Arc, he heard footsteps closing in behind him. He gripped his cane and turned. "Oh! It's you, Aleem. You were told never to contact me outside the café. Under any circumstance. That's a cardinal rule."

"But, Monsieur d'Hiver, you left something behind." Aleem wiped his palm on the towel at his waist and produced an envelope from his jacket. "The maître d' insisted that I give this to him. But I refused."

Jacques tapped the unopened envelope. An Arabic message to be decrypted. Money to cover his expenses—to keep his silence—all for the ultimate good of the Company. "Aleem, the contents would be of no interest to Cavell. And you are well paid for your delivery service."

"At the risk of my job at the café."

"Lose that one, and we will find you another."

"Cavell threatens to have me sent back to my own people."

"So he suspects both of us? Cavell is meddlesome." He patted the envelope again. "I'll make arrangements to receive this elsewhere next time. You'll be safe."

Aleem pointed to his dark skin. "What is it that your God says, monsieur? 'Can the Ethiopian change his skin or the leopard its spots?' No more than you can arrange to wipe out my past."

No more than I can wipe out my own. Jacques understood Aleem's fears. Tasted them himself. They had met not long after Aleem fled Yemen. "I promise you, you will not be sent back."

"Cavell says mademoiselle is a problem."

"She's just a talkative tourist."

"But she's curious, that one."

"Say nothing to Cavell. If pressed, tell him I met the woman at the Rodin Museum. I invited her to join me at the café...but, Aleem, follow her when she leaves. Keep her from harm's way."

"Does she know who you are?"

Does anyone know who I really am? He puzzled on that for a moment. The reminder of no family or friends to call his own blackened his mood even more. Once the house of his youth had vibrated with friends' voices. Now there was no one except Brigette and the children. But did even Brigette know who he was? So much of his past had been blocked out, veiled, destroyed by his resentment. Exchanged for his legend. He felt like a deceiver, lived like one.

But he was committed to the deception.

"Aleem, mademoiselle thinks she knows me."

The other man's black button eyes narrowed. "If she comes back to the café, I will ask her to leave."

"No, welcome her like any other guest."

"Is that wise? Cavell will recognize her. Tonight he stopped her from following you by bumping into a waiter with a full tray. The wine stained her beautiful clothing."

"Miss Winters won't like that."

"I slipped away while Cavell was apologizing to her."

"If she comes back, follow her, Aleem. I must know where she is staying."

He frowned. "Cavell—"

"Leave word for me at the café with blue awnings."

"Will you go home this evening, monsieur?"

"To my family?" Jacques stared into space. His country had asked him to sacrifice his identity, to choose oblivion for the sake of national security, to protect his family and his Muslim friends. Too late he realized that even this had been a betrayal, a cover-up. It had not been his country that asked, but one man at Langley. Refuse, and he knew he would go home in disgrace as his father had done. Or not live to go home at all.

He felt a fresh fury at the American woman who had forced herself back into his life, reminding him anew of all that he had lost.

"Will you be all right, Monsieur d'Hiver?"

"Yes, I'll take a taxi home to Brigette."

Aleem looked toward the street. "You're going in the wrong direction. I can try to stop one for you—"

"No, Aleem. There's always a taxi line by the Arc, off the Avenue de Friedland. Always tourists stopping to see the eternal flame. Go back to the café."

"If the maître d' questions me...?"

"You worry too much. We will not risk your safety. You are too valuable to us."

"Cavell does not trust you, monsieur. He plots against you."

"He does not know me."

"It is the distrust of those not born Muslim."

Jacques allowed himself a wry smile. "But who better than I understands the Arab mind, the Arab unity? The disunity? I studied the Middle East for years. I speak Arabic. I've lived in the Arab world. I care about your people."

Aleem nodded to the envelope in Jacques's hand. "But you are not one of us."

Jacques had no answer for that. He turned, pushing on alone, bound by his own commitments, bound by his own duplicity. As he drew near the magnificent Arc, he thought of Napoleon's promise to his men: "You shall go home beneath triumphal arches."

Long ago, sitting in a tent in Saudi Arabia, someone had made a promise like that to Jacques. A victorious return home. For a man driven by honor and valor, home remained more foreign to him than Kabul and Kandahar. More distant than Kuwait and Qatar and Bahrain, where young Americans had dug in for the long haul on the war against terrorism.

Victory parades had marched beneath that arch. But Jacques had been denied a victory parade, left behind instead to carry the guilt for someone else. He felt the rub of the Arabic message in his pocket. He was still useful, loyal to his country.

But he hadn't lied to Aleem. He had great respect for his Arab friends. He read the Koran. Chose friends among the Arabs at Sorbonne and, in its unbiased approach to learning and liberalism, found his faith wavering. Once he met Hamad, the young Kuwaiti, he wanted to know more and more about the Middle East. While friends spent their summers in Vienna or hiking the Austrian Alps,

Jacques had taken to visiting Turkey and hard-to-enter places on student visas. Yemen. Djibouti. Pakistan. With little more than a knapsack on his back he had gone into village after village. His discovery of a terrorist training camp on one of his trips in the Middle East almost cost him his life.

Was he betraying Aleem? He gave him work. Was that not enough? Was Aleem's blood and safety on his hands? He knew the answer, but he needed Aleem. Jacques knew there were terrorist cells in Paris. One right there at the café. The American embassy had been a target recently.

In Jacques's mind everything fanned out from Paris, and then came back again. His leg might be useless, but his mind was good. Send him on an intelligence mission, and his physical limitations would be cover enough. But which country would consider him fit to go? His adopted land, with President Jacques Chirac giving him the marching orders? Or should he present himself, a man without a passport, to the American president? Even without a game leg, he'd be forced to stay in seclusion, silenced by those he once knew and served with in Kuwait, forced into divided loyalties as Miss Winters's brother had been.

He allowed his gaze to rise to the rooftop of the Triumphant Arch where he had spent long hours viewing the splendor of the city that he loved even more than his birthplace. But not this evening. He had no strength for climbing, not with his stump swelling and the metal rods of his artificial leg tearing at his skin.

He queued for the taxi not far from the eternal flame. Moments later he dropped into the backseat of a cab, his cane braced between his knees.

He left the taxi a block from his apartment complex and walked along the quayside. Electric lights dotted the stone bridges over the dark waters of the Seine, the water as foreboding as the powers in Washington that denied his existence.

Tonight he would leave a chalk message on the Pont Neuf Bridge, trusting that his old contact on the Avenue Gabriel would see it. He'd offer himself for a surveillance mission anywhere—in exchange for Aleem's protection and for the guaranteed safety of Brigette and the children. Better to be a dead hero than to go on without hope of redemption or forgiveness, never having the chance to go back home.

Reaching the brick residence overlooking the Seine, he let himself in with the latchkey. Brigette stood by the windows, motionless. She turned. "Where have you been? I've been so worried."

"I'm sorry. Are the children asleep?"

"Yes. We waited supper—"

"I'm sorry."

He crossed the room and looked down into her worried face. Her tapered fingers touched his cheek, her skin soft against his face. "What is wrong, Jacques?"

He reached out and drew her to him. "My world has just fallen apart."

CHAPTER 10

Watching from her hotel window, Adrienne mused that the City of Light never seemed to sleep. The wisp of an evening breeze touched her bare arms. Still she sat there on the window seat, clothed in her thin negligee, her hands clasped, her eyes on the world passing below her.

Where were they going—these Parisians who had shaped her childhood? Where had they been? The city boasted countless restaurants, theaters, cinemas, and the opera house.

The opulent Opera de Paris Garnier.

She liked the ring of the words and envied the people below whose hearts and minds were filled with the beautiful music. Were they heading home to pillow their heads? If so, she envied them even more.

Just past midnight, she went back to her king-size bed, but the man who looked so much like her mother's son caused her to twist and turn. She pounded her pillow and fluffed it again a dozen times.

The luminous clock ticked away the hours. At three in the morning, humiliation crept into the darkened room with the same intensity with which this morning's rain squall had blown against her windowpanes. Adrienne felt pulverized. Had she chosen a part in a Broadway play, she could not have acted with greater flair. Her mother would be delighted in how well she played the part of a fool. Shakespeare in full costume. She flipped the sodden pillow over and nestled her cheek against the dryness. If darkness did not prevail outside, she would check the address for the nearest

Parisian hospital, hail a taxi, and commit herself to the psychiatric ward—if they had one.

Of all the foolhardy tricks, this was the worst. Accosting a stranger. Following him. Forcing her place at his private table. Dumping her burdens on him.

If only she could sleep. Tomorrow's maddening schedule would take her back to the fashion houses of Paris. She'd study the elegant suits and sleek evening dresses. Silk scarves of every style and design. One-of-a-kind creations in jewelry. She would covet the diamond necklaces. Dangling earrings that glittered like gold and cost even more. She'd scheduled last-minute visits to specialty boutiques advertising matching shoes and purses in a wide price range.

"Be selective. Choose well," her CEO had advised.

Her work was cut out for her, but that moment in the Rodin Gardens had turned her world topsy-turvy. Paris and her brother were one, the bittersweet memories of both stirred by the stranger in the gardens. At four she gave up on sleeping and paced the room, stumbling over her shoes where she had discarded them.

Jacques d'Hiver. Jon Aaron Winters. Coincidental? The last name was the same in either language. Winter. The winter season that Jon had loved. It meant probing the depths, climbing the heights, conquering the ski runs. It meant being alone, isolated from the cares of the world. Being himself. Surviving the elements. The outdoors intoxicated Jon. The higher the mountain, the bigger the risk. A spirited man, he knew no strangers and yet remained an unknown element to those closest to him. Summer or winter he would go into countries where few dared to venture. What drew him? Where did he rendezvous? Whom did he meet?

She saw none of Jon's prowess, valor, or stark independence in this Jacques d'Hiver. The Frenchman seemed provoked, inflamed within, driven by some inner force she could not define. Was he agitated with her? No, something different…

As she stubbed her polished toe on another obstacle on the rug, she wondered what her father would do—and knew. She visualized

Harry Winters sitting at his desk in the library, picking up the Book, turning to its words. She remembered him trying to calm her anxiety with thoughts on God. Trying to coax her away from the wide road to anger and bitterness.

"That's not the path for you, Adrienne."

The memory of her father's gentle voice filled the hotel room. "If we believe something with all our hearts, Adrienne…"

Yes. She believed that the stranger was Jon Aaron.

Cold shivers tracked her spinal column. A childhood memory awakened as she stared into the semidarkness. The stranger in the café had a scar on his index finger. She allowed the memory to creep back from the depths. How old was she when she pushed Jon Aaron into the backyard swing and his hand caught in the chain and tore? Ten? Eleven?

Jon had teased her about Robbie Gilbert, and she had charged toward the swing, railing at him. She could still picture the shocked look on Jon's face as he supported the wrist of his bloody hand. "Now see what you've gone and done, little sis."

Adrienne stopped pacing, her mind made up. She had to find Jacques d'Hiver. But where, in a city of millions? If he never returned to the Café le Grand Royale, how would she ever find him?

For the next few days Adrienne persuaded her new friends from the fashion show to dine with her at the café with the red awnings. Kalina Papanastasious, the stunning magazine editor from Athens. Isabelle Conti, the elegant model from Milan. Maddie Travers, the stylish Londoner with a dry sense of humor.

Belle Goujon, a petite Parisian, latched on to them on the second day. She wore a turban like a crown on the top of her black hair, a sleeveless yellow dress, and thick-rimmed sunglasses. Dark locks hung down on both sides of her face. Her hands were slender, her skin bronzed. Without waiting for the others to check their menus, Belle ordered a crème de cassis to drink and a lunch of scallops garnished with sliced mushrooms in a shell cushioned with a piping of mashed potatoes.

Studying the others through her dark sunshades, Belle tilted her head. "Why the same café as yesterday? There are many restaurants in my city."

But only one where Aleem waits the tables and holds a private table for Jacques d'Hiver. "I'm looking for someone, Belle."

"Aren't we all?"

Adrienne flushed. "I didn't mean it that way. I'm looking for an old friend."

Isabelle's brows arched. "In Milan we would ask how old a friend?"

Adrienne fingered her menu. "He'd be thirty-six now."

She smiled. "Too old for you. Just right for me. Why not tell us what is troubling you?"

Adrienne set her menu down and told them about the stranger in the Rodin Gardens, about following him to this very café. She nodded toward Aleem hovering nearby—a perpetual scowl on his swarthy features. "Aleem waited on us that day too."

With her voice lowered, she told them about the scar on Jon's index finger and the chain link that had lacerated his hand. "The stranger looks so much like my brother, and his hand bears the same scar."

Isabelle's brows arched again. "Has your brother been away for a long time?"

"He's been dead for a long time." Adrienne used her napkin to dab her eyes. "Or so we were told. Now… I'm sorry, but if he is alive, and if this stranger cloaked as a Frenchman is my brother, then Jon Aaron has rejected his place in the family. As children we were friends. At least I thought we were. He was my hero."

The touch of the Londoner's hand turned to a squeeze. "Maddie Travers, at your service. How can we help, Adrienne? We don't have much time to find him." The others nodded as Maddie sipped her hot tea. "But you know this city, Belle. Where would you begin searching for our mystery man?"

Belle lowered her sunshades, her eyes dancing. "In my dreams—or back at Rodin's."

Adrienne sighed. "I plan to go back there on Saturday."

Belle studied her for a moment. "If that fails, I'd go straight to the American embassy. It's on Avenue Gabriel. I could show you the way."

"I know the way—I just don't think they could help me. He's—he's going by a different name now."

A frown creased Kalina's smooth forehead. "Is he in trouble?"

Belle twirled a fresh drink in her hands. "What do you think? Why else would someone use a false name?"

Kalina pondered this. "I don't know. Amnesia, maybe."

Adrienne was startled that someone else should come to the same conclusion. "He acts like he doesn't know me—so it could be amnesia, Kalina."

"Or a car smash?" Maddie suggested.

Adrienne averted her eyes. "A war, I think."

"Or maybe he doesn't know you."

Even when Aleem busied himself waiting at other tables, Adrienne avoided telling them about her brother's CIA connections or the clandestine life that Jon had lived. She had to cover for him. The more questions the Parisian raised, the more doubts surfaced. "I just have to find Jon again."

Maddie peered over the top of the menu. "If you find him, what will you do?"

She hadn't a clue. "I just want to talk to him."

"That's jolly good. Anything else besides him being good-looking? He is good-looking, isn't he?"

"Yes, Maddie, quite handsome. Dark as though he came from your country, Kalina. He has an artificial leg. He uses a cane."

Maddie beckoned for an herbal tea refill. "That narrows it down to several thousand. Think, Adrienne. What else did he tell you?"

"He likes art. Dabbles in it."

"My dear, don't tell me he is one of those street artists in the Montmartre district? Granted, some of them are excellent painters. I almost bought one of their pieces for my flat in London."

Adrienne shook her head. "I don't think he would go there. He wouldn't be able to stand on his artificial limb that long. He takes art lessons in a sculpturing studio not far from Rodin's."

"My dear girl, we need to know more than that."

"Oh, Maddie, I'm certain he told me the name of his instructor. I just can't remember."

"*Think*," they chorused.

"I think it began with C. No an A."

Maddie's dry humor rallied again. "Good. At home I would use a phone directory—to be more accurate, I would ask my secretary to use the directory."

Belle jumped in. "If it is near Rodin's, then it is on the Left Bank."

"Good, Belle." Maddie smiled at Adrienne. "That narrows it down to one side of the River Seine. I think our evening's work is cut out for us."

After settling their account with Aleem, they left the café and headed back to the hotel. Two hours after pouring over five phone directories, they had compiled a list of art shops. Belle read down the list for a third time.

At one name, Adrienne jumped up. "That's it, Belle. *Angelo's*."

Maddie cocked her head. "Of course. That begins with C. We should have thought of that."

Midmorning the following day, Adrienne's new friends saw her into a taxicab. "We should be going with you. There's safety in numbers."

"I'd rather go alone, Maddie."

"That's a bit unfair. You get all the fun. Hurry back. We'll want to know everything. And, Adrienne, if you can't locate him there,

I think Belle is right. You must contact your embassy and tell them he's missing."

"He is."

She already called the American embassy an hour ago and was passed from one person to the other. Yes, she repeated numerous times, her brother was missing, yes, he was an American citizen.

But when they asked his name, she hesitated. "Jon Aaron Winters. Thirty-six...from Virginia...over six feet...dark hair."

"When did you see him last?"

Several years ago. "Several days ago. Here in Paris. We ate at the Café le Grand Royale—on the Champs Élysées."

She'd been put on hold so many times that she was about to hang up when a cocky voice announced, "Hello there. I'm Rick Mendez. If you're an American in distress, I'm at your service. How may I help you, Miss Winters?"

Just the offer of help was enough to nearly reduce her to tears. Now, as the taxi merged with the traffic, Adrienne relaxed against the backseat, her eyes closed. She hadn't a clue what she would tell Rick Mendez when she kept her appointment with him at one. But he sounded anxious to help and was specific with his directions to the Avenue Gabriel.

The taxi driver deposited her at the end of a one-way street. He pointed with a stubby finger toward the studio. "That art shop you are looking for is just a few doors down. But if you are planning on buying, I wouldn't make my purchase there. There are far more elegant shops."

The shingle for Angelo's Art Studio was cracked and faded, but the sculptures in the window display showed the work of skilled craftsmen. Inside a man with a barrel chest and expanded waistline hovered over what looked to be one of his students.

Adrienne pushed through the entry door and heard a tinkling bell announce her arrival. The instructor looked up and plodded toward her, wiping his clay-caked hands on his smock. "Bonjour, mademoiselle. I am Angelo. How may I help you this morning?"

She matched his smile, though hers broadened a bit at his sagging chin. It came in three folds, the lower flap resting on the top of his smock. "I'm looking for one of your students, monsieur."

"Ah! I thought you were about to become one of them." With a sweep of his hands he indicated the men and women bent over the worktables.

"I was hoping to find Jacques d'Hiver."

He shoved his black beret back on his balding head, then shrugged. "*Aujourd'hui? Non. Hier? Non. Demain?* Perhaps. He has not been here for days. You understand?"

"Yes. He did not come today. Nor yesterday. But perhaps tomorrow. So he doesn't come often?"

"He has not been here for several days, but the last time—" Again he shrugged. "He was unhappy with his work. I told him to study the masterpieces of Rodin and then come back. He may still be in the Rodin Gardens, keeping company with *The Thinker*. He thinks much, that Jacques d'Hiver."

She remembered how her brother had been in his art studio—craving perfection, despairing at imperfections.

"You are friends—this Jacques and you?"

She had to clear a catch from her throat before she could speak. "We were close once, a long time ago."

Behind the clay-smudged lenses, his eyes turned sympathetic. "I see. Back in the days when he allowed himself to remember? And yet you do not know where he lives. You come instead to Angelo's..."

"I know his residence overlooks the River Seine, near the Pont Neuf Bridge."

Angelo whipped his thick glasses from his face and wiped them with the corner of his smock. "He is a solitary man—many gifted artists are. Have you seen his work?"

"Not for a long time."

He led her to a worktable at the far end of the room and pointed to a half-dozen unfinished sculptures. The models depicted the ravages of war, yet the facial expressions registered hope.

"The faces—they're marvelous, Angelo."

"Jacques would not agree with you. He is still at war with himself. Always starting over, and yet you see how gifted he is. His figures are always in motion. Alive."

He picked up a smaller sculpture and held it out to her. "This is a model of his son. He's proud of him."

Adrienne balanced the model in both hands. The sculpture was of a small, barefoot boy sitting by a pond, the tips of his fingers touching a sailboat—the sail and the boy's hair windblown. A kitten stretched beside the boy. The details were exquisite. The child's happy face. Scrawny legs. Wiggling toes. His hands lifelike. The smile etched on the boy's face was so complete that the eyes squinted, the mouth opened in laughter.

It was as though Adrienne held the fragile, fragmented heart of her brother. She handed the sculpture of her nephew back to Angelo. "It's magnificent…but it's not finished."

"Art is like that. Some of the unfinished works of art are today the most remembered."

She met Angelo's steadfast gaze. "He always wanted to be remembered… Have you met the boy? Is the sculpture very much like him?"

"Jacques brought Claudio with him a time or two when he was making the original sketches. But the studio is not the place for a rambunctious little boy."

"He loves the child, doesn't he?"

"And Claudio knows it. He loves his papa back."

She glanced once more at the work of art. The sculpture was alive, realistic, and somewhere on the Right Bank of the River Seine dwelt the living image of the statue—a little boy who called her brother *Papa*.

CHAPTER 11

In Washington, D.C., Robbie Gilbert sat in a high-back library chair, his shirt sleeves rolled to the elbow and his gluteal muscles aching from long hours of sitting. The archive records spread out on the long table in front of him held the truth. Somewhere. The truth that would set the Winters family free.

But would it affect his relationship with Adrienne? He rubbed his bleary eyes. He'd dated other women who found him charming enough—at least available—but even sitting across from a Washington beauty or an intellectual journalist, his thoughts wandered back to Adrienne. He'd sit with coffee cup in hand, his gaze riveted on the woman with him, his mind on Adrienne. But she remained as elusive as the truth in the archival files.

For days now—ever since the declassified material had been opened for scrutiny—he'd pored over casualty lists from wars and terrorists attacks from the last twenty years. He drew a cutoff point at September 11, 2001.

It was what happened before 9/11 that mattered. He knew which memorial star at Langley represented Adrienne's brother. Again yesterday, Robbie had reviewed the Defense and State Department personnel lists and checked their memorial walls for the names of men and women who died while serving their country. He'd gone back over the Gulf War obituaries, checking military records to see if by some chance Jon Aaron Winters had served with the army or marines. Nothing. He'd smudged his hands with cemetery records and death certificates and ended up with nothing but paper cuts on his fingers.

Resting his eyes once more, Robbie loosened his tie and tugged at his shirt collar, clenching his teeth as the button snapped and tracked across the table in a zigzagging spin between the paper maze. The offending button stopped in its tracks as it hit his attaché case. He picked it up, fingering it like a fistful of coins before stowing it in his pocket.

En route back to his empty apartment, he'd head to the men's shop that kept late hours and charge another shirt or two to his father's account. Sewing definitely wasn't among his attributes— nor was it among his father's, a world-renown journalist. But Robb had one up on his father: He could handle himself in the kitchen, with excellent tossed salads and steaks or filet salmon cooked to perfection. He had a Thursday woman who did the cleaning and took his laundry home. Maybe, just maybe, she would sew on a button.

As he scowled over the papers in front of him, the librarian with thick-rimmed glasses and a frozen smile appeared at his side. "Mr. Gilbert, this is all I could find of the records you requested."

He glanced down at the Gulf War file marked March 1990–March 1991. "They've declassified other files on the Persian Gulf. They have to be on record here. Available to us. Perhaps someone else checked them out."

She nodded toward the empty tables around him. "I'll have my clerks look again. They're still searching for the Parisian file you requested."

"Good of you. Thank you."

"An hour, Mr. Gilbert."

He matched her frown. "No time to even open the file."

"Rules, Mr. Gilbert."

Yes, she would die by the rules. "Then I'll come back tomorrow. Maybe you could keep the file handy for me."

"We're not open on Sunday."

"Then Monday."

He went back to work, not wanting to miss a minute of his allotted sixty. As she walked away, his gut muscles tightened. He was as eager for information as he was afraid of finding it. Twenty minutes into the file, his eyes combed the words again. He ran his fingers over them. There it was! Proof enough that in 1990 and 1991 intelligence gathering was to be channeled through Central Command. Before the Kuwaiti invasion. Definitely after it. That meant General Schwarzkopf's command. Not Central Intelligence.

He backtracked a few pages and reread the scathing notation recorded by Central Command: *Suspect unscheduled covert activity taking place in Kuwait. CIA and military denials.* And Schwarzkopf wanted answers.

Jon! Was this file talking about Jon? Was Robbie grabbing at nothing, or did he have a puzzle piece in his hand?

Two pages later, another notation: *Langley still denying a three-man mission in and near Kuwait City, summer of 1990.* He scratched notes on his memo pad. Drew in his own time line. Noted the smidgen of information that might relate to Jon Winters. Jon and two others? At first, Adrienne and her parents had been told Jon entered Kuwait on a student visa. Alone. Died alone in an explosion. An accident.

Robbie flipped his pencil, end to end. Tapped it on the table. A student visa? No way. A traffic accident? An accident of any sort? No way.

Not according to the date on Jon's death certificate—the day the Iraqis crossed the border into Kuwait.

Robbie had been that route months ago. He'd covered a twelve-month period. No visa had been issued in Jon's name. Had he gone in under a false passport? Jon with his adventurous, tight-lipped manner would have tried anything.

Robbie was close, he knew it. But he felt as far from the truth as he was last week. Hours ago he had discovered Jon's death certificate listed in the county seat. How had Robbie missed this one? Or was it a recent transaction, a doctoring of records straight down from the bureaucracy? A defense against declassified secrets?

A blasted ache started at the base of his skull, trekking itself into a blinding headache. Robb took an aspirin packet from his attaché case and swallowed two pills without water. His mouth and tongue felt so dry that the pills lodged in his throat long enough to leave a bitter taste in his mouth.

That taste was no worse than the bile rising in his throat at the thought of Jon going into Kuwait on a covert mission. But Robb had no proof. No names.

Toward the end of the file he read: *Embassy transmission suggests American using code name the Fourth Season spotted at Rumailan oil fields outside Kuwait City.*

Robb shook his head. *Impossible.* The only way they'd record a code name was if the operative's cover had been blown.

He jotted words on his memo pad: *Summer, fall, winter, spring.* He scribbled a line through them and wrote: *autumn, winter, spring, summer.* He crossed them out with jagged lines. This time he started with spring, the season that Adrienne loved best: *Spring, summer, autumn, winter.* Winter—the last season of the year. The fourth season. Had Jon chosen his own code name? Lined it up with his family name? Jon loved a play on words.

Winter. Winters. While the rest of them bundled up against a wintry blizzard, Jon Aaron always made for the extreme ski runs. Took the risks. He loved the isolation of winter. The solitary escape. He loved the beauty of snow-covered mountains. The glacier slopes in Alaska. The ranges in Colorado. The Italian and Swiss Alps even more. The Jungfrau. St. Moritz. Zermatt. The Matterhorn. It didn't matter which country he skied in. He excelled at foreign languages. A man with such diverse loves. Sculpturing and skiing. Creating. Being alone. The skill of being the center of attention, yet walking away an enigma to those who had crowded around him.

Jon was the puzzle piece.

Start with him in Kuwait. Why was he there? Who sent him?

Robb ran the scenarios through his mind again. *If the file referred to Jon, where were the men who had gone in with him?* As far as Robb knew there were no other stars on Langley's Memorial Wall from that same time frame. *If the others survived, were they still with the Agency? If so, why the cover-up, the veiled truth regarding Jon?*

The librarian stood at his side again, this time her expression more sympathetic. He glanced at the wall clock. He'd gone well past his hour. He started to close the file.

"I didn't realize who you were, Mr. Gilbert. Why I've read Robinson Gilbert's column for years. Marvelous writing."

He ran his hand through his hair, roughing it even more. "Robinson is my father. Great man."

"Oh, I'm sorry."

"No need to be. I'm proud of him." He thumped the file in front of him. "Someday I trust to measure up to his greatness. Then he'll be proud of me."

She studied him with a smile. "We'll be closing at ten. That should give you another thirty minutes."

He bent over the file again, latching on to every second. If only he could get an assignment to Paris or a visa into Kuwait. He'd run it by his editor, but held out slim hope of convincing the man the trip was newsworthy. What he needed was tangible proof. Personal letters or diaries written by the three men.

All he had was the supposition that Jon was one of them.

As the library lights blinked their five-minute warning, Robbie packed up his attaché case. He'd be back first thing Monday to study the archival records again. He was still listed on the intelligence beat. He'd call Sheridan Macaroy over at Langley and request another visit. Or play friendly with Colin Taylor and gain another interview at the Pentagon, maybe a three-minute one with Rumsfeld.

If nothing else, he'd take a moment of reverence at the Memorial Wall in that cavernous CIA lobby and just remember his old friend Jon.

But where could he learn the names of the men who traveled into Kuwait with Jon? Or had Jon gone solo? He needed access to private letters and diaries. Had Colin's mother-in-law kept her daughter's letters from Jon? Kris Keller had eyes for no one but Jon long before she married Colin.

He locked his case and scooped up the files to return to the librarian. He had as much chance of retrieving Jon's letters from Colin's mother-in-law as he did gaining free entry to the national treasury. Who else would have such letters? Jon's mother? Mara never threw away anything that belonged to her son.

"We'll see you then on Monday, Mr. Gilbert?"

He nodded at the librarian. "Yes. And thank you."

"A pleasure to have helped Robinson Gilbert's son."

He smiled and felt his features relax. "It's a pleasure to be that son."

Burning tire tread on his T-bird, Robb made it to Winterfest Estates in record time. He passed through the open gates, a sure indicator that company was expected, and took the wide stone steps to the double doors and rang.

Rolf swung back the door. "Robbie, we weren't expecting you."

"Who then?"

A conspiratorial grin lit his weathered face. "Mr. Taylor—your friend and mine."

Bad timing. "Are you going to invite me in? I have to see Mara before Colin gets here."

"Madame is sleeping. I don't wish to disturb her."

"Then you help me, Rolf."

Rolf's arthritic shoulders went rigid. "Me, sir? How?"

"I need to see Jon's last letters to his family."

The warmth of a moment ago vanished. "I'm certain madame tossed those away."

"Madame"—Robbie met the man's eyes—"never threw *anything* away that concerned her son. There must be correspondence from Jon somewhere. Now, are you going to invite me in or not?"

From the top of the stairs Mara called down, "Rolf, I never let my guests stand out on the porch."

Rolf stepped aside, clearly seething.

"Thank you, Mrs. Winters."

"Oh, it's you, Robbie. We were expecting Colin. But how nice of you to drop in. Have you been in touch with my daughter?"

"Not today. I've been going over the archival records on the Gulf War."

Her voice trembled. "That war is over, Robbie."

He craned his neck, staring up into a face almost as beautiful as her daughter's. "Not since September 11. The Middle East is still in turmoil."

"I'd forgotten. I find the news depressing."

She descended the stairs, her progress painstaking as she managed one step, then another, gripping the handrail with both hands. At the bottom, she collapsed into Rolf's arms, and he eased her into her wheelchair.

"So why are you here, Robbie?"

"I want to see Jon Aaron's last letters home or any communication from him in the last weeks of his life."

"For some article you're writing? Some exposé?" She clutched her chest with one hand. "They were private letters. Private correspondence. I don't share them, though I can quote almost every word to you."

"But you won't?"

"No, I won't. Rolf, take me into the sitting room."

Robbie was startled to see Rolf brush a lock of hair from her face. "Will you have your dinner in there?"

"Yes, *with you*. And set a place for Robbie. He's hungry for news. We'll give him steak instead."

"Mara, did Jon write to his father?"

"Yes, but we never shared Jon's letters. They were private matters, you see. It was never 'Dear Mom and Dad.' It was never the same letter to both of us."

Robbie felt a surge of hope. "May I read those letters?"

Her smile mocked him. "I have no idea where they are. Perhaps in Harry's old room. If I find them, maybe I'll share them with you."

"Soon?"

Those magnificent translucent eyes rested on him. Challenged him. "Is it that important to you, Robbie?"

He nodded, but she had already turned her eyes toward the spacious sitting room. His approach had been all wrong.

From the sitting room, she called back. "I never dared keep a diary, but Harry did. Well, he kept a journal. Perhaps what you are looking for is in there."

He followed her into the room. "May I see it?"

"If we find the letters, the journal should be there. Ask Rolf. He knows every speck of dust in Harry's room."

Rolf's fist came down on the arm of her wheelchair. "There is no dust, madame. I see to that."

Mara's smile was just a shade tolerant. "So you see, Robbie, Rolf handles the affairs of the estate. He takes care of everything. Including me."

For a moment, tenderness flashed in Rolf's eyes as he looked down at Mara. Then the veil of professionalism was back in place as he inclined his head. "That is my responsibility, madame. And my pleasure."

"Of course." Mara folded her hands in her lap as Rolf stalked from the room. "Well, Robbie, I've done it again. I've angered the man. But he will cool quickly. That's what I like about him."

"Then why don't you tell him?"

"And spoil our sparring game? Never. Now, let's talk about Adrienne. The next time you speak to her, Robbie, assure her that all is well. You do hear from her?"

"I've called her several times."

"Then we're both disappointed she doesn't call us."

Robb held back a wry grin. Mara saw more than he gave her

credit for. "I won't stay for dinner, but please, if you find the letters or Harry's journal—it's important for Adrienne."

Mara tilted her head as she looked up at him. "You never give up, do you? Sometimes I pray you succeed. You could take her off my hands. She won't consider Colin. It's always Robbie this and Robbie that."

It was the first good news that Robbie had heard in a long time. "I'll be on my way then before Colin gets here."

It was too late. Colin's car roared up the driveway. Robbie watched through the window as Colin unraveled from the driver's side and beckoned to his young son, Gavin.

"The boy's here too," Robbie warned.

"That's good. In spite of what Adrienne thinks—or Rolf desires—I like the sound of a child's voice in the halls at Winterfest. Otherwise there is nothing but the dull routine of day after day. I'm not too excited about this long, drawn-out dying process." Her dark eyes clouded. "If things had gone right—if Jon had lived and married the girl he loved, Gavin would have been my grandson. I think of him that way. I would have cherished Kristy as a daughter-in-law."

They heard the front door open and a child's footsteps running. "Mara! Nanny Mara!" Gavin came into the sitting room at full speed, braking only when he flew into her arms.

Robbie expected Mara to push the child away, but she nestled her cheek against the child's. "It has been far too long. I'm so glad to see you, Gavin."

"I told Daddy you'd be happy to see me."

"Always. You are always welcome in my home."

Gavin glanced up as Colin entered the sitting room. "Do you like it when my daddy comes?"

She tousled the child's head. "Sometimes."

Robbie chanced a glance at Colin. Colin jammed his hands in his pockets, his face expressionless, and for the first time Robbie pitied him.

Mara smiled as Gavin propped his elbows on the arm of her chair and cupped his cheeks in his hands. How she enjoyed his visits. He was so much like Jon had been as a child. Bright. Alert. Inquisitive.

"Nanny Mara, may I come live with you for the summer? Starting tonight."

"The whole summer?" She feigned surprise. "That's a long time, Gavin. Your grandmother would miss you."

"She's sick again."

Mara met Colin's cold gaze. "What's wrong with Nel?"

"The cancer's back. More surgery and radiation."

"I'm sorry. I'll call her."

"Don't. She doesn't want anyone to know."

"So, Nanny Mara, can I stay?" Gavin's eyes were wide with anticipation. "Rolf will take care of me, and I'll help take care of you. And I can ride Rolf's horse."

"He might have something to say about that."

"No, Rolf likes me. We talk grownup-like. I can ride Rolf's black horse, and you can read *Black Beauty* to me."

"You still like that old book?"

"Rolf says it's a class act."

Mara smiled at that. "A *classic*, dear. I don't think we have a copy."

"Yes, you do. It's in Jon's old room."

Jon's book. Rolf's Tennessee Walker, one of Jon's favorite horses. It took so little to make this child happy. Being with Rolf. Being with her. "Yes, Gavin, we'll read Jon's book."

"Every night."

"We'll see. But first we have to decide whether you are staying."

She caught Colin's eye. "You should spend more time with your son. Can't you rearrange your hours at the Pentagon?"

His careless shrug set Mara's nerves on edge. "Not with all the problems going on in the world. I'm trying to make the world safer for my son. What do you think, Mara? You have a sizable staff—they can help you."

"And who picks Gavin up when he breaks his neck riding down the banister?"

"I won't slide down the banister this time. I promise."

Mara looked down at the eager face. A child in the mansion again, the boy who should have been Jon's son! The staff was ample, and the boy scrawny enough to challenge Gretel's cooking. Mara thought of childish giggles ringing through the rafters. Of a freshly shampooed six-year-old cuddled against her for story time.

The prospect of Gavin falling asleep in the crook of her arm like Jon did when he was a boy made her choke up.

Her silence encouraged Gavin. "Can I, Nanny Mara?"

"*May* I," his father corrected.

Mara touched Gavin's soft, freckled cheek. "Why don't you run and ask Rolf what he thinks about a summer guest?"

Gavin flew, his feet winging over the floor. She called after him, "And ask Gretel what she thinks of making chocolate cookies all summer long."

"That was a quick turnaround, Mara."

She turned to Colin. "I owe your father one. Bedford was good to me."

One fine brow arched. "And that's the only reason?"

"You know what the child means to me."

Colin flashed an uneven smile. "Even though I am his father, not Jon."

She would not be baited today. "Admit it, Colin. For all of this battle with Parkinson's, I am better than a boarding school. But the decision is up to Rolf."

"Does Rolf control everything?"

"He does when Adrienne is gone. He makes our executive decisions. Few others could carry the burdens of the estate as well as he does."

"Then why do you treat the man as a servant?"

She flushed. "Do I?"

Colin sank into the wingback chair across from her. "With Nel ill, we'll both be grateful if you can help out."

"Colin, Gavin deserves better than a weekend father."

He flinched. "That's not fair, Mara. I spend as much time with the boy as I can. You know my time at the Pentagon keeps me busy."

"I was thinking of your time with Gavin."

They looked up as Gavin charged back into the room; Rolf stepped in behind him. Gavin was gnawing a cookie, his grin spreading from ear to ear as he ran to Mara. "I told Gretel I like sugar cookies best."

"It seems we are going to have company, madame. I can do with some help in the stables. I'll take the boy up now and get him settled in his room. You can read to him later."

Mara gave Rolf a grateful smile. "Then we are in agreement. I'm pleased."

But she was *not* pleased with Colin. He didn't even kiss his son good-night. As the boy left the room, she fixed his father with a firm look. "Colin, is Rumsfeld sending you abroad on the heels of Washington's newest mole?"

There was a flicker in his eyes, but nothing more. "What are we talking about, Mara?"

"I still have friends in high places. Scuttlebutt comes across the Potomac straight into Winterfest Estates. There is much talk about that elusive traitor. But this time, don't pick on an innocent man like Harry. That's the one thing that has always disappointed me about your father. When they falsely accused Harry, Bedford distanced himself from us."

"Not from you, Mara. Never from you. But don't blame the father's sins on the son."

She felt her head shake and gripped her hands to calm the tremors. "My dear Colin, I am more concerned about the sins of the son."

CHAPTER 12

Adrienne spotted Old Glory and the bronze eagle and knew she had reached America's corner of Paris on the one-way Avenue Gabriel. The U.S. Embassy was multistoried, cream-colored, and gated. It stood within walking distance to famous landmarks: Concorde Square, the Hotel de Crillon, and the historic church la Madeleine. The embassy itself was unpretentious, but solemn-faced gendarmes and concrete barricades convinced her that America was on alert.

She was stopped at a sidewalk checkpoint, produced her passport, and was waved through a revolving iron gate. Finally, after a thorough search of her purse, she was escorted inside.

A smartly dressed marine ushered her into a private office. A man with a pleasant face and an outstretched hand crossed the room to meet her. "Miss Winters, I'm Ricardo—Rick Mendez. I'm sorry if I kept you waiting."

"According to my watch, you are right on time."

She did a quick appraisal, both of the man and the room, and could not blend the two. The room with its faint scent of Chanel was well organized, the desk without clutter or personal photographs. The computer screen saver was set to Monet's paintings. Had Mendez borrowed this office for their meeting? He gave the impression of a man fresh from the basketball court—long-limbed, agile, casual in appearance. His crisp dark brown shirt matched the boldness of his eyes. Other than his bladelike nose, his features seemed ordinary, his manner polite as he offered her the soft guest chair.

Taking his place at the desk, he consulted a pocket notebook. "Oh, yes, you're the American tourist with a missing brother. In my job, most of the people I meet have missing passports or stolen traveler's checks."

"What is your job, Mr. Mendez?"

"The official one? Diplomatic attaché. But my day still majors in lost passports and traveler's checks."

His humor hackled her. *I don't care about tourists with missing passports. I'm looking for my brother.* "Perhaps I'm in the wrong department. Should someone else help me?"

"No, I'm the one. Now, let's talk about your brother."

"I'd rather find him."

"Of course." He checked his notes. "Adrienne Winters, in Paris for a fashion show, staying at the Continental—ah, great hotel. I'll be able to reach you there, right?" His pen was poised. "Give me the facts again. Your brother's name. Date you arrived in Paris. Your last point of contact. Whether he's staying at the same hotel."

For a moment their eyes locked. *How much checking had he done since their phone call this morning? And why? Did he believe her brother was missing?*

"Have you been with the embassy long, Mr. Mendez?"

"Not long enough to retire. I'm working toward that, say in about another fifty years. I enjoy helping stranded tourists. So...back to your brother."

"My brother's name is Jon Aaron Winters."

She spoke his name as someone alive—as someone who had just stepped from their presence. The words echoed back in the silence of the room. For seconds Jon's name hung like a wall between them, then she and Mendez responded at the same time. Ricardo's eyes narrowed, his fingers tightening around the pen; her stomach muscles contracted.

"I arrived in Paris alone, Mr. Mendez. I think my brother makes his home here in the city of Paris." She realized her tone had grown edgy and tried to soften it. "As I told you in our phone conversation, I last saw him five days ago—at the Café le Grand Royale."

"On the Champs Élysées. The café with red awnings and white tassels. You took a back table."

She flushed. "On the phone, those details seemed important to you."

"Only in the event that we had a missing person."

We do. My brother! What had Belle gotten her into? Go to your embassy, she said. Why had Adrienne ever listened to her? A growing irritation crept in. She wanted to flee. Coming here to the American embassy could put her brother's life in danger. She didn't know who he was anymore, why he was living in Paris. He was using an assumed name, wasn't he? Perhaps with illegal undertones.

"I think I'd better leave."

"I think you'd better stay. You've done the right thing coming to us. Where else would you go?"

Where else, indeed? The police? No. The embassy was her contact with America. Did they want to help her? Not if they recognized Jon's name. Not if he was living in Paris with clandestine ties to the CIA. Not if they knew where he was.

The echo of her father's soothing voice came to her. Stay calm, Adry. Play their game. Protect Jon. Family loyalty demands it.

She drew a steadying breath. "I must leave."

"You said that already."

Her fingers clenched on the arms of her chair. What if she was filing a report on an innocent Frenchman? A stranger? A stranger, yes—a stranger, either way.

The air filled with their brooding silence. Finally Mendez spoke. "I want to help you. You were telling me about your meeting at the café—"

The café? Yes, the café. He was confusing her. More words tumbled out. "At first we had little more to eat than a basket of bread and jams. Jon took coffee—café au lait, to be precise."

The pen was poised again. "No meal? No wine?"

"I don't drink, sir. And my brother—I think he took red wine and ordered a light lunch of lamb cutlets."

"Well done?"

"I didn't taste them. Aleem—that was our waiter—worried over the monsieur not eating enough. He rather looked at me as though it were my fault."

"So you and your brother were quarreling?"

"No, just talking. I was doing most of the talking."

"You left the café together?"

She blinked back tears. "He left ahead of me. I would have followed him, but the maître d' blocked my leaving."

"You mean he detained you?" His mouth twitched.

She grimaced. "One of his waiters spilled a tray. It ruined my suit. It wasn't Aleem. He's very efficient."

"Do you have your brother's address, Miss Winters?"

She shook her head, tears brimming again. This man was supposed to help her—that was his job, after all—but like a chameleon, he seemed to keep changing. His words said he believed her. His mocking eyes said something else: He did not trust her. Did not believe her.

He leaned back in his chair, notepad closed. "Miss Winters, since we spoke this morning, I've had my people checking with the airlines, with immigration, and with the police prefecture."

So he was not the low positioned attaché he claimed. He had resources and people at his disposal. But why had he gone to such lengths?

Because he knows Jon.

"And what did you find, Mr. Mendez?"

"In the last ten days, customs reports no American tourist by the name of Jon Aaron Winters entering Paris. Or leaving it. On any of the airlines."

It was time for her to take control. "And the police?"

"No recent records. As you indicated in our phone conversation, your family spent several years here in Paris. But there were no recent arrests. No missing persons reported by that name. No injuries. I can't help you unless I have more information, Miss Winters."

He was right. She had withheld information. "I don't know where he lives. And we can't look him up in an address book. I tried that, but it doesn't work… You see, he doesn't use our family name."

She saw the slight twitch at the corner of his mouth. "Then why don't you tell me the name he goes by."

In a split-second decision, she risked telling him. "Jacques d'Hiver."

He looked away, his gaze fixed on Monet's *Blue Waterlilies* on the computer screen. "I'm going to make some calls. Do some more checking." He turned back to her. "I want you to give a full description of your brother. I'll ask Private Meyers, one of the clerks, to help you with that. And Miss Winters, I will be back in touch with you."

"Should I make another appointment?" She'd never keep it, but she determined to be polite. To do what was expected.

He stood, rising to his full height. "I think it will be more comfortable for you if we meet elsewhere. Perhaps you would have dinner with me? Or we could just meet in one of the parks."

Play his game. "There's a park across the street."

"That would be like having lunch in the corridor at the embassy. No, let's choose something more picturesque, something more appealing to a woman in the fashion world."

She flushed. *Or else someone might see you with me.*

"Let's make it the center of the Tuileries Gardens. There are some nice benches under the lime and chestnut trees. Picturesque. Quiet. We can talk there."

"Yes. I know the place. I'll wait to hear from you."

"I promise, I will get back to you and soon."

As the door closed behind the young American, Mendez pocketed the notepad. He jerked his knotted tie. How could he placate Miss Winters and still maintain Jacques d'Hiver's cover?

Adrienne was charming, in spite of her irritation with him. She spun magic with her presence, those large mahogany eyes so intent and purposeful. She swept from the room with a simple, Southern grace that left him longing to chase after her, to know her better.

Jon had spoken often of his sister. Talked with longing about Winterfest Estates, where his family lived in Virginia. But once he was given a new legend—lied to for the sake of the Company—Jon broke all family ties and filed his past into a locked compartment.

They were playing a game with high stakes. But the beautiful Adrienne had become a pawn in their hands. Jon would not be free to protect her. Not when they were so close to tracking the terror-ist cell that stemmed from the Café le Grand Royale and reached back into Kuwait and on into Afghanistan and Iraq.

Rick tugged his ear. His self-loathing merged with the excuses of others. Was Jon a coward, as Sheridan Macaroy said? Was he blacklisted, lied about in those sealed files at Langley? Or had he been betrayed, as Jon insisted? Whatever the truth, all of them had used Jon's cowardice—perhaps his betrayal—to their own pur-poses.

Utterly unaware, Adrienne Winters had stepped into the deadly game of intrigue. He realized in their brief encounter that she would not be silenced. She was spirited, much like her brother. Loyal like her father. Her brother had sacrificed everything.

Ricardo recoiled at the thought...but perhaps the sister would be another burnt offering.

Or had he at last—after all these years—reached the point of redemption? In their last contact, Jon called himself a man in need of redemption. Ricardo scoffed at that, but now he saw himself trapped in the same pit, in constant jeopardy, hopeless without a bloodbath.

Once Mendez worked out the details, he'd see Miss Winters again. He'd enjoy the leisure of talking to someone other than embassy personnel. And why not? His marriage was in the pits.

There was just one problem... If he couldn't convince Adrienne that Jacques d'Hiver was a true Frenchman, what excuse could he offer for a brother she once adored betraying them? Could he convince her? It would serve no purpose to tell her he was part of the team sent into Kuwait. If he identified himself, she'd insist on knowing the name of the third man.

One other possibility existed. Recruit her. Use her to trace the terrorist cell back to Kuwait. Use her for the ultimate end of his own redemption once he broke ties with those controlling him. He'd maintained a life of secrecy and deception to keep Jon Winters alive. In his own way he was a double agent, serving on both sides of the war. He was Jon's only friend, although Jon didn't know it.

Mendez gazed out the window. Adrienne's attitude was obvious. She wouldn't keep the discovery of her brother's existence to herself nor play conspirator with him as they had done in their childhood.

Mendez left Naji Fleming's office as spotless as he had found it and made his way to his own small corner of the embassy. Shutting the door, he picked up his secure line and placed three phone calls. One to Angelo's Art Studio. The second to the concierge at the hotel where Adrienne Winters was registered.

The final, more important call, went international.

CHAPTER 13

Sheridan Macaroy slammed the receiver down, severing the call from Paris. Scowl lines cut deep ridges in his brow as he hurried down the well-lit DCI hallway of Langley for his appointment in the foyer of the Old Headquarters Building. He never walked there without intense disappointment that his own portrait did not hang in the corridor. Other men made it. Men like Maj. General William J. Donovan, who had paved the way with the Office of Strategic Services in World War II.

Donovan's successors—men who served as directors of Central Intelligence—hung on the wall beside him: Rear Admiral Souers and Lt. General Vandenberg. Helms and Colby. Webster and Woolsey. But not Sheridan Macaroy. His copybook was forever tainted from his blunders in Kuwait.

As he passed the row of portraits, his taste turned to bile. He hadn't even made it to deputy director. *A man is nothing if he hasn't reached his dream.*

When he reached the security checkpoint in the lobby, the guard on duty greeted him. "Good morning, Mr. Macaroy."

"Morning, Sam. I'm expecting a guest." He glanced at his watch. "He won't be late. He has a built-in timer."

He turned his back to the guard, cutting off any possibility of small talk as he watched the comings and goings through the front doors. As he waited, he reflected on his first time through those glass doors. The lure of adventure had brought him.

Deception kept him here.

The CIA headquarters stood on high ground on the Virginia side of the Potomac River. Seven miles across the river lay the White House. What would have happened if he had followed his original plan? Graduate from West Point with a strong background in military law and philosophy. Spend twenty-five years in the military. Marry the girl he was dating. Have kids. Retire as nothing less than a brigadier general.

He came out of West Point at a time when there were no battlefields or wars to net him rapid promotions. Terrorism existed in all corners of the world, but it was too distant from American shores to consider a declaration of war. Four years later with just first-lieutenant bars on his epaulets, he was sent as military attaché to the American embassy in Paris.

The assignment infuriated him. He wanted action. He considered leaving, but the army was all he knew. His salvation from boredom came from unexpected sources. He liked to think of it as two taps on the shoulder. One from the Saudi Arabia businessman at the top of the Eiffel Tower. Another from the low-level clerk at the embassy, a bookish American recruiter for the CIA. Those two taps on the shoulder came at just the right time.

His marriage had ended. Another opportunity for promotion had slipped beyond him. He had come to like Paris; he enjoyed the glittering revues at the Moulin Rouge and the nightlife in the Latin Quarter. But he hated the financial demands of supporting a set of twin girls and a son with a deformed foot. They named him Sheridan Gerald Macaroy. *Gerald* to the family—the boy who would never go to West Point.

At that low point in his life, intelligence gathering for either country appealed to Sheridan's quest for something better. Take a job with the CIA, and they might send him on covert assignments that would help him forget his washed-out marriage. Or contact the Saudi and exchange his frustration for money in the bank to meet his ex-wife's demands. One night, with two drinks too many under his belt, he had taken out the phone number for the Saudi and dialed the number. "Let's talk."

Over drinks, he told the Saudi about the CIA recruiter. "Splendid! Accept that offer. Once inside the Langley headquarters, you could be of untold value. We would pay you well, Mr. Macaroy."

"Lieutenant Macaroy."

Once sober, Sheridan turned down the Saudi's invitation to spy and filed his application to the CIA. But as the application process dragged on, the Saudi's invitation lurked at the back of his mind. Paperwork. Interrogation. Psychological testing that should have wiped him out of the program before he began. He'd never forgotten the question that turned him into a grease spot.

"Lieutenant Macaroy, have you ever been approached by a foreign government—?"

"No, sir."

Why they had not given him a lie-detector test, he'd never know. But his service record was good, and his marital problems were separate from his military career. Weeks later he packed his gear, flew back to Washington for the final interviews, and on to intense training at the Farm.

From that first day on the Langley campus, he saw the portraits in the hallway and determined to be one of them. That ambition drove him until he had security clearance at the top level, but the advancement he craved did not come—not with the acting DCI opposing his aggressive methods.

He lost touch with his wife, but she hadn't lost touch with his address. The operations for his son's deformed foot and wasted leg were endless, but out of a sense of duty to the boy he didn't know, he continued to provide funds. The boy deserved a chance at normal life. Boy? He was already a young man.

Sheridan's debts mounted. With every unpaid bill, he spent added hours at the corner pub. No matter how he juggled his accounts, his spending exceeded his income.

After his son's seventh operation—and five years into his intelligence career—he dialed the Saudi again. His desire for monetary gain caused the fatal mistake. Taking things into his own hands, he sent a three-man team into Kuwait just before the invasion. Losing Jon Winters was a personal affront to the director. But before Webster could discipline Macaroy, Robert Gates took over as director. With the change of leadership, Macaroy's blunders were swept under the rug.

"Sir!"

He shot a glance at the security guard. Had he spoken out loud?

"Is that your man, Mr. Macaroy?"

Sheridan saw his guest entering the front doors. The colonel looked trim and efficient in his uniform. Macaroy straightened his tie and went forward to meet him.

A s they walked up the stone steps and entered the Old Headquarters Building, the Impostor smiled down at his CIA escort, a young woman in her late twenties. He glanced at her hand. "Married?"

"I will be soon."

He flicked his visitor's badge. "This is a nuisance."

"Necessary, sir." She had a pleasant voice and noncommittal answers. He liked her style.

"Have you been with Central Intelligence long?"

"Six years."

Long enough to recruit her. "Your wedding will end your time here."

"No. My fiancé works here too. My dad encouraged us both to come on board, but I waited until I finished my university studies. I find I like working for my country."

I did too, once.

Sheridan Macaroy met them as they reached the large CIA seal embedded in the floor. Macaroy dismissed the girl with a brief nod. "I'll ask the security guard to notify you when it is time to escort my guest back to his car."

When she was out of earshot, his hand extended in welcome. "Good of you to come, Colonel."

"Good of you to see me."

The Impostor stood with his right toe on the beak of the Eagle, his heel planted on one of the sixteen spokes of the compass rose—the symbolic declaration that all intelligence data came into a central location. "Jon Winters used to say everything fanned out from Paris."

"Cut the sarcasm, Colonel. Perhaps Winters was right. Look, let's get down to business. I don't have long. I'm meeting with the DCI in thirty minutes."

"So you can report on my visit?"

"He doesn't know we're acquainted."

The Impostor followed him away from the Memorial Wall to the life-size bronze statue of William Donovan. His eyes grazed over the words above Donovan's statue: *And ye shall know the truth and the truth shall make you free.* "Sheridan, are you aware that Adrienne Winters is in Paris again?"

"Ricardo Mendez confirmed it for me a half-hour ago"

"Rick? You said he left the CIA after the Gulf War."

"Colonel, I told you he left Langley. He's been undercover at the American embassy for several years now."

"Why wasn't I informed?"

"The need to know. Remember? But we have a bigger problem. Miss Winters has contacted the embassy. In Rick's words, she's become a meddlesome tourist."

The Impostor shrugged. "She's an American citizen. Maybe she's having trouble with her passport. She tends to be careless with her purse."

"She wasn't looking for a passport. She was looking for her brother."

"What?"

"Startling, isn't it, Colonel? Our mission in Kuwait explodes in our faces again. To quote Dwight Eisenhower, 'Success cannot be advertised. Failure cannot be explained.' It seems we never explained failure to Miss Winters's satisfaction. It's up to you now."

Macaroy eased him to the left to stand in front of a single star. The Impostor fixed his eyes on the words above it: *In honor of those members of the Office of Strategic Services who gave their lives in the service of their country.* The names on the plaque meant nothing to him. "Why would Miss Winters be asking about her brother?"

"She insists she saw him in Paris."

The muscles in his neck tensed. "Impossible. I swear he was bleeding to death when I left him in Kuwait."

"I've known for a number of years that his injuries were not fatal. There was no need to tell you." Macaroy's lip curled. "Your mistake, Colonel. Jon Winters should never have left Kuwait alive."

"Have you checked out her story? You can review Jon's files, change them if necessary."

"They're sealed."

"Then open them! Make him the betrayer. Or do you have a better suggestion?"

"Calm down, Colonel. Jon Winters was declared dead. All you have to do is convince his sister that she's made a serious mistake. I want you to fly there and make certain she understands our position. And if not—"

"I won't bloody my hands with her life."

"You had no problem trying to eliminate her brother. Never mind, I can arrange to have our Saudi contact meet you there. Gresham can take care of Miss Winters for you."

"I don't have holiday time coming. Besides, there's not much military traffic going into Paris these days."

"I'll speak to the president. The director has the flu. I'm filling in for him. With him sick, I can tell the president that the latest intelligence reports indicate that terrorist cells are active in Paris. Ones that lead back to Kuwait. I'll ask him to have you released from your duties at the Pentagon—on a temporary basis, of course. That way I can send you to Paris in the line of duty. Whatever happens, we're in agreement, are we not, Colonel? We must reach Miss Winters before she finds her brother again."

"What happened, Sheridan? You had more ambitious goals than kowtowing to the director. You wanted that position."

Sheridan's pupils narrowed. "Kuwait happened."

Suddenly it made sense. The Impostor studied his companion. "You didn't have permission to send us in, did you?"

"It didn't turn out the way I expected." He glanced around. They remained out of earshot of those passing through the lobby. "It's unwise for us to keep discussing this here. A hidden camera or microphone could pick us up."

"Still, this is much less obvious than a clandestine meeting in your pub in Georgetown."

"You have no complaints, Colonel. If it weren't for me, you wouldn't be positioned there in the Pentagon."

"But my promotions were my own doing. So what happened back in the Gulf War, Sheridan?"

"Back then the DCI was a personal friend of the Winters family. If he had remained in office, my position would have been threatened. He went. I didn't. But whatever he wrote in my file killed my chances to replace him. Now, every time I'm eligible for promotion, someone else fills the vacancy. A man is nothing if he hasn't reached his dream."

"It's your drinking—"

"You're just fooling yourself, Colonel. You whitewash everything. But it will catch up with you someday. I just drink socially."

Sheridan's call came through five hours later. "It's all arranged, Colonel. You fly out from Andrews Air Force Base in the morning."

"My rank doesn't qualify me for a designated flight."

"It does when you fly with the secretary of state."

That surprised him. "So what do I tell Rumsfeld?"

"Your commanding officer will be at your desk any moment to ask you to represent the Pentagon at the meeting with the French ministry of interior. I'll have two men on board myself. They'll brief you en route."

"You're not sending me on one of those air force Lear jets?

That's a twelve-passenger job. And worse luck for me. We'd have to refuel en route at Shannon Airport in Ireland or the Mildenhall AFB in England."

"Does that kind of flying make you nervous, Colonel?"

"One takeoff and one landing are ample for me."

"I know from experience that the C-37A is a commercial Gulfstream V. It's smooth. Efficient. Comfortable."

"Just like one of those UC-35s I flew on in Europe? Too small for my taste. No food. Just bottled water."

"What's the matter with you, Colonel—a big six-footer like you afraid of flying?"

He could taste his own fear. Whenever an airliner flew low over his apartment complex, his stomach knotted at the memory of the jet crashing into the Pentagon—taking his wife and unborn child with it. But he didn't let even a whisper of his anxiety show. "I won't be able to carry my Beretta on board."

Macaroy's gruff, irritating chuckle came over the wire. "You wouldn't carry it on a commercial liner either."

"I know a private gun shop on the Left Bank in Paris."

"Forget carrying—just be at Andrews on time. Once you reach the air terminal, you'll be driven to the VIP lounge. It's a comfortable waiting area—phones, TV, beverages. When the plane is ready for boarding, you'll be escorted to the flight line. Just keep your cool, Colonel. Take your clues from the other passengers. You're part of a special mission."

"So I'll be expected to attend the meetings in Paris?"

"That's the arrangement. Trust me. Traveling with a cabinet member, you fly first class all the way. The 89th Airborne's safety record is excellent." Another gruff chuckle mocked him. "You're in capable hands. You'll be on board the Air Force C-32A—that's the military equivalent to a Boeing 757. The embassy team in Paris will arrange your hotel reservations."

The Impostor started to hang up, but not in time to cut off Macaroy's final words.

"And, Colonel, don't make any mistakes this time."

CHAPTER 14

The air force jet was airborne. The Impostor leaned back in his plush leather seat. He preferred the anonymity of first class on a commercial liner without a seat companion, but his VIP flight on the Air Force C-32A was authorized and free except to taxpayers. He never liked those seconds before lifting off the runway, but takeoff on board this private flight was smooth, efficient. They were still climbing, and he found himself urging the pilot to climb higher, faster. September 11 still unnerved him.

But a new exhilaration flooded him—had been doing so since he reached Andrews Air Force Base three hours ago and saw the gigantic blue-and-white Boeing 757-200 with an American flag painted on its vertical stabilizer and UNITED STATES OF AMERICA emblazoned on its fuselage. From the moment the entourage drove out to the flight line and he ran up the rollaway stairs into the aircraft, he saw luxury like he had never known on any previous military flight.

Flying at the cabinet level was almost like flying presidential, like being on board *Air Force One*. He'd enjoy the triumph of running up those red-carpeted steps on *Air Force One*, of turning to wave and announce, "See, your Washington mole is heading to Paris in style."

The air force had a full crew on board and, unlike the twelve-passenger Lear jet, food. Traveling with the secretary of state was pleasant enough, but being in the company of some of the top brass from Washington was mind-boggling. Everything was available, from the secretary's private quarters to four-man conference tables, a staff room, and a secured communications center. He dared not go that way—he wanted no reason to be tempted with classified recall when he met with Gresham in Paris. This Boeing aircraft had been gutted and transformed into first-class luxury. That's what he wanted to remember.

The Impostor had a final glimpse of Andrews Air Force Base and the lights of Washington in the distance, then there was nothing but the roiling waves of the Atlantic beneath them. He turned from the window and glanced forward at the secretary's familiar well-shaped head, the close-cropped gray hair, the round chin. The Impostor admired the man and envied the patriotic fervor that drove him. If protocol permitted, he would have chosen a seat beside the secretary and thrown out his political views on Washington, his opinion on the war on terrorism, and his silent conflict with Rumsfeld. As the aircraft leveled off, the secretary pushed his glasses back on the rim of his nose and listened as one of the flight crew reviewed the safety instructions.

The Impostor turned to his flight companion. "Remind me, when do we reach Paris?"

"If the weather holds, we'll hit Paris by sunrise."

He had greeted the sunrise this morning. Why not another? "I'm not much for flying."

His companion smiled. "Then it's a good thing we're on a non-stop flight. The crew boasts thousands of accident-free flying hours and unparalleled safety, comfort, and service."

"I guess the one missing amenity is the red carpet on *Air Force One.*"

"No sweat. With the secretary on board this plane, the Parisians may roll out a red carpet on their end to impress us. They often do that for foreign dignitaries. Protocol, you know."

The man's babbling irritated him. "Wake me when they serve the filet mignon."

The fat jowls bobbed. "I'll do that. But I believe the boys in the galley won't want to give the impression of living large off the taxpayer. They'll probably serve a pasta dish or baked chicken."

The Impostor was too preoccupied with the troubles that lay

ahead to worry about filet mignon. Both the emergency meeting with the French ministry of interior and the closed meetings at the embassy would focus on terrorist threats to Americans abroad and on the need for French and American unity. The contact with Ricardo Mendez was unavoidable. The face-to-face encounter with Adrienne not yet scheduled.

When a steward made his way between the passengers, he glanced at the Impostor's attaché case. "Could I stow that for you, Colonel? Make you more comfortable."

"No, I have some work cut out for me during the trip."

"If you change your mind—just tell one of the crew." With a marginal salute he made his way back to the cockpit, leaving the Impostor with his own worries.

The steward's interruption set his flight companion to talking. "Do you have a family, Colonel?"

"I'm a widower. My wife was killed back on 9/11."

Nothing silenced him. "What's your specialty, sir?"

"Classified."

The rebuff proved ineffective. "Are you working on that search for the Washington mole? We'll get him—and I hope they hang this one by his toes or sizzle him. A life sentence isn't enough for a traitor. Don't you agree?"

The sudden tightness at his uniform collar choked the Impostor, but the fat man rambled on. "I'd hoped we'd fly on the C-40. The modified Boeing 737 is the latest addition to the fleet. But we're still part of that long list of dignitaries that have flown on board before. The first lady. Members of Congress. Foreign heads of state. The vice president. Nice perks for serving the government in Washington."

"But you're not a senator?"

He flashed a toothy grin. "I wondered when you'd get around to asking me. I'm one of Macaroy's boys."

The colonel glanced at him. He was midthirties and overweight, give or take thirty pounds. Scarred chin. Shrewd eyes. A mocking smile. A smooth tongue as he said, "We're to stay close this flight, Colonel, except for bathroom breaks. That way you avoid being questioned."

He nodded, waited.

"Sheridan wants you to skip that shopping trip to the Left Bank. He's arranged for the item you want to be delivered to your hotel suite. Got it?"

A trickle of sweat prickled his brow. The last thing he wanted was to be under Sheridan's remote control. But his legacy of deceit forced him back to the sand dunes of Kuwait, suffocating him with sweltering desert memories. He mopped his brow with the back of his wrist. At moments like this, he despised himself as nothing but another Philby. Another Ames or Hanssen. A despicable traitor. He'd long fooled his superiors, himself, everyone. Yet in a matter of seconds the search for the mole could lead back to him. With each sunrise he considered himself lucky. With each sunset came the dread of night.

And the nightmare.

With each news edition came the fear that an ad would appear in the classifieds: FIREBRAND REUNION. E-STREET COMPLEX. ROOM 7 THURSDAY 9 A.M. Whatever day they used he would add two days. Whatever hour listed, he would subtract three. The E-Street location would remain the same, a clandestine meeting on the Capitol Mall, just beyond the Washington Monument. The Impostor considered meeting there a risk. With one lone ad, he'd be forced to find more revenue for terrorism. For the sake of his son and his own protection, he'd be forced to pass some classified document for filthy lucre and the damnation of his soul. Or perhaps he would ignore the ad this time and wait for his controller to seek him out, destroy him. It would be a blessed relief.

He had not expected to sleep through the flight, but after the dinner—he'd chosen the chicken—exhaustion took over. As they neared France, he awakened to darkness and the low mumble of the voices of men who couldn't sleep.

He buzzed his jaw with a battery-run razor and felt more presentable for it. With the razor still in his hand, the black clouds outside the plane turned to gray and then to the brilliance of a sunrise. As the other passengers stirred, the plane cut through ribbons of coral and split the clouds into streamers of ocher and crimson.

They landed at Orly, nine miles south of the capital, and were met by an embassy team headed, he noted, by an attractive young woman. She smiled at the secretary of state. "I'm Naji Fleming, Mr. Secretary. My team will guide you through customs and on to your hotel."

The secretary glanced at his watch. "What's our schedule, Miss Fleming?"

"You will have two or three hours to freshen up. Time enough to catch a quick breakfast. That's already ordered."

"And the meeting with the ministry of interior?" he asked. "I have it down for ten."

"That's correct, sir. We will have embassy transportation for you around 9:15." Her smile was beguiling. "And your usual security escort, Mr. Secretary."

She studied the passengers as they deplaned. Spotting him, she said, "Colonel, Mr. Mendez sent his apologies. He was unable to meet the plane."

"When will I see him?"

"Tomorrow at the earliest."

"That runs against my time frame. Ask him to call me at the hotel this evening."

Her gaze cooled. "He said you would tell me that."

On that same sun-beaten Wednesday in Paris, Adrienne awakened resolute to find Jacques d'Hiver. She hadn't heard back from the embassy. The clock hands were racing, her time in Paris limited. "Oh, Robbie," she called out to the empty room, "I wish you were here to help me."

But she had to discover for herself the loophole that linked the stranger with her brother. Even as she chose to leave the hotel and have breakfast alone on a small pavement café on the Champs Élysées, the old sibling rivalry needled her. She was always on the losing side, driven by the longing to please her mother. Jon, dead or alive, seemed always the favored child. At least she had stayed by her family and not betrayed them.

The café was bustling with Parisians—some on the way to work. Others were enjoying the Parisian's way of life over a newspaper and a cup of steaming coffee. She envied their contentment, their unhurried pace as the day began. She poked at her baked egg and picked at her croissant roll, keeping an eye on the café across the street. But Jacques d'Hiver did not appear.

She allowed her gaze to wander over the broad, shady avenue. The Champs Élysées was flanked by museums and theaters, luxury shops, and international airline offices. Two doors down, in the heart of this business district, a discreet sign was framed in the window of an elegant shop. The general public was not welcome, just the wealthy, secluded clientele, such as those attending the fashion program.

As she reached the fashion show, she was surprised to see someone sitting in the assigned seat beside her. "I'm sorry, but that seat is reserved for a friend of mine."

The girl flipped through the program brochure. "I told your friend she had a phone call. My name is Naji Fleming. You are to go to the café alone today."

Adrienne's breath caught in her throat. "Will Jacques d'Hiver be there?"

"We can't be certain. But we sent a message to him."

"Did Angelo send you?"

"I came on my own."

The girl was attractive. Her accent was East Coast, American. "You look familiar, Naji, but I haven't seen you at the fashion show before."

The girl smiled. "I am not a guest." She stood. "Remember. Please go alone. You have to trust someone."

"But not a stranger."

"You're looking for a stranger."

Maddie was ticked when she got back. "Some charming young woman sent me on a fool's errand."

Adrienne put a consoling hand on her friend's arm. "I suspected as much. She wanted to talk to me."

Maddie's brow arched. "You have the strangest friends."

"And you're one of the best. Will you forgive me when I tell you I can't have lunch with you today?"

"Am I to run interference for you with the others?" Despite Maddie's light tone, there was concern in her eyes. "I'm afraid for you, Adrienne."

"I'll explain everything when I see you at the hotel."

"And if you aren't there when we get back, we'll go straight to le prefecture de police and post a notice with them: MISSING AMERICAN."

She managed a smile. "That's comforting, Maddie. I'll be careful."

For the next two hours, Adrienne forced herself to concentrate on the fashion show. The models on the catwalk were glamorous, the excitement all around her contagious. At 11:15 Maddie leaned closer. "Go now. The others will think you are going to powder your nose."

Thirty minutes later she stepped out of the hot sunshine and into the Café le Grand Royale. The usual guests filled the wicker chairs: Parisians and tourists with carafes of wine on their tables. An ever-increasing number of men from the Middle East occupied the room as well—striking figures with unsmiling dark faces and cold brown eyes. Their beards were well trimmed, their bright headdresses in place.

She had not noticed Aleem, but the moment she took Jacques d'Hiver's unoccupied table he was at her side. His swarthy complexion soured with his scowl. "This table is reserved, mademoiselle."

"Monsieur d'Hiver is expecting me."

He glanced toward the maître d'. "But this is our busy hour. You must order something to hold the table."

She settled on mineral water and crêpes suzette in tangerine sauce. Later, when he seemed anxious again, she ordered a basket of bread and slices of cheese. She waited an hour.

Aleem reappeared. "He is not coming, mademoiselle. Your presence is causing questions among the staff."

"I'll wait a little longer."

Then she saw him. Tall and handsome, a slight hunch to his shoulders, his eyes downcast. But he had noticed her. He was coming toward her.

"I see you already found my table."

"Naji said you would come."

A frown pinched his brow. "Naji?" He took her hand, brushed it with a kiss. "You must not come here again, Miss Winters. Promise me."

The deep rich voice that used to resonate through the halls at Winterfest had no vibrancy to it this morning. He squeezed her hand with a gentle grip. "Don't pull free. People must think we are friends of long standing."

"We are, Jacques."

His smile did not reach his eyes. They remained distant, sad. "Aleem tells me you have come every day, but it is not safe for you to be here anymore."

"My friends and I don't have to sit at Aleem's table."

"Coming back again risks Aleem's safety."

"Oh! Should I leave now?"

His fingers dug deep into her shoulders. "And have people think we're quarreling again? Today we established a close friendship for anyone who may be watching us." He hooked his cane over a decorative flower pot. "I informed Aleem that we were quarreling the last time. He will pass the word along to the right people."

He took a gardenia from the vase on the empty table beside them and held it out to her. She felt her eyes brim with tears. So he remembered how much she loved flowers…how fragrant the gardenia bush was, climbing over the fence back home. How sweet the fragrance when it bloomed.

"You remembered!"

He scowled.

A crimson flush burned her cheeks. She stared, uncertain. "You know…the gardenia bush that grows by Mother's bedroom window at Winterfest. The one Rolf planted for her."

He settled in the chair across from her and folded his hands on the tabletop. "I only remember that women like flowers—even from a stranger."

She dropped the gardenia by her silverware. Her jaw jutted forward. "Then perhaps you should know. I prefer roses, Monsieur d'Hiver."

CHAPTER 15

Now that she faced Jacques d'Hiver, she wanted to believe that this was her mother's son. Like Jon, d'Hiver had good bone structure, thick dark hair and a trimmed mustache. But his features were troubled, his complexion sallow. Dark circles shadowed his eyes as though he hadn't slept. Saddest of all, that easy laugh that defined her brother was miles away, perhaps gone forever.

The day that Jon Aaron went away—when he told her he would play his role well—he gripped her arms and eased her into a chair. Jon's hands were strong and supple as he knelt down beside her. He took his handkerchief and wiped the tears from her face. "Don't be angry with me. I have to go away, Sis."

"I hate it when you go away."

"It's my job." The pressure of his fingers had tightened. "I'm not sure when I'll be back."

"Where are you going this time?"

"Europe. The Middle East."

"Will you come right back after that?"

"No, that's why I'm leaving you in charge. Dad can take care of himself, but if I'm delayed getting home, promise me you'll look after Mom."

Her tears flowed. "*She's* supposed to be looking after me."

"I know. But you know how it is with her ever since we left Paris. So I'm going to need your help."

When she agreed, his grip on her arms relaxed. "Now, walk me out to the curb, little sister. My taxi will be here any minute." He swung his suitcases up in both hands and smiled at her. "If I stay away long enough, you can have my room."

"Really?"

"Really."

Adrienne blinked back tears. She wanted to tell Jacques d'Hiver that she had never used her brother's room. Instead she pulled an envelope from her purse. "I was able to get you two tickets for the fashion show—I thought you could take your wife. You do have a wife, don't you?"

He forced a smile as though her presence intruded on his space, his contemplation—and well it did. He sat like some great poet forming his words and rhyme, and she had broken the rhythm. "Is that curiosity, or have you been sipping my wine, Miss Winters?"

"I'm just curious."

He rubbed his jaw. "I have no wife."

No, the girl you were going to marry married someone else. The girl who never wore your ring. Never saw you again. Will never see you again.

"Then you are alone?"

"I didn't say that." He gazed beyond her, his expression blank, as though he saw her but didn't know her. "I have two children, and their French mother adores me."

Another sudden flush burned her neck. "Then take her to the show."

He palmed his chin in that old familiar way and between splayed fingers mumbled, "I have embarrassed you."

"A little... Tell me about your children."

His expression warmed. "Colette is the oldest. Prim and proper, much like her mother. And my son?" His features came alive. "Claudio is four—small and spare for his size, but such a busy young man." Again his dark eyes challenged. "We named him for a friend of mine."

Claudio. Jon's older friend. She broke off another bite of roll and shredded it. He watched, amused. She couldn't take her eyes from his hands.

He shifted in his chair. "I can see that I trouble you."

"It's the scar on your hand. My brother had a scar like the one on your index finger."

137

He extended his left hand and studied it. "Most people have scars from childhood."

"What happened to you?"

"Shrapnel, I think."

"An accident?"

"An accident of sorts. A battle scar. I served in the Gulf War, you know."

Her heart thumped. "My brother died in Kuwait."

"Was he part of the ground forces?"

"American intelligence, I suspect."

He locked his fingers, hiding the scar, his gaze drifting over their surroundings. In their childhood, Jon had always looked people straight in the eye, challenging them with an unblinking gaze.

Now his eyes looked like deep swirling pools of emptiness.

"I'm sorry about your brother, Miss Winters." Picking up a crisp, golden baguette from the wire basket, he hacked off the end piece and with a thump of his forefinger produced a resonant sound. "The bread and cheese are good at this café. Try some."

When she hesitated, he tore off another piece and held it out to her. "You should buy a loaf to take back to your hotel, but it's best if you can store it in a wooden box."

She shuddered. She was opening a Pandora's box. How far could she push his memory? What words sprinkled in their conversation would draw him back from oblivion—from Jacques d'Hiver to Jon Winters? Did she dare risk his mental stability?

Now and then a quick flicker showed in his eyes, a sudden glance that soon became veiled again. She felt boxed in and had boxed him in as well. Was Jon dead? Was this man just a look-alike?

Was Jon in a wooden box somewhere in the sand dunes of Kuwait? Or would they even bury an infidel on their holy soil?

Her throat caught. A *wooden box? Was that all he received for going into their country to help them?*

"Miss Winters?"

"I'm sorry. I was thinking about my brother and how foolish I am insisting on talking to you about him. You must think me wanton, bold, brazen—"

"No, I do not question your motives." He glanced around the room. "We are friends, remember? And as a friend, I consider you troubled. If you are troubled, Adrienne, you should talk to a clergyman."

"I don't know any in Paris. Do you?"

"I know of a priest south of St. Lo. The city of Paris is full of cathedrals."

"I used to visit some of them with my father." She hesitated. "Am I boring you, Monsieur d'Hiver?"

"On the contrary, I find your story quite interesting."

"But not plausible?"

"The last time we met, you told me your brother was your childhood hero. Perhaps Paris makes you think of him."

You make me think of him. "I think of him often. He was also my biggest rival. For some reason, he still is. My parents adored him, my mother in particular." She yearned for the veil to lift. She studied his features again and saw her mother in them. "You have eyes like my mother. Deep-set. Dark. Pensive."

His eyes narrowed. "Is that a good thing?"

"Complimentary to you." She couldn't hold back the smile. "Mother is a beautiful woman, talented, always entertaining friends, very theatrical—superb at putting on airs. But people love her." She sighed and went back in time, praying he'd remember. "Mother had the leading role in *Romeo and Juliet* in a Broadway theater when my father met her... She's ill now. In a wheelchair. Facing the slow process of dying, I think."

A scowl formed above his thick brows. "From inactivity?"

"From Parkinson's. She could be in a wheelchair for years. Or pneumonia or some respiratory illness could take her life. She has no resistance."

His drinking glass shattered. He grabbed his napkin and wiped his hand.

She used hers to wipe up the spill. "Are you all right?"

"Just a scratch. It will heal." He beckoned for Aleem and glared at Adrienne as the mess was cleared.

When Aleem walked away, Jacques's silence invited her to say more. "Mother wants me to bring her back to Paris someday."

"Please do." She heard an echo of misgiving in his voice when he asked, "Did you follow the theater too, Miss Winters?"

"I never aspired to be an actress. My brother mocked the pretense that went into playing a role. But in actuality, we were always playacting, wearing masks. Pretending to be something we weren't."

As I'm pretending now. Pretending to be an innocent from abroad. And you sit there in your mask. Everything inside of me says you are Jon. Everything about you denies it.

His gaze drifted over his surroundings, then focused on her again. "This brother of yours, what did he do?"

"He followed Dad into government work. The government would like us to think that my brother served with the State Department, like Dad did."

"Honorable."

"Not much more. In the end all Jon got for his loyalty and service was a star on a memorial wall. With my father working for the State Department, I grew up not asking too many questions. We accepted secrecy as a way of life. We didn't even hear about my brother's death for weeks after he died."

His gaze wandered. Came back to meet her own. "You must have had the decency of a funeral?"

"Just a memorial service. There was no body to bury."

"Didn't you ask your government what happened?"

"They turned a deaf ear our way and placated us with words. All we knew was that Jon Aaron had left home for Paris."

Jacques d'Hiver formed lines on the linen cloth with breadcrumbs. She was losing him, pushing him away. "Perhaps your brother really is dead and your coming back to Paris has simply reminded you of him. Having lived here, you must know that everything fans out from Paris and doubles back to this City of Light." His voice deepened. "Or perhaps your brother lost his memory—or his right to remember."

Her heart pounded. Risk or not, she had to say something. "I used to lie awake at night wondering whether Jon had been seriously injured in the Kuwaiti invasion. Or whether in the aftermath, he became a victim of amnesia."

The maître d' hovered near their table. Cavell's presence alarmed her. He was a big man, tall and rigid, his large ears close to his scalp. His sharp, roving eyes bothered her as they evaluated the needs of his guests and the efficiency of his waiters. Without knowing Cavell, she disliked him. He acknowledged the Middle Easterners settling at the table beside them with a cordial smile, but he seemed more concerned with Jacques and herself. Was he reading her lips? Protecting Jacques?

She lowered her voice. "I don't trust that man."

"Cavell? He's curious about you, as I am."

She pushed her teacup aside and chose another avenue. "Monsieur d'Hiver, do you climb?"

With a tilt of his head, he listened to the guests beside them. The corner of his lip twitched, and she knew that he understood what they were saying. She drew him back. "Monsieur d'Hiver, I asked if you climb?"

"Climb?"

"You know, the Alps?"

"I did a long time ago." He chugged down another glass of wine, which seemed to loosen his tongue. "The Italian Alps. The Swiss. The French. The German. I did them all. I was good at it. But Kuwait took that from me. I came back with an aluminum leg instead of a medal."

"My brother didn't come back at all."

He shrugged. "I think those who didn't come back are the lucky ones. For the rest of us, the war goes on."

How dare he think that death was better, that memorials were more comforting. And yet this man sat there, listening to her bare her soul. Did he pity her? Or was he seeking release from his own battle scars?

"My aluminum leg doesn't bend on mountain slopes."

She caught his fragment of self-pity. "Other amputees climb mountains. Some ski."

"Do they? I haven't tried either since Kuwait."

"At least you came back." She moistened her lips. *Tell him now. Don't keep forcing the past on him. Just drop the truth into his heart, one word at a time.* She hesitated, making certain that the Arabic speakers beside them were too engrossed in their own world to be bothered with hers. Their muffled words were heated, argumentative, too soft for Jacques d'Hiver to interpret.

"I lost both my brothers in Kuwait. My oldest brother was stillborn while my parents served in Kuwait City."

"And the other brother?" He lowered his voice as Aleem appeared again. "What do you think happened to him?"

She wiped a croissant crumb from her lips. "I think the CIA sent him into Kuwait on a solo mission."

"I thought your intelligence operatives were under Central Command before the Gulf War, waiting it out with General Schwarzkopf."

"The CIA likes to gather its own intelligence data. You know, for national security reasons."

"Should I know about national security reasons?"

"You were there. The Americans didn't go it alone. The Brits and French were there—"

"Side by side with our Arab brothers?"

"Only one brother mattered to me. But after he was reported killed in the line of duty, he became little more than a nameless star at Central Intelligence."

"He must have been more than that?"

She feared that at any minute d'Hiver would leave and she would never see him again. "They told us my brother was killed in an explosion, one of the casualties of the Gulf War." She fought the swelling in her throat. "A friend of mine—an investigative journalist—could never find my brother's name on the casualty lists."

She was talking too much, making a fool of herself, trying to keep him from standing again and walking away. She considered leaving herself, putting an end to the madness of exploiting this man's patience. But it pained her to watch him fill his glass once more. And she, who never took a drop, found her tongue as loose as his.

He twirled his half-filled wineglass as he studied her. "Men are lost in every war. Many unaccounted for."

Their eyes met over his wine carafe, her own gaze as stony as his. "Easy enough for you to say—I was still fifteen when word came that my brother was gone. All I could think was I'd never see him again."

Her hands trembled in her lap. Like somebody else's hands. She stared beyond him to the Arc de Triomphe in the distance, where twelve avenues struck out from its center. Twelve detours. Twelve escape routes.

D'Hiver's gaze followed hers. "France's unknown soldier lies beneath that arc. It represents all of France's fallen."

"Then Jon should be buried in that tomb—in this city that he loved so much."

"You can't grieve forever. Nor nurse your misgivings. You're too young. If he's dead, let him be dead."

She flicked tangled strands of hair behind her ear. "I won't let it go. You see—I don't think he is dead. But if my brother is alive—and his memory is still good—then he has allowed his family to weep for him for more than a decade. If he is alive and remembers us, he should return home while his mother is still alive."

He palmed his hands to his lips, a simple gesture that reminded her of a ghost from her past.

"Jacques, I have to ask you—I just can't walk away again without asking." She heard the tremor in her own words. "I think you're my brother. Are you my brother?"

He leaned back in his chair. "Your dead brother? Or is that a universal question? The brotherhood of mankind?"

"I'm not a philosopher, Jacques. I told you, I'm a fashion buyer. But what I want to know…are you Jon Aaron? Because, if you are my brother, you can't imagine how much your mother wants to see you again."

Straightaway, his eyes seemed awash with pain. "My mother?" He asked the question as though she had never existed. As though he of all men was born without one.

"You really are Jon, aren't you?"

Without a flicker he pushed his plate aside. "I must go, mademoiselle."

"What about the people who are watching us?"

"They will think we have quarreled again. The staff here knows I have a family." He shrugged. "They will see the two of us as—"

"Friends. Friends who must meet at the café."

As he reached for his cane, he gave her shoulder another gentle squeeze. "Forgive me, Miss Winters."

Adrienne watched him walk away in that halting gait, a proud man slowed by an artificial limb. It was a determined stride—strident. Resolute. He glanced back once and waved, a hint of a mocking smile on that solemn mouth.

So now you know, it seemed to say. *You have found me, but I must go away again.*

CHAPTER 16

Mara Winters watched Rolf coming down the wide corridor, a key ring dangling from his hand. She sensed a strange stirring, a revival of her deadened heartstrings. She wondered...did he know how to dance? Something fast and rhythmic. The tango. The rumba. Music that would make her whirl around the ballroom and feel young and well again.

She imagined him in formal attire, smiling instead of frowning. His voice romantic, not condescending. Yet despite all the years she'd known him, she knew little about him.

Had he ever been married? Had he ever been in love? She had known him forever, yet he remained a stranger. Distant from her because she had placed him there. He was a plain man with a narrow face and faded hazel eyes, his arthritic knees more bothersome than he liked to admit. He'd been part of the Winters household since the day they left for Paris. Before that he was her father-in-law's friend, not hers. In the old days he served as butler and secretary for Harrison Winters, but Harrison and Rolf's relationship was more of friend and confidant than employee and employer. Sending his family away to Paris had troubled Harrison, so he begged Rolf to leave Winterfest and serve the family abroad.

To shadow me, she had thought then. Harrison had been a wise old man, leery of her, loyal to his son, Harry, and devoted to Adrienne from the day she was born. And why? Because Adrienne was so much like Harry. Honest. Loyal. A Winters to the core. Adrienne loved the grounds where the house stood. Harrison intended for her to have it.

In Paris, when the State Department accused Harry of treacherous wrongdoing, Rolf proved to be her husband's strength. He oversaw the packing and the closing up of the house and the flat in Burgundy. Mara had been too distraught to do it herself. And when the awful news about Jon came, Rolf sat in the library with Harry for days after. Mara was no comfort to her husband. She was too busy blaming him for Jon's death. She wanted Jon to be an artist, not a government employee. Not a dead hero.

Even when Harry died five years later, Adrienne insisted that Rolf remain with the family. It was a wise decision. He was, in a sense, the man of the house, the old standby who befriended Mara even though he'd never approved of her.

As he glanced down at her now, she felt both vulnerable and defiant, dependent on him and her wheelchair. She saw something flicker in his eyes—gentleness, caring, sympathy. The man had to be in his midsixties, maybe a smidgen over, but he didn't have a tinge of gray in his sandy hair.

"Good morning, madame." The thin mustache that covered the old scar on his upper lip bobbed when he spoke. "I've brought the key for Mr. Winters's room."

"Then open the door."

"But you have not gone in there since your husband died."

"Then it's time I did. What's the matter, Rolf? Is the room dusty?"

His shoulders reared back, making him tall again. "The room is clean, madame. I see to that."

Yes, he would do that for Harry and Harrison. Rolf was as meticulous as the men who hired him and made him part of the family. Mara was the one who insisted on the uniform to keep him in his place.

"Hurry, please."

With deliberate movements he selected a key from the ring and inserted it in the lock, turned it, and pushed the door back on her past. A musty odor assailed her as she rolled her wheelchair into the room.

Without waiting for her order, Rolf opened the windows and allowed the spring breeze to sweep across the room. It ruffled the curtains, stirring her memories.

"Mr. Harry always liked the windows open."

That would be important to Rolf, doing things the way Harry wanted them. An old photograph of herself sat on the bedside table, taken when she was a zillion years younger. Harry took it the day after they met. She waited for the sudden beat of her heart to slow, the tremor in her hand to calm. She had loved Harry in her own selfish way, but she had never been fair to him. Oh, perhaps in the beginning with that first flush of being loved by someone so sought after by others. Dashing. Charming in a reserved sort of way. But Harry was going places with the State Department. From the moment he paid her attention, she had been intrigued with what life would offer her as Harry T. Winters's wife. *Harry Thaddeus Winters*. The *Thaddeus* she deplored, but marrying him offered an open door to the lifestyle she craved and to the mansion she wanted to possess.

But Harrison Winters's legal wrangling ensured that Winterfest Estates would never be hers. It would go from his son Harry to his grandchildren, and Harrison had warned her against contesting that decision.

Rolf stood by her wheelchair now, his probing eyes on her. Hearing his steady breathing, she allowed her gaze to sweep the room again. It was Victorian in its furnishings, yet it was a man's room. Harry's personality showed in the rows of history books stacked by size in the walnut bookcase and the locked display case of canes. Some of Harry's canes still hung on the wall—the eighteenth-century violin cane and the ebony gun cane, with its carved bone knob handle.

"Something is missing, Rolf."

"Madame?"

She pondered. "Harry's Remington gun cane and the old torch cane used to hang above his dresser."

"The one with the duck's head?"

"No, the well-crafted Pettibone from Cincinnati."

"Mr. Harry had me put them away just before he died. He said they were too valuable to leave on display."

"Nonsense. Why would he do that? Guests never came in this room."

"For your safety, Mrs. Winters."

"My safety?" Or in that last minute change, had Harry left behind a clue to his past—answers to his dismissal from Paris? She did a quick survey of the room again, her eyes settling on Harry's vast Victorian wardrobe. "Is that where he kept his guns?"

"Some of them." Rolf crossed the room and swung the doors back. "His favorites are here, but Miss Adrienne had me store the others on the third floor."

"Harry often said that owners stored personal papers or maps in the barrels of the guns. Was the Pettibone capable of this or the Remington?"

Rolf's wry smile mocked her. "Mr. Harry never confided in me regarding that."

"But he trusted you with his life—with his secrets."

Harry's cane collection annoyed her, although she often gave him a cane for Christmas or his birthday because she could think of no other present that would please him more. It entailed no laborious selection, no aimless shopping. She just wrote a check or sent Rolf to an auction show to bid, whatever it cost.

"We should get rid of that collection—or auction it off. It would bring in considerable money."

Rolf's lips thinned. "Miss Adrienne would forbid it. She wants nothing of her father's disturbed."

And Adrienne would have her way. Stubborn girl. She considered anything her father loved as much a part of the old house as the wide, white pillars on the front porch.

"That will be all, Rolf."

He cleared his throat.

She glanced up and saw his reflection in the elegant Victorian mirror. He held his ground. "Madame, you might need me to lift things for you."

"Rolf, I'll be just fine. I want to spend some time alone with Harry."

If he questioned her motives, he showed no surprise, but gave her a polite bow. He nodded to the bell by the bedside—the one Harry had used to call for help during his illness. "If you need me, madame, just ring."

"Leave the keys. I may want to sift through Harry's desk drawers. Maybe review his private papers and throw out some things that are no longer of value."

He eyed her for a long moment. "Then I'll leave you, madame."

"Please do." *And will you wait outside the door and linger until I am out of this room?*

But as his footsteps faded down the corridor, she forced herself to focus on the massive bed where Harry had died alone while she hosted one of her tea parties out in the garden. Even when Rolf came to tell her he was struggling for each breath—didn't he always?—she'd brushed him aside. "I'll tend to Harry after my guests are gone."

Later, she recoiled when she saw him helpless in death. He'd always been her strength, her handsome husband who opened the doors to Washington society for her. She treasured France and all the other exciting posts where they'd served. After Paris they drifted apart, always struggling for something to say to each other. He thought she blamed him for their exile. Mara knew better. She knew what had happened in Paris.

A fresh burst of grief overwhelmed her. "Oh, Harry, it cost you everything you worked for! Even when you faced the humiliation of friends and government turning against you, I protected my own reputation, salvaged my own place and position at the Winters Estate."

She rolled her chair closer to the bed and ran her hand over the coverlet. "I didn't deserve you."

Harry's stroke had estranged them more. It left him with a partial paralysis and that sickening twist to his drooling mouth. When he kissed her good-night, she turned away, allowing his kiss to fall on her cheek. When he put that limp hand over hers, she wanted to scream. She hated his weakness.

And now! She glanced down at her own hands, her own body. Parkinson's was destroying her as the stroke had robbed Harry of his strength.

She struggled to roll her wheelchair over the thick carpet to his desk. She opened the drawers one by one. Nothing. Not until the last drawer—for there she found the letters from Jon, banded together with a purple ribbon.

She fought back tears as she saw her son's handwriting. The first few letters were chatty, father-son reports on his visits to old friends at the embassy, the visit to the American Academy, a renewed friendship with an old Langley contact, and a disappointing visit to the Sorbonne University. *"Didn't see a soul I knew. Even Hamad has stopped his studies and returned to his country."*

Hamad? Had Jon ever mentioned this Hamad to her? She couldn't recall.

She read and reread his last letter from Paris. "Dear Dad, It's great to be back in Paris. I didn't want to worry Mom, so I didn't warn you that I wouldn't be here long. Of course, Colin and I have been doing the town. All the night spots. Climbed the Eiffel Tower. Did the art museums. Colin's interest in art leaves much to be desired…"

His paragraphs ran as one. "Tonight we'll be having dinner with Claudio and his wife. Kind of a farewell dinner. You remember them. Great friends. They treat me like a son. They didn't want Colin to come, but what was I to do? I'd already invited him to join me."

She puzzled over the third paragraph. "I owe you an apology, Dad, railing on you about my parentage and all. You're the greatest dad a man could have. I'm still determined to clear your name."

She ran her hand over the familiar scrawl, seeking the courage to keep reading. "I know you told me to let it go, but you were on to something, weren't you, Dad? I think you had your fingers on some acts of terrorism. Maybe something going on at the embassy. Whatever it was, you protected someone else. Mother, I suspect or some close associate—"

She winced. Where had he gone from Paris? Kuwait, of course. "Dad, I've been asked to be part of a team going into the Middle East. That's about all I can tell you. No, it's not Saudi Arabia, but you're getting close. The Company may be rushing into this one, but I'm ready. Pray for me, Dad, that I do my job well. If something happens—no, I won't go that route. I'll just plan on getting back as soon as I can. Give that freckle-faced girl of mine a kiss for me, will you, Dad? Jon."

After reading the letter through a third time, she wasn't certain what she had missed. Whatever he was saying between the lines had been for his dad's eyes.

"Oh, Jon, why did you take such risks?" She bundled the letters together again. There were no letters beyond Paris. Perhaps no time to write them.

She searched again for Harry's journals, but without success. After all these years, she was desperate to discover what Harry had recorded about Paris—perhaps she would find some link with the truth that she should destroy before her illness prevented her from caring for herself.

For Harry's sake, and before she died, she wanted to remove anything that would hurt Adrienne.

M rs. Winters."

She spun her chair around. "Robbie Gilbert."

"One and the same."

"What are you doing here?"

His gaze traveled to the desk. "Perhaps the same thing you are. It's been three days since you promised me you'd look for Jon's letters."

"I found them."

"Were there any letters from Kuwait?"

"None."

"Are you certain?"

She clenched her hands on the letters. "And what do you mean by that?"

"Colin told you about the declassification of some of the records from Paris—and from the Gulf War."

"And am I supposed to be interested?"

"Isn't that why you're here, searching for answers?"

She dismissed this with a wave. "Robbie, you're the one who begged me to find Jon's correspondence. But I didn't find Harry's journal."

"I wasn't certain you would look for them." He glanced around the room, then faced her again. "Are you going to let me read Jon's letters?"

She sighed. "I keep forgetting that you and Adrienne are no longer children. I think you both grew up while I was grieving for my son."

He seemed suddenly embarrassed. Unsure of himself. "You've been crying, Mrs. Winters."

Her throat caught. "Why wouldn't I? This is Harry's room. Just being in this room reminds me of him—and his love for his son. I haven't been in here since—"

"I'm sorry. I just want to help you."

She shoved the bundle of letters across the desk to him. "Whatever you are trying to discover, I think you are doing it for Adrienne. I admire that about you."

He picked up the packet. "Did Jon talk about Colin?"

"Just that they were in Paris together—enjoying the nightlife."

"Did he mention their assignment to Kuwait?"

"He mentioned the Middle East. But I'm certain Colin didn't go with him or he would have told me. You see, Colin was here the day we got that dreadful news—"

"I know. Mrs. Winters, I've spent all this week—and most of this morning—poring over the declassified records. These letters will help."

"Are you looking for anything in particular?"

He stopped fidgeting and stood there, his jacket flung over one shoulder—a grown man now with unflinching blue eyes and a packet of her son's letters in his hand. "Mrs. Winters—"

"Robbie, why are you calling me Mrs. Winters? It's been Mara for years."

"I know. But tonight—somehow tonight calling you Mara seemed disrespectful. You see, I know what happened in Paris, when your husband was asked to leave."

She caught her breath. Her panic rose. "You can't know. You were just a boy then, a child like Adrienne."

"You've known all along, haven't you?"

"Get out, Robbie. Leave these premises now."

"And if I don't?"

"I'll ring for Rolf."

He glanced at the cord dangling by the bedside. "Should I ring for you, Mara?"

Her courage wavered. "No, please just leave me alone. Haven't you done enough damage already?"

"I'm here to warn you that Adrienne is in danger."

"She'll be safe. Colin flew to Paris to be with her."

He thrust his face in hers. "When?"

"Yesterday—or the day before. I'm not certain, but he flew on board an air force jet. He plans to see her as soon as he can break free from the meetings he's attending."

If the look on his face had been stern, it was now downright grim. "Then, Mrs. Winters, I'm afraid she is in even more danger than ever."

CHAPTER 17

Rolf stretched to ease the searing pain between his shoulders. Working the stables and walking the remaining horses took its toll. These days he had the added burden of young Gavin underfoot. A good boy. A great little buddy.

Rolf smiled. Here he was, in his midsixties being a grandpa without ever having been a father. He held out his hand and allowed Gavin's new pony to nibble at his callused palm.

In the early days—so long ago—he oversaw the trainers and stable boys. Now he left the pony's stall and patted the sleek neck of Adrienne's thoroughbred. With a final sweeping glance of the stable, he dimmed the lights and trudged up the hill.

At the mansion, he kicked off his mud-caked boots, slipped into his loafers and, brushing the remaining hay from his worn jeans, entered the back of the house. He found the cook in the kitchen and grinned. "Smells good."

"A roast, but that's not good enough for Mrs. Winters. She's getting much too thin. Wants to die if you ask me."

I didn't ask you. "She misses her daughter. Did you ask the nurse to take a tray up to her?"

"Mrs. Winters squelched that one. She told the nurse to leave. Said she was going up to her bedroom to rest."

"Is Gavin with Miss Mara?"

"No, the nurse put Gavin to bed before she left."

"I'll pop in on him. If he's awake I'll read to him."

She shoved another cook pan in the sink, splashing the room with soapsuds. "Mrs. Winters aggravates me, but she is good with the boy. Treats him like a grandchild. Makes me sad." She plunged her hands into the soapy water again.

"So Mrs. Winters is upstairs?"

"In her room, I suspect. Can I dish up your dinner, Rolf? My feet are raw standing on them."

"Please, just put something in the warming oven for me before you leave. I'll eat after I check on Mara."

The name just slipped out. The cook took no notice. "Soak your dishes, Rolf. I'll do the wash-up in the morning."

He checked the library and sitting room before finding Mara's wheelchair and Gavin's fire truck deserted by the stairwell. He went up the spiraling stairs, his steps muffled by the thick carpet. After peeking in on the sleeping youngster, he knocked on Mara's bedroom door.

A cold sweat accompanied the silence. He knocked again. "Madame, it's Rolf."

A muffled cry came from the third floor. Rolf bounded up the stairs and on the final landing found her leaning against the railing, sobbing. He approached with caution.

"Madame, it's Rolf." He sat beside her. "What's wrong? You have to talk to someone. It might as well be me."

"I...found...my husband's journal."

"Harry never meant for you to find it." *Nor did I.*

"I heard Robbie prowling around so I came up."

"How, Mara? You are as unsteady on those legs as—"

Through the muffled tears, she gave a weak chuckle. "I bumped my way up on my backside. One step at a time."

"I'll carry you down."

"What a pair we'd make." She turned to face him, her cheeks streaked with tears. "I dumped Harry's journal back in the storage bin with the canes. I think you hid it there. Poor Harry! He knew the truth all along, didn't he?"

"Yes, he knew." He put his arm around her and drew her against his chest.

"Why did Harry bear that awful burden alone?"

"Because he loved you."

Her tears soaked the front of his work shirt. "Rolf, you must have known all along too. Why did you stay?"

"For the same reason that Harry did—I love you."

He felt the galloping beat in his chest and knew it was not the racy heartbeat of an old man nor the arrhythmic beat of a weak heart. He'd hidden his emotions for so long, and now his heart was in a wild beat at her nearness. They'd labeled his crooked bones arthritic, but not his heart. In that regard he had the strength of an ox. Of ten oxen. His arms tightened around her.

She pushed away and stared at him. "You love me? As cruel as I am to you...I never guessed."

"I never intended for you to know. I couldn't leave feeling the way I do. Besides, I promised Harry and his father that I would take care of you and Adrienne. And if I left, who would tend the memorial garden for your son?"

Again, her eyes brimmed with tears. "You've been so kind to all of us. Oh, Rolf, Harry used to say the truth would make you free so why do I feel so wretched?"

"Because you keep turning your back on the One who would give you peace."

"You know I don't believe the way Harry did."

"You will someday—once you make your confession."

"I can't do that. How could God forgive me for what I did to this family? I must go on hiding the truth from Adrienne...how long did Harry know?"

"Before we ever left Paris, he guessed. We were back here at Winterfest Estates for months before he knew for certain. We talked about it. I told him to turn you in."

She recoiled. "I never meant for him to be sent home in disgrace. I never thought his friends would desert him. And I hated it when he didn't defend himself."

"How could he? Harry couldn't bear for the mother of his children to go on trial for selling out her country."

"That's not what I did."

"What you did would have netted you twenty years or more. Harry couldn't face that—even to save his honor."

Her fist clenched. "I *didn't* steal those documents."

"When you unlocked Harry's vault and turned aside so someone else could steal them, you were guilty."

"I didn't realize—"

"I think you did."

She sent him a ghost of a smile. "I'd had a glass of wine or two. I was angry at Harry that night. It seemed just a dare—and afterward—" She shuddered. "Afterward, I was obligated to protect my side of the family."

"Harry and the children were your family, too, Mara. But you chose a second cousin over them."

"You have to understand. I came from a poor family in rural Spain—I thought I was helping my cousin. He was born in America, but later his family went back to the village. What I did would have ruined it for all of the family back there. My parents—his parents—would have been ostracized. Without resources. Harry was heir to Harrison's fortune. He would never have a financial need."

"But think what your lies did to his career."

"He was so respected at the State Department—I never dreamed that honest Harry would be accused of wrongdoing."

"Of stealing government secrets for financial gain."

"It wasn't like that. When I saw what was happening, I tried to get my cousin to tell the truth. He threatened to harm the children. He reminded me that I had a wealthy father-in-law. He assured me that Harrison Winters could salvage Harry's name and career. I had to believe him."

She was a beguiling woman, but his heart thundered. He had to go on protecting her.

"My cousin promised to have the documents back in Harry's vault before morning."

"And you believed him?"

"I made a mistake, Rolf. That was when Harry was working out of the house—he was recovering from surgery. Remember?"

He put his hands on her shoulders. Was it impossible for her to admit the truth, or had she believed the lies too long? "Listen to yourself, Mara. Instead of making amends, you make excuses for your mistakes."

"At least *Harry* was not a mistake. He was the best thing in my whole life."

"Perhaps I will be the second." He patted her hand. "We'll work it out, Mara. Do you think Robbie read the whole journal?"

"I'm certain he did. When I found him up there his hair was cobwebby. His jacket in a heap on the floor. His smile sheepish. He didn't apologize but handed me the journal and asked me where the missing pages were."

"Missing pages?" *She knows about the missing pages.*

"Harry left the last notation incomplete. He stopped in the middle of a sentence. That wasn't like him. You know Harry never left anything unfinished. Do you think Robbie took those pages, Rolf?"

"He would never take anything without asking. And he didn't say anything about the journal when he came out to the stables to say good-bye. He was upset, but I thought the two of you had quarreled."

"We did. I told him to leave and not come back. Rolf, what did Robbie expect to find in Harry's journal?"

"The truth about Harry's dismissal from Paris."

"Then you don't think he was looking for these?" She held up several snapshots, pictures of Colin and Jon together. "They're nice memories, but why would Harry keep these with his journal? There are none of Adrienne."

He glanced at the side-by-side baby photos of Jon and Colin. Pictures of them as toddlers and little boy pictures of their days abroad. As he saw their faces, he knew why Harry had packed them away together. *For a comparison.* "They looked so much alike as young men."

"Yes, both of them tall and good-looking. Jon's hair was darker than Colin's. And look at this one—both of them sporting sideburns and mustaches."

"They look like brothers."

She stared at him. "Is *that* what Harry told you? I never saw that much resemblance, but Harry did, didn't he?" Her lip trembled. "He thought the worst of me. He thought Bedford and I—"

He waited for the bomb to explode. She remained calm. "Harry thought Jon was Bedford Taylor's son, didn't he? He went to his grave believing that. So that's why their friendship died?"

He nodded. "I think so. But he knew the truth when he died."

Rolf helped her stand and supported her as they made their way down the stairs to her room. She leaned against her pillows, regret in her features. "Harry adored Jon as any father would. If I had known, I could have told Harry the truth. Jon was his son."

Rolf had no reason to doubt her. This was something Mara would have to deal with. She had not mentioned the DNA chip. While she slept, he would make certain that the medical report was still in its hiding place. "Shall I pack the pictures and journal away again, Mara?"

"No, burn them." Her hand slipped from his. "Leave the light on in case Gavin awakens. I'll rest now."

"Do you think you can sleep, Mara?"

A twinkle sparkled in her eyes. "I'll try. But it is not every day one discovers a suitor in her midst."

He felt an unaccustomed heat in his cheeks. "I was out of line, madame, telling you that."

Her smile deepened. "On the contrary, Rolf, I am grateful. Have you listened to yourself? You've been calling me Mara all evening."

He flexed his fingers. Caught hers again. "I've grown tired of calling you madame."

"I'm glad. You will stay on, won't you?"

"But do you need me? That's what's important to my future. Important to both of us."

"I'll need you to help me get this mess unraveled. And Gavin needs you."

"I will be here."

She closed her eyes, then they flickered open again. "I destroyed Harry, didn't I? And you still want me?"

"Harry never held it against you, Mara. He loved you."

"Love is blind, isn't it? This evening Robbie told me he knew what happened in Paris. At first I didn't believe him. He was just a boy then—fourteen. But he wouldn't be searching for the journal without just cause. Can you call him and find out how much he knows?"

Rolf took the blanket from the bottom of her bed and spread it over her legs. "Mara, Robbie is flying to Paris this evening. He's booked out of National at midnight."

"Just like that! Flying off for no reason?"

He scratched his head. "He wants to be in Paris for Adrienne, so he wrangled a ten-day working holiday. He promised his editor the moon—it was that or he'd resign his job with the paper." He leaned down and patted her cheek. "We must trust Robbie where Adrienne is concerned."

"Will anything ever come of it? Between the two of them?"

"Will anything ever come of the two of us?"

At his gentle question, her gaze rested on his face. "You want me, knowing the truth?"

He laid his hand over hers. "We could grow old together. I want to take care of you. Harry would want that."

"Is it the land or me that you want, Rolf?"

Her word landed on tender soil, furrowing to the quick. Anger flashed, but he quenched it. "The land is not yours to give, Mara. We both know that. My position would not change. I would still oversee the care of the property for Miss Adrienne. I love the land, as you know. But I have never owned anything. It's too late to start now."

He met her wide eyes. "What I do want is to marry you."

"I'm no longer young and vibrant, you know. And the side effects of the medicine I'm taking—"

"There's more to marriage than that. Companionship. Kindness. Let me take care of you. Hold you. Love you."

"Oh, Rolf. You are offering me a second chance."

"A second chance for both of us."

The tremor in her hand was uncontrollable. "You won't rest until I give you my final answer. I won't rest until we clear Harry's name. I owe my daughter that much. My son wanted to restore the family honor. Dear boy! How I miss him."

She was silent for a moment. "When my daughter comes home, I will want her forgiveness. Robbie is the one who will have the courage to tell her the truth. Could you reach him at the airport and let him know I want his help?"

"Of course." Rolf started to walk away, then turned back. "I'm keeping something from you."

"It's about Jon, isn't it? I was on my bedroom phone—listening to your last call with Adrienne. I know she thinks she's found Jon in Paris." Her eyes misted, yet her words remained strong. "She's not a foolish girl. She must have good reason to believe she found her brother, not just some look-alike."

She must have seen that her unexpected calm frightened him. She smiled. "Don't look so stricken, Rolf. I never believed my son was dead. But I've always wondered why he never came home again. Perhaps he questioned his own parentage. That would have kept him away from Winterfest."

"We may never know, my dear Mara. Adrienne found him, but she lost touch." He turned the knob on the bedroom door. "It is possible that he is in serious trouble. If Jon needed a place to hide in Paris, where would he go?"

Her answer was spontaneous. "To Claudio and Dominique's— that older couple Jon stayed with when he was at the university."

Rolf considered this. "Would he be safe with them?"

"They were fond of him. They treated him as a son." Mara was silent for a moment, and when she spoke her words were determined. "I must get word to Robbie before he leaves. Tell him where to look."

"Dare we take that risk, Mara?"

She met his gaze, and he was surprised by the understanding he saw there. "There is far greater risk in not telling him."

She was right, of course. Rolf only hoped it wasn't already too late.

After a frustrating delay at the security check-in, Robbie ran the length of the terminal, his ticket and boarding pass in his pocket, his long legs making double time in his race to see his dad. They were flying out within an hour of each other. His dad to Montreal. Robbie to Paris.

Thanks to his dad's air miles, he avoided the cost of a last-minute reservation. He just wanted to say thanks, share a handshake, and wish his dad well. They didn't spend near enough time together. He caught a second breath. Switching his laptop to his other hand, Robbie sprinted toward the Montreal flight, expecting the airport police to waylay him any minute.

He'd have another mad race back to his own departure gate, but any time with his dad was worth it. Gil Gilbert spotted him first, giving him a frantic wave and booming above the commotion, "Over here, Robbie."

His dad wasn't satisfied with a handclasp. He bear-hugged his son.

"Dad, I got the ticket. Thanks heaps. How can I ever thank you enough?"

"You being you is thanks enough for me, Son. You'll be wanting another favor before the month's out. I'm used to it. I'm just glad I had enough frequent flyer miles to send you to Paris."

He grinned as his father studied him. Robbie was struck afresh with his father's good looks. In spite of his thick silver hair and hearing aid and the stubborn set of his square jaw, women still found him attractive. But no one could love and respect his dad more than Robbie did.

"Do you have your Sword with you, son?"

With his hearing level diminishing, his dad's voice boomed louder. "Take it easy, Dad. You'll have the airport police carting us away as suspect."

"Well, do you have the Book?"

"You know I never leave town without it." He thumped his laptop. "But I have it on computer now."

"You still get your direction from God's Word, right?"

"You know I do, Dad. I wish you did."

"Well, I'll worry about that later. Right now, no sermons. I'm doing the talking, and I want to give you a little advice, Son." They were already boarding the first-class passengers. "You know I'm fond of Adrienne. I'd like her for a daughter-in-law, but I don't think it's going to happen."

Robbie felt the old warning coming. "I know, Dad. It reminds you of your courting days with Mother."

"I pursued your mother until she married me. And you know what happened to our marriage. She was a good woman, Robbie, but we couldn't make a go of it, not when we both wanted a career. Adrienne is ambitious, like your mother. I can't fault her for that."

He clapped Robbie on the shoulder as the last boarding call was announced. "I don't think Adrienne is ready—or will be ready for marriage and children. Not for a very long time."

"Dad, that was your last boarding call."

"I hear you, Son. But are you hearing me? I want you to be happy. Not to go running clear across the world chasing a dream." Robbie urged him toward the boarding ramp. "Promise me, Robb, that you'll make certain your priorities are where they belong when you see her."

Robbie lifted his laptop. "I promise, Dad. I'll check it out the minute I board my flight." There was another bear hug, and his dad disappeared down the boarding ramp.

Robbie made his own international flight with eleven minutes to spare. Once aboard, he reached out three times to place a call to Paris. Three times he felt his father's restraint. His Father's restraint.

Sighing, he turned on his laptop and scrolled through to the Bible file. He made random choices. A flip through Psalms. Then the Gospels. Then Jonah. Then back to the sixth chapter of Matthew where he knew he should land. Three words glared up at him: *Seek ye first.*

But I love her, Lord.

He felt the pinprick of a man on a Damascus Road. The burning inside. He felt the urgency to prioritize, to put first things first. He refused dinner on the first invitation. *But I love Adrienne, Lord.*

But do you love Me?

The question was as clear as though it had roared above the clatter of food trays. He knew the answer. He was negotiating with a king—*the* King of his life. And there on the flight to Paris, he surrendered his stubborn will. He let go of the arguments that favored marriage. He loved Adrienne enough to let her go. Once again he made Christ his first priority.

He was wide-eyed with exhaustion as his plane neared Paris, but he was at peace—the kind that passed human understanding. He dashed off an e-mail to his dad: *Dad: Thanks for the good advice. Fought it. Followed it. Weather good during flight. Storms ahead when I meet with Adrienne. She won't believe her life's at risk. Robb.*

CHAPTER 18

Adrienne sat alone on the stone bench in the Tuileries Gardens, soaking up the Parisian sun as she waited for Ricardo Mendez to keep his appointment. Mendez had chosen this meeting spot between the Concorde Square and the magnificent Musée du Louvre, but would he come? Did she care?

As she waited, she savored the beauty that surrounded her. The splashes of green lawn. The vibrant flower beds. The graceful swans skimming the pond. The clippety-clop of a donkey-drawn cart caught her attention, reminding her of her happy, pampered childhood. She smiled and was still smiling when she spotted Ricardo coming toward her with his decided swagger.

"I'm sorry, I'm late." He pointed to the empty space beside her. "May I?"

"*S'il vous plaît.*"

He gathered his thoughts in silence, sitting sideways on the stone bench, his lanky legs stretched out and crossed at the ankles. He kept his hands on his knees, his bold brown eyes on her face.

"Miss Winters, so far we haven't—"

She interrupted. "I've seen Jacques d'Hiver again. I wasn't certain you would find him for me."

A crack appeared in his smooth demeanor. He moistened his lip. "I'm sorry I let you down."

"You don't believe I saw my brother."

"Here in Paris? No, not your brother Jon. I used an embassy computer—a secure line back to Washington. You were notified of your brother's death twelve years ago. Your family set up a memorial garden for him at Winterfest Estates. There were attempts to pay the death benefits, but your parents never signed for them."

Scarlet lines streaked his neck. "Your family attended a private ceremony at Langley where your dad was presented with an Intelligence Star—posthumously in your brother's memory. Should I say anything more, Miss Winters?"

She heard the defiance in his voice, felt her own anger mounting. "You are well rehearsed, Mr. Mendez."

"You have to understand our position."

"Your lies."

He ignored her. "When you came to the embassy, we weren't sure what kind of game you were playing. So let's be honest with each other."

"I *was* honest with you, Mr. Mendez. I saw my brother here in Paris. Where else was I to turn? The police? There was no crime involved. We're both Americans, so I came to you. Isn't that what a concerned U.S. citizen should do?"

"You came to us about a dead brother."

"Yes, we were notified of Jon's death, Mr. Mendez, in the privacy of our own home. But Mother never believed Jon was dead. Not when they couldn't find his body. She still maintains he was forced to slip into oblivion for his country's sake."

"Are you accusing your own country of—"

"Of lying to us?" She met his glare with one of her own. "Yes. I think I am. At first we were told Jon was a casualty of friendly fire. But how could he be? General Schwarzkopf was still building up his fighting team, preparing for the air sorties and ground battles. They called Jon's death an accident from an explosion. Before they admitted he had been lost the day the Iraqis invaded Kuwait."

"And now, here in a city of millions, you want us to believe you found your brother?"

"I did it with the help of a girl named Naji."

"Naji?" He wiped his palms on his trouser legs. "We met in her office at the embassy."

She'd thought Naji was from Angelo's Art Studio, but she decided to keep that information to herself. Or had she already, by some slip of tongue, divulged that aspect of Jon's life? She collected her thoughts. "She's from the embassy? I think she said her name was Naji Fleming."

"Fleming is her professional name."

"And both of you thought I was a fly-by-night American coming to you with a whopper of a tale?"

"Our records showed your brother was dead. We didn't know what you were up to. At the last minute, Naji insisted that I use her office."

"Why? So you could record everything we said?"

Again a streak of scarlet ran the length of his neck. "I'm certain Naji wouldn't do that."

"But if someone ordered her to record our meeting?"

His expression registered a sense of betrayal from someone he trusted. "I'm sorry, Miss Winters."

"You're sorry? What is going on, Mr. Mendez?"

His eyes warmed as she flung a lock of hair behind her ear. "Jon told me you were stunning even when you were angry. He didn't exaggerate."

"Then you know him."

"Yes, we were friends once."

"We were *family* once. Kuwait took that from us. I know you are just doing your job, but what happened to your friendship?"

"I'm still his friend—he just doesn't believe it. We worked together on Special Ops missions a long time ago."

You just gave yourself away. He's still your friend? "A diplomatic attaché *and* a CIA agent? Oh, it's all right, Rick. My family has been in government service all my life. I won't blow your cover. All I want to know is why my brother won't admit who he is. Why won't he go home? My family owns land in Virginia. It was left to Jon and me."

"He used to talk about Winterfest Estates."

"When my father died—"

"Jon's father is dead?" Again a frown furrowed Rick's brow. "We were never informed."

"Why would you be? In your books, Jon was dead. There was no longer a need to keep surveillance on his family."

He glanced over his shoulder, his gaze lingering on the park benches yards away. Two of them were occupied.

Adrienne understood. "Is someone watching us?"

"There'd be no reason."

"Yet Naji found me. She's the one who told me to go back to the café and wait for Jon." Her knit brows squeezed into a headache. "Now I find she works for the embassy."

For a moment she felt sorry for him. She didn't trust him, yet his eyes seemed pained, uncertain. His slick dark hair touched the back of his collar. His suit jacket looked a fraction short for his long arms. The veins in his neck pulsated as he processed what she had said.

"Why would the two of you work against each other?"

"Naji and me? A lack of communication..."

She rubbed her hands together. "Or someone above both of you gave the orders. You will check on that, won't you?"

"I owe it to both of us."

"And you will check on Naji Fleming?"

His jaw tensed. "Rest assured of that."

"I understand about government employees and the old guard from Langley. They're loyal. But for twelve years Langley wanted us to believe that Jon had lost his life."

"You have to understand—"

"I'm trying, but you didn't endure the heartache of losing a brother. Or being told that he was gone. Why can't the Agency be loyal to the families who sacrifice their loved ones?"

"We shield you from the truth to protect you."

"You lie to us."

"Not on purpose. But on any covert operation, others are involved. We have to protect them."

"Nine and twelve years later?"

"Sometimes *thirty* years later. It's the one way we can maintain national security."

She shook her head sending strands of hair across her cheek. "Jon used to say that people live in the shadows and die in the shadows. But he never considered himself at risk. He thought of himself as a survivor."

"I'm sure your brother expected to make it."

"The death benefits you mentioned—the ones that my dad refused to accept—that wasn't all. Jon had no family of his own, so months after the report of his death, checks started coming to a local bank account for my education. Dad put a stop to that too. We didn't need the money. Besides, my dear dad was government through and through. He never asked why Jon had been sent to Kuwait. Never questioned how he died. He cautioned the rest of us to accept whatever the government told us."

"And you never questioned them?"

"I never could. I told you, it was weeks before we knew that Jon had been lost in the actual invasion of Kuwait. And more than three weeks after his death before the Agency sent two of its own to our home to break the news to us. One of them was a friend of my parents—a man who had known about Jon from day one. The other man was high up in the Agency. Sheridan somebody."

Something flickered in Rick's eyes. "Sheridan Macaroy."

"I think that was his name. But we live on the Virginia side of the Potomac, in close proximity to the federal bureaucracy. Why did it take so long to tell us?"

"Perhaps they didn't get word—"

"You know better than that. I think they needed time to come up with a cover story. I'm surprised they didn't tell us he died in a street accident in Paris or fell through a manhole into the underground sewer system. But then, they would have had to come up with a body. Instead they said Jon died in an explosion near Kuwait City."

She thrust back another breeze-blown lock of hair from her face. "Because of the secrecy—because of what I always thought of as *deception*—I could never put meaning to Jon's sacrifice. In the end, it destroyed my father."

"So the invasion of Kuwait was the start of it all?"

"Saddam Hussein's greed for oil and power started it."

His words remained guarded. "Are you aware that Iraq's crossing the border into Kuwait happened overnight? Tanks. Crack troops. Kuwait City was surrounded within hours. Your brother was probably caught in that crossfire."

She brushed the facts away with a sweep of her hand. In the sudden movement, the sun reflected off her diamond watch. "I've come to resent the fact that Jon was nothing more than a number and code name. After all these years, he's still a nameless star in the CIA's Book of Honor."

Tears surfaced. "But you know all about that. You're one of them. They honor my brother, but those memorials don't depict the man he was. Tell your people that as a child my father taught me not to ask questions. To accept secrecy and silence where the government was concerned—all for the safety of the men and women risking their lives in strategic areas in the world. Giving their lives. But I'm sick of pretending my brother died in an accident while serving his country."

Her gaze strayed back to the park benches and the occupants there. "I think Jon became a scapegoat for our country. Back home, he was always the favored child."

"And you felt left out?"

"Wouldn't you? I was jealous. I'm still angry, and Jon is still the favored one. Do you understand what I'm talking about? Do you have a family of your own, Rick?"

"My family is back in the Bronx. It's just my wife and me here in Paris, trying to patch up our differences."

"Is that what you want? A patch quilt?"

"I haven't known what I wanted for a long time. God. Family. Paris. My job. They all feel like burdens on my back." Sudden red crept into his cheeks. "I guess I shouldn't call God a burden, but I'm as confused about His place in my life as I am about my marriage…I'd like to save my marriage."

"Maybe you should go home to the Bronx. Start over from there and find your peace and yourself and your God."

A grin crept across his face. It made his ordinary face look handsome. "Can't God be found in Paris?"

She felt the scarlet flush on her own cheeks now. "Of course, but wouldn't it be best to go back to the place where you lost your peace? I wish my brother would return home while he can still find the way back. The Jon I met in the café is anything but the happy Jon who skied mountains and hiked through the sun-scorched hills of the Middle East. We thought he traveled as an innocent tourist with a knapsack on his back. But with his features, perhaps he blended in with the people, gathering intelligence data."

"You have a vivid imagination."

"I have had a long time to think about it. I want Jon to go home again. Half of the Winters's property is his, now that I'm convinced he's alive."

His smile faded. "Would you understand if I told you your brother can't go home? According to all the official records, your brother is dead. For the safety of those who worked with him, it must remain that way."

"That's the rules of the game? Jon told us not to worry if we didn't hear from him. He was convinced that the Company rescued their own. It didn't work out that way for Jon, did it?"

"I'm sorry, Adrienne."

"That's the one thing my family longed to hear all these years— that the Agency was sorry. I don't think they know the meaning of the word. There's no apology when a man is expendable. If I never see him again, at least I should be grateful—proud even—that there's a star embedded in the marble wall in Jon's memory. Oh, they honor my brother on a marble wall in that cavernous lobby of theirs, but have they forgotten that he was once flesh and blood?"

Struggling to her feet, she adjusted her silk neck scarf. He stood beside her. "That buttercup yellow makes you look vibrant like springtime."

"But inside, I feel dark and cloudy like winter."

He leaned forward. She felt his warm breath whispering across her cheek. "I'm sorry how things turned out, but when your fashion show ends, go home. Forget all of this."

She pulled back. "Forget my brother? Maybe *you* can forget an old friend, Mr. Mendez, but I cannot forget my brother. When the fashion show ends, I'm staying on for a few days of holiday." She smiled at his expression. "Don't look so alarmed. I won't bother the embassy again."

"Not even to let me know if you see Jon again?"

"Least of all if I find Jon. I'll warn him he would be safer if he left Paris."

"Please. Go home. I promise that if I am ever free to tell you anything, I'll contact you at Winterfest Estates."

"Or some other agents from Langley will come knocking at my door to tell me that Jon is dead, this time for real."

"You don't trust us?"

"How can I? My brother is alive—and my government—the country that I have loved all my life—has allowed my family to go on believing that Jon died in Kuwait! Trust you? No."

She shook her head. "When you report to your superiors, tell them I'm glad Jon doesn't know that Father is dead. That he doesn't have to see Mother in a wheelchair. But I wish he knew how much we love him. How much we miss him."

She turned and walked away, not expecting a reply any more than she'd expected help. But with each step, she grew more determined than ever.

Jon Aaron was alive. And she would find a way to take him home.

CHAPTER 19

While his family napped, Jacques d'Hiver slipped behind the Fleming tapestry that hung on the living room wall and into his secure communications center. This was the one room off limits to Brigette and the children. The system offered him worldwide transmission and reception and state-of-the-art electronic equipment. The interior renovation and the entire system were provided for and maintained by the Company. Because they needed his skills? Or his silence?

He often spent long hours in this room, late into the night and the wee hours of the morning to keep the neighborhood complaints of poor television reception to a minimal. To date, neither his neighbors nor the distraught custodian had tracked the interference to Jacques's condo.

He stared down at the latest message intercepted at the café. The Arabic symbols and configurations, foreign to so many, formed words for him. Compared with the other messages that Aleem had passed to him, it became clear that the café was a front for more than fabulous French cuisine.

But Jacques needed another intercept from Kuwait, Yemen, or Afghanistan to tie it all together. Every day he kept Aleem at the café risked the waiter's safety. Warn him—give him the opportunity to choose—and an already nervous Aleem would flee. So far, the American embassy had little interest in protecting the Yemeni immigrant.

Without more proof that the café was a hotbed for terrorism, Ricardo Mendez would brush off Jacques's findings, saying, "The threat to peace invades every country."

The friendship he and Ricardo shared a decade ago had long been forgotten. Didn't Ricardo understand? The proud Parisians, like so many others, were now immune to the threats of terrorism, defiant of those who would destroy their way of life.

Jacques massaged his forehead to relieve the pressure. If he dared ask any of them, the Parisians would shrug. After all, the Eiffel Tower still stood. The Arc de Triomphe immortalized past military triumphs. Notre Dame drew the faithful. Their elegant city set the fashion trends. The Seine went on flowing. The aged men in their black berets continued to spend their leisure moments playing boules under the trees or a game of chess on park benches. Unhurried. Unworried. The Parisians' uniqueness and diversity remained complex, harmonious. The al-Qaeda in other countries would not stop their love of life.

How could he convince them a threat was near? Was it worth remaining on the payroll of a country that still rejected him and doubted his intelligence data? How long did he have to grovel before someone in authority awakened to the problems at the café? Jacques's gut told him Cavell had been undercover at the café for years, heading up a terrorist network. Waiting. It was amazing, really—the patience of a revolutionary, of a terrorist cell awaiting orders.

Jacques reworked the translation, checking the words that had confused him with their double meanings. Arabic script had such expressive beauty, like the ancient Himyaritic writings engraved on stone. From an artistic view, the calligraphy was magnificent. Aleem spoke of it as the sacred language of the Koran, and with growing misgivings passed the messages on to Jacques.

Yes, the café was involved...but where would they strike? American targets perhaps, the embassy for one. Like they struck without warning in Kenya and Yemen—they could strike the symbols of Parisian life, taking out monuments that every Parisian held dear.

Jacques's finger froze on a list of names, aides, lieutenants, and training camp commanders with al-Qaeda. One name leaped from the pages: Hamad. Location: Kuwait.

Hamad, his friend! He would be forced to go back to Kuwait and rescue him. Or take him down, if necessary. In their university days, Jacques counted Hamad and other Arabs among close acquaintances. Now, apart from Angelo at the art studio, Jacques allowed himself few friends. The isolation had been difficult for Brigette. They still did not know their neighbors on the same landing. Yet his father—living in this same building twenty years ago—took time for the custodian and gardener; he had called the fisherman on the quays of the Seine by name and counted them as friends. Even his mother thrived on the recognition rendered her by the maître d' in her favorite restaurants and the social elite of Paris.

Jacques never mentioned Hamad to Brigette and never spoke of their studying together at Sorbonne before the Gulf War. He reflected on those days now. They'd spent hours reading about the French revolutions. Arguing about Napoleon. At Hamad's urgings, he'd read parts of the Koran for the sheer pleasure of debating its philosophy. Hamad's subtle approach had drawn him into the Arab conflicts. There had been pleasurable times, too, on the ski slopes, eating with the Vernettis and reading through Victor Hugo's *Les Miserables* in French. From time to time he and Hamad visited the Arab World Institute on the Left Bank of the River Seine, with its incomparable view of the Notre Dame Cathedral and all of Paris.

"Paris should belong to us," Hamad had told him.

What had Hamad meant? The Arab's mind was like the lattice-work controlling the lighting at the institute—one could see out, but no one could see in. The institute was a cultural gold mine, with its ceramics and sculpture, its collection of carpets on the fourth floor. But Arab nationalism and the good that the institute fostered could be damaged by a cell of radicals acting under the guise of the Islamic faith.

In Jacques's quest for knowledge on the Middle East, he'd neglected his once-fervent pursuit of godliness. Now, when he needed divine guidance, he wasn't certain how to find his way back—or whether the man called Jacques d'Hiver would ever know peace.

He looked up from the translation work on his desk and started.

The indicator line on his phone was blinking. His secure embassy line was set to flash, never to ring, to avoid disturbing his family. He reached for it. "Bonjour."

A monotone voice responded. "Urgent appointment with old friends. Musée des Egouts. Entrance Pont de l'Alma. Four this afternoon."

He glanced at his watch. *Old friends? Ricardo? Macaroy?* It had to be someone connected with the embassy. He grabbed his cane and locked the workroom behind him.

The Impostor glared at Ricardo. He'd been waiting long enough. "Will he come?"

Ricardo's expression was unreadable. "He never fails to appear."

"Then you meet with him often?"

"We use a courier. Naji frowns on direct contact."

"So the embassy works him like a puppet."

"We exchange information—quite often at the bridge near his home and sometimes through Angelo's Art Studio."

The Impostor lifted one brow. "Angelo's Art Studio? So Jon is still trying his hand at sculpting."

"He's good at it."

"Good?" He let himself smile. "He never settled for less than outstanding...for achieving better than the rest of us."

"That's your evaluation. I admire Jon's skills."

"You keep him on the payroll. I would say you are funding his artistic nature."

Ricardo's gaze hardened. *Clearly he doesn't care for my tone of voice.* The Impostor smiled again. *Too bad.*

"We owe him." Ricardo's tone was as hard as his eyes. "Whatever happened in Kuwait, I trust him. It's my colleagues who won't heed his warnings."

"Warnings?" The Impostor let his word sharpen.

"He insists a terrorist cell exists here in Paris."

"They're worldwide."

Mendez shifted in his chair. "He's narrowed it down to the Champs Élysées. We have the Café le Grand Royale under observation and an informant working there as a waiter. For your report to Washington, the waiter's name is Aleem, a young Yemeni. There's little else we can do without more proof."

"I'm puzzled, Rick. Once Jon was found alive, why wasn't he shipped home for trial, for discipline, at best? Instead the Company kept him on the payroll. The man failed to do his duty in Kuwait."

"We have no proof of that. And I don't believe Jon was ever a coward."

"That will be for Washington to decide."

"If he lives to get there." Ricardo paused for a moment. "This meeting with the three of us should be held here in the embassy, neutral ground for both of you, not some clandestine meeting in the belly of the earth."

The Impostor gave a high-pitched laugh. "Have you forgotten the unforgettable Jean Valjean?"

"The story of Jean Valjean is pure fiction."

As is Jacques d'Hiver. "But Jon liked Victor Hugo's brooding works, so the sewers are an appropriate place for us to meet again."

"We were all friends once, Colonel. What happened?"

He leaned back in his chair. What would Ricardo say if he told him the truth? "I find traitors abhorrent."

"Then concentrate on tracking the Washington mole."

"I'm in on a number of the discussions regarding him."

"It's catching him that counts. Come on. We'll be late if we don't get a move on."

The Impostor rose, hesitated. "Ricardo, there is no need for you to go. He's more apt to confide in me if it's just the two of us. Maybe there is some reason—some explanation. Then I'll send a report back to Washington."

"No, we'll go it together. Jon maintains that he was betrayed by a friend. I'm not certain how happy he will be to see you again, Colonel."

He smiled and rose from his chair. *Not happy at all, dear Ricardo. Not happy at all.*

There was a bend in the river not far from the Pont de l'Alma Bridge. Within walking distance, the Eiffel Tower dominated the blue Parisian skyline. Jacques crossed the bridge by taxi. He stood looking toward the line queuing for tickets to the Musée des Egouts. When he recognized Ricardo Mendez, he started forward, then halted.

The man in uniform standing beside Rick was the man he'd been hunting for almost twelve years. The very man who had once joked, "Before we face the stench of war in Kuwait, let's do the sewers of Paris."

Now the three of them were about to step back into the Parisian underground, into the obscurity and black labyrinth, the stagnation and dungeon of Victor Hugo's masterpiece. For the first time since entering Kuwait on a secret mission, the three of them would face off again.

Jacques remembered the mission as though it were yesterday, recalled the need to enter the country under assumed names. Sheridan Macaroy's insistence on utter secrecy. Macaroy's last warning that there'd be no outside help if captured. A three-man team. Their leader—twenty-four then—put aside his military career on a temporary basis. Ricardo so sly and quick, daring in his youth—so unsettled now.

And Jon Aaron Winters limping forward to join them.

If he were still a threat to these men waiting for him, why had he been left to walk the streets of Paris without a bullet cutting him down or some traffic accident taking him out as he crossed the boulevard? He was steps from them when the words of Victor Hugo came back: "It was in the sewer of Paris that Jean Valjean found himself." It could well be in the sewers that Jon would lose his life.

Watch it, Jon. You're wearing your bitterness. Your fury. Wait and see how they play the game. Be guarded, but hear them out.

He was close enough now to see that his betrayer wore the insignia of a full colonel. He reached them, ignoring the colonel's outstretched hand. "So we face-off again."

"Not much of a greeting for an old friend, Jon."

He didn't even look at the man. "Let's get on with our meeting. Are we to talk out here or to go inside?"

Ricardo held up three tickets.

The scorn in the colonel's voice mocked Jon. "I chose this place for a reunion because you were once a great fan of Victor Hugo's work."

"I still am."

"In a way, Jon, you remind me of his character in *Les Miserables*, Valjean, escaping through the slime and filth of the sewers. You've been on the run for a long time. How did you manage it?"

"There was no Inspector Javert on my trail."

Something flashed in the depths of the colonel's eyes. "There should have been."

"Ricardo knew where I was. I'm certain Sheridan Macaroy has known all along as well."

He saw a flicker of surprise on the colonel's face, but the scorn remained. "Correct me if I'm wrong, but I believe Jean Valjean spoke of the tunnels as the intestines of Paris. As an abyss. Is that how you see them, Jon?"

He met the man's gaze head-on. "Being left behind on the sand dunes of Kuwait by a friend was worse than an abyss."

False sympathy painted the colonel's features. "Yes, quite a tragedy. If we had known—"

Jon gritted his teeth. "After you."

The fetid odor hit him as he maneuvered down a stone staircase. They went single file through the heavy steel door and with a turn at the corner were in the sewers. The subterranean chambers they wound through were a far cry from the fashion world above them. Security warnings were everywhere: *Don't run. Don't bend over the railings. Avoid all contact with the waste water, walls, and pipes. Wash your hands when you exit.*

He would comply with the hand washing—if he made it out.

"Jon, when I return to Washington, I must make a report that you are still alive and living here in Paris."

He didn't take the bait. "I would think Ricardo had already done that."

"We need to know why you remained behind in Kuwait."

Anger flowed through Jon's veins at the man's pretense. "I was betrayed."

The colonel's brow lifted. "By Hamad?"

No, by you, Colonel. "Strange that you should ask." Jon squinted at the man in the darkness. It was so long ago. He'd been confused...could he have imagined the colonel—a young lieutenant then—standing over him, leaving him to die? "No, it was not Hamad."

If they had something planned for him, it would happen in the next ten minutes. As other tourists wandered through the tunnels with them, he felt the riveting gaze of a tall somber stranger beside him. The tourist's turtleneck sweater was black, the collar of his jacket taut against his neck. No words were exchanged between them, but Jon felt comforted by the man's presence.

As they made their way along a waist-high metal fence, the stranger stayed close behind them. Here the cavernous tunnels looked like the arms of an octopus with a gushing river of rainwater and human waste surging through them, speeding toward the sewage treatment plant.

"Just think, people work here."

Jon glanced toward one of the blue-suited sewer workers. "Yes, Ricardo, but Parisians are proud of this engineering wonder. It may not appeal to our senses, gentlemen, but it is a definite network of ingenuity."

A cluster of pipes hung above them, some of them a maze of drinking water mains. The city's freshwater supply was routed in this abyss through the blue pipes that hung from the ceiling. Gurgling stone tubes swallowed the waste. They had passed the five-ton flushing boat used in cleaning the sewers, the *bateau-vanne*, which resembled a medieval monster. But it worked.

Turning into the Bruneseau Gallery, they encountered a rancid odor. They paused on the footbridge before climbing the stairs into another main sewer. Here the fast-flowing wastewater gave off a muddy green, floodwater appearance.

The colonel nudged him. "Why didn't you leave Kuwait when you were ordered to do so?"

"I never received that order."

"I gave it."

You're lying. "I was told to make two or three more surveys. That's what I did. But I think you blocked my reports from going out in the embassy pouch."

Ricardo frowned. "According to the records, Jon, you failed to send in any reports."

Failed to… Jon bristled. *What happened to those reports, Colonel?* Detailed maps. Locations of the Iraqi buildup. Estimation of Iraqi troops and equipment. Information on the growing strength of the resistance movement. The discovery of a terrorist cell right in the heart of Kuwait City, complete with names and photographs. He'd sent his reports to the embassy each night by way of a courier.

By way of Hamad.

Jon's stomach churned at the odors surrounding them. His heart missed a beat at the memories and the lies. He rested his hand on the railing. "Colonel, you must have seen my reports."

"Nothing."

Ricardo spoke above the gurgling roar of the swirling water. "Jon, the colonel's record is above reproach. You were always the revolutionary."

The foul smell of the underground tunnels and the colonel's putrid lies left Jon gulping for fresh air. Twenty minutes in this abyss was long enough. As he maneuvered the last set of stairs, he saw the lighted exhibits ahead. The gift shop and the museum were yards away. The exit and fresh air just beyond that.

He passed a warning sign nailed to the wall: DANGER. The tunnel walls were coated with rust and grime. In front of him lay another blackened pit of slime and rushing water. Grating, grinding machinery slashed at the muck and mire. The odor was intolerable. Suffocating.

As Jon inched along the railing, he felt a violent thrust against his back.

He tumbled forward.

The boot of his prosthesis caught on the uneven path.

The cane clattered to the floor. His arms flailed.

Tottering. Staggering. Slipping toward the filth encrusted scum, his upper torso dangling over the rail—until a powerful hand broke his plunge.

"Go—" It was the stranger in the black turtleneck handing him his cane. "The exit is just ahead."

"What happened to him?" The colonel's voice came from behind Jon.

Ricardo reached out. Pulled his hand back. "Why were you bending over the railing, Jon? You saw the security warnings."

"Go," the stranger repeated to Jon as he stepped in front of the colonel. "Let's talk about what happened, monsieur."

Without a backward glance, Jon limped up the stairs and into the clear air of the city. No Inspector Javert pursued him. He gulped the fresh air, the stench left behind. His assailant left behind. He didn't know who had pushed him, but he knew the shove had been intentional.

One of the men he served with wanted nothing more than to end Jon Winters's life forever.

Back on the streets of Paris, he got his bearings by the Eiffel Tower and merged with the crowd. He did not have Jean Valjean's nerves of steel, but he must disappear again. Whatever Ricardo knew, the colonel knew as well. They would join forces for self-preservation.

He had to avoid the condo and Angelo's studio. He had to arrange an immediate flight to Kuwait, but there was no time to warn Aleem. For now, Jon's own safety took priority. So much intelligence data was stored in his head. He had to stay alive long enough to prove that he had been betrayed on the day that the Iraqis invaded Kuwait.

At the first phone, he called Brigette. No answer. His watch reminded him she would be out with the children, walking along the Seine or spending an hour in the nearby park. Did he dare return home and risk their safety?

Confusion assailed him. Was he fleeing as Jon or Jacques? As a Frenchman or an American, a man betrayed? He rented a car and drove without purpose as he sorted out his true identity and his next move. Hour after hour. He must protect his family. He needed someone to help him.

For a moment, the thought of his father's God pressed in his mind. But his father's God was distant, kept there by years of bitterness and anger.

Not even God could help him now.

He kept driving, moving toward the coast, heading toward Normandy.

Ricardo didn't ask questions.

As the stranger confronted the colonel, he fled the sewers, not in the direction Jon had taken, but toward the entry. He raced against the foot traffic like a salmon going upstream, shoving against tourists, pushing his way to safety. He barreled past the cluster of pipes and struggled up from the depths of despair into which he had entered.

He knew from the stranger's angry words that Jon hadn't stumbled. Someone pushed him. The one man in close proximity was the colonel. And with that realization, the whole miserable twelve years fell into place. Jon told the truth. He'd been left behind, betrayed by a friend.

The colonel wanted Jon dead. He would try again.

When Ricardo reached Naji's apartment, he put his thumb to her buzzer and refused to let up until she answered.

"Yes." He heard impatience in her voice. "Who is it?"

"It's Rick. I have to see you."

"Oh, can't it wait? I've just run my bath."

With perfumed bubbles and all. "I'm in trouble, Naji."

"I could see you at the embassy in the morning."

"Please, Naji. The police may be involved."

She released the lock. He pushed in and ran up the steps to her third-floor apartment. She cracked the door, and he slipped in. Naji was in her toweling robe, her shower cap in her hand, the fragrance of bath oil about her. He was about to compliment her when she said, "You smell like the sewer."

"A stinking mess. And with good reason."

"I've run the bathwater. Maybe you should jump in."

"I don't have a change of clothes."

"Something tells me this will be a long session. I keep the coffee perking. I'll get you a cup."

He followed her into the tiny kitchen. The whole apartment was compact, smaller than his own place. He was shocked to discover she made do with little more than bachelor accommodations.

"I didn't realize how small your place was."

"It cuts down on scrubbing and cleaning. Besides, I thought it was only temporary."

"Your choice. I never asked you to leave." He grabbed the cup of coffee and leaned against the kitchen sink. "I'd better drink this here. I don't want to ruin your good sofa."

She stood facing him. "So what happened, Rick?"

He poured out the story in fragments. How the three of them had descended into the sewers before Kuwait. How the colonel thought a reunion there would be humorous. How Jon and the colonel were at odds as they faced each other. He mentioned the stranger who attached himself to them—walking when they walked. Pausing as they entered each galley.

"Like some guardian angel?"

"I guess." He took another sip of coffee and told her about the pipes and the flushing machines and how Jon had stumbled toward the muck and mire. He rocked on his heels as he ended his story. "Naji, it wasn't an accident."

"A deliberate shove? Was the stranger a policeman?"

"I don't think so, but he looks like that priest who works for the embassy from time to time. If he involves the police, they'll look for me. I swear I did not push Jon. But it will be my word against the colonel's."

"It's been that way for twelve years, hasn't it?" She opened the refrigerator and pulled out a cold plate of pizza and a bowl of grapes. "Heat the pizza if you want."

"It's good cold." He met her gaze. "I arranged for the colonel to meet Jon at the underground museum. I set Jon up. In the back of this brainless head of mine, I considered it a golden opportunity to prove that Jon was a coward. That would let me off the hook—free me from this miserable guilt."

"So it's all falling in place for you, Rick?"

He nodded. "The colonel rose in the ranks—he's well positioned. I just couldn't conceive he'd betrayed Jon."

Was that sympathy in Naji's eyes? Pity? She tossed her shower cap on the kitchen counter and popped a grape. "You'd better sit down, Rick. I have something to tell you." They faced each other, nibbling pizza. "The colonel has been under surveillance for weeks."

"Because of Jon?"

"It's far more involved than that—"

Understanding was as immediate as it was inconceivable. "You're not telling me he's the Washington mole? That's ridiculous, Naji."

"Is it? You just said Colonel Taylor tried to shove Winters into muck and mire in the tunnel. Why would he do that?"

She folded her arms in front of her, warding off any argument from him. "He's been on the short list for a number of weeks now. They couldn't bring themselves to consider him, not after his wife was killed on 9/11. But when the initial shock of that blew over, they began to reconsider. He's been in the right place more than once. Had access to missing documents. When they knew he was flying to Paris, they took me into their confidence."

"Is he spending money at random?"

"No, he has a luxury apartment, but little else to cause eyebrows to pucker. It came about because his son said something to his teacher in the after-school program. He said, 'My daddy's a spy. He talks about Rommel and has a gun collection.' But the tip-off came when the child said his father kept money in a Swiss bank account. They've monitored Taylor's every move since then."

"An innocent kid."

"I'd rather it be the innocent child, Rick."

"Why, Naji?"

"There were two names at the top of that short list."

"Two? You mean Jon?"

"No, I mean *you*."

A piece of crust fell from his hand. "You thought *I* was a traitor because I served with Colin Taylor?" He buried his head in his hands. "What a fool I've been. I'm losing you. My work has grown sloppy. I doubted Jon, and all the time you were building a case against me. No wonder our marriage fell apart."

"No matter what happens, Rick, I'll stand with you."

"That could cost you your job as station chief."

"Better the job than you." She touched his cheek as he stood to leave. He longed to stay, to spend the night with her. She pushed him out the door, but even then her hand was gentle. "I'll see you at the embassy in the morning, Rick. You must trust me. Together we can trap Colonel Taylor."

CHAPTER 20

Jon recognized the small Catholic church nestled among the trees, with its cross on top and its whitewashed stone walls. The paint on the weather-beaten south side of St. Maria's was chipped near the rafters. It was so unlike the magnificent cathedrals that stood across France—and so isolated that it went unnoticed from the rural road. If he had two good legs, he'd offer to apply a fresh coat of paint—not because he was a faithful parishioner, but because this was where Brigette had grown up. Been baptized and confirmed. It was her refuge when she sought to confess her guilt and seek spiritual counsel.

On such days she returned to their condo withdrawn, unhappy. More often than not, they quarreled. Yesterday Brigette left the children in the care of a friend and made the journey alone. Last night their tempers flared. Exploded.

He took the same route today in the rented car, oblivious to the traffic behind him. As he neared the beaches of Normandy, he felt the cool breeze whipping through the window. Until the jolt of fresh air, he had not known why he had come this way, refusing to admit to himself that he needed the advice of Brigette's priest. He turned the Citroen south from St. Lo, drove into the country village where Brigette was born, and went past the farmland that had once belonged to her grandparents. Apart from the village, this area of France and Normandy was just part of history to her, but her parents and grandparents remembered the Normandy invasion.

As in Paris, there was an increased migration of Jewish residents on one side of the village and a growing contingency of Muslims on the border of the next town. Jon could see a mosque in the distance. Neither group of people cared about the village parish. Perhaps this was the reason St. Maria's was no longer the center of activity it had once been.

With a grip on the iron handrail and the use of his cane, he went up the twelve steps and through the heavy, double doors into the vestibule. Silence. Emptiness. He recoiled at the musty smell of time. The odor of old wood in an airless room. He paused by the granite bowl. *Holy water. Brigette would stop here in reverence.*

He made his way down the center aisle and took a front pew. Bracing his cane between his knees, he rested the foot of his game leg on the kneeling pad.

He fingered the missal on the pew rack, but didn't bother to read it. Instead, his gaze took in the stations of the cross that occupied small alcoves on either side of the sanctuary. High above the front altar, sunlight diffused the colors in the stained-glass window. To his right were flickering candles. Had Brigette lit one of those candles—a prayer of thanksgiving for the children, a desperate cry for the sanctity of marriage for herself. No, that candle would long have ceased to flicker.

"May I help you, my son?"

His head shot sideways. He had not heard anyone approach. The stranger who met his gaze was in the garb of a priest—a priest with a wholesome face and eyes as sharp as crystal. He looked to be not much older than Jon himself.

Their eyes locked, an uncertain recognition striking them both. "I didn't hear you come in," Jon said.

"Then you're losing your touch."

Could this be the priest who counseled Brigette? A sense of betrayal slapped him. Hadn't Brigette implied that Father Rafael was an older man? He would have to be since he'd celebrated Brigette's birth and held mass when her parents died.

The priest pointed to the space beside Jon. "May I?" Sitting sideways, he asked again, "How may I help you?"

Jon considered the place that brought such comfort to Brigette. "I'm here to talk to you about one of your parishioners."

"The list is not long. You might say that we have a dying congregation. I buried one of them today. Our younger members have moved on as well, many of them to Paris."

"I'm talking about Brigette Bebear."

The tongue-in-cheek banter ceased. "So you are Jacques d'Hiver?" He leaned forward and gave Jon a nonchalant grin. "I'm Father Matthias, but this is not my parish."

Those riveting eyes had focused on him once before. The rooftop of the Arc de Triomphe came to mind. But no, that stranger's features were caught in the shadows. Perhaps a clandestine meeting along the quaysides of the River Seine? But he'd never met with a priest.

He swallowed. "Brigette was here yesterday."

"Looking for my uncle, Father Rafael, the old parish priest. He plans to retire in Bordeaux. I'm fresh from seminary—just filling in until a replacement is found."

Jon looked at the baptistery, remembering his infant daughter in the arms of an older priest. His firstborn. His pride and joy. He'd sat alone in the back of the church, listening to Brigette promise to bring Colette up in the faith. He had not come for Claudio's baptism.

Anger needled him as he turned back to Father Matthias. "Yesterday you advised Brigette to leave me."

"No, she asked me whether she should leave you."

"Did you know that our children were baptized here?"

"Were you married here as well?"

"We're not married."

"Is that a sin of omission, son? You must know that marriage is one of the seven sacraments?"

"I am not Catholic."

Again amusement crossed the priest's face. "That does not change the sanctity of marriage."

"It is impossible for me to marry."

"Are you already married?"

He raked his hair and felt disheveled from head to toe. "I was engaged once. That was all."

Father Matthias glanced at the cane. "Then you are not well? Does Brigette know?"

"I can't offer Brigette and the children the life they deserve. She grieves that we are not married."

He nodded. "When she seemed so troubled yesterday, I told her the first stage of penance is sorrow for sin."

"We quarreled over that last evening. She told me the second stage of penance is confession. How many times must poor Brigette confess her pain...her sin?"

"Perhaps until you confess yours." The priest drummed his fingers on the back of the pew. "If my uncle were here facing you, he'd say, 'We should pray now, son.' But I'm not my uncle, and I think you would be turned away by a prayer. So how can I help you?"

"I may be forced to go away. I'm not certain I will ever be back. But, Father Matthias, I love Brigette."

"Just not enough to marry her?"

"That's why I came here. I want you to marry us."

"You know that's not possible within the church...but you could have a civil ceremony. Something that would not be sanctioned by the church."

"She would insist that we marry at St. Maria's."

The drumming on the pew back continued. "You could convert. We would have to meet together for several weeks."

"I don't have much time. Besides, I wouldn't believe anything you taught me. I did once. But God is no longer important to me. He is important to Brigette. In case I don't come back, it would comfort her if we were married."

The priest heaved a sigh. "Marry her and leave her? And are you destined for some faraway shore?"

Back to Kuwait on a special mission, but I cannot tell you that. His next moves were classified. Dangerous.

"Brigette lit a candle for you yesterday."

"Did she? You have to help us, Father. I owe that much to her and the children. If something happens to me—"

"You said you may be *forced* to go away. That spells trouble to me, Jacques d'Hiver."

Jon ran his hand over his chin. "We have few friends. My fault. I don't know what will happen to my family."

"Is there no place where they could shelter?"

"I was thinking here at St. Maria's."

The priest shook his head. "You cannot expect my uncle to take care of two small children and their mother. Do you not have a family somewhere, Jacques?"

He thought of Adrienne. Of his mother and father. "I did once. My parents think I'm dead."

"Have you no contacts in Paris?"

I'm on the embassy payroll. "My daughter goes to the American Academy, but I avoid it."

"So they won't recognize you? You have burned too many bridges, Monsieur d'Hiver. There must be someone. Brigette said she thought you had American citizenship once."

He started. "I never told her that."

"When you dream, you sometimes speak in English. The woman who loves you hears, listens. She came to my uncle—and yesterday to me. She worries about your past. Worries whether you will ever have a future."

Jon glanced beyond the priest toward one of the stations of the cross.

"Brigette longs to help you. If you are an American, why not go to the American embassy? Ask their help."

"I dare not. I can think of just one old friend. I named my son for him. But he thinks I am dead."

"And how do I find him—in case the need arises? I will keep it in strictest confidence."

In a dozen years or more, he had seldom allowed himself to think of them, let alone speak their names "Claudio and Dominique Vernettis. They're an older French couple who housed me when I attended the Sorbonne University. They treated me like a son." The lump in his throat was miserable. He missed Claudio's camaraderie, Dominique's cooking. "Yes, if they are still alive, they would protect my family. They owned a flat in Paris and a country place in Burgundy. My family would be safe there—"

Father Matthias took a pad from the rack in front of him and noted the addresses.

Jon moistened his lips. "They knew me as Jon Winters. They would not recognize me as Jacques d'Hiver."

"But if I talk to them, I think they will recognize you as a man in need of their help. And if they are the kind people that you say, Monsieur Vernettis would be glad to know your son bears his name."

"Then you will—"

The door of the sanctuary creaked open. They turned, but there was no time to take cover before the bullet whizzed past Jon's head. The priest bolted for the foyer before Jon could scramble to a standing position. As he sprinted, Father Matthias lifted his cassock above his ankles, revealing a pair of blue jeans tight against his lanky legs. He shoved the door open, then turned back, his eyes blazing as he stormed back down the aisle.

"Whoever it was is gone. This is a quiet village, Monsieur d'Hiver. That bullet was not intended for me."

They traced its course, saw where the bullet had zinged through a candle, splitting it and burrowing into the wall behind it. They blew out the candles surrounding it.

Jon wiped his dry mouth. "Whoever took that shot intended to miss me. I'm sorry I brought my troubles to you." He started toward the front door.

"Where are you going, d'Hiver?"

"To the car."

"Sorry, someone flattened the tires." He gripped Jon's arm and led him toward the vestry.

As they stepped into a narrow hall, an older priest came toward them. "What happened, Matthias? I heard a terrible commotion."

"Nothing to alarm you, Uncle."

"And this man with you?"

"He's Brigette Bebear's friend."

The old man's eyes softened. "Is she here?"

"No, Uncle."

He beckoned his uncle aside and they talked in whispers for several minutes. Father Rafael eyed Jon as they talked, his gaze sympathetic one moment, perplexed the next.

The younger priest frowned as he nodded at Jon. "Uncle, I'm going to take this man back to Paris. Can you ride a motorcycle with that artificial leg, d'Hiver?"

"It's been done."

"If you're uncomfortable, we can strap that contraption to the cycle. It might throw your balance a bit, but you'd make it."

"I need it for my footing. But the car—it's rented."

"I know." He turned to his uncle. "Arrange to have his car towed in for service. I'll take it from there."

The old priest made the sign of the cross, his eyes taking an upward glance. "If anyone asks after him?"

"That's the beauty of being a priest, Uncle. We never share what goes on in a confessional. Come on, d'Hiver. We'll take the tunnel. That's one good thing that came out of the war with the Germans." He crouched down and tossed a rug aside revealing a trap door. "Here we go. Can you manage a ladder?"

"I've managed worse challenges. But I'm not sure—"

Father Rafael nodded. "Go. My nephew will lead you to safety."

As they worked their way through the tunnel, Jon glanced at the priest beside him. "Who are you—what's your game, Father Matthias?"

"I'm a priest, like I told you."

"Then why are you getting wrapped up in my problems?"

"Isn't that why you came—seeking my help? Besides, I have orders to look after you. Trust me. I'm on your side."

Their voices echoed in the dank, dark corridor. Matthias took surefooted steps. Jon followed.

"Are we being fair to your uncle?"

"He's cagey. I told him you were followed here all the way from

Paris. Whoever took a shot at you will be stopped before he reaches St. Lo."

"You expected me?"

"When you turned south at St. Lo, we guessed your destination. That's when we were advised to expect you."

"Someone followed me? What is a priest doing getting mixed up in this kind of business?"

"I lost a brother in Afghanistan. It changes a person's perspective. He was a good man. Killed by terrorists. That's when I went to the American embassy. I thought they would laugh me right out of the place. What good would a French seminarian be? They saw some value in me, saw the priesthood as a great cover. Now and then I'm able to help."

"My father would say that belittles your calling."

"I'm at peace regarding it. All my life I wanted to follow my uncle into the priesthood. But I have definite political opinions. I feel called to defend my country. And yours."

The priest's arresting gaze stirred a memory again. "We've met before, haven't we, Father Matthias?"

He turned at the end of the tunnel. Their eyes locked. "Yes, d'Hiver. I'm the one who made certain you didn't slip into the waters at the Musée des Egouts."

Jon's throat went dry. "Then I owe you my life."

"I'm trying to save it again. But perhaps you should thank God instead of me."

"That sounds like something my father would say. In a way he was like a priest. He was a God-fearing man—committed to his job and family. He stayed in an unsettled marriage because he had pledged to do so, and I guess because he loved my mother no matter what she did. But he was a rock, a tower of strength in my life."

"Then I would say that God still has part and parcel in your life, d'Hiver."

"If we were in the underground tunnel together, how did you reach St. Maria's before I did?"

"You went the long way. But I prayed you would seek sanctuary in the church. Perhaps a cathedral in Paris. A man in flight sometimes seeks solace."

The priest's Ducati motorcycle was parked at the end of the tunnel where the door opened into a private warehouse. Matthias gave an all clear, then pushed his cycle outside.

"It won't be a comfortable ride." He folded his cassock and collar and stowed them in the saddlebag. "But at least we are way ahead of those who followed you into the village. When we reach Paris, I'm taking you straight to the American embassy."

"No. That is the last place I want to go. I'm going to see Brigette before I do anything."

"That's unwise."

"I won't leave her without saying good-bye this time. I called her, and when she didn't answer, I thought she might have come back here. She told me once that if she ever left me, she would come to Father Rafael."

"I called Brigette as well and advised her to leave the condo until she heard from me again. She refused. She won't go anywhere until she can talk with you."

"You didn't tell her what happened in the sewers?"

The priest clapped Jon's shoulder, his eyes twinkling. "Some things are best left unsaid. The fresh air on the ride back may remove all scent of your visit there." He secured the strap on his helmet and gave Jon another reassuring smile. "Your embassy will want to get you and your family to a safe place."

No, I must find my own place of safety. And for my family's protection, I must put distance between us.

"Father, someday, if it works out, I would still like you to conduct the wedding ceremony for Brigette and me."

"Just stay alive long enough." He handed Jon a helmet. "That and dark glasses are your best disguise. By the time they realize it's you, we'll be back in Paris."

Jon sensed Matthias's excitement as he gripped the throttle

with his gloved right hand and revved up the engine. He gave a backward glance to Jon. "Hang on."

He leaned into the wind, and they were off. As they sped over the rural countryside and swerved onto the motorway between two Citroens, Jon felt the old exhilaration of taking a risk—the excitement of being alive, of defying the elements. The adrenaline rush of taking the mountain slope—the higher the better. The fear— and the utter elation—of running ahead of his pursuers that day when he hiked through Afghanistan as a collegian and saw first-hand what terrorist camps could do.

He felt the thumping of his heart. The pulsating of blood. It was like bracing for the windstorm when he was lost in the forests of Lebanon.

It was like that moment of all moments, when he cradled his firstborn in his arms.

M oments after the old priest covered the trap door with the rug and positioned his prayer bench over it, he made a phone call to the service garage. The car in front of the parish would be picked up within the hour.

Then he took out young Matthias's laptop. He understood the old wireless sets used fifty years ago, but not these modern new-fangled instruments his nephew brought into his parish. He read over the instructions again, connected the wires to the outlet, and with three fingers typed out Matthias's message:

> From: Father Rafael, St. Maria's Parish
> To: Ricardo Mendez, American Embassy, Paris
> 1500 Hours
> Subject Jacques d'Hiver en route to Paris. Traveling single motorcade. Sniper's fire within sanctuary. No injuries. Please replace the cost of candles and wood paneling.
> Rafael R. Benefield/Parish Priest.

Colin Taylor leaned back in his chair as Ricardo left him alone in the communication center at the embassy and stepped down the corridor to Naji's office.

Perfect. Colin smiled. Naji Fleming has chosen the wrong moment to question her husband's motives. Rick has chosen the wrong moment to leave.

Rick had even been foolish enough to say on departing, "Guess I can trust you, Colonel. Won't be a minute. I jump when my wife summons."

Colin patted the arms of the chair, contemplating his next move. The communication system, even with its intricate capabilities, had limited access. Top clearance only. The chosen few who needed to know. The encryption machine on the back table was larger than a computer mouse, smaller than a tape recorder. He guessed from a glance that it was similar to the one he used at the Pentagon, no doubt a smaller version of the one at Langley. But he needed an access code. What about Sheridan Macaroy's code number? Colin had lifted that on one of his last visits to Langley.

He had to risk it. Pushing himself to a standing position he strode to the back table and within seconds had entered Macaroy's access code. The machine hummed in response. He addressed his message to the top brass in Washington, and indicated the DCI's name at Langley as the sender. That should get quick action.

He was sweating as his fingers skimmed the keys. For a second he thought someone was at the door. He waited for the knob to turn. Nothing. Then his fingers raced again.

> Urgent. Top security. All references and
> records for Jon Aaron Winters, A-436, Code
> name the Fourth Season, to be purged from
> files ASAP.

He repeated the same message, addressing it to Naji Fleming, Chief of Station, American Embassy, Paris, and signed it *Sheridan Macaroy.*

Before the hoax could be discovered, any records on Jon Winters would be erased, untraceable. And Colin's two companions from Kuwait would be unidentifiable.

Until now his Kuwait companions were a crooked cog in the wheel. He smirked at his deception. Yes, the error of command might be discovered, but not in time—not before Sheridan Macaroy's position at Langley was in jeopardy. Rick Mendez would be on the losing end as well, his career at the embassy finished before the truth was unraveled.

Colin had taken a major risk. He was just settling back in the chair when a message came in. He pushed the receive button and read the message. It was from some parish priest.

He tore it from the machine and smiled as he tucked it inside his briefcase.

So, "Jacques," it would seem I finally have the edge in finding you. His smile broadened. *And that's exactly as it should be.*

Rick Mendez slipped into the chief of station office without knocking and scowled at his wife.

"Did he fall for it?"

He nodded. "Like a bird without wings."

"Don't look so glum, Ricardo. Putting him in the communications center was my choice, my one option."

"A major gamble—and not your wisest move."

"We don't know where the leak is—if Taylor's source is in the hierarchy of Langley, we're on our own."

She leaned back in her chair. "Give him ten or fifteen minutes, I don't think he'll need any longer. A mole blunders sooner or later."

His wife—the risktaker, the attractive woman who caught eyes and never blinked back. She started out as a CIA courier and, with nerves of steel in Beirut and Zaire, had moved up in the ranks. But she was always his superior. In rank. In office space. In the respect of others. From that first day when he walked into the embassy, he'd been smitten by her beautiful face and clever wit. He knew too late that the Agency was her first love. Marriage came second. Children were out of the question. Did she even remember he called on her last evening? Needed her?

He glanced at his watch.

"Sit down, Rick. Your pacing irritates me." Her eyes brightened as she watched the closed-circuit monitoring of the communications center. "Our bird is taking flight. Give it another eight minutes, Ricardo."

He eased down on the corner of her uncluttered desk. Since his contact with Jon Winters's sister, he carried the weight of Kuwait on his shoulders again. Until that moment with Adrienne in the Tuileries Gardens, he believed Jon had betrayed them in Kuwait. He considered Jon a fallen hero that the Agency kept alive because he was useful. Rick had little respect for a man who sold out his own identity. Took on a legend. Now, after that miserable twenty-minute trek through the sewers of Paris, he knew the truth. Whether Jon had his finger on a terrorist cell in Paris was still a question mark, but that possibility kept him on the payroll. They had to play it his way. If they were lucky, he was telling the truth. There was so much wait-and-see to this business.

He hated waiting. Hated the way it jangled his nerves. "Naji, let's call time. If something else goes wrong in there, I'm at fault. You know no one but authorized people go into that room—ever."

"I authorized taking Colonel Taylor in with you."

"Without embassy clearance. If he's what we think he is, he'll do more collateral damage while he's in there."

"You worry too much. We have to know whether he's involved and how deeply. Who his contacts are."

"If we're wrong, Naji...if Colin isn't the mole, if he's just a man with a personal vendetta against Jon—"

"We have one other choice for a spy, Rick. You."

He bit back what she mockingly called his short fuse. Ever since she stepped into the role as chief of station, they'd drifted apart.

True, it was a temporary position until the Agency could find a more permanent replacement. But five months had elapsed! He resented taking orders from his wife, resented the way they locked horns on important matters. And he hated the possibility that she no longer remembered eating cold pizza together last evening.

He still roiled over her intervention in arranging that second meeting between Jon and his sister without asking his advice. At times like that, he doubted Naji's ability to handle a man's job.

Five months ago he told her he didn't think a woman—*any* woman—should be a station chief. She said it was his childhood in the Bronx. His dislike of women. His egotistic mastery. His anger at being bypassed for the promotion. She was right, of course; but her appointment to the post, however temporary, might well be the end of their marriage.

"You're scowling, Rick. What's wrong?"

"I was thinking about us."

She laughed. "Don't. Not on company time."

She ruffled his thoughts as though she were shaking the wrinkles out of a pillowcase.

"I'm worried about Adrienne Winters, Naji."

"There's no time for worry in this business."

"If we can't prove Colin's guilt, she won't be safe."

Naji's eyes narrowed. "Then recruit her."

He stared at her. "She despises us."

"But she's good. She won't let this business about her brother rest until she knows the truth. Better to have her on our team. If we fail, she can use her wiles to trap Colonel Taylor." She rattled the papers on her desk. "Time. Go back and see what our friend Colin is up to. And if nothing has happened, then we need Jon Winters's sister."

She reached across the desk and ran her finger over his wedding band. "I see you're still wearing the ring. I'm glad, Rick."

"We're still married. The embassy is none the wiser."

"But it's not cost effective to keep two residences." Her voice softened. "When this is all over, Ricardo, what about a holiday? I know you think we're strapped for cash, but I'd settle for some downtime in Burgundy. The farmlands for me. The Alpine forests for you."

When he hesitated, she said, "I'd go trout fishing with you this time... No matter how this ends, one of your friends broke faith with his country. You'll need time to wash Kuwait from your memory. I want to be there for you."

"You're serious about a holiday? Serious about going away with me? What changed your mind, Naji?"

"When you came to my apartment last night I realized how troubled you've been over Jon Winters and Kuwait. Until then I didn't think you needed me—" She looked away, but not before he saw the glitter of tears in her eyes. She met his gaze again. "I'm just suggesting we get away. Give you a chance to work things out."

"Between us?"

"I'm not sure about that. But you need someone to stand with you. I just think I'm that person."

"Like a shrink? My personal counselor? I'm to spill my guts. Didn't I do enough of that last night?"

"I want to keep you out of the reach of the police. I know you well enough, Ricardo, to know you're a good man."

"But you're not certain how involved I was in Kuwait."

"Can we put that aside? Just for a few days. We could stay at a chateau—one that looks out on the vineyards. You used to say I was a farm girl at heart."

"That's why I fell in love with you."

"Then what do you say? If we come out of this one unscathed—and still friends—we need to concentrate on us."

"And start a family?"

She paled. "I'm not ready for that yet." Her hand eased over his. "But I'm not ready to let you go. If we don't do something soon, Rick, our marriage is over."

CHAPTER 21

As they reached the outskirts of Paris, Jon had to shout above the roar of the cycle. "I've changed my mind, Father Matthias. Drop me off near the Rodin Museum."

"At this hour?"

"Yes. I want to go to Angelo's Art Studio—it's on a one-way street on the Left Bank near Rodin's."

"Then you have another friend?"

"Yes, my art instructor. I can't leave Paris without telling him good-bye. He's helped me through some tough times—he believes in my work." With more hand signals and another tap on the shoulder, he directed the priest down the alleyway to the studio. "There."

Father Matthias brought the motorcycle to a grinding stop and whipped off his helmet. He glanced back. "Now, Jacques, if you'll let up on your death grip, I can get off this cycle and help you. Are you certain this is the right place? It looks deserted."

"Angelo never leaves for home before eight or nine and never before he pulls the grate and padlocks the door."

"He did this time. Must have been in a hurry. I think I'll wait around for you."

"Lend me a hand, will you, Father? When my stump swells like this I'm in big trouble."

Father Matthias grinned. "Do you think you can manage after riding in the saddle that long?"

"I'm a bit saddlesore, but just help me land on two feet... There, I have my balance now." As he walked in front of the display window, the shingle above the studio creaked. Jon peered through the plate glass window as a tiny light flickered inside. The eerie light moved toward them, forming shadowy shapes in the window.

"Is one of your sculptures on display, Jacques?"

"I never finish my work."

"Brigette thinks that once your confidence matches your skill, you'll be another Rodin."

"Not in my art form. Perhaps in my lifestyle. Like Rodin, I failed to legitimize my children—failed to marry the woman I love." Jon swallowed back his bitterness. "Right now, talking to you, it sickens me thinking about Rodin and his mistress. Is that how people view Brigette—as my mistress?"

The priest allowed the darkness and his silence to be his answer. Jon's father would have called Jon's question "soul-searching"— but, then, Harry Winters would never have brought dishonor to the woman he loved.

The priest clapped him on the back. "Don't sell yourself short, d'Hiver. I believe you will right that wrong. After all, you did come to St. Maria's today to ask me to marry you and Brigette. You and Auguste Rodin both have a passion for art and beauty. Brigette is one of the most beautiful parts of your life."

Jon balanced on his cane. "Another unfinished part of my life."

The light inside flicked off and on. Receded. The shingle above them creaked again. Did Brigette see similarities between Rodin and himself? They both loved Paris. They had both gone to Italy to study Michelangelo's work. As gifted and prolific as Rodin was, he longed for praise and recognition, yet faced opposition and con-troversy. They both had their critics and scandals to face down. They both wanted to be remembered.

"Why the silence, Jacques?"

"I was lining my life up with Rodin's and didn't like what I saw."

"You were both revolutionaries, which is not all bad. You have your own art styles and commitments. Your loyalty to sis-ters. Give yourself time, Jacques. Rodin waited a long time for recognition. You're not even forty yet."

"Thirty six...I may not live to be forty."

The priest chuckled. "Something inside me believes that you will live long enough to find peace. Jacques, are you familiar with Rodin's *Hand of God?*"

"Yes. I've spent hours looking at that hand, trying to decide what he believed about it. Critics say he was trying to interpret God. I think Rodin was showing us that the hand of God created life from nothingness."

"You're not far from truth, Jacques." The priest rattled the door to the studio. Tapped on the windowpane. "Is this Angelo friend of yours deaf?"

"A little. Knock again."

A man appeared on the other side of the display window. "Is that Angelo peering out at us?"

Jon looked and saw Angelo inside the studio, a flashlight in his hand. In the beam of the light, his face looked puffy, distorted. "Angelo, it's Jacques d'Hiver. Let us in."

Angelo opened the door, waved them inside, and with a trembling hand locked the door behind them. Jon turned to his friend. "Angelo, this is Father Matthias."

Angelo didn't acknowledge the priest, but using his flashlight, ushered them back to his office. They stumbled in the darkness behind him. As the light switched on in the cluttered cubicle, Jon stared at Angelo's bruised face. One eye was blackened. Blood caked his right nostril. With his familiar beret missing, the deep scratches on his balding head were evident.

Alarm rushed through Jon. "What happened to you, Angelo?"

He wiped his hands on his clay-smudged smock. "I couldn't answer the man who came asking for you."

Jon's stomach clenched. "Someone from the embassy?"

"I never saw him before. He towered over me. Dark hair. Dark eyes. Well sculpted features. He spoke French with an American accent. He was not the usual courier. Too well-dressed for that. Called himself the Impostor. I don't think he intended to say that, but he was enraged at not finding you. He would have destroyed everything—but some ruffians screamed outside the studio, pounded on the window like they sometimes do. And then the ringing of my phone—that helped. He was frightened off. He almost knocked one of the little hoodlums down when he left…I'll never scold those children again."

"We've got to get you to a doctor."

"No, Jacques. The man warned against that."

"Look at you. You're hurt. Where are your glasses?"

He nodded toward his desk. The frame on his thick-rimmed glasses was bent, and one lens was shattered. "Jacques, you must stay away from the studio until your problems are settled. I can't risk the safety of my other students." He patted his swollen cheek. "You had another guest a couple of days ago. An attractive young woman who said you were old friends."

It could only have been one person. "My sister, Adrienne… I'm going away, Angelo. That's why I came here tonight—to say good-bye and to ask a favor."

"And leave your art behind? You must not do that. Just stay away for a few days."

Jon glanced at the priest. "Father Matthias is a friend. If you need to reach me, you can go through him."

Angelo nodded. "And that favor?"

"Don't destroy my feeble works of art in my absence. If I don't get back, ask Father Matthias to take them to Brigette and the children. He'll know where they are."

"Then you are in trouble. That man who came here—"

"He wants to silence me."

"You mean…kill you?" The beady eyes squinted in the semi-darkness. "The saints be preserved. That's what he tried to do to me. What have you done, Jacques?"

"It's a long story."

Angelo frowned at the priest. "One that you won't tell old Angelo. Not now. Not ever. Jacques, you come here with this priest, still hiding your past from me."

Jon touched his arm. "You told me once that the past does not matter. But, Angelo, don't let anyone destroy my work."

"Destroy your work? Never! Did you see your sculpture in the window, Jacques?"

He turned, his jaw twitching. "You never put my work on display."

"You forbid it. But that's what I was doing when the stranger came. It's the sculpture of your son and his sailboat."

"But, Angelo, that's unfinished."

"It is one of your best works."

Father Matthias cleared his throat, pulling Jon from the conversation. The priest's eyes were apologetic, but somber. "Jacques, we must go. I think we should send Angelo to the seminary. He will be safe there. When I get back I will tend to his cuts and bruises."

Angelo hesitated. "And Jacques's sculptures?"

"Leave them for now."

Jon nodded. They helped Angelo lock up the studio, then waited with him at the corner for a taxi. "Do what Father Matthias said, Angelo. Go to the seminary. If the stranger is still watching, he won't know where you live."

The priest's eyes twinkled as the taxi drew to the curb. "Your assailant will think twice before breaking into our gated community. We look with disfavor on break-ins. And—we still have marbled saints on duty at the gate."

There were tears in his instructor's eyes as the priest held the taxi door open. He pulled Jon against his solid chest and embraced him.

They watched until Angelo's taxi disappeared from view, then rode through the streets of Paris, along the River Seine. A block from the condo Jon insisted on going the last few yards alone.

"You've had enough of motorcycles?"

Jon slid from the bike. Caught his balance. Took his cane in his right hand. "I've had enough of a lot of things."

They quarreled for an hour, Brigette's unhappiness growing when he refused to tell her where he'd been. Toward midnight they made up with greater tenderness than Jon had ever expressed before.

Now, as she lay asleep in the crook of his arm, the street lamps of Paris reflected on her long burgundy hair. He twisted a silken lock and watched her rhythmic breathing, savoring the warmth of her body nestled beside him. Easing his arm free, he relinquished her to the rolling crest of her pillow. She stirred, then slept again. He kissed her bare shoulder as he tucked the sheet around her.

Ten minutes later he was in the children's room standing by their bedsides. Agony tore through him. Would he ever see them again? Colette slept on, her body thin like her mother's, her hair spanning the bolster in damp tendrils, her wistful brown eyes closed in sleep.

Jon picked up the baby doll that had slipped to the floor and placed it on the pillow beside her. He saw little of himself in Colette, much of himself in his son. Sometimes his daughter's insecurities and sensitive nature annoyed him. But he embraced that first memory of holding her in his arms, of marveling at the miracle of her birth.

The children seldom questioned what he did, where he went when he was not with them. Time had mellowed him, freeing him to laugh at Claudio's mischievous antics or melt with pleasure sitting beside his daughter, reading together. His children had turned his empty existence into a muted joy.

In the morning when Colette found him gone, she would run to the window and pound the pane with doubled fists. She would never forgive him for not saying good-bye. He bent down and kissed her hot cheek. Still she slept.

Outside the bedroom window, the black clouds of night swept across the Parisian sky. He hurried across the room to his son's bedside, almost stumbling over Claudio's toy trucks. This was the son of his loins, a willowy little boy with knobby knees poking out from the covers. His thinness belied his hearty love of food.

Jon rested his hand on the headboard, amazed at how many times Claudio thrashed and turned. He allowed himself a moment to picture the children safe and running free at Winterfest Estates. All he had to do was admit to Adrienne that he was her brother, and she would find a way to take them safely to Virginia. His parents would thrill to the shouts of their grandchildren. He choked at the thought of his father lifting them onto his lap, of his mother taking a special liking to Colette and her feminine ways. He imagined Rolf lifting the children up on a pony for their first rides. Colette afraid. Claudio shrieking with excitement.

He had robbed them of so much.

The boy opened his eyes as Jon stood above him. "Papa!"

He tousled the raven head. "Go back to sleep. We must not wake your sister."

As Claudio buried his face in the damp pillow, Jon leaned down and whispered in his ear. "I love you, my son."

Stumbling through the sitting room to the front windows, he looked out on the river that divided his city, the river that would soon separate him from his family. From where he stood fighting his demons, he saw the quaysides of the Seine. Notre Dame and its church spires reflected in its waters. Even now barges traversed the river. Between the lampposts and the lights on the bridges, he watched the River Seine wending its way toward the sea. Bridges crossed its gentle waters, linking the two banks and threatening to sever him from all he held dear.

He palmed his chin, thumb to cheek, and considered the wisdom of crossing the bridge alone. But there was no other way. He blinked against the darkness, his senses heightened. Somewhere out there, someone was watching the condo, waiting. But Jon saw no one. Just a parked car or two. A truck beyond that. And an unmanned motorcycle.

Three men waited inside the surveillance truck.

"Nothing, Phil," Kurt grumbled, adjusting the headphones. "Kids' voices. The woman saying prayers with the children. Nothing since midnight."

The older man—fat and all of sixty—stretched his shoulders. "Don't forget the big squabble earlier. It's just like being at home. What do you think, Father?"

Father Matthias sipped hot coffee and smiled. "Phil, I think Monsieur d'Hiver is smarter than you credit him. If you had bugs in the bedrooms, he was clever enough to find them. After all he's worked for your Company for a long time."

"We just bugged the living room. No more time."

"If you want my opinion—"

"We don't."

Father Matthias shrugged. "It's free."

Kurt crossed his arms. "Then spill it."

"Jacques won't make a move to leave until morning. And when he leaves, I don't think he will take his family with him. Someone took a shot at him back at St. Maria's, and I don't think it was one of you. So why don't you trust him?"

"He blew it in Kuwait."

"Firsthand knowledge, Kurt? If it's true, why is he going back there?" Father Matthias swallowed the last of his coffee. *D'Hiver doesn't have a fighting chance. Whatever he knows, he's expendable the minute they find it out.*

"Father, we don't know any more than you do. But it bothers me that a priest has his hands in politics."

"Kurt, my business is the protection and spiritual needs of people. I'd say d'Hiver needs both."

From the brief hours with Jacques, he knew the man deserved a friend. Was it Brigette and the children? No, he wanted to protect the whole family. Hadn't he made the man a halfhearted pledge? *Stay alive, Jacques, and I'll figure out a way to perform a wedding ceremony.*

The older man passed his binoculars to Matthias. "Take a look, Father. Help my myopia. Isn't that someone standing in the window? Second floor. Corner apartment."

He focused on the darkened room where an evening breeze fluttered the curtain. Behind the curtain stood a shadowy silhouette. "Too dark to determine... No. Wait. That's d'Hiver. At least he's tall like that."

There was little he could do to help d'Hiver now, but he would do his best to lead Brigette and the children to safety. He had memorized the names of d'Hiver's friends. He would take them there.

He feigned a yawn. "I don't think d'Hiver is going anywhere this evening. I think I'll call it a night. I brought him back to Paris for you. Now he's all yours."

Down on the darkened street, Jon saw a flash of light as someone stepped from the truck. A lone figure made its way to the motor-cycle, donned a helmet, and drove away with the headlights off.

The condo was under surveillance!

He had only to awaken Brigette and confess who he was. To beg her to flee the city with him. But there were other considerations: his family's safety. The stepped-up surveillance at the café. His betrayer back in town. His sister still in Paris. The threat of a ter-rorist attack erupting.

Things were moving too fast. He should warn Aleem. But Jon could no more protect him than he could Adrienne. The cell of terrorists that hid behind the doors of the café had awakened. American intelligence had identified many al-Qaeda leaders, the military operational chief from Kuwait among them.

Jon was a time bomb waiting to explode. Once he had been a man of honor and valor, but the shadowed reflection in the win-dow glass was haggard, unreadable. He was on a solo mission back to Kuwait, on a personal search for Hamad. Prove Hamad's inno-cence and perhaps he could prove his own. But Kuwait was no place for Brigette and the children.

The Rodin Gardens had ruined everything. This kid sister of his waltzed back into his life grown, mature—more beautiful than he had ever imagined. Her stubborn streak and her dogged pursuit of truth still shaped her. He denied any relationship between them, yet she knew. But did she understand why he had to go on pre-tending? Finding him spelled danger for her. She'd torn away the rusty lock of his past, broken into his legend as Jacques d'Hiver. He'd lived as Jacques d'Hiver for so long that it was almost impossible to remember being Jon Aaron Winters.

With either name he was a security risk, but too valuable for the Company to eliminate. He understood the Arab way of thinking. The Company needed him to intercept and decipher Arab intelligence as it passed through the Café le Grand Royale. Even now, Ricardo Mendez was preparing a passport for his return to Kuwait. As Jacques d'Hiver? Or Jon Winters? Or was he to go in as someone else? Pierre du Pont, perhaps.

As Jacques d'Hiver, he could go on living. They paid him to let Jon Winters die. But nothing could stop him from living like Harry Winters's son. Family honor drove him. Love of country burned deep inside him. His sister's appearance had strengthened his resolve. He had to pass on to Adrienne the need to go on searching for the truth about their father's betrayal. About his own.

As Jon made his way out the condo, he prayed that old Claudio and his wife were still alive. He locked the door behind him and limped to the elevator. As the door slid open, Father Matthias was waiting for him.

CHAPTER 22

Adrienne flipped through her clothes closet looking for just the right outfit for the fashion show in the morning. She settled on the periwinkle designer suit with its slimming lines and exclusive label. Standing before the mirror holding the outfit against her, it looked as though an artist's brush had painted a sky blue background for her dark eyes and lashes. She chose the accessories to go with it—the necklace with blue diamonds and matching earrings that Robbie had given her last Christmas.

She considered running down the grand staircase to the patio tearoom for a midnight snack, but her thoughts turned to the luxury of soaking in the Jacuzzi tub. She stripped and slipped into the hot water running to the rim. The perfumed bubbles washed over her, some of the water splashing onto the hotel bath mat. She leaned her head back against the tub and closed her eyes, her thoughts winging back to Winterfest.

She had mentioned the land to Jon, but had she told him that the land was half his? Would it stir enough longing in him to go home again? From the massive iron fence that surrounded the property, you could see the forest behind the mansion and, to the right, the sparkling river that ran below the terraced lawns. She had told Rick Mendez that half of the land belonged to Jon—that Jon would find peace by going home to the valley and forest and memorial garden established in his name.

What she didn't tell Rick was that for a time after they heard the dreaded news about Jon, the land had returned to bracken and prickly thorns—the unkept state her grandfather had found it in. When her grandfather Harrison paced out the property lines, trampling the briars and brambles beneath his heavy boots, he'd been wise enough to envision the beauty of Winterfest Estates. But Grandpa Harrison would have been horrified to see the briars that had crept back over his sprawling land after his grandson's death. But thanks to Rolf the land had been restored again.

Adrienne added more hot water from the tap, then relaxing again, she pictured the garden as it existed now, filled with gardenias and roses and garden lilies. In her mind she traced the delicate violets thriving on the edge of the garden, shaded by trees. Imagined the crocus along the border breaking ground after a harsh winter. She remembered the yellow primroses and irises bending with the wind. The sweet-scented lilac hedges blooming in the spring. The vibrant pink camellia bush in the summer. The sturdy chrysanthemums and petunias in the fall.

Yes, thanks to Rolf's ingenuity, the hills at Winterfest had long been ablaze with a kaleidoscope of color—reds and yellows, orange and lavender—changing with the seasons.

Oh, Jon, like you changed from Jon to Jacques.

You need the beauty of Winterfest. The solitude. I know if you would go home with me, you would find peace. If you could see Dad's library. Your old room—it's just the way you left it. Pennants on the wall. Pictures of the mountains you climbed. The photograph of you and Kris Keller. If you could see your boyhood home. If you could see the land again. A lump rose in her throat. *If you would talk to Mother, perhaps—perhaps then, you'd remember being Jon.*

She was lounging in her silk pajamas and the hotel toweling robe when her room phone rang.

"Adrienne, I am coming right over. Let me in at once. I'd rather no one know we're together."

"That sounds mysterious, Maddie."

"It is important."

"I'll open the door right now."

As she did so Maddie slipped inside. "I'm glad you're home, Adrienne. I—I was worried about you."

"Worried?"

"I wanted to make certain no one followed you back to the hotel. You weren't expecting a guest, were you?"

She frowned. "Like in a date?"

Maddie flashed a sheepish grin. "Oh, never mind. My imagination is running wild. But now that I'm here, I think I'll just chat a while. So tell me, how did the visit at the café go, Adrienne?"

"Not well. I accused Jacques d'Hiver of being my brother. He didn't answer me, but I knew by the expression on his face that it was true."

"Will you see him again?"

"Not apart from a miracle. He told me it was safer for both of us not to be seen together again. He asked me not to go back to the Café le Grand Royale."

"But their food is scrumptious." Maddie slumped down on the thick carpet and leaned against the wall.

Adrienne crouched down beside her. "Something tells me we're in for a long session. Should I order room service?"

"No. Let's just talk—about anything."

"Then, Maddie, forgive me. I'm always talking about my brother. I've never asked about your family. Are you an only child?"

Maddie stopped fidgeting and smiled. "Don't I wish! I grew up in a household of five brothers that left me feeling as unsettled as a windstorm. I was awkward and insecure and tall as a beanstalk."

"You're still tall and elegant."

"I didn't make much of an impression in the beginning. When I was born, my father lined my brothers up like stairsteps, waiting for the birth announcement, but when it came they were speechless. Even my father greeted my arrival with utter bewilderment. 'Maddie is a girl,' he told them."

"That was cruel."

"That's the way it was. As far as my father was concerned my being a girl eliminated any future in the House of Commons, Scotland Yard, or M-I5."

"Is your father proud of you now?"

"He didn't stick around long enough for me to find out." Her eyes combed the room and settled for a moment on the door. "My brothers filled positions that pleased him, but for all my scholastic achievements, I never quite measured up."

"Families are funny, aren't they?"

"Hilarious. I can laugh at it now, but my mother wasn't too pleased with my gender either. With a household budget to maintain—they were saving for Oxford for the boys—she considered buying a girl's wardrobe a needless extravagance. I spent my childhood in my brother's patched jeans, coveralls, and polo shirts...And you'll love this one. When mother lined us up for our haircuts, her fingers were stiff by the time I sat on the cutting stool for my weekly boy's bob. That and thick glasses blew my self-esteem across the Thames."

Adrienne shook her head. "I'm embarrassed. I was born into wealth and position. I guess I never questioned it. On school days the chauffeur drove me to a private girl's school in Washington. At night we followed the same crowded motorway back to Winterfest."

"Easy street all the way!" Maddie sighed. "Not for this London girl. But don't pity me, dear girl. I learned to live in a man's world. I didn't always like it, but I survived. They didn't even make a place for me in the fox hunts. They considered riding to the hounds a man's privilege. I just watched them mount their horses and ride off across the countryside over the fences and streams, the dogs yapping at the heels of a terrified fox." She shrugged. "They may be proud of me now—but I wouldn't know it. They don't say, and I don't ask."

They pressed their heads against the wall in an uncomfortable silence. "Growing up in a house full of brothers wasn't all bad, Adrienne. Now and then, Jeffry Earl and Charles came to my rescue.

That meant cuts and bruises and bloody noses for the other three."
Her eyes twinkled. "Charles broke Edmund's nose once. After that
Edmund kept his distance, and Peter and James were more careful
with me."

"A tough way to gain their favor."

"It never went that far. There was always sibling rivalry, but
now and then Jeffry Earl would come out into the kitchen and help
me with the dishes or some other task assigned to the only girl in
the family. There was always a fairness about Jeffry—"

"Was he the oldest?"

"The middle brother. He took the most knocks from the others—
showed the most love to me."

Adrienne heard the wistful cry in her words. "Do the two of you
stay in touch?"

"He lives in London. Easy access, in a way. When I'm in the
pits, I call him. Then we have dinner at one of his clubs. Never on
holidays and never with his family. But they're good times
together. We laugh a lot. Hash over old times. Laugh about
Edmund's broken nose—it's still crooked. Jeffry Earl always brings
a book along or a pair of expensive clip-on earrings to cheer me.
Poor dear. He's never worked it out that I prefer pierced earrings. I
don't wear his gifts, but I treasure them."

"He sounds like your favorite brother."

"As important to me as Jon is to you." She massaged her forehead. "Adrienne, does it ever occur to you that Jacques d'Hiver
may not be your brother?"

Her throat caught. "I believe he is. In any case, I'd still like him
to go home with me."

Maddie gave a side glance. Shook her head. "What do you want
him to do? Pretend to be your brother? That tops the cake."

"Would that be so wrong? He's the spitting image of Jon."

"You are crazy, Adrienne. You could never fool your mother. A
mother would know."

She fought to keep her voice steady. "I think it would work. I'd
make it work. It would be healing for all of us."

"Healing for you, Adrienne, but not for the rest of your family. You would add to their pain."

"Don't you understand? Going back to Winterfest would be so peaceful for him."

"Apparently your brother didn't think it was safe. Otherwise he would have gone home twelve years ago."

"Was it fair to us for him to stay away?"

Her gaze riveted on the door once more. "Let me play the devil's advocate. Let's say that Jacques d'Hiver *is* Jon. Could it be that he has amnesia? Some posttraumatic syndrome as an aftermath of his injury? Or perhaps he was a life dropout. That happens, you know."

"A life dropout? Not Jon. In many ways my brother was a loner—content in his own company. Challenged by his dreams. Quick in his studies. Steadfast in his pursuits. But he loved life."

"Maybe he didn't like being a rich boy. He had the Winters's financial backing, Adrienne."

"That's true. Had he not been declared dead those many years ago, Jon would have inherited a vast fortune—first from our grand-father Harrison and then from Dad. When his friends and class-mates were earning the money to go back to Sorbonne in the fall—"

Maddie looked at Adrienne. "He went there?"

"Yes, and did his family proud. But while everyone else was forced to earn tuition, Jon trekked to some of the hot spots in the world that the State Department labeled as seedbeds for terrorism. Unsafe for American travelers."

"And he went anyway?"

"Since we lost him—since we *thought* we lost him—I believe he went on government business."

"Intelligence work?" Maddie cooed the words. "Just like my brother Charles with M-15. Your brother was still in school. All the better to recruit him."

"But they used him."

Maddie shrugged. "And he let them."

"He didn't come home."

"His choice, perhaps."

Adrienne turned away for a moment. "I haven't told you, Maddie, but we knew my brother was an intelligence operative when he left home. We just don't know what he was doing in Kuwait when he was reported killed there. The war hadn't started."

Maddie whistled through her teeth. "Very unBritish of me. But now things are beginning to add up, and I don't like the sum of them. I'm staying over after the fashion shows. I want you to travel through France with me."

A tug of uncertainty hung between them. Maddie drew her knees to her chest. "I plan to go to Burgundy and do a bit of wine tasting. But I don't think I can persuade you to do that. I don't know what it is about you, but I rather think it is a God-thing with you. Some religious scruples."

"Not religious. But I do believe in God."

"I thought you were more certain than that."

Certain? No, I'm struggling. "I'm on the fringe, Maddie. Wanting God. Not wanting Him. Knowing that He loves me. And shying away from loving Him back. I'd like to be more like my father—"

"Deliver me from that one. My father went screaming into eternity saying there was no God."

Adrienne choked up. She wanted Maddie to know Harry Thaddeus Winters—to know that apart from that one period of despondency after Jon's death, her father was a man of faith. "My father was at peace when he died."

"What about you, Adrienne?"

"I'm not dead yet."

Adrienne stared at the carpet. *You want to know what's ticking inside me. Don't ask, Maddie. Don't ask. I'm trying to find my way. I know God loves me—but if I believe as my father believed, I will have to let Jon go. I will have to ask God—what would I have to ask God?*

She cast a glance at her friend. Angry. Defiant. "What about me, Maddie?"

Maddie shrugged. "I'll back off. New topic. What about Burgundy? Will you go with me? It has vast farmlands and crystal-clear rivers for canoeing."

"I need to stay in Paris and look for Jon."

"What about the herb-scented hills of southwest France? Beautiful harbors. Lots to tempt your appetite. Dried sausage. Sweet-and-sour rabbit. Goat's cheese."

Adrienne couldn't help smiling. "And more wine tasting?"

"I would forgo that as long as we get out of Paris."

"Maddie, I'm staying here."

Maddie's sigh was deep. "Then I have no choice. I will stay on with you and make certain you get on board a plane for home—back to that Winterfest Estates you are always talking about."

"Why the sudden concern for me?"

"Because—I think someone did follow you to the hotel. An hour ago there was an American army officer down at the desk asking for your room number. The truth is, that's why I'm here—to make certain you are safe."

An American army officer? Here in Paris? "Was he good-looking?"

"A real love, but I had to remind the receptionist that it was not hotel policy to give out a guest's room number." Maddie fidgeted again, locking and unlocking her fingers. "A woman was waiting for him in the hotel lobby—that same woman who took my seat at the fashion show."

"Naji Fleming? She works for the American embassy."

"I told the officer you were out for the evening, catching the late, late show at the Moulin Rouge."

"You knew I wouldn't go there. Why lie to him?"

"So I'd have time to talk with you. When I got here, I felt foolish. I didn't want to alarm you about the stranger in the lobby. And I'm still trying to figure out why you insist that Jacques is your brother."

Adrienne settled back against the wall. "You'd have to know what it was like in those first awful months after the news of his death. My dad was too grief-stricken even to go horseback riding with me. Jon was the second son they lost." She hesitated. "On top of that, a scandal hovered over Dad's career. He was innocent, but the accusations followed him home from Paris."

"My dear girl, I know about the upsets in government service. We don't have a Philby in our family, but we know something about the deceptive road to power."

Adrienne hugged herself. "My dad worked for the government too. After we lost Jon, all I cared about was doing my best so my parents would see me as the favorite child, even better than Jon. I was fifteen—almost sixteen—consumed with my interests in the fashion world and tennis. Angry at Jon for dying. And all the time, Jon was alive. But Rolf was always there to jolt us back into reality."

"Rolf?"

"He was Grandfather's groomsman and Dad's confidant. He still oversees the care of Winterfest and wheels Mother into the gardens whenever the weather permits. Our property is beautiful, thanks to Rolf." Adrienne angled a look at her friend. "You must come for a visit. Come when the cherry blossoms are blooming in Washington. It's a beautiful time of year."

Maddie clicked her tongue. "Then I'd meet that journalist friend of yours."

"Yes, Robbie is part of the landscape. Sometimes he lends a hand when Rolf's arthritis is on a rampage." She smiled, thinking of Robbie, thinking of the garden.

"In the springtime we have azaleas and rhododendrons, daffodils and tulips, and Mother's rambling red roses. Except for winter, the memorial garden is always alive with brilliant colors. There's a rock garden near the river with stone steps leading down to it and a millpond and waterwheel. You will love it, Maddie, from the minute you ride up the winding drive to the house. As a teenager I used to think my grandfather had patterned Winterfest after Manderley."

"The Manderley in *Rebecca*?"

"Yes, but that was my childish thinking. Other than the iron gate and the winding drive, Winterfest is my grandfather's dream and the memorial garden was Rolf's dream."

"It sounds as though Rolf knew Jon would come home again someday."

"I think he wanted it more because it would make Mother happy. The memorial garden was started before Langley invited us to the CIA headquarters to honor Jon."

"With a garden?"

"With a medal and a memorial star embedded in marble."

A knock at the door startled them. Adrienne stared at her friend. "Who can that be, Maddie? It's 1:00 in the morning."

Maddie looked from Adrienne to the door. "Oh, maybe the army officer came back. I told him you'd get home late."

The knock persisted. "Who is it?"

"Room service, mademoiselle. Fresh linens."

The voice was masculine, deep, and distinctive. There was no doubt in Adrienne's mind as to who it was. "I don't need any. Not at this hour."

"Oh, Adrienne. Just open the door."

She shot a glance at Maddie and rose to her feet. "It's okay. I know him. I don't know what he's doing in Paris, but I do know him."

Maddie pointed to the bathroom. "I'll wait there."

When Adrienne opened the door, Colin towered above her. She seldom saw him in his uniform and was impressed with how striking he appeared. His hair and mustache were dark, like her brother's. He eased past her and stood in the alcove. She kept her back to the open door. "Hello, Colin. What are you doing in Paris?"

He leaned down and kissed her, his lips like ice chips on her cheek. "Is that all the greeting I get? I flew over with the secretary of state on government business. When you called and told Rolf about seeing Jon alive here in Paris, I was shocked. We all were."

Alarm sang through her. "You didn't tell Mother?"

"I don't recall, but I did contact Sheridan Macaroy at Langley.

That sent shock waves through those sacred halls. He doubted the truth of it, so he asked me to come over and check it out."

"You said you flew over with the secretary of state? On what kind of business?"

His lips curled in a small smile. "You know that's classified."

"Or did you wrangle a place on the plane because you knew Jon and could recognize him?"

His eyes narrowed. "My rank doesn't get me a designated flight. That's reserved for generals. But this is a special mission with the secretary of state. As part of the team, he invited me to fly over with his entourage."

"And knowing you, if that hadn't worked out, you would have inveigled another way."

His smile was back. "You're right. I would have caught a regular air force flight into Ramstein Air Base in Germany."

"You did that once before, didn't you?"

"More than once. And from Ramstein, I hitched a ride on a turbojet into Paris. That took all of an hour."

"And made you airsick, didn't it?"

"At least I enjoyed the spectacular view of Paris better this time. I like flying in style."

His arrogance annoyed her. Or was it her weariness? He seemed unaware when the bathroom door squeaked, but he did turn his head for a quick appraisal of her luxurious surroundings. "Elegant. Your company provides well too."

"It's feminine."

"Like you."

She wished he would leave. "I can't tell you anything about Jon—and that's the truth."

"But if Jon is alive—there are serious complications. It means he has deceived us. Deceived his country. It's been twelve years and not a word from him."

"Or it means someone compromised him."

A loud thumping on the wall in the room next door was

accompanied with an impatient growl. "Quiet in there! Some of us are trying to sleep!"

Colin polished the visor on his cap. "Let's not quarrel. But we have to know how your brother got out of Kuwait. Who helped him. Why he chose to stay behind. Why he remained in Paris. All of that points to betrayal on Jon's part."

You're lying to me. "He almost didn't get out of Kuwait. And when the Company found out he was alive, he no longer counted. Who do you think has been supporting him all these years?"

"Is that what he told you?"

"It doesn't matter. I need some answers too. What about your posting at the Pentagon? Did they just up and release you to fly over here and find my brother?"

"We know Jon worked with resistance cells in Kuwait. He may have been in contact with terrorist cells as well. Langley wants answers."

She pulled back when he touched her shoulder.

He let his hand fall to his side. "Macaroy has contacts all over Washington, so I was cleared to come. The secretary was gracious enough to offer me a space on the plane."

"In other words you still have clearance with the CIA? Have you been working for them all along?"

"You know that after Jon…left us, I went back into the service. After that, Macaroy was able to get me on at the Pentagon. Good references and all."

"Under military cover—isn't that what they call it?"

"Adrienne, can you arrange for me to meet Jon as soon as possible?"

Her stomach coiled into tiny knots. "I can't do that."

She marveled at the cool, detached mask he wore. That well-remembered expression. "We can find him, Adrienne. We will find him."

"In the city of Paris?"

"You found him."

"I think God brought him across my path." Adrienne kept herself from pulling away as he took her hand and lifted it to his lips.

"Then perhaps this God of yours will do the same for me."

As Colin left, the bathroom door squeaked again.

"Oh, Maddie, come on out."

Maddie leaned against the doorjamb. "That lover boy is as slick and slimy as a fish on the end of a hook. He reminds me of two of my brothers. Snide. Arrogant. An attack dog ready to strike if you don't give him his way."

"He's not that bad. He lost his wife and unborn child in the disaster at the Pentagon."

Maddie mellowed. "How awful. But, Adrienne, does that give him license to be so rude to you—to dislike your brother so much? Look at you. You can't stop trembling."

"I know. Colin upset me so, I didn't think to ask him about Gavin."

"Don't tell me there are two of him?"

"No, Gavin is his son—a really sweet little boy."

"Then thankfully not like his father. I'm glad you don't consider Colin a right proper suitor."

"Never." Adrienne collapsed on the edge of the bed and tried to smile. "Maddie, do you dislike *all* men? Is there no one significant in your life?"

Maddie turned scarlet. "There's one significantly absent when I need him. He's a Londoner—but he lives in Cambridge and teaches at the university. He's more mad about research than about me." Her flush deepened. "I can't get him to the vicar for a cup of tea, let alone to the altar."

"Does he have a name?"

"A real handle: Archibald Sebastian Finhold. And that's *Sir* Archibald."

"Then you could be Lady Finhold."

"Not in the next five years. It will take Archy that long to discover he's in love with me. By then I may fit into his research formulas. But forget me, what kind of a mess are *you* in? Until I heard soldier boy talking about your brother, I thought Jacques d'Hiver just didn't add up. Now...well, I'm staying on to help you. I'll put Burgundy on hold. I can catch the chunnel back to Paris anytime. On a long weekend, maybe."

"But I'm spoiling your plans."

Maddie waved the objection away. "It's not like I haven't seen Burgundy. But you need to know something. I was at the café when you met with Mr. d'Hiver that second time."

Adrienne stared at her friend. "I didn't see you there."

"The waiter Aleem saw me. He served me a sweet roll and tea. Oh, don't look so irritated. I was worried about you. I had to know you were all right. I didn't tip Aleem because he was anything but courteous. He's an edgy sort."

They both jumped when they heard a distinct tap on the door. Maddie grimaced. "Don't tell me your soldier boy is back?"

Adrienne jammed one hand in her toweling robe. "He is not *my* soldier boy."

"That settles it." Maddie planted her hands on her hips. "I'm staying with you tonight, or you're going to my room where we can get some peace and quiet. Something is going on and whatever it is, we will face it together."

The tap persisted. "Room service."

Adrienne cracked the door as Maddie disappeared into the bathroom again. A waiter in a white shirt and black bow tie bent over a trolley loaded with silver tureens.

"I didn't order room service."

He glanced to his left. "The gentleman over there ordered for you."

She peeked around the casing to find a young man, his jacket slung over his shoulder, standing in the door of the room next door. His broad grin warmed her from the inside out. "Hi, Adry."

"Robbie!" She threw open the door.

Stepping toward her, he reached up and ran his hand through his hair. "Are you going to invite me in or not? The food's getting cold."

She tightened the terrycloth robe around her waist. "You just missed seeing—"

"I know. All of Virginia is dropping in. I'm checked in to the room next door, so I heard you squabbling."

"*You're* the one who thumped on the wall?"

His grin was utterly unrepentant. "One and the same. The colonel doesn't know I'm in Paris. I want to keep it that way."

"Colin is here on government business."

"So am I. According to your mother, he flew over on official business with the French ministry of interior."

"You don't sound like you believe him."

"I think it was his excuse for coming. He has every reason to want to find your brother…and so do I. Now are you going to keep me standing out here, Adry? I'm hungry."

When she stepped aside, he dismissed the waiter and pushed the trolley into the room himself. "You can tell your friend to come on out. I think there's enough food for the three of us."

"How did you—?"

"I saw her reflection in the mirror."

"Oh, Robbie. I haven't had anyone to talk to."

"You had me," Maddie protested as she came into the room. "I was beginning to think I was in America's Grand Central Station. Quite a lot of traffic through this room in the last hour or two. And not just the maid turning down the coverlets."

He extended his hand. "I'm Robbie Gilbert."

"You must be Adrienne's journalist. I'm Maddie Travers. London born. London bred. Consider yourself among the fortunate, Mr. Gilbert. The last guest didn't get past the threshold. Maybe it was the uniform—"

"And you, Maddie?"

"Adrienne and I attended the fashion show together. And that business about finding her brother, I think she's telling you the truth."

Robbie's arm went around Adrienne's waist, and she leaned against him. "Oh, Robbie, I still can't believe you are here."

"I told you if you got into trouble I'd catch the next plane."

She couldn't fight back the tears. "I can't tell you how many times I've wished you were here."

"I consider that a good sign." He smiled that rakish grin of his and thumbed away a tear from her cheek. "Do I take those tears to be tears of joy at seeing me?"

"I—I think so. You said you are here on business."

His smile melted, and Adrienne felt a stab of alarm at the somberness in his gaze.

"I'm here, dear Adry, to make certain nothing happens to you."

CHAPTER 23

Colin lunched at the sidewalk café, planning his strategy as carefully as Rommel, the Desert Fox, would plan his. From the table where he sat, protected by a big red umbrella, he studied the faces of the passersby on the Champs Élysées, and took note of those who entered the café. The plate-glass window reflected the street and the waiters moving among the tables, but he could see inside the café.

Jacques d'Hiver's table remained empty.

Colin's waiter refilled his water tumbler. He smiled. "On my last visit, another young man from the Middle East waited on me. His name was Aleem."

"He's still with us. He always serves inside."

"Perhaps you could point him out to me."

"I'll tell him you are asking for him."

Moments later an anxious young man appeared, looking puzzled. "You asked for me, monsieur?"

"Yes. You waited on me several months ago."

"I don't recall."

Colin studied his prey. The man's dark, riveting eyes were full of sadness, the rest of his features stony. His close-cropped beard and sideburns covered his narrow jaw. Colin pictured the Yemeni as a tribal warrior generations back wearing his tribal wraparound skirt, a turban on his head, a ceremonial dagger at his waist. As a waiter, the Yemeni was defenseless.

"You are from Yemen…in fact, you left Aden Harbor in a hurry." Colin allowed the implication to take shape in Aleem's mind. "Don't leave, Aleem. Sit down."

The waiter collapsed in the chair. "What do you want?" His voice—low-keyed, hostile—held none of the respect and affection for guests that would be expressed in his home country.

"I'm looking for Jacques d'Hiver. I believe you serve him when he takes his meals here."

Aleem's olive skin paled. "I've not seen him of late."

"Then tell me how to reach him."

He shoved back his chair. "I have no way of knowing that."

"Don't leave. Many people migrated from your country to Europe. But I understand that you came here right after the bombing of the USS *Cole*."

Not a muscle moved. "I had nothing to do with that."

"But some Yemeni are still being deported to your country—just for questioning." He had no knowledge whatsoever whether this was happening, but it was getting Aleem's full attention.

"I was forced to leave my country."

"Why?"

"They say my country is a prime source for terrorist training. They tried to recruit me...would you have stayed behind and let them recruit you, monsieur?"

No, but I am involved against my will. Providing funds for the terrorist training camps. Involved because my father was money hungry. "I must find Monsieur d'Hiver. We both know he believes in freedom. Is that why you serve him?"

Aleem braced his hand on the table and stood. "Of late he has taken his meals with an American woman."

"A girlfriend?"

"She calls herself his sister." He shrugged. "But I cannot be sure. She and her friends have a reservation here this evening." Aleem's eyes remained guarded. "When I see Jacques d'Hiver again, I will tell him you are looking for him."

"You don't know my name."

"But I can describe you, monsieur." With that, Aleem rose and hurried away.

Colin pushed his plate aside. The snails looked slimy, unappetizing. He grabbed his half-empty glass of water and drained it.

He was blundering every move—throwing caution to the wind ever since Jon eluded him in the underground tunnels. He wouldn't lose. Dared not. Winters alive was a threat to his own safety and career.

Winters the competitor. The overachiever. The skilled skier. The rich kid who had filled him with envy. No matter what they did, Jon always did it better. But in military rank, Colin had come out on top. And when Jon was reported dead, he took great pleasure in winning the hand of Jon's fiancée. Taking Kristina Keller as his bride had been one of the greatest days of his life. It was like hurling another clump of sod Jon's way. But part of Kris never forgot Jon; Colin was never first with her, not even when he married her.

Seeing Jon for the first time in years awakened the old jealousies. He brooded afresh that Kristina was gone. Knowing Jon was alive—knowing he remembered everything, was like gall and wormwood, the bitterness and rancor so deep Colin could not sleep. Could barely eat. He could see Jon now, limping toward them at the museum—without haste, a cane in one hand. But he wasn't a cripple. He was still that rangy, suave acquaintance from university days, scholarly and lettered. Older, yes, his sideburns fringed with silver. Stone-faced, yet composed. Those black eyes blazing, challenging. His manner commanding. His words sharp, crisp, unafraid. Without pointing a finger, Jon condemned Colin for his lost twelve years.

Apart from the Parisian interfering, Jon would have lost his balance in the tunnels and fallen headfirst into the muck and mire. Humiliating, if nothing else. And if he'd timed it right, Jon would have fallen in and cracked his head on one of the sharp dredgers or cleaning apparatuses. But Colin still had the advantage. Jon couldn't be certain which man had pushed him forward.

He twirled the water glass. When had he pushed to the edge of madness? When had he become two people? Colonel Colin Taylor and the Impostor. No, he was sane, and yet the good that he would do, he did not do. The evil that he would not do, he did. Forget the row of ribbons and merits he wore on his tunic. Forget the insignia on his shoulder.

In spite of the cup of steaming coffee that the waiter placed beside him, shivers clung like icicles to his spine. It was that same quivering sickness he felt whenever Jon's father talked to him about God. Harry Winters's last effort to call him to redemption thundered in his mind: *"A carnal man allows sin to dwell in him until he is held captive by it. Don't wait too long, Son."*

Too long for what? The cleansing of the inner man? The conflict still waged war inside Colin. If hell existed—Harry declared it, while his own father denied it—but if it existed, he already felt the flames licking at the soles of his feet.

He could blame his long list of betrayals and failures on his father, and did in part. How much he had wanted to please Bedford Taylor. But the thought of being well-to-do, like the Winters family, had drawn him like a magnet.

"One theft and we can live in style, just like the Winters," his father had promised. *"I have a buyer."*

"For what, Dad?"

"A couple of defense files from Harry's office. A Saudi diplomat, a friend of mine, wants to photograph them. We'd have them back before Harry knows they're missing."

"That doesn't sound legit, Dad. I'm not helping some Arab. Besides, the embassy vaults are impregnable."

"Then it's a good thing Harry is working out of his condo since his surgery. The files I want are there."

"Come on, Dad. You're crazy. I can't break into his house and come up with the combination to his vault."

"Someone will be helping us."

What a fool he'd been—the gullible teenage son eager to please his father, anxious to deceive the father of his greatest competitor. The thought of outwitting Jon persuaded him. That first theft was exhilarating. He was almost caught when he ran into Mara Winters on the stairwell. She seemed a bit tipsy, but she didn't question him. He knew now that she had been aware of what was going on. Knew later about the bond that existed between Mara and his father. The bloodline that suckered him in.

As he waited for his bill, a shadow fell across his café table. He looked up into the maître d's face.

"Cavell."

"Was it wise for you to come here, Colonel?"

"No one will recognize me."

His brows lifted. "In that uniform, sir, can you be certain?"

"I'm anxious to find Jacques d'Hiver."

"We received word through one of our clients that he is returning to Kuwait."

Colin frowned. "To find Hamad? Then things are moving fast."

Cavell nodded. "I suggest you leave before any attack occurs in Europe or this city."

He was right. Colin laid out some coins. "You must do something for both of us, Cavell. Aleem cannot be trusted."

Cavell gave a curt nod. "I will see to it."

"One other thing, Cavell. Has Gresham the Arab arrived?"

"Last night. He's available if you need him."

"Better that we not meet this time."

When Colin left the café, he strolled the streets of Paris for hours until his feet burned. All he ever wanted to be was an army officer. To serve his country. To be like Erwin Rommel and have his one last chance at glory.

Colin had committed more thefts after Harry Winters went home from Paris in disgrace, and after that, he got his military dream all right—but at what price.

Much of his father's illegal fortune lay in unnumbered bank accounts, accessed by terrorist networks worldwide. What should have been his own inheritance fed into the al-Qaeda training camps. To buy silence, Colin still provided the names of wealthy businessmen and entrepreneurs who could provide a continual flow of money into these camps, not for political favor, but to protect their miserable reputations. He no longer channeled classified documents from the Pentagon, and yet he, too, was a wretched man.

Confronting Angelo at the art studio yesterday had been another major mistake. He was taking too many risks, making too many bad choices that would reveal his identity. It was dark when he reached the hotel and placed a call to Sheridan Macaroy.

Macaroy's words snarled through the phone lines. "I've just been informed by Ricardo Mendez that you risked meeting Jon in the sewage tunnels."

"With good reason. I had to find out what Jon remembered about Kuwait. The minute I saw him, I knew he remembered everything. Now he is going back to Kuwait."

"What? Then follow him and *leave* him there this time. If you work it right, we can still convince the powers that be—including Mendez and that wife of his—that Jon is the mole. Our careers depend on it."

That, Colin thought as he hung up, *and our lives.*

Aleem left the café from the back entry and walked into the unlit parking area. A midnight breeze whipped through his thin jacket and blew against his face. He considered turning back, but it was just a few yards to the boulevard. He increased his speed when he realized that his footsteps were not the only ones echoing through the night.

In the shadowy mist, someone was coming toward him. Someone behind him. A taste of fear rose in his throat.

It was like fleeing a dust storm in Yemen. This evening's windstorm resembled a *shamal,* with its dust blocking visibility. Instead of tiny sand particles, beads of perspiration clung to his skin. The race for cover from the dust in his home country replayed in his mind. His desperate flight from Yemen. He ran.

His thoughts plummeted with each beat of his heart. For months he had dreamed of sailing back through the Port of Aden, of going home. He had waited too long. *I will never see Aden again nor the village where I was born.*

He had taken one risk too many for Monsieur d'Hiver. In the background, the engine of a Peugeot roared into drive, tires squealing. The man approaching cried out, "Aleem, I must have a word with you."

Cavell's voice. Commanding. Threatening.

The car drew beside him now, its door open.

The back of his shirt and armpits were wet with sweat as his assailants overtook him. From the corner of his eye, he saw the man on his heels moving closer, arms upraised. He felt a thin wire scrape over his face. Felt himself screaming silently for oxygen as the wire tightened against his throat.

"You are in too much of a hurry, Aleem," Cavell said.

Aleem knew with terrible certainty those were the last words he would ever hear.

A half-mile from the Pont Neuf Bridge, the car made its way along the river with its headlights off. It turned onto the bridge, the engine hiccuping, until the driver pulled to a stop between street lamps. He popped the hood, turned on the emergency blinkers, kept the engine running. Cars sped by them; one swerved around the disabled vehicle, but the driver did not stop.

Glancing in both directions, the stocky man on the passenger's side stepped from the parked car and hurried to the railing. The half-moon cast a hazy gleam over the rippling river, leaving the quaysides in darkness.

He waited as a motored flat-bottomed barge drew closer. Its squared front was visible now, its heavy cargo holding the barge low in the water.

"Now."

It took two of them to lift the waiter's lifeless body from the backseat. One shoe fell off as they dragged him between them. "Make sure we throw him clear."

Grunting, the other man gripped Aleem by the trouser legs. Up and over. They gave a final push. The limp body plunged headfirst, landing with a horrendous splash—then a thud as body and barge collided. The crushed body slipped from sight as the barge towed its cargo under the bridge.

The men slammed the hood shut and scrambled back into the car. As they sped across the old bridge, Cavell smiled. "He was a good worker. A quiet man. But he won't even be missed until he fails to report for duty in the morning."

CHAPTER 24

Adrienne discovered Rick Mendez waiting for her outside the fashion house. "Mr. Mendez, what are you doing here?"

"I left several messages for you at your hotel."

"Two," she corrected. "I thought we settled everything between us the last time we met."

He pulled her away from her friends. "The embassy is arranging a flight home for you as we speak."

"Whatever for? I have my own return ticket. You aren't robbing me of ten more days in Paris."

"You are an American tourist. It is my job to protect you."

"Because I wanted *you* to find my brother?"

He remained somber, his grip on her forearm insistent. "Miss Winters, Aleem, the waiter from the Café le Grand Royale, is dead."

"Dead." Her knees caved. Mendez steadied her—an unexpected act of kindness. "What happened, Rick?"

"He was pulled from the Seine early this morning."

"A suicide?"

"A man who kills himself doesn't bother to kick off just one shoe. We believe he was thrown in after he was dead—sometime after midnight—by someone who knew him. The police notified the American embassy."

"Aleem was not an American citizen. He's a Yemeni."

"We know. The police are looking for Jon—for Jacques d'Hiver—in connection with his death."

She shuddered. "I saw Aleem at the café yesterday. He seemed all right then. Why him, Rick? Robbery?"

"Because he could identify you. And Jon... No, don't be alarmed. Jon is safe for the moment, but he refuses to remain in hiding if you don't fly out today."

Her lip quivered. "I won't go without seeing him."

"I told him you'd say that."

She glanced at her friends, waiting a few steps from them. "My friends and I are on our way to the café now."

"No, the café is off-limits."

"But their meals are superb. I didn't like the maître d', and Aleem was annoying—"

"Stop it, Miss Winters. Aleem was a point man. Jacques d'Hiver had a permanent table there."

Light dawned. "Then I came along and interfered. They were working for you. That's it, isn't it?"

"Aleem worked for Jacques. Your presence at the café drew attention to both of them. Jacques tried to warn you."

"You're trying to blame me for what happened. How dare you." She sucked in her breath. Blinked against the sun. "I'm sorry—but I'm not leaving Paris until I see Jon."

"I'll work something out. But you must leave with me. Just tell your friends you've had bad news. They'll have no difficulty believing you. You are white as a sheet."

Maddie Travers sauntered over. "I don't like the way you look, Adrienne. Is this man bothering you?"

"I'm all right, Maddie. Mr. Mendez...knows my brother."

"Then tea with us is out?"

Mendez nodded. "I need some time with Miss Winters."

Maddie pointed her finger at Adrienne, but her threat was aimed at Mendez. "We'll go back to the hotel to eat, but don't be long." She glanced at her watch. "Two hours. I'll give you two hours. Three, maximum. One tock past three, and we're reporting you missing."

Rick frowned. "But I'm from the American embassy."

"Reason enough to scare me."

As she left them, Ricardo took Adrienne's arm and guided her toward the Arc. "Let's grab something to eat. It will give you time to collect yourself. Then we'll take a taxi back to your hotel so you can pack. I'll accompany you to de Gaulle."

"De Gaulle is out."

He eased her toward a pavement café and urged her to sit under a shade umbrella with him.

"I'm not hungry, Ricardo."

"I am. At least thirsty. And I need to make a call." He glanced around, his gaze darting from face to face as he dialed his cell phone.

"Expecting someone?"

"I have to make certain no one is following us. Yes. Yes," he said into the phone. "Rick here. Let's keep that appointment."

As they sat sipping tea, Adrienne studied the man across from her. "Ricardo, I don't believe I need protection, so why are you trying to send me away?"

His gaze was stern. "Adrienne, Aleem was murdered. Your brother is convinced you may be next."

She put her cup down before it slipped from her fingers. "Stop trying to frighten me."

"I'm risking my career telling you this—but the Café le Grand Royale has been under surveillance for months."

"Why the sudden candor? You didn't trust me on our last two visits."

"But Naji Fleming did. She's my wife. She's also acting chief of station here in Paris."

"She's CIA. You're married to Naji?"

"I told you we are working out our differences, in particular our disagreements about Jon. Naji worked at the embassy when I was assigned there. We needed special permission to marry. In the end they thought her work would complement mine."

"You mean cover it?"

He neither denied nor confirmed. "Adrienne, don't you understand? Jacques d'Hiver is in serious trouble."

"Because of me?"

"Your meeting with him at the café raised suspicions."

She closed her eyes. "I put my brother in danger?"

"Innocently so."

Adrienne opened her eyes and thanked him for that with a smile.

He met her gaze, his eyes troubled. "I've had time to sort through all we talked about the last time. I believe now that you were telling me the truth about Jon. About Kuwait. *You see, I was there.* I went in on a three-man team with Jon just before the invasion of Kuwait."

"You?"

He nodded, his expression miserable.

"You and Jon? You should have told me sooner, Rick."

"I know. I thought—"

"No, you didn't think at all." The couple at the next table stared at her. She didn't care. "You tried to protect yourself. You deceived me. Played me for a fool." Her voice rose a pitch. "Who was the third man?"

"It doesn't matter. Just another intelligence officer. Foolhardy. Willing to risk his life for our country. When the report came back that Jon was severely injured—I believed it was impossible for him to survive."

"But he did. You did."

Ricardo shrugged. "I was one of the lucky ones. I came out unscathed, on the outside anyway. The years haven't erased the inner scars."

Adrienne's fingers gripped the table. She lowered her voice. "*Nothing* erased my parents' pain when they were told Jon was dead. But you—you went free."

"For many months I thought your brother was dead. Then word filtered down that Jon chose to remain behind. That he failed to send in his reports."

She stared at him. It couldn't be true...

"I was ordered to fly to Saudi Arabia to interrogate a released POW. Several of us met under a tent in the hot desert. When I walked into that interrogation center, Jon was there. I was asked—no, *ordered*—to testify against him."

"As a deserter?"

"Sheridan Macaroy convinced me."

"Macaroy." Adrienne leaned forward. "He's the man who came to Winterfest to tell us Jon was dead."

"He's the man who sent us into Kuwait."

She absorbed his words, then leaned back in her chair. "What happened to the third man?"

"He wasn't there. He wouldn't have recognized Jon anyway. Jon's leg was missing. The stump infected. His cheeks hollow. His olive skin blanched. He had no meat on his bones. They accused him of being a traitor. Of staying behind in Kuwait to help out a terrorist organization."

Rick stared at his tea. "I couldn't meet Jon's eyes when he asked to go home and put it all behind him. Even when one of the Saudi officers accused him of choosing to stay behind, Jon made no effort to defend himself. Macaroy was unyielding too. He said intelligence data indicated that Jon had hidden out with a terrorist group in Kuwait."

"Lies. All lies. I know my brother."

"I couldn't think with a clear head then. I thought Macaroy was being merciful when he offered Jon a new identity—a chance to redeem himself using his knowledge of the Arabic world. Macaroy insisted that if we kept him on the payroll as Jacques d'Hiver, we'd find out which country he was working for. Otherwise, he said, Jon's returning home to be judged as a traitor would just add to his father's disgrace. May God forgive me, Adrienne, but I ended up thinking if he stayed behind by choice, then he was a stinking coward."

She wanted to hit him. To throw something at him. Instead, she just glared. "And you call yourself Jon's friend?"

He at least had the grace to look ashamed. "I had dysentery so I had to leave before the interrogation ended. All I knew beyond that was a brief communiqué from Langley. Jon had been listed as dead. His file sealed. That was Macaroy's final word."

"You *knew* better."

"I only know what Langley wanted me to believe. Live with a lie long enough and you believe it. But when I was reassigned to Paris, Jon and I met by accident at the Louvre. He told me he was on the CIA payroll. I checked the files. There was no Jon Winters listed, but Jacques d'Hiver's name was there. The age and statistics bore a resemblance."

It was too much. Adrienne could take no more. She stood and ran.

Ricardo caught up with her, grasping her arm. "Hear me out, please! I followed him out of the museum to a bench near the glass pyramid. We never met again that way—although I have sent couriers to meet with him."

"Ricardo, what irrational excuse—what *threats*—persuaded Jon Aaron to become someone else?"

He slowed their pace. "The safety of his country. His family. The safety of the men who served with him in Kuwait."

"You and this third man?"

"Jon loved the Kuwaiti people. The Arab way of life."

"He loved being an American too. Loved the Winterfest way of life. I know there's more to it than what you're admitting, Ricardo. You're sworn to silence. But don't tell me my brother was a coward, and stop trying to convince me that he came out of Kuwait in disgrace. I've been that route before—a long time ago when they lied about my father."

His Adam's apple bobbed in protest. "You have to understand, Adrienne. We were in Kuwait at a dangerous time. Invasion was imminent. It was our job to help establish a resistance movement among the Kuwaitis. Jon kept telling us that he had discovered a terrorist cell as well. The third man on our team insisted that with the impending invasion we had a job to do. Do it."

As they neared the unknown soldier's tomb, she stopped and let the crowd surge around them. "What do you believe now, Ricardo?"

"That Jon told the truth all along." His eyes combed the crowd, searching. He led them to a shaded area so they could stand with their backs against the wall.

"Did Jon lose his leg in an explosion?"

He faced her, his gaze tormented. "The other day Naji showed me the medical file on Jon—the one she was supposed to destroy." His voice hardened. "She tossed it across the desk to me and said, 'Read it. And maybe you'll finally believe your friend.'"

Adrienne stared at him, numb. "Did he lose his leg in an explosion?"

This time he didn't flinch from her gaze. "According to the medical records, Jon was caught in the fire of an Iraqi helicopter on the day of the invasion. Later, when he was hiding out with some of the resistance forces, he endured the brutal amputation of his festered leg without medication so no one would discover his native tongue. That sounded like Jon."

For a moment she thought she would be sick, but the wave of nausea passed. "That doesn't sound like a coward."

Ricardo's smile was grim. "No, he is still a gutsy, intelligent man driven to prove himself the betrayed, not the betrayer."

"And you've done nothing to unravel the truth. Oh, Ricardo, does his friendship mean so little to you? Jon's betrayers went on with their lives and their promotions. They may have risen in the ranks—may be wearing a row of ribbons on their tunics."

"One of them does. He went back and fought in the Gulf War and later in Bosnia."

"Is the man who betrayed my brother here in Paris?"

"That's classified."

"Classified or not, arrest him."

"Nothing is ever that easy. He's under surveillance, but we want to arrest him on his home soil. Before we can do that, we have to know who he's working with. We're certain it is someone at Langley or the Pentagon. It may take months before we can identify his contact. Without evidence we have nothing."

She felt sick inside, unable to separate her father's betrayal from Jon's. Unable to comprehend why Ricardo had let his friend down. Other men bore their sins, tasted their dishonor, felt the sting of disgrace, the condemnation of their own countrymen. But why her brother? Why her father? They were good men. Honorable men.

Ricardo searched the crowd again. Adrienne followed his gaze. "Are we expecting someone?"

He glanced back at her. "I'm not certain he will come. But before he does, I need your forgiveness, Adrienne."

She felt her jaw sag. "You can't be serious?"

"I'm desperate. This whole thing has washed over me again. I feel responsible for you—because you are Jon's sister. Jon wants you to go home, but I have another suggestion. You could work with us, Adrienne."

The man had to be mad. "With the embassy? The *CIA?*" Shock rolled over her as the truth dawned. "You're trying to *recruit* me. The next thing you'll do is ask me to be friends with Jon's betrayer so you can capture him. Whoever he is—he left my brother on the sands of Kuwait to die."

His eyes told her she was right. "You may be the only one who can trap him. We need your help, Adrienne."

"I'm a woman. Not some snake charmer."

He inclined his head. "A beautiful woman."

Adrienne stood there, breathless. Angry. "Why have you brought me here, Ricardo? Is it a symbolic effort on your part? Are you asking me to pretend that Jon is dead and go on with my own life, as though I never had a brother?"

"Please. It would be best. For his safety—for yours—he must always be Jacques d'Hiver."

"I can't accept that."

"You must. There's too much at stake."

His face twisted as he nodded toward the curb where a taxi had pulled to a stop. Jon stepped from the cab and limped to the unknown soldier's tomb. She started to go to him, but Ricardo put a restraining hand on Adrienne's wrist. "I brought you here so you could say good-bye. Whatever you do, don't break his cover."

She let her eyes tell him what she thought of him, broke free, and crossed to stand beside Jon at the eternal flame.

Ricardo sat on the stone bench and watched her go—a lithe, graceful young woman slipping through the crowd to stand beside her brother. For seconds they stood without speaking, two strangers in the crowd looking down on a plot of hallowed ground that honored France's unknown soldier.

The very reasons that lured Jon to this place of solitude and solace kept Ricardo from coming. He avoided this place, and yet it was the starting point for parades and victory celebrations, for marching troops and cyclists from around the world. His wife liked the upscale shops and magnificent chestnut trees. He admired it as an architectural wonder. Jon's feelings for it went a step further. He had even memorized many of the French battles and warriors carved on its walls; he was haunted by the unknown warrior from World War I. It was understandable—Jon longed to be remembered. Perhaps that was why he came here so often to identify with the soldier who was honored by an eternal flame with the golden arc his canopy.

The soldier's tomb was squared off with a low chain surrounding it, and beyond that the roped off area forbidding onlookers from going further. Black-booted French military in traditional black berets and green scarves stood at one end of the tomb, their hands clasped behind their backs, their faces somber, their glances beyond eye contact. Two placid gendarmes in dark, gold-braided uniforms took up guard facing the eternal flame, swords to their shoulders instead of rifles, the tricolor of the French flag snapping in the breeze above them.

Adrienne and Jon stood in the crowd, their eyes focused on the tomb, their lips moving. They walked, paused, then moved again.

One moment they stood by the military guard, the next closer to the gendarmes. From there, Adrienne pointed to the brilliant red, orange, and yellow wreaths that honored the dead soldier.

Adrienne was indeed beautiful. Not at all like Naji, who was petite, brisk, swift in speech and manner. No, Miss Winters was elegant, charming. Naji's beauty was lost behind her efficiency and her determination to move her status as chief of station from temporary to permanent. And when she did—*if* she did—what would become of him?

He leaned against the stone wall and closed his eyes against the glare of the sun. Naji would be angry about this meeting between Adrienne Winters and her brother, but he was fighting for more than his wife's approval. The foolhardy daring of three young men twelve years ago had never gone away. Other men drowned their pain with liquor.

But nothing could quench Ricardo's turmoil except reconciliation with his wife—and with his past.

CHAPTER 25

When Adrienne stole a glance up at him, Jacques d'Hiver seemed lost in his own troubled world. Strands of raven hair fell over his left eyebrow. Graying sideburns gave substance to his thin cheeks. His eyes remained downcast, but she knew them to be black like her mother's—and angry as he stared down at the tomb. Beneath the immaculate summer shirt she saw a flutter. Perhaps his heart pounded as fiercely as her own.

Adrienne didn't care what name he was forced to live by if only he would admit who he really was. "Please say something."

"You're like a bulldog, hounding me. Why can't you just leave me in peace?"

Leave you in peace? You are a man tormented. But I'll play your game. "My brother used to say I was plucky."

"Gutsy."

She smiled. So he did remember the word game of their childhood. Was that as far as he would go? She had no other clue. No other confirmation from him.

His sigh was deep, as though it came from the very depths of his soul. "What do you want from me, Adrienne?"

"The truth."

"And apart from that?"

"Fly home with me. Pretend to be my mother's son. The likeness is keen. Perhaps she'll embrace you as her own."

"You're quite mad. Don't ask me to deceive her."

"You know what happened to me in the Rodin Gardens. It will be the same for Mother. She will call you Jon Aaron. She always calls you that... It would bring her such joy. She's been sick so long. Rolf would wire the money."

"Rolf." It didn't come across as a question, but more like a well-loved name rolling across his tongue.

"Rolf is still at Winterfest, seeing to Mother's every need, brushing aside her complaints. When I called him, he assured me Mother would want to see you again."

"My family is dead."

"Must you go on denying us?" She looked up at him again. "I still want you to go home with me. You see, Monsieur d'Hiver, when my brother went away all those years ago, he never said good-bye to Mother. Perhaps you could do that for him."

"And weave another tangled web of deception?"

"Only one thing would keep you from going home—your commitment to the CIA. But they betrayed you."

He eased around the unknown soldier's tomb, never glancing her way. She felt a broiling revulsion. "Why did you let them give you a new name? A new residence?"

"For security reasons."

"But they broke your spirit sending you back here."

He chanced a steadying look at her. "Coming back here was my choice. Please, I want you to go home, Adrienne."

"Without you? I'm just to forget the last few days—is that it?"

She strained to hear his answer. "As if I have forgotten the last twelve years."

Beneath his disquiet, she still saw her mother's son. "Am I to look Mother in the face, Jon, and pretend I never saw you? I couldn't bear that."

"And I won't risk her safety by going back. The men who killed Aleem are the same breed of men who hijacked an airliner and flew it into the Pentagon."

"Terrorists?"

He put a finger to her lips and guided her to a spot distant from others. "The café where Aleem worked was a front for such activity.

247

Some of the staff belong to al-Qaeda and are committed to a holy war. There are those even now looking for me, Adrienne—from both sides—but it will take a few hours before they realize I am not returning to the condo."

"We're in a public square with gendarmes all around."

His impatience was clear. "I'm anonymous in this crowd. No one would think to look for me by the unknown soldier's tomb."

"Ricardo Mendez did."

"Those were my instructions when he called on the cell phone. He was to bring you to me so I could convince you to leave Paris. Don't you understand? My life is in danger."

"You could hide out at Winterfest."

"And desert Brigette and my children?" He shaded his eyes and looked down the busy boulevard. "I want you to remember something, Adrienne. It all began here in the city of Paris. Everything fans out from Paris. Someone I respected and loved was betrayed in this city. I'm still looking for answers to clear his name."

Our father. His name had not passed between them. Jon's emotions were too vulnerable. Fragile. Guarded. Dare she tell him the truth now? Add shock upon shock. She swallowed. "You don't have to search any longer, Jon. Harry—Harry Winters died several years ago."

He froze. His eyes went watery.

He looked at her then, his tears still brimming. "I'm sorry. I'm so sorry, but someday I'll know what really happened in Paris." He leaned forward, both hands on his cane. "I have to go away, Adrienne—more than ever now, but I need your help. You have to trust me, but you have to trust me as Jacques d'Hiver."

"I can't be part of your conspiracy."

"I wouldn't ask you to do that."

"You're still determined to go on another covert mission? Won't that be dangerous on your artificial leg?"

He smiled. "I get around on it, Adrienne. I'm going to Kuwait. If I don't come back this time, it will be up to you to clear the family name. I can tell you this much—what happened in Kuwait goes back a long way."

"To my father's dismissal in Paris?"

"I think so."

"Then I'll go with you." Whatever name he was forced to use, she wasn't going to lose him again. "If you try to send me away, I'll expose this deception. This double life you're living. Even now, you won't admit to being my brother, but in my heart, I know. I'll go to Langley and demand that your place be ripped from the Book of Honor and your star torn from the Memorial Wall."

For the first time, laughter filled his dark eyes. "They won't like that."

"I don't like what they've done to you! I don't like the stranger you've become. *I know you are Jon.* Yet you insist you are Jacques d'Hiver. Jacques d'Hiver wouldn't know about our family... If Langley won't remove your place in the Book of Honor—I'll do it myself. I'll break that steel case right off the marble wall."

"Destroy government property?" A chuckle escaped his lips. "What a tigress you are. But don't go to Langley."

"Will the sacred walls cry out?"

"Yes." The muscles in his jaw tensed. "Someone in high position at Langley betrayed me. At least someone there may have given the order that sent me into years of obscurity."

She stared at him as the shadows in his eyes darkened. "You're saying that more than one man was involved—a conspiracy at the top level?"

"Yes."

"So you're telling me the truth at last. But why can't you admit that you are Jon?"

"I must not go that far. Please trust me." He turned, his tormented eyes on her. "Please, Adrienne, go home while it's safe for you to do so. I'd give anything for you to forget what happened here these last few days."

"Never."

His lips twitched. "I thought you would outgrow your stubbornness."

"I perfected it. You want Ricardo to put me on a plane for America. In exchange for what?" She cut off his reply with a lift of her hand. "Never mind. It doesn't matter. When I told him I wouldn't go, he offered me an alternative plan." She met Jon's gaze. "He wants to recruit me. So let me help you."

He closed his eyes. Forced them open again. "The truth is I need your help. But for everyone's safety, help me as Jacques d'Hiver. Find a way to talk Brigette and the children into going away with you."

"Back to Winterfest?"

"If something happens to me, yes. But right now we have to get her out of the condo without Ricardo or anyone else knowing. I don't want anyone to interrogate Brigette—"

"Even if she agreed to go with me, where would I take her?"

He leaned on his cane, a grimace of pain on his face. "Do you recall the friends who thought of me as a son?"

"Claudio and Dominique? Yes, of course."

"The Vernettis, yes. They would protect my family, Adrienne. Would you recognize them if you saw them again?"

"I think so. Claudio wore a tweed hat like an Englishman and a raincoat even when it wasn't cold. He always joked about being prepared for any storm."

"Do you remember his face?"

She nodded. "A kind face, with small brown eyes."

"Don't forget the bulbous nose and the stirrings of a mustache. He always went marketing with his wife so he could barter for better prices."

"Dominique made the best upside-down apple tarts."

"And raspberry ones." Jon's smile was warm. "The children will love them. Do you remember where the Vernettis live?"

She hesitated. "On the Left Bank, I think. Yes, I'm certain I can find their place."

"Adrienne, will you take my family to them? Keep looking at the tomb or the crowd. Anywhere but at me."

She blinked against the intensity of the sun. "But I don't know where you live."

"But you do. In a three-story pink building on the Right Bank of the river—quite near the Pont Neuf Bridge."

"Our old apartment!"

He nodded.

She remembered the homes of her childhood in expensive apartment complexes and summer homes in the country. Her father was endlessly trying to please his wife, picking social settings comparable to the diplomats of other countries. "Dad used to say Mother would force him to steal just to keep her happy—force him to break faith with himself just to support her."

"I know. And yet she loved that building near the river. I figured no one would expect me to move back to the familiar." He plucked a dying leaf from one of the memorial stands. "You were always good with numbers, Adrienne. It's a private cell phone. Brigette will expect me on the other end. As soon as she answers, tell her what you need."

As he gave the number, she sealed it in her memory. "I'll call her tomorrow."

"No. Right away."

She glanced toward Ricardo. "Rick will take me back to the hotel—that should give you the time you need."

"Good girl."

She wanted to grab him, to never let him go. "Jon...will I see you again?"

"I don't know. Someday perhaps. Will you be all right, Adrienne?"

"Of course."

"Will you forgive me for not going home?"

She swallowed the tears that threatened. "There's nothing to forgive." Because he *was* going home. She didn't know how or when, but she knew this much: Somehow, she was going to make it happen.

Jon was going to go home.

Colin strolled along the quayside, humming, "The Last Time I Saw Paris." His life had been less entangled then. In his boyhood he often ambled along the river, browsing at the book stalls that lined the street. Once he had tried his hand at painting, imagining himself more skilled than Jon Winters.

He increased his pace to a brisk stride, anxious to reach the d'Hiver condo before the police or the embassy found Brigette. With Aleem dead, d'Hiver would become more elusive than ever. Colin rehearsed his plan. He would tell the woman that Jacques had been injured in a fall. He'd persuade her that he was an old friend, that he would take her to him. Once he had Brigette and the children in his control, this Jacques d'Hiver—as he wished to be known—would stop at nothing to rescue them.

It would be a simple confrontation. He had blundered in Kuwait, certain that Jon would bleed to death. Yesterday he failed at the Musée des Egouts. He would not fail again. If Jon came back alone, Colin's nine-millimeter Beretta would take care of him. A shot between the eyes would be quick, complete. But if the woman and children returned first, he would force them to leave with him.

Without checking for a street number, he knew he had found the right complex. The place where the d'Hivers lived was a magnificent old building with a steep sloping slate roof and an unobstructed river view. The afternoon sun cast a pink glow over the limestone bricks, its plain facade was relieved by flower boxes filled with flaming red geraniums. He settled his gaze on the corner apartment on the second floor where ivy entwined itself around the wrought-iron balcony. A dove perched on the top railing outside the narrow shuttered window. How clever of Jon Winters to choose the very place where he had lived with his parents. He pictured Jon laughing in the face of authority, controlling some of his own fate.

Colin crossed the street and went up the steps to the entry. Should he risk announcing his arrival by ringing the buzzer? His problem was solved for him as a woman labored up the steps. He charmed her with a smile and relieved her of her heavy parcels. As she undid the latch, he slipped into the building behind her. Once she took her parcels back, he ran up the stairs two at a time.

No one answered his knock. He scowled at his watch. Of course…d'Hiver's mistress would spend time with her children in the nearby park. The breaking-and-entering part of his training was a long time ago, but he was still an expert. He swung the door back and stepped inside.

He remembered the apartment from the days when Mara Winters entertained. Back then there had been an indoor stairwell leading to the next floor, private quarters for Harry Winters, all funded by the State Department. He went up those steps just once. The image of the room was sealed in his memory: rows of library books, a massive vault, a corner set up as a sitting area where Harry entertained foreign dignitaries. Now there was not even a patch in the ceiling visible to the naked eye where the stairwell once stood.

He inspected the condo. Two bedrooms, the larger one with a simple brass bed and an eiderdown quilt. Wooden shelves in the dining room with its collection of Haviland plates. The old-fashioned kitchen was a Parisian classic. Back when Jon lived here as a boy, the kitchen didn't matter because Jon's mother spent little time in the kitchen. A maid did the cleaning; a cook prepared the meals.

Two bathrooms held deep enamel tubs on cast-iron claw feet and large matching basins. But something was missing. Where was the bedroom Harry Winters used as his downstairs study?

Colin took another quick survey. The study had been to his right—over there where a woven tapestry hung on the wall. No light filtered through the thick, woven threads. The tapestry could hide a door to Jon's art studio—a door that kept the children from his clay models. It could be a library filled with books on Rodin and Michelangelo, too classic to be touched by children. Or could it be where Jon worked unhindered on Arabic memoirs or a scandalous exposé on renegade intelligence officers?

He strode across the room and tugged the paneling.

"What are you doing in my home?"

At the frightened voice, Colin spun on his heels. No wonder

Jon had been smitten by this woman. She was easy to look at, even when she was frightened.

Her eyes were dark with alarm. "Please leave at once."

"I'm sorry." He inched closer. "The door was open—I'm a friend of your husband's. I was hoping to catch him."

"He is not here. And no, the door was not open."

A scrawny little boy peered around her side, "What does he want with Papa?"

An unexpected nostalgia hit him. The boy was younger than his own son. He had never been a good father, but his son was all he had left of Kris.

"What do you want?"

He smiled at Brigette. "Your husband and I are friends."

The ringing of a cell phone from deep within her purse broke off his explanation. He had to get her and the children to leave with him. If he grabbed the boy—or the girl cowering behind her—

Brigette snatched the cell phone from its dungeon. As she listened a frown troubled her brow. "Yes—I mean no, we're not alone. A man is here. He says he's a friend."

She backed into the hall, still gripping the phone. "I did ask him to leave...I don't know. He hasn't said. He's tall. Dark. No—no uniform."

Colin eased toward the door as her voice grew louder. "Yes, that would be splendid. Yes, you said your name is Adrienne. A sister. Jacques's sister? But where is Jacques? Is he all right?... Yes"—her glare pinned Colin—"send the police."

The police. Colin was about to make his move when she glanced to the side—and a relieved smile painted her lovely features.

"Oh, we'll be all right now. Father Matthias is coming down the hall."

The fool woman had outsmarted him. He shoved his face into hers and took pleasure in her fear. "Tell that sister I will come back." He crashed past her and ran.

Brigette crumbled against the wall, her children huddled around her as Father Matthias reached them.

Her fingers gripped the cell phone. "He's gone now, Adrienne," she sobbed. "No, I don't know who he was. He said he was a friend of Jacques's. Oh, tell Jacques I love him…it doesn't matter what he's done."

She caught her breath as the priest lifted the children into his arms. "Hurry, Brigette. Tell Jacques's sister we will meet her at the seminary. That man will be back. Hurry."

CHAPTER 26

The complex where Dominique and Claudio Vernettis lived was a four-story building checkered with red window awnings. Ivy stretched between the narrow balconies, putting a touch of color to a building that had aged with soot as gray as the slate roof.

With each step to the third floor, Jon's uncertainty grew, but once his hand gripped the familiar wrought-iron knocker, his confidence came back. Claudio Vernettis peered out, squinting into the darkened corridor. He glanced beyond Jon and seeing no one, cried, "Come in. Come in, Jon."

As Jon stepped across the threshold into the light, Dominique made the sign of the cross with trembling fingers. Finding her voice, she wept. "Have mercy on us. The priest told the truth. Our boy Jon has come home."

He slipped his arms around her. Sniffling, she tapped him on the chest. "Now *qu'est-ce que c'est* this nonsense about you being Jacques d'Hiver? My memory may be slipping—and Claudio's more than mine—but you are Jon Aaron Winters. I know *certainement*. And what's this that Brigette tells us about a wooden leg?"

"Silence, Domie," her husband ordered. "Tell the children their papa is here. Then cook up some *moules marinieres* or *noisettes d'Agneau* for Jon. Vite! Vite!"

Dominique tucked in her double chin. "At this late hour? Have you forgotten? We did not go to market today."

Jon grinned. "Anything, Domie. I've missed your good cooking—most of all those upside-down apple tarts."

Her eyes scolded. "Don't let your wife hear that."

My wife. My wife. He must tell Domie the truth, but young Claudio was flying across the hardwood floor, his sister coming a step behind him. Jon opened his arms and engulfed them. "You are safe, *mes petits.*"

"*Bien sûr.*" Brigette sounded calm as she came into the room. "Father Matthias and your sister brought us here."

"We took several taxis," Claudio announced.

Colette shook her head at her younger brother. "Father Matthias said we were escaping from the people who were following us. We went *fast,* Papa!"

"It was just a game, children." But the stark fear in Brigette's eyes denied her words. "Father Matthias likes to tease. But your son is right. We went much too fast." She halted across the room. "Jacques, why did you never tell me about your sister, Adrienne? She is charming. And why did she rush back to the hotel?"

The old man hushed Brigette. "First we eat, my child, then we ask our questions. Go, make up a room for Jon."

Domie slammed a cook pot on top of the stove. "Look at him. Jon is still a young man." She gave her husband a withering glance. "Separate beds are for old folks like us. Brigette's room is made up. That will do... How long can you stay, Jon?"

"I have to leave as soon as we eat."

"Jacques, won't you be with us even for tonight?"

In the room light, Brigette looked more beautiful than ever. Longing welled within him. "It would be dangerous for you if I stayed."

"It would be meaningless for me without you."

"For tonight then." He limped to her side and kissed the top of her head. "But tomorrow—"

"I know. We will talk about Kuwait later—when the children are asleep. Adrienne explained everything."

She looked calm, as though unraveling his past comforted her. When they were alone, he would speak of his mission to Kuwait. But had Adrienne discussed Aleem's murder and its link to a terrorist cell? No, she would not alarm the children.

His son slipped his hand in Jon's. "Papa, we left the house so fast, I didn't get my trucks."

"It's all right," Colette informed him. "Tante Adrienne promised to buy us some toys. A doll for me."

The older Claudio swiped at his bulbous nose. "She will have to mail them to our home in the country."

"Then you are going there, Claudio?"

"Yes, not even our neighbors know our address there. The children will be safe, with plenty of space to play."

The wise old sage. He had guessed that Jon's mission could take time, perhaps knew that Jon might never come back.

"We will talk in the morning, Jon."

Claudio's wife shot him a warm smile. "My Claudio gets up so he can sleep in the chair right after breakfast. But I still like having him around."

Jon tried to remember how old they were and lost count. "I'll leave right after breakfast."

The old man nodded. "And after that or the day after tomorrow, I will drive the children to the country."

"I'll do the driving, Claudio." For the first time in all the time Jon had known them, Claudio did not argue.

Early the next morning Jon said good-bye to Brigette. Her cheek was nestled against the pillow when he leaned down to kiss her, but he knew she was awake, close to tears.

"We can't outstay our welcome here, Jacques."

Alarm struck him. They *had* to stay where they were safe. "You are not happy with my friends?"

"They are good to us—Domie most dear with the children—but we must go home soon."

"Wait until I come back."

"What about our clothes and my Haviland plates?"

"There are those who will be watching the condo. They are

looking for me." He saw her lip tremble and patted her shoulder. "You will be safe with Claudio and Domie. I left money with Claudio for more clothes. And later I will buy you another set of dishes if we cannot go home again. Promise me you will do what Claudio says."

"If I must," she whispered. "Be careful. Come back."

"I will. I have someone to come home to."

"Adrienne wants you to go home with her."

His lips moved close to her ear. "And leave you here in Paris? I love you too much for that. If I go, *you* go. Now, sleep, *ma chère*. It's a long drive to the country." He took a final glance down at her. *If I come back, I will ask Father Matthias to marry us.*

He left her with her face turned from him and made his way to the kitchen. As he sat down beside Claudio, Domie poured cups of steaming black coffee for them. Jon forked his baked eggs. "I don't know how to thank you."

"Thank us?" Claudio shot back. "Since Brigette and the children arrived, Domie has not slept for worrying about them. Now you must go away again and worry her more."

Domie slapped a hot roll on his plate. "Old women don't sleep well."

He ignored her. "Jon, your father wrote to tell us that you were lost in Kuwait."

Domie met Jon's gaze. "Claudio was never the same after that. Nor was I. Our home has always been yours, Jon. We could have died waiting for you to come back."

Claudio gulped the black coffee before blurting, "We never thought of you as a selfish man, Jon, yet you shut us out of your life all these years."

He ached at the sorrow in his friend's eyes. "I couldn't risk your safety."

"Not even to tell your parents you were alive…not even to tell us you named your son for me?"

"I was too ashamed."

"Ashamed?" He shook his head. "Of what? Your betrayal in

Kuwait? Yes, your sister told us as much as she knew."

"It is bigger than my betrayal."

"Your father's betrayal, then? Domie and I are afraid for you if you go away again. What if you never come back? Kuwait sits on the border with Iraq—on the border to trouble."

Jon placed his hand over the old man's trembling one. "I must go. The trip to Kuwait has something to do with a terrorist cell here in Paris." He pushed his cup toward Domie for another refill. "Some months back a young American marine was killed in Kuwait. An Italian oil tanker damaged. An American diplomat gunned down. Missionaries in Yemen murdered. The other day a waiter here in Paris lost his life. Intelligence data indicates a link with Hamad, a Kuwaiti friend of mine."

"And you believe it is your duty to find this Hamad? Was he not that university student that Domie didn't like?"

"Yes. He was my contact in Kuwait before the Iraqi invasion. I recruited him for the resistance movement against the Iraqis, but the rest of my team didn't trust him. Hamad was attending one of the mosques rumored to be a haven for young radicals. Hamad came from a wealthy family, distant relatives of the ruling sheik. He seemed a loyal Kuwaiti in the daytime, but one of the men who went into Kuwait with me called Hamad an Islamic rogue by night. Yet we remained friends."

"You were always loyal to your friends."

"Yet one betrayed me. With the Iraqi invasion, the terrorist cell lost some of its impetus. But my reports on my findings never reached the proper channels in Washington. Someone stopped them."

"So your interest in the Middle East did get you into trouble. We feared as much, Domie and I. Domie thought Hamad was radical in his political leanings even when we met him here in Paris."

"No, he was a good man. Trustworthy. I swear it."

The old man shrugged. "There were those back in our French resistance, before the Normandy invasion, who were traitors. Good, honest men, in my thinking. Some of them were accused of collaboration and hung without ever clearing their names. Others betrayed us. The war on terrorism goes on. There is no end, not with evil. Do what you must, Jon. I have no choice but to let you go. Only tell us how we can help you."

"Take care of my family."

Claudio's rough fingers tightened around Jon's wrist. "You know we would want them to stay on with us, but we will be gone before the children are grown."

"If that time comes, send Brigette and the children to Winterfest Estates. Adrienne would want that."

Claudio nodded. "What else can we do for you?"

Jon felt a sudden tightness in his throat. "Pray. That's what my father would do."

On Tuesday, the CIA station chief arrived in the hotel as the secretary and his entourage gathered in the lobby for their transport to Orly International. The secretary's staff blocked the station chief's approach; and even when they recognized her, demanded to see her identification. The personal slight offended Naji Fleming, but she had only seconds to talk with the secretary.

The secretary stood out in the crowd, a striking presence, his military bearing still evident. His features were big and broad—the "consummate nice guy," according to an outdated *Newsweek* on her desk. In the closed meetings at the embassy, he'd been forceful, determined; in the meetings with the ministry of interior, smooth and diplomatic, an indomitable statesman.

She smiled as their eyes locked. "Mr. Secretary, I was afraid I would miss you."

"We've been delayed, Miss Fleming. One of our party is missing. My aide has sent someone up to his room to hurry him along. Otherwise, we must go without him."

"Colonel Taylor isn't coming. He requested a TDY."

"Temporary duty, here in Paris? That request should go through me." He stepped to the outside of the circle, his hand firm on her elbow. "You are aware of protocol? I prefer my team return to Washington with me."

"He plans to catch another military flight back later. He said he was a last-minute replacement on your team."

"An efficient one."

"But we believe he came to Paris with his own agenda. I was left with a split-second decision when he requested temporary duty at the embassy... You see, he has been under surveillance since he reached Paris."

His locked gaze remained on her. "Did your orders come from Washington?"

She shook her head. "There's not much higher to go than you, Mr. Secretary. But if we're right, the colonel is not working alone, so I couldn't risk clearing the request with the Pentagon or the White House."

"There was no diplomatic pouch? No secure lines available?"

"We believe he plans to fly into Kuwait. If he is who we think he is, he may try to contact the al-Qaeda operations coordinator there on the direct orders of someone in Washington."

The secretary beckoned for his aide. They spoke in undertones, then he turned back to Naji. "The location of the terrorist Mohammed, the coordinator in question, is still unknown. Nor is there any recent word on Ghaith."

"I have two intelligence reports on my desk that indicate sightings of Mohammed back in Kuwait. That's unlikely, Mr. Secretary, but those Mohammed trained may still be in Kuwait." She knew she was risking immediate dismissal as station chief, but she had to go on. "At our sessions at the embassy, we discussed the mole. For those of us on the inside, he's now known as the Impostor."

"I've been apprised of that. And you're trying to tell me you've found him?"

"The colonel may not be the mole, but he's involved somehow. Send him back to Washington now, and whatever leads we have will be lost. We may lose him forever."

The secretary glanced at his watch, impressing her with the time.

"Sir, before the Gulf War, the CIA put an unauthorized surveillance team in Kuwait. Any one of those three men might be able to identify Mohammed or those he trained."

The aide nodded his confirmation. "Winters was on that surveillance team, the operative believed dead for some time."

"He's been living here in Paris under an assumed name, still working for the government. He maintains that he was betrayed in Kuwait by one of the men who went in with him—not by a member of the resistance movement. The colonel was one of two men who entered that country with him."

"Who was the other man, Miss Fleming?"

"My husband."

CHAPTER 27

As she crossed the elegant nineteenth-century lobby, Adrienne ducked behind a marble column. Maddie looked at her as though she'd lost her mind.

"What is wrong with you, Adrienne?"

"Robbie is outside the hotel."

Maddie surveyed the situation. "All I see is the uniformed bellman standing under the awning."

"Look beyond him. That's Robbie, in the chauffeur's hat in front of that car rental. What should I do?"

"With a nice young chap like that? Just go out there and get in the car with him."

"I can't. He's a journalist. He'll ask questions."

"Dear girl, I can tell you one question *I'd* like to hear, and I wouldn't tell him no."

Adrienne felt a sharp prick of envy. But hadn't she turned Robbie down for years? "Maddie, I don't want him to find out where Jon's children are."

"Why? Where are they?"

"With family friends."

"And I'm not to know the address? I'm to go shopping for toys, but I'm not to know what's going on. Your brother is real trouble. Just wash your hands clean of him."

She shook her head. "Jon and his family need me."

"So does that handsome man out there in a chauffeur's cap. I think the poor chap is in love with you."

"That's the problem."

"Well, luv, I would like such a problem. He was such a charmer at breakfast."

"He was trying to impress you."

Maddie's smile was slow. "And so he did. Doesn't he mean anything at all to you?"

Adrienne hesitated, then forced the words out. "We're just friends."

"Then why don't you cut your friend loose?" Maddie looked toward Robbie again, her expression pensive. "He's flown all the way across the pond to be with you. He's here to help you find your brother. If you know where your brother and the children are, you need to tell your Mr. Gilbert."

Adrienne would have stomped her foot as she did as a child. But now as an adult? No, she was afraid it would draw attention to her. "He's not *my* Mr. Gilbert."

"He'd like to be. I will go shopping alone—you just go settle things with Robbie." She ripped off a page from a magazine and shoved it in Adrienne's hand. "In case we lose touch, write down the address of your family friends."

The concierge stood at his desk, nodding in their direction. Maddie snatched the address and key card from Adrienne. "Go. Or you will have to face that gentleman from the embassy. Thanks to the concierge he's heading our way."

Adrienne groaned. "Not Ricardo Mendez?"

"Yes, I'll head him off. Maybe he'll treat me to tea."

"The lobby bar isn't open yet."

"I'll think of something."

Maddie met Ricardo Mendez in the middle of the lobby. "I'm sorry, but Miss Winters had a pressing engagement with that young man in the chauffeur's cap."

Ricardo's jaw twitched. "Who is he?"

"An American journalist. A friend of Jon Winters."

"A friend in search of a story?"

She gave him a pointed look. "No, Mr. Mendez, a friend who is looking for the truth. Over breakfast, he seemed well informed. Now, how may I help you? Or perhaps you would go shopping with me?"

He glowered. "My wife does the shopping."

"But you are acquainted with the stores in Paris. I'm looking for toys for a little girl and her brother."

His gaze sharpened. "You have a family in London?"

"No. Adrienne asked me to buy them for her."

He lowered his voice. "If we are talking about Jacques d'Hiver's children, we want to know where they are."

"I just buy the toys, I don't deliver them."

She turned to walk away, and he grabbed her arm. "How much do you know, Miss—Miss Maddie, wasn't it?"

Maddie pushed his hand aside. "Maddie Travers. My mother told me a thimble full of knowledge is a dangerous thing. But I think you know I met Adrienne's brother."

"You mean Mr. d'Hiver?"

"Call him what you want. Adrienne is convinced he is her brother, Jon. I'm staying on in Paris until she can figure out how to rescue him from the mess he's in."

She saw by the fire in his eyes that he was weary of her banter. "Don't make light of something dead serious."

Her humor chipped away. "Are you referring to the waiter from the Café le Grand Royale? Adrienne had nothing to do with that...nor did I, before you ask."

"The man you call her brother may have."

She blinked against the horror.

"Jacques d'Hiver is missing, Miss Travers. He disappeared right after Aleem's death."

Maddie leaned against the marble column. "You are not saying— you don't think...then I must stop Adrienne."

"Her car just drove off."

Maddie gripped her hands together. "If something has happened to Mr. d'Hiver, then Adrienne may be in danger as well."

"You are both at risk. To protect Miss Winters, we must move her from this hotel. The chauffeur, as you called him, has already checked out of the Intercontinental. He will take Miss Winters to the new place later today."

"To the Bristol or the Balzac? Or the de Crillon?"

"It won't be so glamorous—and nothing like this"—he cast a sweeping glance around the lobby—"but it will be safe until she leaves the country. I have someone from the embassy coming over to pack her luggage and cancel her reservation here."

"She won't like that. And I won't like not knowing where she is." Maddie considered the man facing her. She didn't know what he was up to, but she'd play his game. For now. "Perhaps I can save you time. I have the key to Miss Winters's room. I can pack Adrienne's things—and mine. And when your embassy staff comes, tell them to plan on picking me up as well."

"Then take her luggage to your room and wait there, Miss Travers. I'll check her out right now. The concierge is always quite cooperative with the embassy."

Maddie wrapped her fingers around the address that Adrienne had given her. Without another word, she walked toward the lift. She'd pack Adrienne's' luggage as Mr. Mendez had instructed—but she would not wait for the embassy personnel to pick it up.

The uniformed bellman held the door of the Intercontinental open as a lovely young woman swept past him. She ran the last few steps to the young man waiting at the curb. His suit jacket was oversized, his wild tie distasteful, out of character. The chauffeur's cap rested on top of his sunshades. As the girl reached him, he grinned and pointed to the open door on the passenger's side.

The bellman grimaced. These foreigners were so unpredictable. There he was tipping his hat and swooping low to greet her. A boyish grin spread over his face as he ushered her into the passenger's seat.

Why not just come courting in the proper manner? The bellman shrugged and waved them off. There was no tip for him, but he took pleasure in seeing the happiness on the chauffeur's face and the teasing glance that the girl gave him as they drove away.

He looked again, puzzled. Another car was pulling away from the curb, and he had the uneasy feeling that the driver was following the young couple. He felt it his duty to report his suspicions to the concierge, but before he could do so, a taxi full of guests pulled up. He stepped forward, smiling. "Welcome to the Intercontinental."

Maddie couldn't believe how arrogant Ricardo Mendez was. American embassy or not, she didn't like him.

The crushed address in her hand might lead to Jacques d'Hiver. She stowed it in her bosom and flattened her blouse against her breast. In spite of her outward appearance of calm, Mendez made her feel vulnerable—taking her back to a painful childhood in a household of brothers.

It wasn't that she didn't like men. She did. Adrienne was foolish to let one as charming as Robbie Gilbert slip away. Certain chaps had changed Maddie's own life, given her confidence. Andrew for one; they loved going to the steeplechase races, yet it was casual Andrew who had handed her a fashion magazine and convinced her she could be anything she wanted to be. With Andrew's prodding and a new hairstyle and contact lenses, she was transformed.

Maddie took another step, her thoughts on Basil, the handsome chap who made her feel special over candlelit dinners. She reached the top step thinking about Archibald Finhold, her latest ongoing relationship. Archibald, ten years her senior, had a place at Cambridge, but he also had a place in his heart and life for Maddie. He didn't mind that she was tall and enjoyed flattering her for her stylish world, her easy manner, her pretty face. There were times when she thought Archibald was about to propose, but in typical absent-minded fashion, his conversation would drift to his latest scientific interests.

If only he could win the Nobel Prize, then maybe he'd center his thoughts on her. She was not opposed to marriage. If Archibald ever got around to asking her, she'd gladly give marriage a go.

On reaching the landing, she made her way down the corridor toward Adrienne's room. She considered Americans frivolous, so friendship with Adrienne had been unexpected. It was not the other woman's beauty and warmth that swayed Maddie's opinion, but her plucky spirit. Adrienne would throw aside everything to help Jacques d'Hiver.

But Maddie was fairly certain Adrienne was walking into a danger zone, and she had no intention of letting her American friend stumble alone. *In for a penny. In for a pound.* She was going to stand with Adrienne until she saw her on board a plane at de Gaulle, heading home.

Putting Adrienne's key card in the lock, she opened the door and stepped inside the luxurious suite. The door clicked shut behind her. She had just seconds to catch sight of the dresser drawers balanced on their hinges and Adrienne's clothes strewn about the room before she realized she was not alone. Two men with olive skin and dark, angry eyes stared back at her.

She recognized Cavell, the maître d' with the brush mustache from the Café le Grand Royale. The other was a stranger with a razor sharp gaze and a pistol in his hand.

Cavell spoke first. "Where is Jacques d'Hiver?"

Maddie shrugged, hoping to buy time—but to no avail. Searing pain raged though her as a bullet tore into her chest.

She spun.

Drifted.

Collapsed.

As their Arabic words trailed to a faraway murmur, she heard Cavell say, "You fool, Gresham, you shot the wrong woman."

And in a voice that rumbled in her own ears, she cried, *"In for a penny. In for a pound."*

The ambulance sped away from the hotel. As the wail of the siren faded, a frantic concierge picked up the phone and dialed the American embassy.

On the Avenue Gabriel, Naji Fleming jotted down the hospital address and glared across her desk at her husband. "I *told* you to get Adrienne Winters out of the hotel—and now, with your negligence, Ricardo, someone shot Miss Winters in her hotel suite."

He glared back. "Impossible. She left the Intercontinental before I did. The woman in her suite must have been that friend of hers. She was there on my orders."

"Explain," his wife snapped.

He adjusted his tie. "The injured woman must be Maddie Travers, a British subject. How badly injured is she?"

"The concierge said she was a bloody mess when they carried her out. So get back to the Intercontinental, Ricardo, and find out anything you can about her before the place swarms with gendarmes. Then get over to the hospital before we have an international scene on our hands."

He snatched the hospital address from her. "Naji, I'm going to stick with you until we settle this problem with Jon Winters and his sister. But after that, I'm calling it quits." He sliced his hand beneath his chin. "I'm up to my neck with what has happened between us. I'm going to Burgundy, with or without you."

In the emergency room, the nurse stripped Maddie's blood-drenched clothes from her body.

"She won't be wearing these again." She dropped them in a patient's garment bag.

As the doctor worked over the unconscious form, he said, "She won't be wearing anything if we don't get this bleeding stopped. The bullet nicked a main vessel... Has the family been notified?"

"She came in without identification, Doctor. There's this sheet of paper with an address scribbled on it, but it's so bloody I can't read it... Would you like me to call for a chaplain?"

He dropped a saturated gauze on the tray. "What about that priest who helped us before?"

"Father Matthias? The patient may not be Catholic."

He glowered. "At this point, it may not matter."

They were hanging another unit of blood and waiting on a thoracic surgeon when Father Matthias and Ricardo Mendez rushed into the emergency room together.

"Did they call you too, Mendez?" The priest looked surprised. "Then the patient must be an American."

"No, Maddie Travers is British. We've already checked the contents of her purse and luggage. That's what took me so long. Keys, purse, notes from the fashion show, but we didn't find any next of kin to notify—just a business card on Archibald Finhold, Cambridge University." Mendez tossed her purse to the priest. "See what you can find."

Father Matthias was still searching the handbag with its Italian label when they reached the gurney behind the drawn curtains. He was shocked at the pale appearance of the unconscious woman lying there, but he was not unnerved. It was a familiar scene. The beeping of a monitor echoed in the cubicle, its erratic pattern racing across the screen. Oxygen hissed. Fluids flowed into both arms. Mendez turned chalky and gripped the handrail.

The priest lifted Maddie's limp hand, then leaned down and whispered in her ear, "I'm Father Matthias. I'm here to pray for you. You're going to be all right."

Mendez shook his head. "You're all the same, you doctors and priests. Promising the moon when the girl might not make it out of surgery."

"She'll make it." Father Matthias held up a letter. "It looks like she has someone waiting for her in England. This Archibald Finhold is more than a Cambridge professor."

"Then we'd better notify him."

The priest reached down to the foot of the bed and lifted the chart. "Gunshot wound! Mr. Mendez, when they called me, they said an accident case. Was this a robbery?"

"No, a mistaken identity. She was in the wrong room at the wrong time."

As they drove out of Paris, Adrienne smiled at Robbie. "Where are we going?"

"To the gardens at Giverny."

"Jon loved it there."

He laughed. "So did Monet. We know he painted some of his best work there. You looked so worn out that I wanted to get you out of town. In spite of the crowds, Monet's gardens are meant to inspire. Besides, we need time to talk—just the two of us."

For three hours they wandered through the scented gardens, hand in hand. For the first time in days she felt a sense of peace, walking among the crimson poppies and the lavender wisteria that rose above the pond and wrapped itself over the Japanese foot-bridge. Magnificent roses reflected in the pond, among the floating water lilies.

Robbie didn't hurry her as she told about discovering Jon at the Rodin Museum. Nor did he seem to doubt her conviction that it was Jon. As she expressed her fears, he linked his fingers with hers. "Adry, after pouring over the declassified material in Washington, I believe anything is possible. Even Jon's survival."

Around them, clumps of yellow flowers poked their heads above the earth. White daisies and the last of the tulips tumbled across the footpaths. They were caught between two seasons—the end of the profusion of spring flowers and the blossoming of summer. The hollyhocks and wild yarrow of the first days of summer were already budding. Everywhere they looked, deep green foliage hovered above the gardens and shaded them as they strolled.

When she ran out of steam, he told her that he'd read Jon's last letters to her father. He mentioned her father's journal and told her that Rolf had shown him several pictures of Jon and Colin together.

"And why not? They grew up together."

"You're right, but I don't think Rolf likes Colin."

"That's not fair, Robb."

"Where Colin is concerned, I'm not fair." His smoky blue eyes clouded. "Did you know that your brother went into Kuwait on a three-man mission?"

"How would you know that, Robbie?"

"Those same declassified materials. The dusty archives are rough on my sinuses, but very revealing. Jon was the only one left behind in Kuwait. One of those men is working at the embassy here in Paris as a diplomatic attaché."

"Ricardo Mendez? He's CIA. I met him." She wanted to ask about the third person, but her skin prickled. "We'd better get back to the Intercontinental. Maddie will be worried about me."

"We're not going back there. Mendez told me to take you to another hotel for your safety. He plans to have someone pack up your things and check you out in our absence."

She bristled. "I don't want some stranger packing my clothes. I'm not going."

They walked a few more yards along the pebbled path toward Monet's pink stucco house, past the calico cat. "I don't trust Mendez, Robbie, and neither does Jon. I think Mendez is trying to keep me from Jon."

"Or trying to get you to lead them to his family."

"You're frightened for me?"

"I'm frightened for both of us. We've been under surveillance since we left the hotel. I fear for you. I wish I could shield you from the truth."

"Does it have something to do with Mother and home?"

"Yes, but I must talk with Jon first. Are you okay with not doing what the embassy wants?"

She arched her brows. "I'm already in their disfavor. They want me out of Paris."

"We could head to the top of the Eiffel Tower, but overnight accommodations are lousy. Any better ideas?"

They were silent for several minutes. "Robbie, do you remember Claudio Vernettis and his wife—the couple Jon stayed with? Jon's family is there now. We could go there, but I won't have any clothes except what I'm wearing."

He grinned. "I have an extra pair of running togs. You'll swim in them, but they'll do until we can buy something for you to wear... Will Jon be there?"

"I don't think so. Oh, Robbie"—she turned to him—"Jon is so lost. So unlike the Jon we used to know. We have to help him."

Robbie's hands were gentle on hers. "I agree. So where do we find him?"

She hesitated. "He's returning to Kuwait. If he goes, I'm following him."

"Well, I'll get my editor's okay to go too. I'll tell him I'm onto a big story. Now if we're going to the Vernettis', we can't take the same car we came here in. Whoever followed us may still be out in the parking lot, waiting by our car. Do you see that group of people over there? We're going back into Paris in their tour bus as soon as they're ready to leave."

"But the car rental?"

"I'll call them and have it picked up."

"They won't like that."

"They will if they want their car back."

He pulled her down to rest on a bench near an arched trellis entwined with pink and white roses. He caught a strand of her hair and tucked it behind her ear.

"Adry, I must talk with Jon before he flies into Kuwait. I haven't wanted to worry you, but I'm certain I know what happened in Paris, when your father was sent home. Friends betrayed him. I can't say any more until I talk with Jon. You see, the same so-called friends—at least the same family—may have betrayed Jon in Kuwait."

Her heart pounded. "Then it's not safe for him to go into Kuwait again."

"When did Jon ever consider safety first when he was on a mission? I know we can help him, but we have to convince him that we fly in together."

"He'll never go for that."

"We have to try."

As he sat there, he loosened his tie, stowed it inside the chauffeur's cap along with the dark sunshades, then leaned back and hid them behind a bush. Removing the suit jacket, he rolled up his shirt sleeves. Now he looked like the Robbie she knew, his blue eyes studying her. Eyes that were so much a part of her life…of her heart.

Realization came. Robbie meant a great deal to her. More than she'd ever admitted.

With a shy smile, she said, "Robbie, you haven't asked me to marry you since you arrived in Paris."

His grin faded. "I'm not going to ask you, Adry."

She searched that well-loved face and felt her heart constrict. She was losing him. He looked as he always had—handsome, his auburn hair impossible to tame. His smoky blue eyes steady and glowing—but not for her. "Is—is there someone else?"

There was tenderness in his expression. "No, but on the flight over I had time to size up my life. I couldn't sleep, so God and I had a little chat."

"About me?"

"About us. About my priorities." He extended his hands, palms up. "I almost called you during my flight to tell you I was coming. But I knew six miles up there above the telephone wires that you were a treasure I'd clung to far too long. You see, I always thought you'd break down and marry me."

She blinked back tears. "Ask me again. Maybe I will."

"Not this time, Adrienne. You see I told God it was okay—I'd let you go. I settled it before we even came in for the landing at de Gaulle."

"What if I don't want you to let go?"

He reached over and squeezed her hand. "I still love you. I guess you will always be part of me. But right now, I want nothing more than for Christ to be King of my life."

She managed a smile. "Has there ever been a question about that? The first time I met you, you were toting a Bible in your knapsack."

"You know where I stand, Adry. At least where I thought I stood. God first. Everything else after that. But these last few months, I mixed my priorities because I wanted you to be my wife. I couldn't admit to myself that God wasn't number one with you either."

Adrienne stared straight ahead. She was losing him, and it was all her own doing. "You sound like Dad, Robb."

"Your dad was a great influence in my life. I miss that camaraderie. I miss his wisdom. He was a good man, Adrienne. If ever anyone put God first, it was your dad. And if anyone ever kept on loving his wife, it was your dad. He stood tall in a tough battle and died without favor in Washington, but there's not an acquaintance of his there who could ever deny Harry Winters's faith."

He turned to break off a rose and a clump of blue forget-me-nots from the bush behind them and pressed them into her hands. "You will always be special to me—I think you know that."

Her tears spilled on the rose petals and washed over the forget-me-nots. "Robbie, I don't think you are supposed to steal flowers from Monet's garden."

He wiped the tears from her cheeks with his thumbs. "You weren't supposed to steal my heart, but you did."

She wasn't certain her voice could squeeze past the lump in her throat. "Can—can we still be friends, Robbie?"

He held her against him, her face buried in the crook of his neck. "Adry, I'll always be here for you. But you don't have to worry about me proposing every time I see you. I've settled that one."

"I don't know what to say."

He tousled her hair. "You don't have to say anything."

CHAPTER 28

Sunday evening, Adrienne left the Vernettis' apartment without telling anyone she was going to the evening organ recital at Notre Dame—the place where her father found peace in the midst of his turmoil. With Colin or Ricardo Mendez somewhere on the streets of Paris hunting for her, her friends would only worry about her safety. But no one would think to find her at the cathedral—except, perhaps, Father Matthias.

She approached majestic Notre Dame at an angle, which gave her a somewhat distorted impression of the structure. The two towers with their high windows appeared as one. She wound around to the main square where the towers became two, and a growing crowd ambled toward the entry portals. Just inside the cathedral, her spirits soared with the immensity of the sanctuary, its timeless beauty, its quiet. Once, so long ago, her father told her that in the hush of this sanctuary, eternity made its presence known.

She went on feathered feet up the center aisle. Past a forest of flickering candles. Praying people. Majestic statues. In one chapel off to the right she glimpsed a priest offering the sacrament of reconciliation to a visitor. She wondered what music would be played this evening: Brahms, Mozart, Beethoven. She enjoyed them all. But as she made her way down the aisle, the guest organist pulled out all the stops, filling the old pipes and the room with the haunting, lilting theme of "Going Home" from Antonín Dvořák's *New World Symphony*. The sounds transported her.

"Going home, going home, Lord, I'm going home..."

She was grateful for the apprentice butcher who found his way into hearts through the music he had composed so long ago. Grateful that his words were as alive for her today as when he'd penned them all those years ago.

Going home.

Longing filled her as she made her way to the South Rose Window, where she and her father had sat together.

She searched her own heart in her quest to find God's. There was no doubt, she was His from childhood. Standing there, surrounded by memories of her dad, she closed her eyes and waited for the healing to be complete. She did not pray aloud, so unaccustomed was she to hearing herself speak in such a way. But she whispered in her heart, *Lord, I've come to make peace with You—not because of Robbie, but because my decision is long overdue. I want to know Your forgiveness and love once again.*

She could still hear Antonín Dvořák's music in the background. Like the prodigal, she'd come home. Peace engulfed her. The last rays of a sunset filtered through the stained-glass window, bringing ribbons of light into her heart and soul.

In Paris the following day, Colin settled his account at the front desk, changed into civilian clothes, stored one suitcase with the concierge, and made his way out the servants' exit. He cut through the park and hailed a taxi on the boulevard.

"Where to, sir?"

"Charles de Gaulle International."

With those words and the squeal of the taxi's tires, the Impostor began his journey back to Kuwait.

Father Matthias smiled across the desk at Naji Fleming. He considered her an attractive woman, cagey, patriotic. They puzzled each other with their strange commitments to Langley. She guarded her feelings about faith; he committed himself to it. She held objections to a French citizen, particularly a man of the cloth, working with them. Once he took a parish, his work in Paris would end. For now, any strike he made against terrorism was a personal triumph—an acknowledgment that his brother had not died in vain.

"The Café le Grand Royale was cordoned off."

"That's the gendarme's doing, Father Matthias."

"So thanks to the police, Jacques d'Hiver's long months of surveillance have been wasted."

"Not everything is lost. We are on high alert. But the men who used the café as a front will not slip away without targeting Americans. The French, too, of course."

"And you can't arrest them?"

"The gendarmes have their own way of doing things. So what do you have for me this morning, Father Matthias?"

"I spent late last evening with Archibald Finhold."

"And I'm supposed to know him?"

"He flew to Paris to accompany Maddie Travers's body home."

"She's dead?"

"No, but in a drug-induced coma. I rather imagine the order to put her in that state came from your office. That way she could not be questioned before she left."

"I believe *interrogated* is the proper word."

He liked bantering with her. "As you requested, I accompanied Miss Winters and the American journalist to the airport. Mr. Finhold asked that Adrienne be told nothing except that Maddie was ill and flying home. He even suggested that Miss Winters would want to attend their wedding."

"She's that much better?"

"I told you—a drug-induced coma, but Finhold prefers the bright outlook. He's a don at Cambridge. Brilliant scientist. He said it took almost losing Maddie to realize how important she is to him."

"Forget Maddie Travers. Did Jon Winters catch the flight to Kuwait?"

"Yes. We spoke for some minutes. Before you ask, Miss Fleming, I cannot and will not disclose the whereabouts of Jon's family. Based, of course, on the sanctity of the confessional."

"Of course."

"As far as I know, Colonel Taylor did not see me. They all boarded the same plane—the colonel escorted on board at the last minute. He does have his contacts."

"Now everything depends on Jon Winters?"

The priest nodded. "And, perhaps, his sister."

He tapped his fingers. "I'm curious. Periodically the U.S. urges American civilians to leave Kuwait, unless absolutely needed there. With travel and safety conditions still far from perfect, Americans are flying into Kuwait with no questions asked."

"Really?"

"Why do I feel so convinced that you arranged passports and visas for all of them? Maybe even a new legend for Jacques d'Hiver? You're risking their lives, Miss Fleming. For what?"

She was like a snapping turtle, the way her neck jerked and her eyes narrowed. "Sometimes we have to consider the ultimate good of all concerned."

"*Your* ultimate good? Does success guarantee your position here in Paris?"

Her lips tightened, but he saw regret in her eyes. "Padre, I'll take care of their entry permits; you take care of praying for them."

Sheridan Macaroy sat behind a massive, government-issued desk filled with his personal belongings. For days he'd been putting papers through the shredder; others he stuffed into his briefcase each night when he left Langley. Weeks ago—after he was bypassed for yet another promotion—he opted for early retirement. He would move to the Cayman Islands under an assumed name and enjoy spending the funds hoarded there.

Since 9/11, he had transferred vast holdings into an unnumbered account in Grand Cayman. His son would be repulsed at the thought of tainted money, but Sheridan had a second major Swiss account in his son's name. No matter what happened in the days ahead as the search for the Washington mole came to a close, his attorney in the Cayman Islands had assured him that no one could freeze his assets.

Two photographs of his son sat on his desktop. He stared at the boy at six...the man at twenty-six. Why could he never think of his son without remembering the affliction, the day he was born?

They had named their son Sheridan Gerald—Gerald after his ex-wife's father. Sheridan remembered how he'd rushed up to the nursery window just as a nurse lifted a crying baby from his crib. The blanket and cap were blue. It had to be a boy. The blanket fell away, and he saw the shriveled leg, the twisted foot. He pitied the child. Pitied the parents, whoever they were.

The nurse tucked the blanket around the baby and stepped into the corridor. "Would you like to hold your son, Lieutenant Macaroy?"

"My son? That crippled child is my son?"

"But, Lieutenant, he's a beautiful baby."

He looked down at the scrawny face, red and wrinkled and screaming, and recoiled at the thought of touching him. He tore at the blanket and uncovered the shriveled leg. "Do you call *that* beautiful, Nurse?"

He felt blind rage at his wife. Fury at God. A frenzied madness at the fate that had placed a crippled child under his care. He ran from the nursery and down a flight of steps. Shoving past those who blocked his way, he stumbled out into a snowstorm and retched. This was the son who would never grow up and attend West Point. Resentment burned in his chest. How could it be that he, Sheridan Macaroy, had produced a deformed child like that?

Six hours later the army doctor called Sheridan and his wife into the privacy of his office and told them their son had a birth defect. "We'll refer him to specialists. The prognosis is good. Everything else seems normal."

"Will he ever walk?"

"I'll let the orthopedic specialist and neurologists discuss that with you. Do you have other children, Lieutenant?"

"One-year-old twins."

"Girls," his wife whispered.

"Your son will require constant care." The doctor met Sheridan's gaze. "Perhaps you will consider the wisdom of not having any more children."

He stared at the doctor. Wasn't it ample that the boy was crippled? Was the doctor putting restrictions on his manhood as well? "You're blaming *me* for the baby's leg?"

"No one is at fault, Lieutenant. Statistically—"

He had no interest in statistics, and little interest in his marriage after that. Because of his son, the debts mounted. Because of his son, he drank too much.

As he'd done again last night.

Sheridan grimaced. And why shouldn't he drink? For twenty-six years it had helped him wipe out that first glimpse of Gerald in the army hospital. He longed for a drink, yet his mind had not cleared from last night's overindulgence. No matter how he tried, he couldn't drown out the miserable mistakes he'd made. Or the shame he felt whenever Gerald limped into his presence.

In reality, he was as crippled as his son, but there were no surgical corrections for Sheridan's condition. Only mounting debts. He caved in at Gerald's seventh surgery, contacted the Saudi businessman, and agreed to his terms: top secrets in exchange for money.

A man is nothing if he hasn't reached his dreams. With his double existence, dreams eluded him. Big promotions went to others. With every small advance, his ex-wife took him back to court for more money. He heard from her on a regular basis, but had seen little of her since the divorce except for those times when they ran into each other after Gerald's surgeries. Once he had taken the twins for a weekend, but they were so much like their mother he never offered to do it again.

He never spent a weekend with his son—the little boy with crutches and a gigantic smile. A little boy, with an elevated platform on his shoe, running awkwardly toward him.

Gerald grew into a handsome young man, confident and sure of himself. A year ago they had faced each other again. Gerald walked into his father's office with a visitor's badge attached to his lapel, the DCI personally escorting him. Sheridan and his son had been meeting ever since.

The more he became acquainted with his son, the greater his sense of shame as Washington searched for its mole. Once they arrested Colonel Taylor, his own discovery was imminent. The dragnet was closing in.

Today, when he took the elevator up to the seventh floor and entered the DCI's office, the director slapped his desktop. "We've got him! The mole is not one of our own. He's the Pentagon's headache. Once he's back in Washington, we've got him. Thanks to a little boy's innocent remarks to his teacher. Actually told her his dad was a spy. Proud about it. Dates, facts checked out. All of them confirmed by our embassy in Paris."

Sheridan waited, silenced by fear. The director didn't mention the mole by name, but the man's defeat marked his own downfall.

"You're looking unwell, Macaroy."

"You kept me from another promotion."

The director's features hardened. "It's your drinking. Why don't you see one of our doctors—get yourself straightened out?"

"I'd rather take that holiday I discussed with you."

"But you're retiring in October."

"I need a break. I'm thinking of leaving tomorrow."

"That soon?" The director nodded absently. "You'll miss the big show when Taylor comes back to Washington."

Macaroy felt detached, almost relieved that it was almost over. Perhaps remorse would come, but right now escape was uppermost in his mind. Or death. Tonight he'd walk through the gates of Langley and drive to the flying club. Or would he be banned from flying the Cessna as he had been banned from using a top-security line this morning? *Access denied.* He'd file a flight plan with the tower. Once airborne, he'd switch off radio contact and fly over the ocean into the clouds until his gas tank ran dry.

He pulled out another desk drawer, stared at the contents, then slammed it shut. He didn't care what happened to his ex-wife and daughters, but he couldn't shame his son with such a cowardly act as suicide.

At fifty-two he felt like a man ten years into his federal pension. He needed a vacation, one last chance to go away with his son. One last opportunity to set the record straight. Would Gerald agree? What about some tropical island where they could fish and sail? Where he could prepare his son for what lay ahead.

Where he could apologize for betraying his country.

Sheridan reached out and dialed his son's number. He let it ring, giving Gerald ample time to reach the phone. "Hello," came the deep voice. "Gerald Macaroy speaking."

"Gerald, it's your father. Can you get away for a three- or four-week vacation? I'm overdue for a holiday."

Silence.

Sheridan blundered on. "What about a tropical island? Hawaii? The South Pacific? Or the Cayman Islands?"

"What about my sisters?"

"Come on, Gerald, just the two of us. You used to talk about Portugal and the Canary Islands. What do you say?"

"Let's make it the Cayman Islands. Okay? You won't be embarrassed to see me in a swimsuit? Or limping and stumbling along in the sand?"

He winced. "I deserved that, Gerald. I'm sorry."

"No need to apologize. I've come to accept you on your terms. Are you sick, Dad? Or just diagnosed with cancer?"

"Let's just say I woke up after a long, long sleep. The trip's on me. I've talked to the DCI. He's okayed a vacation for me. I'd like to leave in the morning."

And never come back.

"Fishing and diving in the Caymans sounds great to me. And, Dad, I don't intend to watch the beauty of the undersea world from a glass-bottomed boat. I'll put in a vacation request as soon as we hang up. But since I'm the assistant manager, I see no problem…

Thanks, Dad."

Tears stung Sheridan's eyes as the call ended. Tonight he would write a letter to his son, a letter that would not be delivered until after Gerald came back from their trip. He'd be careful not to blame Gerald for his own decision to sell top secrets to the Arab. He couldn't excuse a double life, but he wanted the record clear between his son and himself. He'd spell out how he had sent a three-man team into Kuwait and its dire consequences on the Winters's family. He'd describe that day when he sat in the tent under a blistering heat in Saudi Arabia months later and condemned an innocent man to a legend in exchange for more money. He would apologize to his son and his country for collecting the funds channeled to terrorist training camps.

But for three weeks, four perhaps, he would be a real father for the first time in his life.

For the last time in his life.

CHAPTER 29

Kuwait City was several kilometers from Kuwait International Airport, but Adrienne caught a glimpse of the palm-lined boulevards as the plane came in for a landing. Below her lay a bustling metropolis with high-rise buildings and ultramodern hotels, a country quick to rally from the Iraqi invasion and months of occupation in the nineties.

She longed to sit with her brother, but he had been adamant. Once they boarded the plane, they went their separate ways. If they met at all, it would be as strangers. It was obvious that he still saw her as the stubborn, pesky kid sister tagging along at the wrong time.

As the plane lowered, she felt a growing concern for Jon and his mission. He was right. She was strong-willed, like her father. Headstrong, like her mother. And all she had done was add to Jon's burden.

When she stepped from the plane, she was hit by a stifling blast of desert heat. Even inside the terminal, sand filled her nostrils. Her mouth tasted like gravel. Prickles of self-doubt needled her as she inched her way toward the customs desk. It gave her no comfort that Jon was in front of her, Robbie somewhere behind her. They were entering as strangers in a country continually braced against the threats of its Iraqi neighbor. Jon had warned them that the situation remained unchanged since his prewar visit. With the ongoing war on terrorism, Kuwait and the other countries on the rim of Arabia proved perfect locations for terrorist networks to melt into the crowds and flourish. Security remained tight, foreigners caused concern, and a non-Arab—especially a woman traveling alone—would be viewed with suspicion.

She entered the country under her own name. In front of her, Jon was entering in the same deceptive way that he did the first time, with a passport bearing another man's identification and nationality, his own blurred photo in the corner. The favored child in the Winters home in Virginia no longer existed.

The custom's officer scowled at Jon. "Name?"

As though he had already severed himself from all ties, he said, "My name is Pierre du Pont."

"Nationality?"

She heard him lie again. "French."

As the customs agent studied the photo, Adrienne's spine stiffened. The man glanced up, his eyes like chunks of coal. He flipped the lid of Jon's luggage back against the countertop. The search was thorough, but having dealt with clean shirts, underwear, and shaving gear, he shoved the suitcase aside and demanded, "Occupation?"

She waited for Jon's next lie. "University professor."

A hint of interest crossed the man's face. "Sorbonne?"

Jon nodded. "Middle-East studies."

"Purpose of your visit?"

He met the official's fiery glance. "I'm here on holiday."

"Your address in my country, Pierre du Pont?"

"The Sherwin-Kuwait."

"Do you need assistance, Mr. du Pont?"

"*Je pense que non.* I have my cane."

The customs officer handed him the passport and waved him on. "Next."

Adrienne stepped forward, and stared into the man's unsmiling eyes.

"Name?"

"Adrienne Winters." She wet her lips and hoped that he had not noticed her nervous gesture. She fumbled for her passport and transit visa and held them out, her palm sweaty.

As the agent finished studying her passport, he did a cursory search of her luggage, patting the blouses and skirts and checking the contents of her cosmetic bag. Shoving her suitcase aside, he demanded, "Occupation?"

"Fashion buyer."

He did a quick appraisal of her stylish suit. "For Middle-East clothing?"

She shook her head.

"Country of origin?"

"United States."

"New York?"

"No, near Arlington, Virginia."

"Traveling alone?"

She hesitated. Perhaps he was about to advise her on safety in his country. "I'm meeting friends at the hotel."

Her eyelids felt gritty, her thirst unquenchable. She dared not look back for Robbie. Short of an emergency, she would have no direct contact with him until they reached the hotel.

"Your address in my country?"

She blinked trying to recall the name of the hotel. What had Robbie told her? She knew from the guidebook that Kuwait City and the hotels and mosques were sixteen kilometers from the airport. *She* was registered at one of the hotels on the palm-lined boulevard near the American embassy. The name? The name. What was the name?

"Your address in my country, Miss Winters?"

Tears pricked her tired eyes. "I don't remember."

"Perhaps Pierre du Pont's hotel at the Sherwin?"

She flushed and nodded. "Yes, that's it."

"Purpose of your visit?"

To protect my brother. "It's my first holiday in your country."

Once she reached the hotel there would be no turning back. They would slip into oblivion and, with any measure of luck, make contact with Jon's Kuwaiti friend, Hamad. Knowing the truth depended on it. Protecting her brother depended on it.

Her attention jerked back as the customs official asked, "Religion?"

Denying the God of his boyhood, Jon had said, "None."

She considered following his example, but couldn't. Not after that commitment at Notre Dame. Not when she remembered the ribbons of light touching her face, her heart. "Christian." She sensed peace as she said it.

His interest waned. The entry stamp came down hard on her passport, the seventy-two-hour visa stamped in red. Again the official held out his hand, a twitch tugging at the corner of his mouth. "Destination when you leave my country?"

Adrienne produced her ticket. "Bahrain, then Paris."

The man returned her papers with a curt nod and with another quick appraisal looked to the person behind her. "Next."

As she picked up her suitcase, she expected to hear Robbie announcing, "Robb Gilbert, American journalist."

But the deep voice she heard, though familiar, did not belong to Robbie. "*As-salaamo, alaykum.*" With equal politeness the customs agent responded, "*Wa alaykum e-salaam.*"

She moved away in haste as she heard, "I'm Colonel Taylor—Colonel Colin Taylor. American embassy."

She had only been ten or fifteen minutes behind Jon, another five until Robbie caught up with her outside the terminal. Other passengers queued in the transportation line, but Jon and Colin were nowhere to be seen. She turned to face Robb. He brushed his lips with his finger. *Wait*, his gesture said. *We're still strangers.*

But sizing them up as a couple, the Kuwaiti driver waved them into his van. "Sherwin-Kuwait," Robbie instructed, then fell silent.

Outside the van window the land was flat, with gentle, rolling sand dunes. The Gulf War had set the country back, but they built again—a progressive country made rich by oil. Cars and trucks roared over the modern motorway. Date palms grew beside it.

Beyond the highway were scrub bushes. A Bedouin riding his camel. A falcon taking flight in the distance.

Jon had been here when the tanks rumbled through the streets and the sky filled with Iraqi helicopters. He'd seen the damaged palace. Witnessed the slaughter of soldiers. Heard the reports of citizens killed, tortured, raped. Resistant fighters were caught and murdered, foreigners treated as infidels.

Adrienne closed her eyes. It was a miracle Jon had survived at all. She offered a swift prayer against the apprehension that he— and they—might not be so fortunate this time.

Adrienne signed her name in the hotel registry. "I'm meeting a friend here. Mr. Pierre du Pont."

The receptionist's eyes narrowed. "Mr. du Pont? He cancelled his reservation this morning. I believe a family emergency pre- vented his visit to Kuwait."

Impossible! We came in on the same plane. He passed through cus- toms just fifteen minutes ahead of me. Was Jon that desperate to be rid of us?

Robbie pushed his way to the counter and extended his pass- port. "Excuse me. I'm Robb Gilbert. I'd like to register, if this lady doesn't mind." He smiled, as though to ease his harshness. "I see we're both Americans. I'm meeting friends too. I'm certain your friend will be along soon."

You're not certain at all. You're worried too. I see it in your eyes.

"Once we've settled in our rooms, perhaps you would join me for a cup of tea, Miss—?"

She nodded. "Adrienne Winters."

"Another journalist?"

"No, my parents lived here many years ago. My baby brother was born here."

"Has he come back?"

He was cutting her off so she wouldn't say too much.

"No. Neither have my parents returned."

"You should have brought them."

The receptionist took in every word. He hailed the nearest porter. "Miss Winters, you and Mr. Gilbert are on the same floor."

They rode the lift in silence. As the porter piled her luggage in her room, Robb said, "Miss Winters, why don't you rest for an hour. Then we can have that cup of tea."

She touched his arm, but he eased away. Quick heat filled her cheeks. Of course, one didn't touch strangers as if they were friends. She cleared her throat. "Mr. Gilbert, did you see Col—?"

He gave a quick shake of his head and his eyes shadowed. "I beg your pardon…oh, I'm traveling alone."

A senseless answer. He was hushing her. Protecting her? But he understood. Yes, he had seen Colin. She could tell it by the concern in his eyes. "What are you going to do?" she whispered.

As the porter moved down the corridor with his luggage, Robb mimicked putting a phone to his ear. "I'll make a few inquires to Dad's journalist friends."

"Be careful, Robbie."

Adrienne's low warning warmed Robbie's heart. He winked and strolled down the hall. Giving her a final wave, he slipped into his room. He was whistling as he shut the door behind him. When he dropped his suitcase, he saw two men. No, three. The two nearest him grabbed his arms and twisted them behind him. He fought. Kicked. Felt the muscles in his upper arm tearing.

He cried out, but was helpless without knowing the language. "You're making a mistake."

"No mistake," the third man said in English. "Inject him, you fools. Inject him. Silence him."

Colin Taylor's voice. Though Robbie's assailant wore a Kuwaiti cloak and headdress, there was no doubt those angry eyes and voice belonged to Colin. Robbie struggled once more to free himself. He felt as though his arms had been torn from their sockets.

The jab was instant. Violent. Stinging. He stopped struggling. Felt himself falling.

Adrienne. *God...please help Adrienne.*

Though Robbie's room was a mere four doors away, it seemed too far. Adrienne would feel safer with him.

She bolted her door and went to hang up her clothes and empty her suitcase. That done, she paced the room. If only Jon would call them. Perhaps Hamad had been waiting for him. But then, why didn't he leave a message? In spite of the air conditioning, she felt suffocated by the desert heat. An hour. Robbie had said an hour. She glanced at the bed and stretched out on top the covers just to rest her eyes for a moment.

Adrienne awakened to a pounding on her door and semidarkness outside her window. A glance at her watch told her three hours had passed. She rushed to the door, pulling it open, expecting to see Robbie. Her smile faded. "Colin, what are you doing here?"

"I've come to take you to Jon."

Robbie awakened, groggy and disoriented, but it only took a moment to realize he was on a jetliner. He could tell by the setting of the sun and the rapidly darkening sky that they were flying away from Kuwait. How far distant he could not be certain. He grappled with his seat belt and tried to stand. His world spun in vivid Technicolor, the cabin of the aircraft turning upside down with him. He squeezed his eyelids shut. His world kept spinning in zigzagged images. Revolving. Rotating. The gut of the plane twirling with it.

"Sir, may I help you?" A flight attendant became part of the swirling maze. His vision was too blurred to read her name. "You're awake now." She sounded pleasant. Spoke English.

He glanced around. "Where's Adrienne?"

"You're traveling alone, sir."

No, I'm traveling with Adrienne. Each time he moved his head, his world swayed. He inched forward. Sickened by the move, he thrust his head back against the headrest. The spinning became unbearable. Nauseating.

"Where's my attaché case?"

"You boarded without luggage, sir."

His mouth felt dry. "What am I doing on this aircraft?"

"You're on your way to Paris."

"No, I just reached Kuwait."

She looked alarmed. "Don't you remember? Your friends checked you in at the boarding gate, and an attendant brought you on board in a wheelchair. We—I thought you had been drinking."

Sweat dampened his forehead. "I don't drink."

He couldn't remember anything after reaching his hotel room. He'd intended to phone friends of his father in Kuwait City. And Adrienne. Where was Adrienne? She was going to rest, and then they were going to have tea together.

"Tea, sir?"

Had he mumbled the word aloud? More nausea swept in, accompanied by jabbing pains. He estimated the steps to the rest room and knew he was too weak to make it. He groped for the disposal bag in the seat pocket in front of him. The action drained him.

Robbie searched his pockets for a handkerchief and realized with growing annoyance that his wallet and passport were missing. The jacket he wore was someone else's. At least the shoes and trousers were his own, and the crushed ticket on the seat beside him bore his name.

The jabbing pains in his stomach grew more violent. "I'm sick."

The attendant rushed off, returning moments later with a

steaming cloth. He pressed it to his face. The spinning subsided, and he risked opening his eyes. "Can we turn back to Kuwait International? I have to help my friend."

She looked sympathetic. "Why would you want to go back? Your friends said you were traveling alone. That you were in trouble. They wanted to get you out of the country before you were detained."

Yes, someone wanted him out of the country. But violence was not Jon's method. "I don't have any friends in Kuwait. No one except Adrienne Winters. She's an American citizen… Something may have happened to her. We have to get in touch with the American embassy—in Paris, if that's where we're going. Ask for Naji Fleming."

The attendant was gone again. He tried to remember. Two men. Yes, two men had been in his room. A third remained in the shadows. His stomach turned into a speedway. Rumbling back and forth. Racing inside out. Running circles in his intestinal tract.

Colin. Colin Taylor.

She was back. "Are you all right?"

He managed a feeble grin. "The pains are worse."

"The pilot wants to see your passport."

"It's gone. Stolen."

"Without that, they'll detain you in Paris."

"Not if the pilot makes a call for me. Tell him someone injected something in my arm."

She remained calm as she lowered his headrest and put a thin blanket over him. "Are you certain?"

Yes, he was certain now. Colin Taylor gave the order. That was the last thing he remembered.

"Do you have a family, sir? The pilot wants to know."

"Yes, my dad. Robinson Gilbert. I'll need my dad."

The thought of his father helping him locate Adrienne and Jon eased his distress. His father would go straight to the top.

In his long career as a journalist and commentator, Robinson Gilbert—*Gil*, to his friends—had made a lasting impression, one as memorable as Edward R. Murrow saying, "This is London." Robinson was as well respected as Harry Reasoner, Walter Cronkite, and Peter Jennings. But Robb's father had no desire to anchor a news broadcast these days. If the war on terrorism didn't let up, his father wanted to be on the front line.

Yes, getting his dad involved was his best hope for protecting Adrienne and Jon. If Robinson Gilbert couldn't open doors in Washington, then he could capture an audience with his headlines.

Like Robb, he'd been on top of the story on the Washington mole and would throw his hat into the ring to help take Colin Taylor down and to establish worldwide concern for a missing American woman and her brother.

"Tell the pilot my girl's—my friend's name is Adrienne Winters."

"I will."

The pain and the chills came in waves. "And tell the embassy I'm going to need medical attention on my arrival."

She put a fresh cloth across his forehead. "I've already told the pilot."

CHAPTER 30

Colin gripped Adrienne's elbow and felt a fresh sense of power as he walked her down the hotel corridor. He'd fancied himself in love with her once.

I offered you everything, Adrienne. My name. My rank. My position in Washington. But it was always Robbie. Robbie strikes your fancy. Robbie. How I despise that man.

He'd known Adrienne for most of his life, but he steeled himself against the sentiment of being welcomed at Winterfest Estates as far back as he could remember. He focused on Adrienne's rejection. Her scorn. Her indifference. Fresh rage gripped him. *I refuse to let the past deter me now, not when you threaten my future, Adrienne.*

Colin's heart quickened with his steps. According to the records in Washington, Jon Aaron Winters was dead. Jacques d'Hiver would disappear in the same way. The duplicity of Jon living and walking the streets of Paris as another man could be crushed. No one at the embassy would stir the waters. In Washington, Sheridan Macaroy would make certain any objections fell on deaf ears. Another scapegoat in the war on terrorism would be a small price to pay.

He could pull it off without even dirtying his hands, then return to Washington with Adrienne and Jon destined to oblivion, and his colleagues none the wiser.

As they reached the stairs, Adrienne broke free and ran back down the corridor. He spun, ready to chase her. "What are you doing?"

"I have to tell Robbie where I'm going."

Foolish woman. "Robbie is en route back to Paris."

She stared, and he saw doubt shade those glorious eyes. "Without telling me?"

He walked toward her. "His papers were out of order. He was expelled from this country."

"I don't believe you."

He allowed a small smile as he reached her. "Not to worry, my dear. I had him...accompanied to the airport."

Adrienne eluded his grasp and ran to Robbie's door. She pounded until a Filipino maid appeared from the next room.

"I'm looking for Mr. Gilbert."

The maid's Tagalog was indistinguishable as she cringed behind her bedding cart. Adrienne turned back to Colin, "What did she say?"

"She said he left the hotel after checking in." Enough. He'd been patient with her, but it was time to go. He closed his fingers around her upper arm. "Come. You wanted to see Jon. I'll take you to him."

O utside the air-conditioned hotel, the desert heat slapped Adrienne as Colin propelled her toward a waiting car. Inside she stared blindly through the tinted windows. She jiggled the handle. He leaned forward and pressed a button to close the window between the driver and themselves.

"There is no need to make a scene, Adrienne."

"I don't want to go with you."

His harsh laugh rankled her already raw nerves. "You have no choice, Adrienne. You wanted to see Jon. I'm taking you to him."

His cockiness grew as they drove out of the city. Adrienne pressed back into the seat. "You're frightening me, Colin. You were always welcome at Winterfest. What would Dad think if he could see you now? He was so fond of you."

"I never saw it that way, Adrienne. He tried to block my enlistment—my promotions. He warned others against my assignment to the Pentagon."

"I don't understand. Why would he do that?"

"You don't know, do you? I wanted to spend, spend, spend like you and Jon did. But I got even—"

She shrank against the door. "You're talking about Paris. About Dad's dismissal."

He nodded. "Your father didn't deserve that, but when I realized he knew and was hoping I would be man enough to turn myself in, I hated him. He couldn't force me to turn myself in. I knew too much."

"You're accusing him—"

A sickening sneer crossed his features. How had she ever thought him handsome?

"No, not honest Harry. Not him."

She wanted to weep. "Why, Colin? Why did you ruin his career?"

"I stole those secret files from your father's vault to please my own father. Dear Daddy Bedford. And do you know what? For the first time in my life, I had access to the same amount of money Jon did"—his features darkened—"and I couldn't *touch* it because of the investigation."

He brushed his fingers through his military buzz. "Your brother couldn't let it go either. *Family honor,* he called it. He was like a raging bull. In the beginning Jon confided in me. He told me how close he was getting to the truth—until that last time together in Paris when he realized how involved I was."

Tears balanced on her lashes. "*You were the third man.* You're the one who left my brother behind in Kuwait."

"I had orders to do so."

She had to escape. She jiggled the door handle again.

"You're wasting your energy, Adry. I didn't mean to hurt your father, but once I stole his files, my own dad wouldn't let me rest."

"So you went on selling out to Russia and China?"

"No. Not to them." He drummed his fingers against the car seat. "That's why it has taken Washington so long to unravel the truth. They're looking in the wrong direction. Looking for the wrong man."

She was safe as long as she could keep him talking. "And after your father died?"

"I was a sleeper." He said it as though the admission exonerated him. "And foolish enough to think I had escaped unnoticed. But just before 9/11, I was threatened with exposure unless I helped them again."

Adrienne knew as he spoke that he never intended her to repeat his words. Fear—stark and clammy—clawed through her. She was at his mercy—and with Colin, mercy did not exist. Her childhood friend had become her enemy, but she dare not let herself think of dying so far away from Winterfest.

"You stole Pentagon files, Colin?"

He met her contempt with forced bravado. "Pentagon, State Department? What difference does it make? My dear Adrienne, you know how much wearing my country's uniform means to me. At first I transmitted classified information, but I had Gavin to think of, so I told my handlers I no longer had access to classified documents."

She shuddered at the icy tone as he spoke. Was he mad? Or had he lived with deception so long that he saw himself as honorable?

"What they wanted then was money. I put them in touch with millionaire businessmen living on the edge—men who didn't want to ruin their reputations or lose everything they had. We never met face to face, but ego at high places finds a special satisfaction in charitable donations to help victims of disasters whether it's in the Middle East or Kentucky. Some want their names in the limelight. Others must cover serious indiscretions. If they suspected where their funds were being channeled, they never asked. Congressional hearings for misappropriation of company funds was a great deterrent for some. Men who can't risk losing their reputations give in liberal amounts."

"And you took pleasure in destroying them?"

He couldn't meet her gaze, his eyes as restless as his hands. A strangled laugh sounded in his throat. "The only good that comes from this is your mother's love for Gavin. I'm not a good father, but I want the best for my son. With you and Jon out of the picture, Gavin stands to inherit Winterfest."

He *was* mad. "What kind of a fool do you take my mother for?"

"Not a fool at all. She's in my debt and knows it."

"My mother always pays her debts."

"How well I know. Your mother's social life has been diminished by Parkinson's, but she enjoys contributing large sums to charity to keep her name in the social registry. A month ago she wrote a check for me, payable to cash. No questions asked. But Rolf intervened and shredded it. That money would have funded terrorist training camps." His words mocked her. "Charitable donations are all she has to offer these days, except perhaps her one real asset— Winterfest Estates."

"How dare you!" Didn't he know the land had been left to Jon and her? Or had her mother boasted ownership?

He turned to watch her. "You are a beautiful woman, Adrienne. So was your mother that day in Paris." She covered her ears. He pulled them free. "It's a shame you won't live to ask your mother about that day in the library when she left your father's vault open."

Adrienne jerked her hands from his and pounded him with her fists. "You're lying!"

He caught her wrists. "No. I am not lying. You're as blind as your mother, Adrienne." His features twisted. "When your mother looks at Gavin, she sees him as *Jon's* son. Do you know how angry that makes me? *I'm* his father, but in Mara's eyes, Gavin should have belonged to Jon. We loved the same woman, but *I* married her. I'm counting on Mara's devotion to my son to give Gavin the chance in life he deserves."

"I'm so glad Kristina never knew what you were."

"I think she knew. I saw her moments before that jet crashed into the Pentagon; she never planned to come back to me." He spat out his contempt. "Adrienne, I loved her, but Jon was her first love, and your family more dear to her than I ever was. I think she suspected I was leading a double life. She wanted to protect Gavin from that. Once, when Gavin was asleep in my arms, she called me a spy. But Gavin wasn't asleep. Still, we kept screaming at each other. I was so angry, I told her the job paid well. I told her we would never lack for a thing—not with the wealth I was accumulating in Swiss bank accounts... I threatened her if she ever told anyone." His shoulders slumped. "I loved Kris, but days later, she left me. She left me and took Gavin with her."

The driver had turned off the main motorway, and the car was taking a throttling from the bumpy country road.

Colin studied her, and she thought she saw a glimmer of regret in those cold eyes. His words convinced her she was right.

"For what it's worth, I loved you. I wanted to marry you."

She fought back her revulsion. "So you would be certain to own Winterfest?"

"I need that security for Gavin. It wasn't right losing my wife and unborn child the way I did."

"It wasn't right that my dad left Paris in disgrace. It wasn't right that you left my brother behind in Kuwait."

"I never meant to hurt them. The Winters were more family to me than my father ever was. But my dad wanted money at any cost—even to the point of betraying his country. I wanted his approval. All I ever wanted beyond that was to be an army officer. To serve my country."

"You are a disgrace to the uniform you wear."

His face went white at that, and they rode the rest of the way in silence. As they stepped from the car, a Kuwaiti in a long flowing cotton robe came forward, head held high. He was wearing the traditional headdress secured by a black rope. His skin seemed weathered by the sun and age, a man at least sixty-four. His facial features were harsh, uneven; his mustache thick, black; his eyes kind.

He bowed. "I am Mahmoud, Hamad's father."

Adrienne caught her breath. This was the head of the Kuwaiti family who counted her brother as a friend and protector during the invasion. His interest in Colin seemed minimal; his interest in her intense.

In desperation, she turned back to Colin. "Jon always thought they were his friends."

A sneer cut across Colin's face. "Jon once called me his friend as well."

As Mahmoud snapped his fingers, she saw that his gold watch matched his gold-toothed smile. The servant who responded, a weapon at his waist, was Egyptian or Syrian.

"Take Miss Winters to her brother." Mahmoud glanced at the sky, then at his watch. "If my son needs me, I will be at prayer."

Adrienne was manhandled and thrust inside a white-striped tent large enough to house eight prisoners. She stumbled on the dirt floor as the armed guard shoved her forward. Catching her balance she took in her surroundings. The tent was windowless, its cotton-thin skin unable to provide shade from the blistering desert sun. The merciless dust crept in. She adjusted her eyes to the changing light.

Then she saw him.

Jon lay stretched out on a cot, his face and neck bruised. Dried blood caked his cheek. His shirt was drenched, his cane lying out of reach.

"Jon, what happened to you?"

He lifted his shackled hands and with great effort put a finger to his swollen lips. When he spoke, his voice was hoarse. "Jacques, please."

She nodded, too frightened to argue.

"Welcome…but it isn't exactly the Savoy. The air conditioning is terrible."

A sandy gust of wind blew through the tent flap. "The air conditioner must be broken," she said crossing over to him. She touched his bristled cheek. "What happened?"

"When I stepped out of the terminal, I was forced into a car. I never reached the hotel."

"Hamad?"

"Young terrorists would be my guess."

A pitcher sat out of Jon's reach. The water was warm, and a bug sat sipping on the brim. She brushed the insect away and filled a glass. Cradling his head she pressed it to his lips.

He swallowed and lay back. "Thank you, Miss Winters."

"Oh, Jon. Even now you refuse to say that you are Jon Aaron. We're playing word games. I know the truth. You know the truth. Can't you please admit that you are my brother? Just once. It would mean so much to me."

"There is too much at risk. Too many lives at stake. I can never be Jon again."

In spite of her fear, she fumed. Her pent-up bitterness hissed like a teakettle. "Go on. Go on denying us. At least we have the same family name. Winters, d'Hiver. But I know your past, my brother's past, is sealed back at the CIA headquarters. Your family is locked out—the way you are still locking us out." She wagged her finger at him. "The Company has fed us bits of truth. Nothing more. And yet they keep thick folders, no doubt, recounting your missions in detail—folders with nothing but your number and code name to identify them."

His tired face crinkled with a smile. "Not much for your brother to leave behind, is it? Number A-436, the Fourth Season."

Blood raced through her body. Was that Jon Aaron's number? His code name? The fourth season: winter. It would be like her brother to pick a name like that.

"Are you the Fourth Season?" she whispered.

"Yes, Adrienne. That's as much as I can say." His long fingers locked around hers.

If she didn't suck in her breath, her breathing would cease. She longed to embrace him, but he was still the stranger, the French-man who must be called Jacques d'Hiver. The Frenchman who entered Kuwait this time as Pierre DuPont. Deception. Nothing but deception. "Then I was right all along. The same blood courses through our veins. No surgeon could change that."

"Some of the blood, Adrienne. I'm not your brother—a half-brother perhaps. That is all. But I'm afraid I must always be Jacques d'Hiver... Don't cry, little sis."

"If you had amnesia it wouldn't hurt so much that you didn't want to be part of our family any longer. You should have come home to us."

"I couldn't. For months, Hamad hid me from the Iraqis. I was ravaged with fever. My leg infected. My friends—the men on the mission with me—deserted me. I couldn't guess how far up the political ladder it went. When Kuwait was liberated, Hamad went to the American embassy and begged for my return to the States."

She offered him another sip of water. He refused as he shifted his leg to ease the pain. "That request was denied. In time, Jon Winters became a nonentity. I had no passport to prove who I was. After the embassy made contact with Langley, I was shipped to Saudi Arabia for interrogation for being in Kuwait illegally. Ricardo was there. And Sheridan Macaroy. In the end, Langley denied knowing me."

"Then why is your star on their Memorial Wall?"

He shrugged. "Duplicity."

"Your country came before your family."

"Not in my heart, Adry. But national security had to come first. Terrorists had infiltrated our fight against Iraq. When Kuwait was liberated, some terrorist cells remained. Finding me might have led them to innocent Kuwaitis. Trustworthy men."

"Is that why your name isn't in the Book of Honor?"

"For the safety of others, my name should never be in a Book of Honor. I must always be Jacques d'Hiver."

She sat on the floor, her hand resting on his. Jon's skin had been bronzed by the Parisian sun and all those clandestine missions in the blistering heat of other countries. Now he looked as sunbaked as the Kuwaitis. But each time she looked at him, the same thought assailed her.

"Will we get out of here, Jo…Jacques?"

"Not without a miracle."

CHAPTER 31

Jon touched Adrienne's face, and she wanted to weep at his tenderness.

"Adry, did Colin mistreat you?"

"He didn't touch me—except on my arm. He was harsh. Arrogant. He bragged about betraying Dad—" She couldn't go on.

"I'm sorry you had to find out this way. There was a time when I could have killed him with my bare hands for betraying me—" He flinched at her expression. "That idea troubles you, Adrienne. But I thought he had gone quite insane."

"I don't think Colin is crazy. Brilliant, perhaps."

"You're so loyal. Even back to our days in Paris, Colin was obsessed with the life of Field Marshal Rommel. You used to sit there bug-eyed listening to him boast about Rommel's heroics. He scared me. He saw himself as another great military strategist like the Desert Fox. He was always heading in the wrong direction."

"He might have turned out all right if he had our dad."

"Adrienne, he made his own choices. Even at the Rodin Gardens, only a few feet separate *The Thinker* from the *Gates of Hell.* It's all based on choices."

She scooped up a handful of sand and let it sift through her fingers. "Where are we, Jon?"

Jon. She had called him Jon. This time he seemed too weary to argue. A crooked smile tugged at the corner of his mouth.

"We're miles from Kuwait City. In a terrorist training camp of some sort. Hamad is in charge; Colin involved."

"Is there no one to help us?"

"With any luck, Robbie is out there tracking Colin's movements and taking photos of Hamad. He'll know enough to report to the American embassy."

She shook her head. "He was forced to leave the country."

"He left Kuwait? Deserted us both?"

"Colin's doing. But wherever Robbie is, he's out there doing everything he can for us. He's a journalist. He'll fight this with words."

"That's not the kind of arsenal we need." Jon sounded so weary. Disheartened. "So Mahmoud may be our one hope. Maybe I can persuade him to help us. Our troops have been stationed here since the Gulf War ended. Mahmoud informs me that fresh troops have arrived and are on military maneuvers in the desert, ready for any conflict with Iraq. They're on night maneuvers too—out there in full packs, stirring up the dust with live ammunition."

She touched her dry nostril. "How do they breathe?"

"With great care. Tonight, when the camp is still, we'll listen for gunfire. Maybe I can pinpoint their location." His smile was sardonic. "We should put Colin out in the thick of the practice maneuvers. With any luck they might mistake him for the enemy."

From time to time Jon dozed. When he did, she rested her head against his cot. The next time he rallied she said, "We must not be bitter against Colin. Or hate him."

"No. Brigette tells me a man can't live that way. If we live through this, I want something—"

"Half of the land at Winterfest is yours."

"Not Winterfest. What I want is Harry Winters's Bible. But right now I need a miracle to get you out of here."

"Walking is out. Colin drove for a long time."

"And we've no vehicle. If I could persuade Mahmoud to find a camel—"

"I'm no Bedouin. I won't ride one of those."

"Not even a one-hump camel?" His bruised face halted his smile. "Their feet don't sink into the sand. They provide meat and milk—"

"No camel."

He was teasing her now, trying to keep their spirits up. "Camels are more trustworthy than a car. Dust storms can clog the car's engine, but camels go a hundred miles a day. It's less than that to the embassy in Kuwait City."

"Have you forgotten? Colin will be there."

"Forget Colin. Just think about your escape. The camel's body is built for the desert. Their eyelashes protect their eyes in a storm."

"Stop joking. I won't leave without you."

"But for the sake of my children, you must."

Late that evening two guards hustled Jon from the tent again. He went with the toe of his prosthesis dragging across the dirt. Adrienne lay in the darkness, waiting for his return, fearing that he would not come. *They will kill him. And then what will happen to me? I'm scared, God. I am so scared.*

She rolled into a ball on the bed, shivering beneath the thin blanket. "Now I lay me down to sleep—" No, that wasn't the kind of prayer she needed. Pray. Pray for Jon. Pray for yourself. "Oh, God, I've forgotten how to pray. But please take care of my brother."

The mumble of voices drew closer. A disturbance at the tent flap. Two guards dragged Jon across the room and tossed him on his bed. He was alive.

She crawled to his cot. His shirt was ripped, his face puffy. She leaned gently on his shoulder and looked into his battered face. "What do they want from you?"

"Information. The names of my contacts in Paris. They insist that I'm still working with the CIA."

"Are you?"

"In my own way."

"Does Brigette know?"

"No."

"Jon, I prayed for you."

"It's a good thing, Adrienne. I've forgotten how to."

She reached out and buttoned the torn shirt. "Maybe we can learn together."

"Maybe." His empty eyes scanned their surroundings. "It's not much of a prayer chamber."

"It doesn't have to be."

He slapped his thigh. "I prayed that I would get out of Kuwait."

"You did."

"With a useless leg. And I prayed that Kris would wait for me. But did she wait for me?"

"Jon, I prayed you would be home for my sixteenth birthday."

He ran his bruised fingers across her cheek. "I left a birthday present for you."

"I know—a saddle for Rocket. I loved it. Rocket is dead now, but I still use the saddle on my new thoroughbred. When we get home, Jon, let's talk to Robbie. He knows all about praying. All about God. He says praying is as easy as riding a bicycle. You set a course and pedal."

He pointed to his prosthesis. "I'd have a mite of trouble pedaling with this contraption." But he smiled. "Ah, little sis, you are always talking about Robbie."

Before she could protest, he dropped into an exhausted doze. In his sleep he cried out for Kristina. A tear stole down his cheek. Still he slept. She let him.

The next time he awakened, she said, "Jon, was your fiancée the reason you didn't marry Brigette?"

"I had nothing but a legend to offer her."

A life of lies. More deception. "Kristy married someone else."

Jon's eyes raked the space around them. "Is she happy?"

"She's dead...she was killed at the Pentagon on 9/11."

He groaned. "Oh, no. She didn't deserve that."

"She didn't deserve the man she married either. He was never right for her." The taut lines on his face changed with the seconds.

Twitching. Easing. She risked it. "Kris grieved for you for three years—before she married Colin Taylor."

He erupted, a human volcano spewing vulgarity, pounding the air with his fists. He staggered to his feet, caught his balance, paced within the confines of the tent.

"Jon...Jon, please."

He stayed in motion. Back and forth leaving his zigzagged, uneven footprints on the dirt floor.

"Jon—sit down."

Finally, he collapsed on the cot and stretched out his boot. "Kris and Colin! And you ask me not to hate him? All through our boyhood he wanted everything I had. Sometimes he lifted what he wanted. I ignored it. Wrote it off. And now you tell me he stole my girl."

"He was hurting, Jon—like you're hurting right now. Compared to us, Colin had so little. Do you think Bedford ever hugged Colin or had a man-to-man talk with him? He was too busy building his role as a war hero. Too puffed up with being a military attaché at the embassy."

"Is that why Colin wormed his way into Dad's favor? Always dropping by for a chat at our condo in Paris or in the library at Winterfest. Suggesting a game of chess. The door always open to him."

"Dad saw potential in Colin that we missed."

"He stole my fiancée... I used to tease Kris about her freckles. She promised to outgrow them before we were married. And if not, she was going to pass them on to our children."

"She did. They had a son. Gavin is six now, and he has freckles on his nose and cheeks. He's sensitive. Sweet. Very much like Kris."

His voice was husky. "For Gavin's sake, I'm glad."

"Mother treats Gavin as her own grandson. She said he should have been yours."

His control button was on again. He met her gaze with the well-remembered steadfastness. "Is Colin good to him?"

"I think so. Gavin adores his father—I think because of the uniform and the important post he holds. Kristina's mother takes care of Gavin most of the time. That way she can keep him in Sunday school and teach him the things that Kris would have wanted him to know."

"All that time in Kuwait, I wanted to live because I loved her. I wanted to survive so I could go back to her."

"She had no way of knowing that, Jon."

"I thought she would wait for me."

"We thought you were dead. Why didn't you send for Kris? She would have sailed around the world to be with you. She would have taken on your legend. Been part of it."

"She took Colin on the rebound. That's it, isn't it?"

"Is that how you took Brigette?" At his sharp look, she lowered her eyes. "I'm sorry...that was unfair. But Gavin and Mother are close. Gavin calls her Nanny Mara. But dear as he is to us, he cannot substitute for your own children. Mother has a right to know Claudio and Colette."

H ow twisted the workings of her mind after a restless night in the desert. Was Jon right? Did she always talk about Robbie? She rarely thought about Winterfest without thinking about him. And in Paris she kept wanting him to come—to solve her problems. He was the family pillar. The family leaning post. The man she and her mother turned to when things went awry. Want something done? Ask Robbie. When a flower bed needed weeding, Robbie would be out there with Rolf, digging in the dirt and loving it. They were two of a kind: bedrock dependable.

Her friends envied her connection with him. The cook pampered him. The editor at the newspaper where he worked praised him.

Was she always thinking about Robbie?

He was easy to talk to. Fun to be with. The two of them—riding the horses neck and neck. Racing. Laughing. He was her favorite dancing partner, but she never told him. She considered it now and found comfort in the thought of being in his arms.

Yet so often she pushed him away. Held him at bay. She liked him too much to marry him. She was too much like her mother, and Robbie was too devoted, like her dad.

Her thoughts and dreams about Robbie were smashed when a Kuwaiti in a white robe entered the tent in the middle of the night and placed a water tumbler beside her. He hovered above her. She held her breath, her throat too dry to scream. Adrienne opened one eye as he stole across the tent to Jon's bedside. She muffled a cry as he yanked Jon to a sitting position.

"Hamad. What do you want?"

The Kuwaiti lifted his hand.

"No, don't, Hamad!" She struggled to sit up. "Leave my brother alone. Don't you dare touch him."

The back of his hand came down with a resounding crack across Jon's cheek. A second strike followed. And then the man was gone, his flowing robe scraping across the dirt.

"Jon." His name came out on a sob.

"Stay where you are, Adrienne. Not a sound."

She froze. "But he hit you."

"I'm all right. Go back to sleep."

She took a sip from the tumbler, and lay back. *God...please help us. Get us away from here.*

The prayer soothed her heart, and she slipped into a deep sleep. When she awakened, it was to the gray of dawn breaking and the sound of Arabic words. Guards were dragging Jon back into the tent. She tried to scream. Her mouth was dry, the bitter taste of an unknown substance on her tongue. The shadowy figures were gone without a word to her.

Her world spun. "What's wrong with me?"

"I think they drugged your water last night."

She pushed herself to a sitting position. Even from across the tent, she saw the deep gash on his cheek. If they dragged him out one more time would he have the strength to endure? "They must stop the beatings."

"Our friends in Paris need time. I must give it to them." He stared at the tent flap as particles of sand blew in. "A long time ago my country denounced me as a man who failed to do my duty. I won't fail this time, Adry, even if it costs me my life."

"Did you fail in Kuwait?"

"Sheridan Macaroy told me the invasion of Kuwait could have been thwarted if I had sent my intelligence reports on time. I know the truth now. It was impossible for Washington to act on intelligence data that never made it into the diplomatic pouch."

He kept a wary eye on the tent flap. "I've spent the last twelve years trying to find out why I was left behind. I'm convinced that Colin sold out his country, but I can't prove it. It would be my word against his."

"He told me everything. But who would believe us? Colin admitted he worked with Macaroy."

"I suspected as much. But Dad was right. There is still honor at the top. Good men serving our country." His eyes darted from the tent flap to her. He grinned through cracked lips. "Men like Robbie. I always thought you'd marry him one day."

"He stopped proposing."

"Is he blind? You're most attractive."

"Right now, I'm a mess. No shower. No makeup. No clean clothes."

He winked. "But you do own a vast piece of property."

Adrienne was torn between laughter and tears. "I finally turned him down once too often. Besides, I don't want a proposal without candles and red roses."

"Then you propose to him."

He shifted his leg and cried out. She was at his side lifting his bloody hand in hers. There were abrasions on his knuckles. "Oh, Jon. How can I help?"

"My knuckles are not broken. It's that blasted leg of mine."

"But your cheek needs stitches too. We've got to get you back to Paris for medical treatment." She knew she was crying and didn't care. There was no fresh makeup to streak. "When we get there, what's the first thing you're going to do?"

"Marry Brigette. What about you, little sis?"

Keep him talking so he won't think about the next beating. "I'm going to have a celebratory dinner at the Eiffel Tower. I want you and your family to join me."

His humor came across dry, unemotional. "Claudio plans to climb to the top of the tower someday when his mother isn't watching. The two of you can climb. The rest of us could catch the elevator up to the restaurant in a tower held together with a million rusting rivets."

"I know we're going to get back to Paris alive. Just hang on, Jon. Will you come to dinner then? And after that will you go back to Winterfest with me?"

His smile was soul-weary as he turned on his back. "For now, Paris is far enough."

Jon closed his eyes, shutting her out. Moments later, he fell into a deep, even sleep. His chest rose and fell. His facial muscles relaxed.

Oh, Jon, how can you sleep so peacefully when another beating may be minutes away?

An hour dragged by. An hour and fifteen minutes. At last he stirred. He glanced her way.

"Adry, I'm sorry. I couldn't stay awake."

"You needed the rest, Jon."

"I think I was dreaming about Brigette and the children. I was trying to tell them where I was, that I was all right. That you were with me. The dream was all mixed up. You were there. We were back at the Rodin Gardens."

"Was it raining?"

"A downpour." A chuckle escaped him. "And we were sitting there nibbling fruit tarts by the reflecting pool, drenched to the skin. Not caring. Just talking about Paris and Winterfest. About Mom and Dad. I still had two good legs—"

She swallowed. Spoke slowly. "I'd like to go back to the gardens again."

Their eyes met across the dusty tent. "I used to take Claudio there with me on those days when Brigette and Colette went off shopping, doing their girl things."

"Does Claudio like art?"

"No, he likes little boy things. He'd splash in the mud puddles and chase white butterflies. He was like a butterfly, flitting from one activity to another." Jon's voice filled with pride. "And after he'd run himself to exhaustion, he'd sit beside me. Not even a breathing space between us. He'd take stubs of crayons and make a picture of the rainbow that hung above the lime trees."

She let him talk. Let him have his moment of healing before they came to beat him again.

His eyes shone. "I used to sit there listening to the church bells in the distance, remembering my own boyhood and wondering what my Claudio would be when he grew up..."

He closed his eyes. "And now I may not be there to see him grow up."

Adrienne could only pray he was wrong. For all their sakes.

On the third night, Jon turned his feverish body toward her. "Adrienne, Colin doesn't intend for us to leave Kuwait. If we are to beat him at his own game, you must do something for me."

"Lie some more?"

"No. I'm carrying some useful equipment. The next time they drag me from this tent I want you to use it. It's a miniature tent city out there, but they always question me in Hamad's tent."

"I can crawl across to that tent and listen."

"No, they would discover you."

"And interrogate me?"

He was silent for so long that she knew he feared exactly that. "I pray not. Colin leaves the nasty business for others." With his shackled hands, he uncovered the prosthesis. "Help me ease the boot off."

She pushed and tugged until the boot broke free, leaving a bloody, stocking-covered stump. "You're hurt!"

"I never wear the boot this long. It causes pressure points. But I had no choice. I never know when they're going to drag me out of here. Please, hold the boot up for me. There's a flat object jammed in there."

She slid her hand inside the sweaty boot, in between the flannel lining. "I think I've found it."

"Then pull it free."

She stared down at an eight-inch collapsible dish. A wire and a bionic ear. She shuddered at the thought of them pressing into his stump, leaving indentation marks and scratches on his fragile skin. And opening him to more infection. "Oh, Jon, why? What is this?"

"Eavesdropping equipment. I want you to test it the next time they usher me over there. Just hold the dish in the direction of the voice and listen. Between us, we may remember all that is said."

As the minutes passed, Jon's frustration grew. "I thought Colin would want to see me. Perhaps he finds facing me too threatening."

"Then we'll track them from here."

She plugged in the bionic ear and strained to listen. A low voice came through clear.

"Should I send for our prisoner, Colonel?"

"Don't be a fool, Hamad." It was Colin. "It's best that Jon and I do not meet. He is your prisoner. We have more important matters to discuss before I leave. It is time to move men into key cities. A few at a time. Our best weapon is to keep the fear level high."

Hamad sounded weary. "Multiple attacks then?"

"A few decoys to small towns and villages near major rivers. That cuts off water supplies and utilizes one of our best weapons—fear."

"Colonel, you know the strength of your own military. Are you not concerned about the growing coalition against us?"

"No, Hamad. Some of those countries are dependent on oil from these regions. They can't risk taking sides and having their oil supply cut off."

"And you're not worried about the endless U.N. resolutions?"

She heard the scoffing in Colin's voice. "They keep running behind our military time line. Politics. Diplomacy. Both play into our favor. But, Hamad, you must be aware we can no longer depend on the al-Qaeda hierarchy. The small cells will have to strike on their own. We need those who will go all the way."

"Suicide missions? Our training camps are equipping men with toxins and poison components... How many men do I send from here, Colonel?"

Her stomach turned at her childhood friend's reply. "Not more than thirty or forty. Others will go in from Yemen, Cyprus, Djibouti to target major cities. We've arranged passage for them. We need replacements in a café in Paris."

"I thought we were to target the training maneuvers here first of all."

"Too risky this time."

"And Jon Winters and his sister?"

"They can never leave your country. But nothing is to happen to them until I'm back at my desk in Washington."

"Be assured your wishes will be carried out."

Anger burned deep inside Adrienne. This from the man Jon trusted. She glanced at her brother, dozing restlessly on the cot, too weak to care that she was eavesdropping.

"Jon Winters's usefulness has run out. Is that it? Until now he served as your scapegoat, an excellent cover for our work. Is that not your point of view, Colonel?"

"Scapegoat? I thought he was dead. I should have been informed he was still alive. Then we could have used him. Now we must be rid of him. Our cause is too important to risk him stopping us. Anyone stopping us."

"Worldwide terrorism. We will triumph, Colonel."

There was assent before she heard the scraping of chairs and

Colin's footsteps fading. She turned to her brother and repeated the conversation. "I'm scared, Jon. I was sure your friend Hamad—"

"I still think Hamad will help us."

Moments later they heard the roar of the rotor blades of a helicopter lifting. "Adry, we could do with a good sandstorm right now to put that copter out of business."

As quiet and dusk settled around them, Adrienne sat on the edge of her cot and fought her tangled hair. Across the tent her brother lay helpless, ill. Silent.

Oh, Jon, I don't know how to help you. I don't know whether we will ever get out of here. I've wasted so many years, so much energy missing you, being angry at you for going away...for not coming back. I don't feel jealous anymore. Oh, God, I want him to know how much I love him, but I don't know how to tell him.

He moaned. Stretched. Turned.

She rocked on her cot. "Jon, are you awake?"

"What do you think? We don't exactly have the best of sleeping quarters."

"We have to talk."

"We've been doing nothing but."

"I mean—we must settle things between us. Just in case—" Her throat tightened. "I don't like the thought of dying out here where no one will even know. But I'm more afraid of dying without your forgiveness."

"My forgiveness?"

She shook her head. "I was always envious of you. You were the favored child. I could never live up to you."

"Forgivable." Across the tent he touched her with a smile. "But it must have been a relief when you thought I was dead."

Another lock of hair stuck to her salty tears. She brushed it back from her cheek. "No, I was more envious than ever. All Mother could talk about was your dream to be an artist... Will you forgive me for being such a bratty sister? I did love you. I do love you."

"I never doubted it. That was Harry's gift to us, wasn't it? Unconditional love and forgiveness. His unending faith in spite of everything that happened to him." Jon sent her another engaging smile. "The slate's clean, Adrienne. It's okay between us."

She sniffed. Fought tears. "Thanks, Jon."

"No problem, little sis. Any time. Isn't that what Dad would say?"

"Yes...and then he'd quote his favorite verses. But I don't know what they were."

"Stop worrying. Try to sleep. I still think that God of yours is going to get us out of here."

They were stretched out on their cots when a woman stole through the tent flap carrying a basin in her slender hands. As she glided across the dirt floor to Jon, the contents of the basin splashed over the sides, leaving in its wake the strong scent of antiseptic blending with the sweetness of an aromatic fragrance.

From somewhere deep within her robe, the woman extracted soft cloths and bottles of medicine. She bathed Jon's face. "He is gone."

Jon's puffy eyelids cracked at half-mast. "Hamad."

"No, your American Desert Fox—Colonel Taylor."

He forced his eyes wider. "Fatima! What are you doing in a place like this?"

"Fighting my own war for the soul of Hamad. Now turn, Jon, and let me bathe your wounds."

He moaned with the effort. As Fatima bared his back, Adrienne cried out, "Oh, Jon. Your back is raw."

"Quiet!" Fatima's harsh whisper silenced Adrienne. The woman looked at her. "We must not alert the others. There are still several armed guards about the camp. Come, help me. Hold his hand. Comfort your brother."

Another Kuwaiti in traditional dress crept in on padded feet, a steaming pot of boiled mutton and broth in her hands. Without a word she placed the pot on a stand near Jon's cot, lit a lamp, and slipped away again.

Fatima worked as she spoke. "Hamad's plan is working, Jon. But you need strength. You have a fever. Adrienne must feed you and take nourishment herself. When it is safe, I will take her to the washroom to bathe." She laughed, a soothing ripple. "Such pretty clothes when she came. Now she looks like one who crawled in the sand dunes with the snakes and the spiders. When you see her again, Jon, she will be in a Kuwaiti robe and veil. Hamad's orders."

As if on cue, a rangy figure breezed into the tent, his long flowing robe slapping at his ankles. His headpiece covered all but his handsome face—his hair no doubt dark like his eyes. He crossed the tent in stealthy silence.

"Hamad."

"Jon, we do not have much time. My father has gone into the city for help—in his shiny BMW. I instructed him to go to the palace, and then to the American embassy."

"Is it safe for your father? He seems unwell."

"Do you remember how you hated the dust storms when you lived with us? Then the burning oil wells during the occupation were indescribable. My father still suffers with lung problems from the ash and oil fumes. He does not approve of the work I am in, but he is my father. He will defend me."

Hamad smiled at Fatima as he pulled a stool beside Jon's cot and took the bowl of broth she handed to him. "You must eat, my friend. It is not the hand of an enemy that feeds you."

He pressed the spoon between Jon's bruised lips. "I'm sorry about the beatings. Colonel Taylor insisted on them. My men waited to see what I would do. Some of them do not trust me. Too much was at stake to shield you."

"I understand, Hamad."

"Then you will understand that I must keep you here until we can arrange your transportation back to the States." He offered more broth. "In the chance that Colonel Taylor reappears you must still be my prisoners."

"If you help us, you risk your own safety."

Hamad glanced at Adrienne, and she could not hold back a glare. He smiled. "Your sister still thinks I'm one of them. But twelve years ago you told me to infiltrate the group in order to destroy them. A few of the men left last evening."

"Then it is too late to stop them, Hamad."

"No, I am with Kuwaiti intelligence—"

"Then why did you come into the tent yesterday and without a word backhand my brother's cheek?" Adrienne's question came out low and fierce.

"Hush, little sis. I will recover. Hear Hamad out."

"Sometimes we must prove ourselves even to the enemy. But, Jon, will you ever forgive me?"

"Just tell me about those teams of terrorists you sent out. How can we stop them?"

"They will be detained at the airport or as they cross the border into Iraq. They will receive better treatment than the collaborators we dealt with after Iraq's occupation. I do not always favor the engagements of war." Hamad shrugged. "But your American president can be quite persuasive at times. He is constantly proving his mettle."

He paused with the spoon midair. "Jon, your arrival was unexpected. I needed time to alert intelligence agencies in Yemen and Djibouti and our embassy in Paris." He turned to Adrienne. "We had security problems before the Gulf War with terrorist cells forming. But back then our main objective was to form a resistance movement to fight the Iraqis when they crossed our border. The terrorist movement is even more dangerous today."

"But you're one of them," Adrienne protested.

"Little has changed. Jon well knows that for a time I wanted to be part of the terrorist cell. There were those of my Arab brothers proclaiming a holy war in the mosques, and I was caught up in it. It shamed my father. Jon told me I could better serve my country by infiltrating the cell once the war ended. It took the war and the Iraqi occupation to bring me to my senses. I watched my people build up Kuwait after the war, and I knew I could never be part of terrorism."

"But you are. I listened to your conversations with Colonel Taylor—"

His handsome face relaxed. "Do you not think that I knew about that crude little listening device of Jon's?" For a moment he balanced the broth bowl in one hand and with his other patted Jon's trouser leg, stopping at last on the tiny microphone attached to the prosthesis.

"So that's where you hid it. You always were the clever one, Jon. Of course, our receiving and sending system picked up your signals, but Colin was unaware. I took your advice, Jon. I rather admired the double life you led, even back in our university days, all for love of country. I even trained in one of the al-Qaeda training camps in Afghanistan. They are a formidable enemy. Once I returned to Kuwait, I presented myself to Kuwaiti intelligence. You can guess the rest."

"If you lose your life, there will be no honor."

"My father will know the truth—and Fatima." He let his fingers entwine the Arab woman's for a second. "What else can a man ask save his father's support and the love of a woman like Fatima? She has agreed to be my wife. She is my family's choice—and mine."

Fatima turned scarlet, the color more vivid because of the light robe and head scarf she was wearing.

His voice wavered, his jaw jutting forward. "There is an old saying among my people that honor is a person's most valuable possession. Colonel Taylor has no honor."

Adrienne shook her head. "You don't understand, Hamad. Colin lost his wife and unborn child in the attack against the Pentagon. It changed him. It left him angry. Depressed."

Hamad's gaze was hard. "There is no excuse for betraying your country or your honor. He is like the Iraqis who invaded my country. They destroyed everything. People and animals. The throats of our horses were slashed. Stores ransacked. Vehicles burned." His voice rose a pitch. "Our women raped, our people murdered. Unexploded mines washed up on our beaches. They torched our oil fields. Our loss and destruction ran into billions..." He stared down at the bowl in his hand. "Colonel Taylor is destructive like that."

Hamad pushed back the stool and stood as he handed the empty bowl to Fatima. "You need rest, Jon. Strength for the journey. Fatima will bring you fresh water and blankets. She will help you bathe and then once again we will clothe you as a Kuwaiti. You always made a handsome one."

At the tent flap he turned back and saluted Jon. "You are an honorable man, my friend. We are still not safe. We are still fighting a war against terrorism, but we must beat Colonel Taylor at his own game. I will come back tomorrow and we will form a plan. Otherwise, Colonel Taylor and men like him will go on destroying our world."

"I have a plan."

"And so do I. But rest now, my friend. Time is on our side. Fatima will bring you rose water for your face and hands. You were limping the last time they brought you to my tent, so you must remove your prosthesis and sleep in comfort tonight. Fatima will tend to any pressure points on your stump. If Colonel Taylor comes back, we must restrain your hands again. But I think he is anxious to leave my country. I will pray to Allah for forgiveness, but I promised Colonel Taylor that you and your sister will die in this country as your infant brother did. He desires for you to never step on American soil again."

His penetrating gaze held them both. "He will be most surprised when you return to America."

Jon lay his head back. "I am not free to return."

"But you will be, my friend. Remember, my father is distant relative to the ruling sheik. That will be an open door to the White House, and once your president hears what we know, you will go home with honor."

Adrienne could hardly believe her ears. "Are you going to let us go free, Hamad?"

"Miss Winters, you must trust me." His brown face was swathed in a smile. "Your Associated Press will be pleased when I set you free. They have made you a celebrity, Miss Winters. That's one reason I had to send my father to your American embassy—to assure them that you are alive. This Robinson Gilbert and his son are very persistent journalists: 'American Woman Missing in Kuwait' they scream in the headlines. Very embarrassing for my people."

The relief that swept Adrienne was so powerful that her knees would have buckled if she'd been standing. "Then Robbie is safe?"

Hamad's smile broadened at the glad tone in her voice. "And no doubt waiting for you."

Adrienne trembled when the guards took Jon away the following morning, but when he returned with Hamad three hours later, he was smiling. "We're going home, Adrienne. We'll leave after dark."

Hamad nodded. "Just be ready. We have agreed to a plan. But, Miss Winters, if you do not like our suggestions, I have an alternative plan. I prefer the alternative plan for a man who has funded terrorism far too long."

Jon turned to Adrienne. "We are to fly to Washington at once. Hamad is going with us, Adry. The emir of Kuwait is quite the diplomat. In exchange for the missing American woman, he has arranged a presidential hearing for us once we reach Washington."

"Will it work, Jon? Will your name be cleared?"

"Hamad kept detailed records of activity of the terrorist movement in this country and the other Arab states. Colin's betrayals are almost over. I will testify that he left me behind in Kuwait. Hamad has photographs to prove that Colin has been here more than once—and proof that Colin is deeply involved in the worldwide terrorist network. He's only the tip of the iceberg, but defeating him is a beginning."

"Hamad said he had an alternative suggestion."

The Arab's face hardened. "Sandstorms kept Taylor's plane from taking off yesterday. Your American Fox flies out later today, unless we take him out before he boards."

Adrienne gasped. "Assassinate him?"

"Our intelligence division has contacts everywhere. We could wait until his plane touches down in Paris. Or"—there was an eager arch to his brow—"we could have a sniper waiting when he reaches Washington. That would be ironic. He would think he was home free."

Adrienne held her hand out to her brother. "Jon, don't let Hamad give that order. Mother and Rolf will have Gavin at the airport to meet his father."

Hamad swept his long, flowing robe tight around him. "Miss Winters, he left your brother to die in Kuwait twelve years ago. He was here to make certain that the two of you never leave this country. We cannot estimate how much money he channeled into al-Qaeda training camps. Other men's money that may have met the expenses of the men who flew into the Pentagon."

She sank down on the cot. "You're saying Colin may have been responsible for his own wife's death?"

"Hers and many others. Speak up, Jon. Your sister finds our methods offensive. You've said nothing. I don't have much time to order a sniper in place at the terminal."

Jon's eyes were fixed on Adrienne, and he finally nodded. "Don't kill him. Let him do life with Aldrich Ames and Bob Hanssen."

Hamad fell silent, then sighed. "I guess you have your reasons, my friend."

Jon eased his swollen stump into the boot. Locked it in place. Positioned his leg for standing. "When I had two good legs—back when we were in university together in Paris—you told me that Arab brother never went against Arab brother. Do you remember that?"

Hamad's frown held a flicker of impatience. "What does Arab brother against Arab brother have to do with Colonel Taylor? He has no respect for this country of mine, nor for yours."

For an agonizing moment Jon looked away. Then he faced Adrienne. Their eyes met, held. "I can't let him die that way...you see, Colonel Taylor may be my half-brother."

CHAPTER 32

Adrienne and Jon were eager for darkness, eager to leave when a scuffle erupted outside the tent. Angry voices sounded. Human fists pounded, made contact.

"I am Hamad! Stop! I command you to stop."

In the twilight, Adrienne saw the shadowy boxing on the other side of the tent skin.

"Fools, I have everything under control. Stop! That's an order." Hamad sounded furious. "The prisoners have not escaped."

"The colonel sent us back, Hamad. He didn't trust you to deal with them."

Jon struggled to stand, but his body was too feverish and ravaged to keep his balance. He fell back on the cot. In the distance Adrienne heard gunfire—but the military maneuvers were too far away to help them. She could not distinguish Hamad from the guards. Two? Three guards? Adrienne wasn't certain. Arms entangled. Someone was pushed to the ground.

Jon sent her a twisted smile. "I thought we were going to get out of this alive. I'm so sorry, Adrienne."

She didn't move. Couldn't. Outside they heard a body being dragged away. The flap of the tent was thrust back, and two guards entered. Ignoring Adrienne's screams, they cut across the dirt floor to Jon and yanked him to his feet. "Come, Pierre du Pont. We are to take you with us."

"My sister—please don't hurt her."

"We have no need of her. The colonel wants you."

As they went out, they grabbed the lantern and left her in darkness. She wept. She heard more voices—Jon's among them. Heard the harsh sound of his face being slapped.

A car engine. Wheels digging into the sand. She'd been left alone. She reached out in the darkness for her tumbler and bumped it. The water dripped down the makeshift table onto her cot, dampening her blanket. More tears.

She paced inside the tent, hour after hour. Feeling her way in the dark. Frightened that a snake might slither in through the tent flap. With every minute, sinking more and more into despair. She prayed for Jon's safety, but feared it was too late. She prayed for dawn to come and saw a starless night hovering about her. The only echo was her own frightened voice and the screech of nighthawks.

She prayed that God would send Fatima to comfort her. In the morning, God sent Mahmoud instead. She heard the rustle at the tent door. Hamad's proud father stepped inside, wearing his long cotton robe and Kuwaiti headdress.

He bowed. "Miss Winters, do not be frightened."

She was too terrified to move. His thick black mustache twitched before she realized he was speaking perfect English. She remembered the gold-tooth smile from their first meeting.

"We must hurry. You have a plane to catch."

She didn't move. "I was left here alone all night with the fear of snakes crawling into the tent and hawks swooping over the rooftop...and now you're going to let me go?"

He tapped his gold watch, his patience clearly waning. "We have transportation—"

"Not a camel?"

His dark eyes turned gentle with understanding. "I do not ride them myself. We shall ride in my BMW. I am to accompany you to Kuwait International." He helped her to her feet and urged her to hurry. "The media anticipates your arrival. We forbid any news media invasion in Kuwait, but you will be overwhelmed in Paris.

You have the world's attention, Miss Winters. We must return the missing American woman intact."

"But my clothes. My hair."

"We will stop off at your hotel so you can change and collect your possessions."

"And Jon?" Her fear dropped her voice to a whisper. "Is Jon all right?"

He said nothing. She realized with a pang that Hamad had been taken away as well. Mahmoud's son. Her brother. Both gone. Dead. Then came the piercing memory: Sheridan Macaroy at Winterfest telling them Jon was dead. When would Mahmoud tell her?

"May I take his body home?"

Mahmoud's thick brows lifted. "We shall see."

Thirty minutes after reaching the hotel, she was back in the car speeding toward the airport. As they leaned against the backseat, Mahmoud turned to her. "I am to brief you. Last evening's fiasco was intended. Kuwaiti intelligence permitted it. Even Hamad did not know what was going on."

Her hands tightened around her purse.

"Intelligence has been infiltrated. We did not know when or the names of those involved. When they went back to the camp to take Hamad and your brother as prisoners, they gave themselves away. We were able to arrest them before they entered Kuwait City."

She whispered a thankful prayer. "And Jon? Hamad?"

"Under no circumstance could we allow the missing American woman to be associated with them." At the airport he stayed by her side, guiding her past newsmen to the departure gate. As she reached it, she saw two young men in Kuwaiti dress. For a moment she thought she would faint.

"Steady, Miss Winters. Say nothing. The three of you will be traveling on the same plane into Paris. After a night of rest, you will be interrogated and then released for your flight back to America."

"Jon is going with me?"

"Your brother and my son have an appointment at the White House. The evidence they carry with them will be enough to arrest the Washington mole."

Colin trapped. She wanted to hug Mahmoud, but knew it was unacceptable. So she shook hands with him. "I don't know how to thank you. You saved my brother's life twice."

The gold-tooth smile warmed her. "Then perhaps you will make it a point to send my son back to me. Safely."

She ran to board the plane, not wanting him to see her tears. As she walked down the aisle toward her first-class seat, she was certain that Kuwaiti intelligence was on board to protect her. Just before she took her seat, her gaze locked with Jon's.

And then she was buckling her seat belt and smiling to herself. They would have Paris for their glad reunion.

The glad reunion in Paris was brief. Jon spent what time he could with his family. But the embassy and the CIA consumed most of their hours. Then the three of them—Jon, Hamad, and Adrienne—were escorted to Charles de Gaulle International for the military flight back to America. Ricardo Mendez was already on board.

Jon's brow ridged with a scowl as their jet neared Washington. Even now she saw his brooding mood reflected in the plane window —still demanding space of his own.

Did the Company still own him? His coming home was a gathering cloud—a quicksand for the family he had denied for so long. For most of their journey, they traveled in silence. He sat gazing out the window with his face turned from her. His hands rested on his legs—fine hands with no sign of sculptor's clay beneath the nails. No evidence that he dreamed of being another Rodin.

Adrienne longed to give him back his youth, with its dappled lifestyle. But she couldn't give him back the lost years. The space of time between yesterday and now had become intangible mists swept away, never to return.

He pressed his forehead against the window as the jet descended over Washington. Adrienne leaned forward—if only the cherry blossoms were in bloom for his homecoming. She wanted to point out the glistening dome of the Capitol and the White House. How ridiculous! Jon could see the old familiar landmarks for himself—the Lincoln Memorial on the western end of the reflecting pool and the marble shaft of the Washington Monument stabbing the skyline. He'd recognize the Potomac River dividing the capital from the Virginia side, where their mother waited for them.

Jon tightened his seat belt as the plane hovered above the runway. She ached for the choices he must make. His future. His reputation. His family. Which would it be? The family at Winterfest? Or the one left behind in Paris?

"You should have brought Brigette and the children with you. Mother is so anxious to meet them."

"Brigette insisted I come alone."

"You're still not certain?"

"I'm not sure Washington will believe me. If they don't, I may end up on trial. That would be humiliating for Brigette. And worse for Mother. No country wants to admit to an officer gone bad. Thank goodness Harry Winters won't know the outcome. Mine or Colin's."

"Jon, why can't you bring yourself to call him *Dad?* Half-brother or not, you will always be my brother."

"I wanted Harry Winters to be my father. But from all I can determine, I'm the son of Bedford Taylor."

"Even if it turns out that way, no one else will know. You will be welcomed home as our father's son. He thought of you as a son. He loved you as a son."

"I never got to tell him how much he meant to me. Never

apologized for doubting my parentage." His voice was choked with emotion.

"I confronted Harry once. I told him what I suspected. I said he owed me the truth, but I wasn't prepared for his answer. 'I love your Mother, Jon. I put aside that one possible indiscretion.'"

He palmed his chin. "Remember how he always looked you straight in the eye? He met my gaze that day and said that he kept silent because he had you and me to think about. I let him have it. I pointed my finger right smack in his face and said, 'But you deceived me—' Adrienne, he put his head down on that big old desk of his and sobbed. When he looked at me again, his face was mottled. I never saw such grief on a man's face before or since. He told me I would always be his son, whether I believed him or not."

"He meant it, Jon. You *were* his son."

"I wanted to be. I felt it was my responsibility to measure up for the infant son they lost. But I kept at it until he said, 'Jon, I have been your father since the day you were born. No one can take that away from me.'"

"Did you ever make it right with Dad?"

"We never talked about it again."

Adrienne wanted to weep as well. "It wasn't his fault. You shouldn't blame him. Mother craved attention. Bedford was there, more than willing to share her life. Does Colin know?"

"That I might be his half-brother? It could be the reason he dislikes me so."

"Dad always said truth lay in Washington."

He smiled as the plane bumped and lurched over the runway. "I've always said the truth fanned out from Paris. I intend to learn the truth before I go back to Paris."

"You won't stay? Winterfest is partly yours."

"Brigette and the children are in Paris."

"Then promise me that you will forgive Dad—and Mom?"

He nodded. "I wasn't to blame for what happened. I've come to accept that."

"Neither was Dad to blame."

"I know that now."

She thought of her father clasping Jon's hand on those return trips from the Middle East. Hushed conversations in the library. Raised voices. Jon leaving the library and slamming the door behind him. Jon never seemed surprised to find their mother in the hallway.

"Jon, you must not quarrel with your father. Bedford Taylor isn't worth it."

Jon had a mind sharp as a whip. A tongue that could wrap around several languages and come out speaking like a native. A gentleman—always a gentleman with their mother as he shielded her from the slander in Washington. And yet he could not accept his parentage. She flinched, for the taste of childhood envy was hers momentarily as she thought of Jon as the favored child. Herself as a castaway. But it slipped away at once. Nothing lingered but love for her brother.

When they met Robbie at the baggage claim, he picked Adrienne up in his arms as though she were a mere feather and whirled her around. "I never meant to leave you in Kuwait, sweetheart."

She wrapped her arms around him. "I know. Colin admitted everything."

"Not everything. He'll be back at the Pentagon tomorrow, proud as ever. But I trust not for long."

"And Gavin? What will happen to him?"

Robbie looked at Jon. "For now, Colin has him."

The whole trip from the air terminal to the family estates, Robbie held her hand. "I'm never going to let you go again. Count on it."

"I'm glad. And, Robbie"—she pointed skyward—"I know who is first place in my life."

The smile that lit his features was as joyful as it was tender. "Good. But I knew it from the look in your eyes. You're not only beautiful. You're peaceful."

He glanced back at Jon. "The cook is beside herself. She's got pot roast cooking—just for your homecoming—and she baked three pies because she couldn't remember which one was your favorite."

Jon laughed. "Sounds great. I'll have a slice of all three just to please her."

"Your mother is so excited about your coming, Jon. When I left, she'd already tried on six outfits. Rolf was trying to persuade her to choose something blue and to calm down."

"Mother will look good in anything."

"Jon," Robbie cautioned. "Parkinson's has taken its toll. She won't look like she did when you left."

"Neither do I."

"She was miserable when I told her Brigette and the children weren't coming, so Rolf settled that one too."

"Oh no. What did Mother do this time?"

Robbie squeezed her hand. "What any grandmother would do. She called Brigette and the children and spoke to them for two full hours. It was quite a mixture of French and English. Mara was crying on this end. I imagine Brigette was blubbering on her end as well. I think they worked out an agreement that Brigette and the children will visit soon."

Adrienne pointed ahead. "Oh, Jon, there's the gate to Winterfest. We're almost home!"

He leaned forward, peering between them. His eyes shone. "It's just the way I remembered."

The sprawling Winterfest Estates lay before them, the lawn a velvety sea of green, the meandering river winding at the foot of the bank. The wooded hills behind the white stucco mansion loomed shaded and beautiful. Two Tennessee Walkers grazed near the stables.

Adrienne put her hand on her brother's arm. "Let's go horseback riding right after dinner? Mother bought a new thoroughbred just for you—" She sucked in her breath. She'd forgotten his amputation. "I'm sorry, Jon."

"It's okay, Adrienne, I have no doubt that Rolf can get me up on a horse again. But tonight, I'm going to spend the time with Mother. Would you mind?"

"Once they feed us," Robbie announced, "Adrienne and I will go for a long walk. Maybe pick a bouquet from your memorial garden."

"Good idea." Jon's eyes twinkled. "The flowers are appropriate. I think Adrienne plans to ask you something—something of a rather permanent nature. It's the modern thing to do, isn't it Robbie, for the woman to propose to the man?"

Adrienne's cheeks flamed, but Robbie just grinned. "Sounds good to me, Jon. Except she insists on candles and red roses to set the mood. I may find some red roses in the garden, but—"

The bantering ceased when Jon saw his mother standing by one of the Doric columns, Rolf at her side. She was waving a white handkerchief, her face wreathed in smiles.

"It doesn't seem right to be coming home with Harry and Harrison both gone."

"I think they're with us, Jon. Inside."

Before Robbie could help Jon from the parked car, he was already standing and catching his balance.

"Wait, let me get your cane."

"No cane, Robbie. Mother is standing there without her wheel-chair and I'm going to walk right on up those steps on my own and into her waiting arms."

Adrienne's mother took her hand from the Doric column as Jon reached the top step and collapsed into his arms. "Oh, my son, my son. My sweet Jon Aaron. I'm so glad you are home."

Early in the morning, Colin Taylor pulled on his uniform jacket, then turned to catch Gavin up in his arms. He hated leaving the boy under the care of a housekeeper. But he had to go to work. "We'll spend time together tonight, Son."

"I want to go with you, Daddy."

"I can't take you to work, Gavin."

"Can I go back to Rolf's and Nanny Mara's?"

"Not today. She said she was expecting company."

He glanced at his watch. A thread from his son's pajamas had snagged on his row of medals. He flicked it free. "I have to hurry, Son. We'll talk more tonight."

His housekeeper met them at the door, a matronly woman with flighty gray hair. "Can you be home by seven, sir? I can't stay much after that." She seemed resigned however, adding, "If need be, I can put the boy to bed for you."

"Gavin can wait up for me this time." He glanced down and tousled the boy's head, surprised at the tenderness he felt. "You are so much like your mother, Gavin."

His mood blackened as he drove to the Pentagon. At his desk, he tried to access three confidential files. The screen went blank on one; access was denied on the others.

He tried again, cursing under his breath. He buzzed his secretary. She looked uneasy. "There have been some changes while you were gone, Colonel Taylor."

He shoved back from his desk and strolled down the corridor to his commanding officer's quarters. At that precise moment, the brigadier general stepped into the hall. "Well, there you are, Colonel. Your secretary called to say you were en route. Welcome back."

"Sir, I'm having trouble accessing some files."

"Yes, we have to talk about that. Right now, I'm on my way to the White House. Things have come to a head in your absence, Colonel. It looks like we have the mole."

Taylor's mouth went dry. "You caught him?"

"He's as good as in our hands. That's what the White House conference is about."

"I'm supposed to be there when you discuss the mole. Let me grab my attaché case."

"Not this time, Colonel. Closed meeting. I'll brief you later. Tomorrow, perhaps. Then we can talk about the top files. We made some changes while you were gone. Even have plans for another appointment for you."

"What's wrong with the assignment I have?"

"We found some reshuffling necessary."

Colin was left standing there, his gut recoiling, his throat and mouth dry. A jolt of adrenaline put action to his feet. Flee. Yes, flee. *They know. They know I am the Impostor.* He calculated the distance to the nearest airport during the snarling bumper-to-bumper traffic. He'd look conspicuous in his uniform, but he kept an overnight case at the office with casual clothes and ample cash in hundred dollar bills. He could catch a flight to the Cayman Islands before they knew he was gone. Wasn't that Sheridan Macaroy's point of refuge?

No, Colin had a second contingency plan, a better escape route. The Canary Islands, a province of Spain. The place where he and Kristy had honeymooned. Totally separate from Macaroy. Yes, he liked that idea—an island in the Atlantic Ocean, off the coast of northwest Africa, a link with his dad's family.

He hurried back to his own office. As he edged the corridor, his thoughts raced. *Perhaps I should head straight to the tiny village in Spain where my ancestors lived for generations. No one would think to find me there... I can take my son with me. Let some distant, well-bosomed aunt take care of Kristy's son and raise him for me.*

He planned each step. Empty the desk drawers. Lock the desk. Fill his briefcase with classified documents. Grab his overnight case. His attaché case. Tell his secretary to hold his calls. He smiled to himself and added a final touch. Tell her you have an emergency meeting with Rumsfeld. And walk out. Walk out of the Pentagon for the last time.

No, he knew as he reached his office he'd have to leave Gavin behind—the boy would only be a hindrance.

As he entered his office, his secretary looked rattled. "Colonel, someone is waiting to see you. He refused to wait. He just barged in."

They've come to arrest me. As Colin thrust his door open, an adrenaline rush exploded like a incendiary bomb in his head. Shock held him in his military stance. He considered the odds of overpowering the man facing him, but if his time had run out, at least he would go out of the Pentagon like a man.

Jon Aaron Winters stood tall, a cane in one hand. Stone-faced. Cool-headed. Composed. His chest heaved, but his breathing was inaudible. Jon dominated the room, controlled it in his silence. Only his eyes were scornful. The stench of the Parisian sewers was gone. The stench of Colin's own sins, putrid. What was hidden in the darkness of the tunnels was illuminated now in this well-lit room in the Pentagon.

"How did you get in here?"

"Like you, Colonel, I have friends in high places."

He seemed to stand even taller. "It's over, Colin, but I had to see you once more. Just in case I misjudged you. I can tell by the expression on your face that it is all true. You betrayed me in Kuwait. You tried to eliminate me a second time in the underground tunnels."

He limped passed Colin, moving out of the office.

"Wait!" Colin turned, reached for him. "I can explain everything."

They were inches apart, both stoic in their bearing. Jon's voice was low and cold. "Can you explain the last twelve years? I have an appointment at the White House. Let me say to you what you once said to me, Colin. My orders are to leave you behind."

His heart pounded. "But, Jon...we're friends."

Jon met his eyes then, and the sorrow Colin saw in Jon's features cut him to the quick. "That's what I thought when you left me on the sand dunes to die. You told me there was only transportation out of Kuwait for one of us. Now there's only transportation to the White House for one of us, Colin... Don't try to run this time. You're under constant surveillance."

CHAPTER 33

Jon had to pinch himself as he sat at the mahogany conference table beside the vice president of the United States. He had met important dignitaries in his father's political world. Even in his own world, he had met the emir of Kuwait and been close enough for digital photos of the French president. But these last eighty minutes in the White House capped them all for the immaculately groomed man across from him on the east side of the table was the president of the United States. The secretary of state sat to the president's right, the secretary of defense on his left.

The room in the West Wing overlooked the Rose Garden. It was an auspicious room that Jon Aaron Winters never expected to sit in and never expected to see again. It was reserved for the Cabinet, the National Security Council, for members of Congress and heads of state, yet for eighty minutes he'd been part of this impressive private hearing. He wanted to seal in his memory the busts of Washington and Franklin and the magnificent portraits of Jefferson and Eisenhower.

Ricardo Mendez and Hamad, in his Kuwaiti robe and kaffiyeh, looked small with all the big guns of Washington present: the CIA director and representatives from the State Department and a brigadier general from the Pentagon; the operational director from Langley who headed up the counterterrorist division; and the agent from the FBI who threw the most questions Jon's way.

Once the meeting began, all eyes turned to Jon. Five minutes into his discourse, he spoke with a fervor that rocked his voice and captured his audience. "I am convinced, Mr. President, that my friends and I have all the proof you need that Sheridan Macaroy,

Colonel Colin Taylor, and his father, Bedford Taylor—deceased now—worked together for years betraying this country. Everything is detailed in those reports in front of you."

"Very thorough," the president said. "It sounds like Colonel Taylor and Mr. Macaroy should be detained at once."

The operational director squirmed. "It's not that easy, Mr. President. Macaroy is away on vacation."

"I saw him last week at a state dinner. He was inebriated, in my opinion."

"It was after that when he requested holiday time. He planned a trip with his son—an escape to some Fiji island as far away as they could get. That way Macaroy could evade the bill collectors for a while and the boy—"

"The crippled one?" The general's scowl silenced those around him. "I thought he died from pneumonia months ago. I figured that was why Macaroy drank so much and spent with such abandon."

FBI Special Agent Wilkins looked skeptical. "If Macaroy told you that, he lied. Gerald Macaroy is very much alive, but his father agrees to his wife's constant demand for more alimony even though the children are grown. His lifetime guilt, I think. But you don't risk Macaroy's type of gambling habits on a government paycheck. He's neck-deep in debt. We've checked his bank accounts, his style of living. He's been on our top surveillance list for some time."

"The Impostor list?" This from the secretary of defense.

"Yes. But we missed Macaroy leaving the country."

Rumsfeld's voice rose a notch. "Then file extradition papers and get him back here."

Agent Wilkins shot back, "We can't risk months of surveillance, Mr. Secretary. We have to be certain that the charges hold when we arrest him."

"Sir," Jon said, "that's why my friends and I are here. We believe Colonel Taylor is your Washington mole, that he's worked under Sheridan Macaroy for years. But their link with the terrorist network is far reaching." He made eye contact, one man at a time. "Everything Hamad told you is documented in the papers in front of you. That's why the president granted an audience to my friend Hamad."

The two old friends exchanged glances, warmth passing between them. "That's why Ricardo Mendez is here from the embassy. We've stopped a terrorist attack in Paris. We've detained several terrorists leaving Kuwait…but that's just the tip of the iceberg."

He played taps with his fingertips. "All of you know the terrorist organizations worldwide have long-term plans—with renewed vengeance because of the troubles in the Middle East."

He looked steadily at the president. "Endless terrorist recruits have been caught up in their madness. Our report includes target cities. Training camps. Names. Details. But those camps can break on a moment's notice. Move on. The task is daunting."

Jon turned again to his friend Hamad. Hamad's gaze darted from face to face, then settled on the president. "Mr. President, some of your operatives joined forces with our own teams in the Kurdish territory in northern Iraq and with dissidents in the south."

"But, Hamad, you must know we use satellites to collect intelligence data."

"Of course, but you also have guerrilla operatives at your command—as guides for any ground troops that you send in."

Jon shuddered. *Hamad, don't stretch your safety margin. You got your point across—say no more.*

But Hamad went on. "Sir, the war on terrorism will not end tomorrow. I am with Kuwaiti intelligence. We know CIA paramilitary teams began moving into the Middle East days after 9/11. It may have escaped the notice of the American people, but your commandos have a guerrilla force in place. If you need us, we are available to help your secret army."

The secretary of state glared at the CIA operational director. "Your clandestine operations have a history of disaster. You're risking lives."

The director's grin twisted. "They risked their lives when they joined the Agency."

From the corner of his eye, Jon saw the director jotting down notes. The old itch to serve in the hot spots tingled Jon's spine. For a second he forgot his prosthesis. *I'm ready to serve my country, wherever's needed.*

A still small voice prompted him. *Don't forget Brigette and the children.*

He swallowed. He loved them, but making their world safer took priority. He stole a glance at Rick, whose elbows were propped on the table, his stubborn chin resting on his hands. The old excitement burned in his eyes.

Was Rick bored with being an undercover diplomat? Frustrated down to his toenails, saddled as he was with the lost passport circuit? His marriage was rocky. Why not volunteer for the Special Ops group again? It risked killing and being killed, but they both understood what Hamad was saying...

Yes, a clandestine mission meant a second chance for both of them.

Eighty minutes after the conference began, the men in the room sat in stunned silence. Jon closed the file in front of him and slid it across the table toward the president. "There are photographs there to confirm everything we've said. Colonel Taylor is your man."

The defense secretary peered over his glasses. "This Bedford Taylor, how does he fit in?"

Colin Taylor's commanding officer checked his notes. "He was Colonel Taylor's father. He was buried at Arlington Cemetery with full honors."

"Then have him removed."

"That would create another scandal, sir."

The CIA operational director rubbed his hands, a smirk tugging his lips. "If memory serves me, Bedford's family in Spain wanted his remains shipped to them for burial. We denied that request—the ceremony at Arlington had already been arranged. Taylor was a Vietnam Medal of Honor winner. We thought we were honoring a hero—"

"Gentlemen." The august assembly turned to Jon. "If this scandal reaches tomorrow's headlines, it will thrust the president's efforts on terrorism to the back pages."

"Do you have a better idea, Winters?" The secretary peered at him. "You have traveled with a well-known journalist from here in Washington. He may even now be wording his headlines."

"Robbie Gilbert—Robinson Gilbert's son—is one of the most honorable men I know. My family respects him. If I had my way he'd marry my sister. We won't have to buy Robbie's silence. The president has merely to ask for it."

The FBI agent snapped back. "From all we've discovered, your mother's reputation could also be ruined."

Jon gave him a hard look. "I think my family has suffered enough. My father went to his grave in disgrace for another man's betrayal."

Ricardo Mendez squared his shoulders. "I agree with Hamad. There's one way to keep the scandal to a minimal. Jon, your legend is well established. You can best serve your country as Jacques d'Hiver. We need you behind the scenes in Paris analyzing intelligence data. That way Hamad's work in Europe and the Middle East can go on undetected as well."

"That's a costly request."

"Mr. President, it would be more costly to tear Jon's star from the wall and delete his name from the Book of Honor. Langley would have to explain to their people that they knew Jon was alive all along."

"Only a few of us knew that, Mr. Mendez," the operational director defended.

The president glanced at his watch. "Let's hear your suggestion, Mr. Winters. Would there be something else on the bargaining table?"

"Three things. First, I must be honest with my sister and explain everything to her. She has that right. And second, we both want to protect our mother's reputation. Any charges against her must be dropped. She's very ill. Having her son and daughter know the truth about her has been ample punishment."

"And the third bargaining tool, Mr. Winters?"

"The safety of Colin Taylor's son, Mr. President. I have a son younger than Gavin. I'd gladly take the boy into my own home, but if not, I want this committee to guarantee Gavin's future."

A smile crossed the CIA director's face. "A satisfactory exchange. At least fair to the rest of us. We'll have ample scandal when the identity of the mole goes public." He turned to the secretary of defense. "We could see about having Bedford Taylor transferred to his family plot in Spain. You know an act of compassion on our part. Then we'd rid the hallowed ground at Arlington of his remains."

Jon nodded. "But not be rid of his collateral damage. I'd check inside the casket before I shipped it."

"Mr. Winters, what do you mean?"

"My mother tells me that it was a sealed casket. What if Bedford Taylor is off on some Fiji island, spending the money he accumulated for selling out this country?"

The president met Jon's gaze. "Bedford Taylor was your father's friend, perhaps your friend as well."

"I grew up thinking of him as…as an uncle."

That familiar half-grin lit the president's face. He folded his hands on the files that Jon had passed to him. His gaze went the length of the conference table to his Kuwaiti guest in the impressive long, flowing robe. "Hamad, we want to thank you for delaying your wedding to be with us."

Hamad nodded. "My fiancée, Fatima, urged me to do so." He glanced at Jon and then back to the president. "My people respect Jon Winters as a true representative of your country. He risked his life for us in the Gulf War. He came back again to help us."

The president's half-grin broadened, then faded. He turned back to the man sitting across from him. "What about Bedford Taylor's son?"

Colin's commanding officer leaned forward. "In agreement with the FBI, Colonel Taylor is going about his routine day, except we have blocked his access to secret documents. Once again he is under the false assumption that Jon Winters will not leave Kuwait alive."

"Correction." The men turned to Jon. "Colin knows I'm here. I went on a fool's errand before coming to the White House. It was the second time we were face to face since he left me in Kuwait to die. The last time was in the sewer tunnels in Paris, where he made another attempt on my life."

The special FBI agent glared at Jon, then glanced at the defense secretary. "Mr. Secretary, we have enough evidence to arrest Taylor today, but his son is with him."

The secretary thumped the table. "That can't be helped! You have surveillance teams on him, don't you?"

"We've had him on watch for months. Home surrounded. Wires tapped. Warrants ready for the federal prosecutor's signature. We've tailed him from the moment he stepped off the plane."

"Then what are we waiting for? I don't want that man tainting the halls of the Pentagon another day."

The DCI interrupted. "If we wait we would know whether Mr. Macaroy was returning from his vacation—or whether we will have to file extradition papers. He can read the headlines wherever he is. And if he reads them, he won't come back."

Jon cleared his throat. "You can't hold off for Sheridan Macaroy's return. The secretary is right. Colin Taylor has gone free long enough."

The president nodded. "Arrest him."

The FBI agent took out his cellular and called the command post. The room grew tense. There was an adrenaline rush. Faces came alive around the conference table. Jon felt a blend of triumph and grief for an old friend. His whole body tingled.

Wilkins's neck went scarlet, his neck vessels throbbed. The room went silent as he said, "This is Agent Wilkins. Everything's in place, right?... Proceed. The pickup is on."

An hour later Jon stood among the crosses at Arlington Cemetery and stared down at the marker for Bedford Taylor. He had little respect for the man, but he felt an overwhelming sadness for Harry Winters. Lying here had been Harry's ambition.

Behind him he heard the creak of a wheelchair and his mother saying, "I thought we would find you here, Son."

He turned. "Mother! Rolf! I planned to be home for dinner."

"Sharply at seven." She smiled. "But I couldn't be certain. We didn't end on good terms last evening. I didn't want you to know about Paris or the way I let your father down."

"Mother, I came to terms about that long ago."

"But not about your parentage. I was angry when you questioned that. But I deserved everything you said."

"No you didn't. You're my mother."

"But I have the answers you want."

He pointed down at the burial site. "Then tell me why Bedford rated this honor and Harry Winters didn't."

"A twist of fate." She said it quietly, as though resigned. "The death of fairness. Nothing played out right for Harry from the day we came home from Paris."

"Your doing?"

"Yes, in many ways. You know, don't you?"

"I guessed." He looked at the grave. "Bedford betrayed your husband, yet you gave up everything for this man."

"Not everything. I never stopped loving you and your sister. And deep down, I cared about Harry."

Jon leaned harder on his cane, his leg throbbing.

"Son, I watched you from the bedroom window last evening— alone out there in the gardens by your father's grave. If I could have trusted my own legs, I would have come out and grieved with you for your father."

"Which father?" The crack in his heart split wider.

Rolf rested his hand on Mara's shoulder. "Not another word like that to your mother."

"It's all right, Rolf. He just wants the truth." She bent her head and put her cheek against his rough hand.

Rolf's jaw tightened. "It was best for Harry to be buried next to his own father. I never liked Harrison's solitary tombstone out there on the property. Oh, I know it looked down on the river and over-looked the city they both loved. It was quiet and beautiful, but those two men belonged together. I built the memorial garden out there."

"In your memory, Jon," his mother said.

"I intended it as a place for the Winters men."

Jon nodded to the older man. "You did a good job, Rolf. But it doesn't answer my question—which man is my father?"

With a quick tilt of her head, Jon saw his mother's proud, elegant features, once so bewitching. "You had only one father, Jon—the man who should have been buried here."

Was she lying? "What proof do you have?"

"Your mother's word." Rolf almost growled the words. "Isn't that good enough?"

Jon turned to the man who had served the Winters family for so many years. "I thought if I ever got home, Dad and I could have blood tests taken. When Adrienne told me he was dead, I knew I'd have to go the rest of my life without knowing." He tried to smile at his mother. "I'm not blaming you. It's too late for that. If only I had tangible proof—"

She squeezed his hand. "I didn't know until recently that you and Harry questioned your parentage. I knew something was wrong when Harry's friendship with Bedford died, but I pretended not to notice."

"But you were always with Bedford. Why, Mother?"

"We were cousins. Second cousins. Your father knew. I thought you did as well. But Bedford preferred we keep it secret. Something about our thick Spanish roots, Jon. Family loyalties that ran deep. I couldn't forget that."

"And what about us? Your husband? Your children?"

"I've been a selfish woman, Jon. My family in Spain had nothing. Harry had great wealth. Bedford felt he had a right to it. We were never lovers, Jon. Just relatives. We argued at times about the way Colin was turning out, but Bedford seldom paid attention to him."

Jon gave the grave another scathing glance. "Then Bedford Taylor is not my father?"

"Of course not. I confess to an affair in Milan that ended before it got started. But my children had the same father. *Yes, dear Jon, Harry Winters was your father.*"

Jon turned from them and wept. Wept with relief. He brushed the tears with the back of his hand. They kept flowing. "If only Dad had known, Mom."

"And if we just had some tangible proof for you—more than my word."

"But, Mara, we do," Rolf said. "After Harry's stroke, he insisted that I help him. I'm the one who tore out the last few pages of the journal so you wouldn't find them. I couldn't risk you destroying the message that Harry bequeathed to his son. I rolled those journal pages as tight as I could and slipped them into one of the canes. Then I sealed it with wax and put it high on the storage shelf so you couldn't reach it."

"One of the Remington canes, Rolf? Did those records concern Jon's paternity?"

"Yes, Mara. Harry had me go to the State Department and Walter Reed Hospital and when my efforts failed, he sent his lawyers. Once Harry discovered his own DNA report, he knew that he must leave it for his son to find—just in case Jon came home again."

She looked up into Rolf's weathered face. "Then, Rolf, all Jon has to do is have his own DNA checked!"

"Repeat it if you wish. But Harry's lawyer managed to get a copy of Jon's medical records from Langley."

Jon started at that. "From my sealed file?"

"From Sheridan Macaroy. It may be the only honest thing Macaroy ever did. Likely he was trying to prevent us from searching further into your service record in Kuwait."

Jon's mother grimaced. "I never liked that man from the day he came to Winterfest Estates to tell us you were dead. Your father never trusted him either."

Rolf patted her shoulder. "I despised him. Forcing lies on us. Keeping Jon's name from the Book of Honor for so long. But I can tell you, the DNA profiles on Harry and Jon were a match."

Jon leaned over his mother's wheelchair, his eyes still red from weeping. She patted his cheek. "Can we put this behind us now, Jon? Harry was your father."

He smiled, feeling free for the first time in years. "Yes. It's settled. Once and for all."

She reached up to touch his face, her fingers feather light. "Jon, I put your father's Bible in your room this morning. Adrienne said you wanted it... Perhaps it will help you find your way."

"Someday, I'd like to believe the way Dad did."

"That's what Harry always wanted."

"What about you, Mom? Did you ever believe the way Dad did?"

She tilted her head and the sun caught her beautiful features. Tears balanced on her eyelashes. "Before we were married, I pretended I did. Afterward, it didn't matter to me. I'd won Harry." A single tear wet her cheek. "And now...I don't deserve God's forgiveness, not after all I've done."

"That's not the way it works, Mom. Dad said God forgives even the stain and guilt of sin."

Her tears overflowed. "Then perhaps we may both find our way someday. Oh, Jon, you are so much like him. And now, before the two of us get blubbery, I have a question. Where were you this morning?"

He grinned. "At a closed session at the White House with the CIA director and Colin's commanding officer."

His mother's eyes widened. "Am I to assume that you used the president's oval office without his presence?"

"No, we used the cabinet room—and he was present."

"And did you settle world affairs?"

His grin melted. "Only the ones on Colin... He will be arrested today, Mother. For espionage against this country."

Jon knew from her pallor, that had she not been sitting, she would have collapsed.

"I failed him didn't I, Jon? I'm part of Colin's downfall."

"No, Mother, Colin made his own choices." *As you made yours,* he thought.

"What will happen to him?"

"If it goes to trial he'll spend the rest of his life in solitary confinement. But I'm afraid they won't reach him in time. You know about his obsession with Rommel. Colin always said that it was a point of honor with Rommel that death was preferable to arrest."

"Take his own life? Oh no. Poor Gavin." She pressed her hands against her breast. "At what price, Jon? What will all of this cost you? Us?"

He touched her cheek. "I agreed to return to Paris as Jacques d'Hiver, Mother. I left loved ones there. Hamad and I will be flying out together."

"Does your sister know?"

"I want to be the one to tell her."

"Can't you even give her a few days? Spend them together at Winterfest. Then tell her."

"No, Mother. Time is something we can't spare. If Robbie agrees, Hamad and I will bunk in with him until we leave."

Rolf shook his head. "No need, Son. We can tidy up the loft out in the stables. If the media comes, you and Hamad can take cover there. We'll keep the front gates locked. If necessary, you can leave the property by way of the horse trails."

Jon gripped his old friend's hand. "All I'll need is another thirty hours. Forty-eight at the most. But first, I must talk to Adrienne. Where is she? Back at the house?"

"Already grieving for you at the Memorial Wall at Langley. At least she planned to be there with Robbie late this afternoon. She must have known you would not stay."

"She's met Brigette and the children. She understands they are waiting for me in Paris."

"There's more to it than that, isn't there? National security. Our country sending you away again."

He couldn't tell her that he had bargained for her freedom. "Langley asked me to leave promptly. Once the news on Colin erupts, they want me out of the country. I can't risk more than a day or two. Colin's apt to suggest that I'm still alive. They don't want to risk the news media swarming over Winterfest asking the wrong questions."

More tears escaped her eyes. "So my son is really dead. What about us, Jon? How are we to tolerate such a separation again?"

"Mother, I want you to visit us in Paris as often as Rolf will bring you."

She managed a trembling smile. "We'll do that, Jon—if you promise to go back to your art. You were born to be another Rodin."

He glanced at his hands, open palmed. "Brigette will insist that I do so. And come this summer"—he smiled—"I'm sure Jacques d'Hiver would like to come back and bring Brigette and the children. Would you like that?"

"Do you have to ask?"

Colin left the Pentagon for the last time, painfully aware he had only one option. But he drove aimlessly for two hours, keeping to the speed limit, checking his rearview mirror from time to time. A dark Corvette lagged three cars behind him. A white Ford to his right. He could not be certain whether he was followed or not. He no longer cared.

It was late morning when he reached his apartment. He stole past his son's room into the library and shut the door. Field Marshal Rommel went out with honor. Colin glanced down at his own ribbons and medals and thought of the man he might have been.

Tossing his uniform jacket on a chair, he went directly to his gun rack and unlocked it. He had a choice—the last one he would ever make. His eyes grazed over the Mauser and Kar rifles and on the 7.65mm Walther tilting on its anchor. Colin fingered his Saiga-20 shotgun. Then considered his smaller firearms—his favorite revolver, his father's old magnum. He chose a 9mm pistol.

His legs felt rubbery as he eased into his desk chair. He checked the chamber. Inserted the clip. It was too late to pray. He lifted the gun and pointed it to his temple.

CHAPTER 34

Daddy, what are you doing?"

Colin stared transfixed at the Luger as he lowered it. He glanced at the photo of Kristy on the corner of his desk, then forced himself to look at Gavin. He was so much like his mother. Fair and good-looking. Freckled cheeks. Freckled nose. Trusting. Innocent. How could he add suicide to the pain his son would suffer?

Gavin leaned against his leg. "Are you okay, Daddy?"

Kristy's voice. Her curiosity. Her concern. "I'm just cleaning my gun, Son."

He emptied the chamber and slid the pistol into the desk drawer. On the crowded street below the condo—on a place that overlooked the Potomac—came the familiar sound of sirens blaring. *Strange. They took Aldrich Ames and Bob Hanssen by surprise.*

No, it was just the police going about their business. Paramedics speeding to an accident scene. Fire trucks demanding the right of way. The sirens grew closer. Brakes screeched. Gavin flew to the window and pressed his face to the pane. Colin opened his mouth to scold and shut it again. He heard excitement in his son's voice. "The big news van is down there. The big blue one. And there are a lot of cars with flashing lights, Daddy. What do they want?"

"Me."

Gavin turned from the window. "Why do they want you?"

"I've done something bad, Son."

He'd been overconfident. As long as the Pentagon refused to believe they harbored the traitor, they would never find him. Now he was encircled. Perhaps he had been under surveillance abroad.

In his absence they must have wiretapped his home. Planted bugs. If so, these men whom he despised knew him better than he knew himself. But what had betrayed him?

Where had he made his fatal mistake? Traveling to Paris? Crossing into Kuwait? Sending those messages from the embassy? He was not guilty of overspending. He'd been careful to maintain an even lifestyle. Drinking was beneath him. His obsession with Erwin Rommel, Hitler's favorite general, and his enviable gun collection were his major vices, not liquor and gambling. His car was two years old. Unlike Sheridan Macaroy, his apartment in an upscale neighborhood was still modest and within his budget. He was a widower. A father. A soldier.

A traitor.

"Daddy, the men have orange jackets and rifles."

That would be the FBI SWAT team converging on the neighborhood. Men and women well armed. He licked his lips with the tip of his tongue. He knew the scenario. The FBI would pour its manpower—hundreds of agents—into this moment. Unmarked cars with red flasher lights on the dashboard would be switched on along with their sirens. They would take the Impostor down, cuff him. Carry away any evidence.

Still he sat immobile.

Would he know the agent in charge by sight? Would it matter? The man would be a squad leader carrying the proper warrants for his arrest. Warrants to search his well-ordered home and tear it to shreds. A warrant to impound his car, freeze his bank accounts. If there was any humor in it at all, he found it amusing how much federal money would go into his well-planned takedown. All roads surrounding the apartment building would be covered by now. His escape route blocked. Agency vehicles jammed against his Camry in the parking garage. No, he had left the car out front. His car was hemmed in.

"Come here, Gavin."

The boy ran to him.

Minutes later he heard the cacophony of running feet in the

corridor. The whispered commands at his door. The whimper of his son cowering by his desk.

He was aware of his son but unable to console him. His thoughts raced to Rommel who had known what was expected of a German officer. It was not surrender. Not arrest. Rommel had suffered bitter defeats in the battle for North Africa, another in his attempt to strengthen the Atlantic Wall against the invasion that crossed the English Channel. Yet even Churchill had called him a great general; even Hitler who ordered his death by poison buried him as a hero. Like Rommel, Colin had wanted nothing more than to serve his country as a soldier. He wanted to die as a hero, not rot in a prison cell.

From where he sat, Colin heard the thunderous knock on the front door. *The knock and notice…*

"This is the FBI. We have a search warrant—"

The housekeeper screamed as a battering ram splintered the door. It swung back on its broken hinges. The agents swarmed into the apartment, their MP-5 rifles aimed. *FBI Swat Team* was sprawled across their bulletproof vests. The housekeeper flattened herself against the library wall, her hand clasped to her mouth. Robbie Gilbert slipped into the room and stood beside her, his finger to his lips.

When Colin saw him, the words of a historian pounded in his mind "Only the final act of self-destruction remains."

His son had robbed him of even that.

As guns were leveled at Colin, an agent shouted, "Keep the news media out of here. Get them back on the streets. This area is secured."

The housekeeper clung to Robbie. He stood his ground as others were shoved from the room. Colin glared at Robbie.

Are you friend or foe, Robbie? Whatever! Whichever, you will defend my son.

As the FBI information officer held the rest of the media at bay, Colin moaned. *It won't take long for the media to identify me. They'll smear my face all over the five o'clock news.* "Are you going away again, Daddy?"

He looked at his son's pale, frightened face and tousled his hair. "Yes, for a long time, Gavin."

As he stood unsteadily an officer cocked his gun. "Not in front of my son," Colin commanded. "He's only a boy."

"You should have thought about the boy sooner." Rough hands slammed Colin against the desk and cuffed his wrists behind him, one at a time. *Click. Click.* He smirked at the squeak of shoes, the snap of gum in the agent's mouth.

"You're under arrest, Colonel."

"For what?"

"Espionage against the United States."

"Wait. I'm Colonel Colin Taylor. I work at the Pentagon. You have the wrong man."

"*Code name Impostor,*" the agent snarled. "You lost your way, mister, when you turned against this country." He felt the man's contempt. Colin saw the semiautomatic on his hip. He noted the efficiency with which the man moved and admired him for it.

His books were taken from the polished shelves. *The Rommel Papers* swept from his desk with his bookmark still in it. The contents of his desk emptied. Behind him someone jerked opened his gun cabinet. He glanced back as they pulled rifles and handguns out with reckless abandon. Someone snatched up his wife's picture. "Leave that alone. My wife is of no value to you. She's dead."

As they yanked him to his feet, he cried out to Robbie Gilbert. "Robb, please take my son to Winterfest." Despite his best efforts, his voice cracked. "There's always a welcome for him there."

A**s he fought off the firm restraint of an FBI officer, Robbie felt only pity for Colin. The shirt of Colin's uniform was torn at the collar. The dark tie lay on the desktop. Colin looked like a dead man, like a sleeping volcano blinded to his own eternal welfare.

"There's no need for protective services to be called in," Robb told the officer. "I'm—I'm a family friend. I can take care of the boy."

"Yes, I recognize you, Mr. Gilbert. We'll be in touch."

"Come on, Gavin, your daddy needs to talk to these men."

Gavin tugged at his hand. "Is Daddy in trouble, Robb?"

"Yes. Serious trouble."

As Robb tried to lead him from the room, the boy cried out. "I won't leave my daddy." He turned to Colin and wailed, "Daddy, don't go away like Mommy did."

"Go with Robb, Gavin. Be a good soldier."

Robb's eyes locked onto Colin's. *At least you are thinking of your son's welfare.* Robb lifted Gavin. The boy's scrawny arms wrapped around him, choking him. His wet cheek pressed into the crook of Robb's neck. As he carried him from Bradbury Towers, the child whimpered, "Do bad men love children?"

"Sometimes."

"Does Daddy love me?"

"I know he does."

"But he's going away."

"I know."

"Grandma Nel is too sick to take care of me. Nanny Mara is getting old."

Again he nodded. "Nanny Mara's son, Jon, was talking about you living in Paris with him someday."

"Daddy lived there once."

They had reached the street level. Robbie pushed through the entry doors of Bradbury Towers and was confronted with the warning: FBI SWAT LINE. DO NOT CROSS. He ducked under the yellow barrier tape, taking the boy with him; he didn't remember taking the stairs with the boy in his arms. He rushed past the cars with their flashing lights. "That's why Jon thought you'd like to go to Paris. Maybe go to the school where your daddy went. You could live with Jon's family. You'd have a brother and sister."

"Would I have a mommy?"

"As soon as Jon can tell Brigette about you."

"But, Mr. Gilbert," he said as Robb secured him in the front seat, "Grandma Nel and Nanny Mara need me."

"But someday—maybe in a few months—when they don't need you to take care of them anymore, what say the two of us fly to Paris? We'll ask Adrienne to go with us."

The boy was crying. His eyes gushing like two broken fire hydrants. His face puffy. The freckles tear-washed. Robb knuckled the boy's chin. "Give me five, Gavin."

Their hands slapped together.

Gavin giggled.

"Okay, soldier." He saluted the boy. "Let's go home to Winter-fest. I promise, everything is going to work out."

He straightened. Swallowed his lie. Raced around to the driver's side and hopped in. For a second he couldn't face the boy, his own eyes blinded with tears.

"Give me a five, Robb."

Robbie did him one better. He took Gavin in his arms and rocked him. "I love you, little man. No matter what happens, remember that."

CHAPTER 35

It was late afternoon when Jon reached Langley. He went up the stone steps and through the multiple glass doors into the familiar lobby with its marble pillars and walls and recessed lighting. The old Company pride soared through him as he walked over the CIA seal. The world of intelligence, enshrouded in secrecy, was his life. His commitment. It was the way he could best serve his country.

On the South Wall to his left stood the bronze statue of William Donovan, dead these many years, yet inspiring him even now, convincing him that he had made the right decision. He passed several strangers, but no one stopped him. Once again he was an employee, his ID card dangling from his lapel. He approached the security post and stopped. Adrienne stood alone beneath the Memorial Wall—her fingers touching the glass-encased Book of Honor.

How many times had he strolled by that wall in the past, unaware of how costly it had been for other covert officers, how devastating it had been for their families? As he went to Adrienne, she was so engrossed in the row upon row of black stars that she did not sense his presence.

He wondered which star was his own. "Adrienne."

She turned as she had done at the Rodin Gardens, that same look of surprise on her face. She rallied quickly. "I wasn't expecting you, Jon."

He pointed to his ID card. "I guess we're some of the privileged few. I had to come. I was afraid you'd destroy government property if I didn't get here in time." His dark eyes teased. "But I see my star is still in place and you haven't ripped my name from the Book of

Honor."

"You didn't give me enough time."

He was struck again with his sister's elegance, but her large mahogany eyes were brilliant with tears.

"Jon, do you remember Miss Fenmeyer from the academy in Paris? She used to give us stars when we did something special. Is that what the star on this wall means—you did something so sacrificial that we must never know about it?"

"It no longer matters, Adrienne."

"It does to your family."

Her lip quivered, and he prayed she would understand what he had come to tell her. "We need to talk."

"Here?"

"It's as good a place as any. In a way, it all started here in the sacred halls of Langley."

She brushed her tears away. "A black star embedded in marble is just a symbol. It doesn't tell anyone who you are or how much we love you. Or how angry I feel for all those years we lost."

"I know. Those stars represent a lot of living. But those other men and women didn't get to reunite with their families as I have." Gently he changed the subject. "I thought Robbie came with you."

She nodded toward the security post. Robbie sat on the top step, his head against the rail; the Agency's escort stood nearby. "He knew I wanted to be alone for a few minutes. How did you know to find me here?"

"Mother told me you'd be here. I was surprised. Langley is not open to tourists."

"I have a friend in public relations. She's most sympathetic. But you didn't tell me why you came, Jon."

"I have an appointment with the director about my future, but I needed to see you first. Mother said to tell you that she's expecting us all for dinner tonight. Seven sharp. And I wanted to be the one to tell you"—he steadied her as he glanced at his watch—"they arrested Colin today."

"Oh, Jon, Robbie told me. What will happen to Gavin?"

"We'll have to sort through the legal haggling, but eventually I'd like to make a place for him in my home."

"Have you forgotten? He's Colin's son."

"Have *you* forgotten?" he countered. "He's Kristy's son, too, so his welfare is uppermost in my mind. Gavin was one of my bargaining chips at the White House. I pointed out that his mother is dead. His grandmother Nel dying. His father facing a life sentence if convicted of espionage."

"It will destroy Nel."

"She's stronger than you think, Adrienne." He rubbed his jaw. "Rolf and I met with her last night—after you and Mother went to bed. I wanted Nel to hear about Colin from me—before any news broke today. Nel never wanted her daughter to marry Colin. Never trusted him. But for the sake of the child, she has maintained a polite tolerance toward him. If Colin hasn't changed his living trust, Nel is to assume responsibility for Gavin as a minor—if Colin dies or is incapacitated. Nel has practically raised the boy anyway."

"But Colin isn't dead."

"But a life sentence will incapacitate him. Nel is the logical one to care for the boy, but she is not doing well, Adrienne. She doesn't have the strength to care for Gavin any longer. But Rolf made a suggestion on Mother's behalf."

"I'm afraid to ask. Mother is not well either."

"We woke Mother on our return to the mansion to tell her our plan. I told her Colin would be going away for a long time. That we had to make permanent arrangements for Gavin. Mother didn't ask why." He swallowed. His voice grew hoarse. "She knew. She's known the truth all along—suspected the outcome. I told her if Colin's lawyers can convince him to relinquish all claim on Gavin, we'd like to move both Nel and Gavin to Winterfest. Nel can afford round-the-clock nurses. That way she can spend her remaining time with her beloved grandson. And Mother, who loves that boy more than anyone, will share in his care. He's happy at Winterfest, and he'd be isolated from the media."

"What are you trying to do? Turn the estate into a convalescent home?"

"We want what's best for Gavin."

Robbie wandered over. "Is everything okay between you two?"

"We're just discussing Gavin," Jon said. "If Colin agrees to turn Gavin over to Nel, she'll rewrite her own trust and make me the caregiver for Gavin when she dies. Eventually, I'd like Gavin to make his home with me."

"Sounds cut and dried, Jon. But what about Brigette?"

"Robb, once I explain everything to Brigette, I have no doubt that she will welcome Gavin as a son." He checked his watch a second time. "I have ten minutes before I meet with the director…and I almost forgot, your English friend Maddie phoned, Adrienne."

"And I missed her call! What did she say?"

"Something about honeymooning in Washington in December—she was wondering whether she and her bridegroom, Archibald, could spend Christmas at Winterfest."

She laughed. "You will like her, Jon."

"Adry, I won't be here then."

Her hilarity died. "You're not staying."

"I'm flying back to Paris with Ricardo and Hamad."

"In three days?"

"Sooner. It was one of the stipulations in the meeting at the White House."

"That you leave the country again?"

He put his finger gently to her lips. "I was in agreement. That way they will not pursue Mother's involvement in Paris. It's a closed file."

"Then Dad will never be exonerated."

"Dad is gone. Mother is ill. Those of us who knew Dad—and that includes the hierarchy in Washington—know the truth. He was innocent. Honorable. We won't stir the waters. Mother's reputation will remain untarnished. She was young and foolish when she left

Dad's vault open—Colin will try to take her down with him, but the proper gag writs will protect her. She told me last evening that Dad didn't even know she knew the combination to the safe."

"You really love her."

"Dad would want me to protect her at all costs."

"And how high was the price?"

"The death of Jon Aaron Winters. The ongoing legend of Jacques d'Hiver. But I'll always be your brother, Adry. I'll be free to travel back and forth between Paris and Washington on a French passport. As a Frenchman. The Agency will see to that."

"You're still with the Company?"

"Undercover, but being headquartered at the embassy in Paris will be easier on Brigette."

Adrienne's gaze went back to the Memorial Wall. "What other conditions did you accept, Jon? What about this star? Won't they have to remove it?"

"Isn't that what you wanted?" He wiped a tear from her cheek with his thumb. "It will remain there. Jon Aaron Winters is already dead. The two missions into Kuwait are not on public record. It's best they remain that way."

"Is that another one of their conditions, Jon?"

"It was a fair exchange, Adrienne. Mother's reputation. My country's national security. They promised to make certain Gavin has a good home. There will be shock and scandal enough on tonight's newscasts and in the morning editions. The three o'clock news has already aired. Having another mole so soon after Bob's Hanssen's treason will not set well with Americans."

She bit her lip. "Why must you be their scapegoat?"

"Hamad suggested that I remain dead. It will help him in his work, and it will protect so many of the people I once worked with."

"What about us? Mother? Me?"

He took her hand, willing her to understand. "I think you love me enough to let Jon Aaron go."

"Does Mother know you are going back to Paris?"

"She guessed. She agreed to travel to Paris soon with Rolf—

conditionally." He felt the crooked smile on his face. "She'll fly to Paris if I go back to my artwork at Angelo's Studio. And I promised to bring Brigette and the children back to Winterfest this summer." His words trailed off. "Mother said that more and more I remind her of Dad. He always kept his wife and children top priority."

"Brigette is not your wife."

How like her to point that out. He smiled. "I plan to remedy that when I get back to France." He extended his hand to Robbie. "Take good care of Adrienne for me, will you, Robb?"

A rakish smile filled Robbie's face. "My pleasure."

With forced bravado Jon leaned down and kissed Adrienne on the cheek. "I will always be your brother, Adrienne. Nothing can change that."

Adrienne listened to Jon's limping gait resounding on the marble floor as he walked away. Her eyes sought her brother's star one more time, and tears brimmed. Robbie stepped forward to stand beside her. "I'm sorry for the way it worked out. You know how much Jon means to me."

"Jacques." She spoke the name, surprised it didn't hurt as much as she'd expected it to. "Jacques d'Hiver."

"A Frenchman, no less."

"But he's still my brother." She slipped her hand in his. "And I still have you, Robbie."

They turned and made their way past the security post to the glass doors. "Did you see Jon's name in the Book of Honor, Robbie? It wasn't there the last time I was here."

"I'd wager the ink is barely dry. But remember, Adrienne, men of honor belong in a book like that."

As they stepped into the sunshine, she shielded her eyes and gazed up at him. "I love you, Robbie Gilbert."

He craned his neck back.

Held her at bay.

He searched her face, his smoky blue eyes dancing. "What did you say?"

"I said I love you." Her voice fell to a whisper. "My brother told me to propose to you."

"Call me chauvinistic, but I'll have none of that." With a gallant Sir Galahad flourish, he swept his jacket from his shoulder, spread it wide on the stone steps, and knelt down. He smiled as he reached up and took her hands. "Tell me once more, Miss Winters."

She laughed and cried at the same time. "You know what I said, Robbie."

He ignored the passersby who paused to watch them and grinned at her. "I've waited a long time to hear you say that. But, my darling Adrienne, let me make it a proper proposal...will you marry me?"

Spontaneous applause began around them and grew louder.

Joy flowed through Adrienne. "Yes, you silly man. Of course, I'll marry you."

His gaze held hers. "You told me once you'd never accept my proposal without candlelight and red roses."

"Robbie, I can provide the candles. What about a candlelit dinner on the porch at Winterfest this evening?"

"Perfect! And I'll bring the roses."

He was back on his feet, slinging his jacket over one shoulder. "I know a great place for our honeymoon."

"You do! Where?"

"Paris." His warm smile sent her heart racing. "Our old stomping ground. What better place? It's where we met." He leaned down and cupped her face in his hands. "I love you, Adrienne. I always have. I always will."

"Oh, Robbie, I—"

The applause crescendoed as he caught her up into his arms and silenced her with a kiss—long and tender.

...TO BE CONTINUED

Enter
www.betrayalinparis.com

GET ACQUAINTED.

Shoofly Pie
—*Tim Downs*

Get to know Kathryn Guilford, from a remote North Carolina county, and Nick Polchak—a.k.a. the Bug Man. When Kathryn receives news that her long-time friend and one-time suitor is dead, she refuses to accept the coroner's finding that his death was by his own hand. Although she has a pathological fear of insects, she turns in desperation to Polchak, a forensic entomologist, to help her learn the truth. Gold Medallion award winning author Tim Downs takes you on a thrill ride as Kathryn confronts her darkest fears to unearth a decade-long conspiracy that threatens to turn her entire world upside down.

ISBN: 1-58229-308-2

HOWARD
Fiction

BECOME FRIENDS.

Sins of the Mother
—Patricia H. Rushford

You'll surely enjoy getting to know country music singer Shanna O'Brian, as award-winning author, speaker, and teacher Patricia Rushford draws you into a story of romance, mystery, and adventure. As dashed hopes are rekindled and a haunting past comes into the light of truth, you'll find yourself caught up in Shanna's complex world. And when the mysterious death of her mother turns Shanna's world upside down, you'll feel her conflicting emotions as she is forced to make sense of her life—despite her fledgling faith in herself, her God, and the man determined to reclaim her love.

ISBN: 1-58229-342-2

ENJOYMENT GUARANTEE

If you are not totally satisfied with this book, simply return it to us along with your receipt, a statement of what you didn't like about the book, and your name and address within 60 days of purchase to Howard Publishing, 3117 North 7th Street, West Monroe, LA 71291-2227, and we will gladly reimburse you for the cost of the book.